M000266218

FATED

KAREN LYNCH

Text Copyright @ 2018 Karen A Lynch
Cover Copyright @ 2019 Karen A Lynch

All Rights Reserved

ISBN-13: 978-1-948392-15-0

Cover Designer: Melissa Stevens at
The Illustrated Author

For Ednah Walters

Writers aren't supposed to be at a loss for words, but there are no words to say how much I miss you, my friend.

ACKNOWLEDGMENTS

Thank you to my family and friends for their love and support, and to the indie community that has embraced me and my books. I've made so many wonderful author and reader friends in this business since I published Relentless that I can't possibly name them all. I couldn't do this without you.

PROLOGUE

Chris

F*ourteen years ago*
       "Is everyone out?"
   "God, I hope so."
   I approached the two firemen shouting over the roar of the flames engulfing a four-story apartment building across the street. The five hoses aimed at the building were doing nothing to stop the fire that was blazing out of control. All the men could do now was try to keep it from spreading to nearby buildings.
   I'd been on my way to meet up with Nikolas when I heard the alarms and saw the fire, and I came to see if there was anything I could do to help. But it looked like there was little I could do here.
   Glass broke on the top floor of the building, followed by a child's scream.
   "Jesus Christ! Someone's up there," one of the firemen yelled. "Get that ladder over here."
   One look at the flames licking at the curtains of the broken window told me the firemen wouldn't get there in time. Engaging my demon speed, I sped across the street and entered the lobby of the old building. The place was an inferno, and smoke burned my throat and eyes as the intense heat surrounded me.
   I raced up the burning stairs that would have collapsed under the weight of a normal man. Only my speed kept me from falling through them and

protected me from the worst of the flames. I'd have a few burns, but nothing that wouldn't heal in a few hours.

The top floor was just starting to burn, but thick smoke made it difficult to see, even with my enhanced sight. I had to find the child and get out of here before this whole place went up.

"Where are you?" I shouted as I ran from one apartment to the next.

A shrill cry answered me, and I followed it. Inside the apartment, I spotted a middle-aged woman lying on the living room floor, and a quick check told me she was dead. Was I too late?

My Mori stirred, telling me there was another of my kind nearby. I whirled around, my gaze scanning the room until it landed on a small form huddled in a corner. I ran over and swept the child up in my arms, relieved when she cried out, letting me know she was okay.

I turned to see flames licking at the doorframe. I could withstand the fire, but the child's Mori was too young to protect her. Running to the closest bedroom, I grabbed a quilt from the bed and threw it into the bathtub to soak it with water. The child didn't move or speak as I wrapped her in the wet quilt and hugged her to my chest. She was in shock, but there was no time to comfort her. We needed to get out of here, now.

I ignored the sting of the flames as I hurried out of the apartment, carrying my precious burden. At the landing, I stared down at the gaping hole where the stairs used to be. If I were alone, I'd jump to the first floor and sustain minor injuries. I couldn't do that with a child unless it was our only option.

At the end of the hall was a door I hadn't tried, and I yanked it open to find the stairs to the roof. Seconds later, I burst out onto the roof and took a few gulps of fresh air.

Smoke billowed out of the doorway, reminding me we weren't out of danger yet. I ran to the edge of the roof and looked down. Between the flames and the thick smoke, it was difficult to see the people on the ground, so I knew they couldn't see us either.

My gaze moved to the next building, and I judged the distance to be around fifteen feet. Backing up, I tightened my hold on the child.

"Almost there," I said to her before I sped forward again and jumped.

I landed easily on the other roof. The child whimpered when I set her down and pulled out my phone. A few seconds later, Nikolas answered, and I wasted no time in explaining the situation to him. I hung up to see to the little girl.

I pulled back the edges of the quilt to reveal a tear-stained face framed by messy blonde curls that glowed like a halo in the late afternoon sun. She couldn't be more than five or six, too young to lose all she'd ever known.

"It's okay," I crooned. "I won't let anything hurt you."

Her eyelids fluttered open, and frightened gray eyes met mine. She stared at me without speaking, most likely in shock after what she'd been through.

I smiled and withdrew my hand to show her she was safe with me. I had rescued a few orphans in the past, and I was good with children.

"I'm going to carry you down now," I told her softly. "If you get scared, you just hold on tight to me."

She didn't say anything as I pushed the quilt off her shoulders and picked her up. Cradling her in my arms, I ran lightly down the stairs and stepped out into the crowd milling around. Without a backward glance, I hurried down the street toward the gas station on the corner where I'd told Nikolas to meet me.

Five minutes after I got there, Nikolas pulled up on his bike, followed by a white van. The side door of the van slid open, and Paulette jumped out.

"Is she injured?" the blonde warrior asked.

"Not that I could see, but I think she's in shock."

Paulette's face softened. "I'd be surprised if she wasn't. She'll be okay once we get her home. You can give her to me."

I moved to hand the girl off to her, but small arms wrapped around my neck, clinging to me. Not wanting to frighten the girl more, I tried to persuade her with gentle words to go to Paulette. But every attempt only made her whimper and hold on tighter. When Paulette tried to take her from me, the girl started to wail, quieting only after Paulette stepped back.

I smiled at Paulette over the girl's head. "I'm due for a visit home anyway."

Climbing into the van, I settled in the back with the girl hugging my neck. Her clothes were damp from the quilt, and she shivered against me even after Paulette laid a thick blanket over us. My Mori warmed her, and I whispered reassuring words until she relaxed against me.

I couldn't help but think of how close we'd come to never knowing of her existence. If I hadn't decided to take that route to the restaurant, if she hadn't screamed at that moment, I would not have found her and she'd be dead now.

She moved, and I looked down at her round, angelic face, streaked with dirt and tears. Her gray eyes watched me with so much trust it made my chest ache, and all I wanted to do was take away her sadness and fear.

"Can you tell me your name?"

She blinked but said nothing.

"I guess I'll have to make up one for you," I said playfully. "How about Goldilocks? You like that?"

She shook her head.

"Hmmm. You're a quiet one, aren't you? Maybe I'll call you Mouse. How does that sound?"

Her golden eyebrows drew together.

"No?" I pursed my lips, pretending to think about it. "I know. I'll call you Dove because of those beautiful gray eyes."

A wisp of a smile touched her lips before she lowered her head and curled into me again.

I smiled down at the mop of blonde curls peeking above the blanket.

"Dove it is."

1

Chris

"We've got company."

I adjusted my grip on my sword as half a dozen cutlass-wielding gulaks ran into the basement, followed by two ranc demons with semi-automatic weapons. I grimaced at the sight of the guns. Ranc demons had terrible aim, and it would take a lot of bullets to kill one of us, but getting shot still hurt like hell.

I'd worked with Nikolas so long that no words were needed. My free hand went to one of the knives in my harness, and out of the corner of my eye, I saw him do the same.

In one fluid motion, I pulled a knife free and sent it flying at the nearest ranc demon. He made a choked sound and fell to his knees as the blade buried itself in his chest. Next to him, the second ranc demon went down without a sound as Nikolas's knife found its mark.

"That's better," Nikolas said, facing the gulaks. "Let's do this."

The gulaks shouted and charged us, and I found myself battling three of the lizard-like demons at once.

I blocked the first gulak's strike with my sword and felt the force of the blow all the way to my shoulder. Spinning away from him, I swung low and slashed open the stomach of the second one. He bellowed in pain as I ducked the oncoming blade from the third one.

Coming around for a counterattack, I landed a kick on the first gulak's knee, sending him staggering backward as my blade sliced cleanly through the wrist of the third one. He roared as his sword hit the floor with his hand still gripping the hilt.

Lucky for me, gulaks were known more for their brute strength than their skill with a blade, or I might have been relieved of a few favorite body parts before I was done with them. With the three of them disarmed, it was easy enough to dispatch them back to the hell they came from.

Too easy.

I looked at Nikolas, who was wiping his blades on the pants of a fallen gulak.

"You'd think a slave-trafficking operation as big as this would have a lot better security."

He nodded as his gaze swept the basement. "I was thinking the same thing."

"How's it going down there?" Sara's voice came over the comm she insisted we wear on jobs now. She could talk to Nikolas through their bond, but she liked us all to be in contact. He and I had never used communication devices, but Sara felt better with us wearing them.

"We're good, *boss*," I retorted.

"How are the humans?" Nikolas asked as he stepped over a gulak body.

We'd entered the four-story building from the roof, and the first thing we'd done was take out the guards on the top floor and free the captives up there. Once the floor was secure, Sara stayed behind with Paulette to reassure the terrified humans while the rest of us cleared the building.

"Few cuts and bruises, but alive." Her voice sounded a little breathless, and I knew she was moving around checking on her charges. "We have fourteen human girls and three mox females up here. One of the demons needs medical attention... Hold on."

She went quiet for a few seconds. "One of the girls said five more were taken away before we got here. They could still be in the building."

"We're on it," Nikolas said. "Raoul, you copy?"

"Copy," Raoul replied. "Three is clear, and we're doing a sweep of two now."

"We'll work our way up to you," Nikolas said.

Sara cut in. "Be careful. Don't make me have to come down there and save your sorry asses."

Nikolas smiled and shook his head, and I was struck by how much he'd changed in the year and a half since he'd met Sara. Dedicated to his warrior lifestyle, he'd been the last person I'd expected to settle down, but one look at my little cousin and my best friend had fallen hard.

He used to almost lose it when Sara was in any kind of danger, and I'd often wondered how he was going to deal with her being a warrior. Now they worked together, and he'd finally accepted that his mate could take care of herself. That didn't mean he didn't worry, though.

We moved silently through the basement until we came to a utility room. Nikolas reached for the knob and stopped, sniffing the air.

"You smell that?"

I sniffed and nodded grimly as the coppery scent of fresh blood hit me.

"Human," I said in a low voice.

We positioned ourselves on either side of the door, and Nikolas turned the knob, easing the door open to reveal a dead girl inside. One look at her ravaged throat told me no gulak had killed her.

I crouched and touched the body. "Still warm."

"We have a fresh vampire kill," Nikolas barked to the team. "Stay sharp."

"I'm not picking up anything," Sara said.

No one questioned her because her "vampire radar," as she called it, was never wrong. She could sense any vampire within a quarter-mile radius and even tell what direction they were coming from. Pretty useful skill to have in our line of work.

Nikolas and I left the room and continued our search of the basement. It didn't take me long to find the open sewer grate in the boiler room where the vampire had exited the building.

I peered through the hole at the blackness below. "What do you think?"

"If Sara can't sense him, he's long gone," Nikolas called from the hallway. "Let's finish down here and head up."

I headed for the door and let out a grunt when I walked straight into an invisible wall as I tried to pass through the doorway.

I rubbed my nose. "What the hell?"

Nikolas tried to enter the room, coming up against the same barrier. He pushed at it with his hand. "Force field. My guess is it's warlock made."

"Nice," I groused. So much for the lack of security. "What now?"

He smirked as he spoke into his comm. "Sara, it looks like you have to save Chris's ass after all. He got himself stuck behind a warlock barrier."

Sara laughed. "I'm on my way. Give me a minute to –" She gasped loudly. "Five vampires, coming fast!"

No sooner had she spoken than the first vampire leaped through the sewer grate. Nikolas battered the magic barrier, and I heard Sara say something, but I was too distracted to listen.

I brought my sword up as the vampire rushed me without waiting for his backup. He screamed as my blade sliced him from navel to shoulder, and he fell backward onto the second vampire coming through the grate. His brethren threw him aside, and he slammed into a pipe, sending water gushing everywhere.

The newcomer snarled at me but kept his distance as three more vampires jumped through the hole in the floor. I quickly sized up the situation. These were not young vampires, judging by how fast they'd gotten here after Sara had detected them. That didn't bode well for the good guys – namely me.

"I don't suppose you guys are up for a fair fight?" I asked as they spread out in a semicircle. "You know, one-on-one?"

The only female in the group looked me up and down lecherously. She was blonde, and she'd been in her early twenties when she was changed.

"I'll do some one-on-one time with you when the boys have had their fun." She licked one of her fangs. "I'll even let your friend watch."

I shook my head. "Sorry, I have a rule. No sex with people I have to kill. It puts a real damper on the romance."

Behind me, Nikolas snorted.

One of the male vampires snarled. "Enough playing around, Jen. Let's do this."

She huffed and tossed her hair over her shoulder. "Fine. You want him, he's –"

A white flash lit up the room. Out of nowhere a slender brunette girl appeared, sprawled on her back between me and the vampires. I couldn't tell who was more shocked to see her there.

She sat up and looked around in wonder. "What do you know? It worked. Sort of."

"Sara, what the hell?" Nikolas shouted at his mate, who had apparently added transporting to her ever-growing list of Fae powers.

She tossed a sheepish smile over her shoulder at him. "Surprise."

"Who the fuck are you?" demanded the female vampire from the other side of the room. She and the others had been driven back by Sara's arrival, but they were inching forward again.

Sara stood and dusted off her jeans. "I'm here to rescue him."

The female stared at her.

"It's our thing. He gets into trouble, and I save him." Sara lifted her hands and let them fall back to her sides. "Men. What can you do, right?"

"Sara," Nikolas ground out.

One of the males barked a laugh. "She's wacko. Look, she doesn't even have a weapon."

I moved swiftly to Sara's side. I'd seen enough of her power in the last year to know what she was capable of, but there was no way I'd let her face five vampires alone.

"New trick? Impressive."

Her green eyes gleamed with excitement. "I can't wait to tell Eldeorin I finally did it."

I smiled at her. "Maybe we should deal with our little problem first before your mate loses it."

"Oh, right."

We sized up the five vampires watching us with a mix of confusion and malice. I was pretty sure they'd never encountered someone so wholly unfazed by their presence, and they had no idea what to make of her.

Sara looked at me. "I'll take the three on the right. Can you handle two?"

I met her smirk with my own. "Try to keep up, little girl."

I was on the first vampire before he knew I was coming. My blade severed his head, and his blood sprayed the shocked faces of his friends. To my right, another vampire screamed, and I glanced that way as he burst into flames.

A vampire took advantage of my distraction and rushed me. His claws scored my stomach and would have gutted me if I hadn't spun away in time. Ignoring the burning pain, I came around quickly and took his arm off at the elbow. Before he could recover, I impaled him through the heart.

I turned to see two bodies engulfed in flames and the female vampire cowering against the far wall, her eyes darting to the sewer grate.

"Want to flip for it?" I joked to Sara.

She opened her mouth to reply but sucked in a sharp breath instead, her hand going to her chest. I knew we had more company before she got the words out.

What I wasn't expecting was for my sweet little cousin to grab the front of my shirt and throw me toward the doorway. I hit the forcefield and fell to my knees, losing my grip on my sword. I regained my feet as another six vampires spilled from the sewer.

Before I could move for my weapon, Sara lit up like a bolt of lightning. I barely had time to make sure I was on dry ground before her power streaked through the water on the floor. Every vampire in the room screamed and convulsed before collapsing in smoking heaps.

I jerked as an errant spark of Fae magic set me back on my ass. It wasn't enough to do damage, but it felt like I'd grabbed the end of a low voltage wire.

I let out a moan. "Son of a bitch."

"Sorry!" Sara fell to her knees beside me. "Are you okay? Did I get you?"

Her eyes widened, and she reached out to pat the side of my head. "Oops. You're smoking a little."

I gave her a suffering look, and her lips twitched.

"Sara," Nikolas growled as Raoul, Brock, and Calvin arrived behind him to stare at the carnage.

She smiled at me and went to dissolve the barrier with a touch. Fae magic beat all other magic every day of the week.

In the next instant, Nikolas had her in his arms, looking like he wanted to yell at her and kiss her at the same time.

"Don't mind me," I called. "I'll just lie here until my legs work again."

Sara laughed, and Raoul came over to grab my hands and pull me to my feet. My legs wobbled a little, and I had to hold on to him for support.

"What happened to you?" Raoul asked.

"What do you think?" I grimaced at Sara. "I can't believe you set my hair on fire."

She looked me over. "It's just a little charred on the ends."

"Great."

Her eyes sparkled with laughter. "Why? You have a hot date tonight?"

"Not yet."

She rolled her eyes, and the others laughed.

Nikolas looked at Brock. "We'll need a large cleanup team, and the human girls should go to the hospital."

"And the mox demons?"

Sara stepped out of Nikolas's arms. "I already called someone for them. I should probably get back to them and the girls."

Nikolas gave her a wry smile. "Take the stairs this time."

She laughed softly and kissed his jaw before she headed to the stairwell, leaving the rest of us with a pile of smoking vampire bodies.

I looked at Nikolas as I ran a hand through my hair to assess the damage. "Did you know she could transport?"

He rubbed his jaw in exasperation. "She and Eldeorin have been working on it, but as far as I knew, she hadn't been able to do it since that first time."

"Well, that should make for an interesting dinner conversation tonight."

I'd had a few laughs at Nikolas's expense since he'd bonded with Sara, and the fun hadn't ended with their mating. Knowing my cousin, these two would keep me entertained for decades.

"When are you two heading to LA?" I asked him.

"Next week. Sara wants to stop by Westhorne for a few days first."

Last year, we'd set up a temporary command center near Santa Cruz, and after we left, it was moved to Los Angeles. Now, the Council wanted to establish a larger, permanent command center there to handle the day-to-day operations in that area. They'd asked me to help get the center up and running, but I'd already committed to a long overdue visit with my parents in Germany. Nikolas had agreed to take over in my place.

We spent the next two hours working with the cleanup crew while Sara and Paulette saw to the girls we'd rescued and delivered them to the hospital. Then, we all met up again back at the safe house in Norcross.

After my shower, I found Nikolas and Sara in the kitchen, discussing dinner options.

I sat on one of the barstools. "You guys staying in tonight?"

"Yes," Sara answered for them. "You are not dragging me to another nightclub like the last one."

Wearing an innocent smile, I rested my arms on the granite counter. "What was wrong with Koma's? You said you wanted to go somewhere laid-back where you didn't have to dress up."

She fixed me with a look of chagrin. "If those people had been any more laid-back, they would have been horizontal. In fact, some of them were."

Nikolas chuckled, and she tossed him a half-hearted glare. "You're as bad as he is."

He tugged her back against him and trapped her with his arms. "How about I take you to Dominick's, and then we'll have a quiet night in?"

Her lips curved into a smile. "That sounds really nice."

I laid my hands on the counter and stood. "And this is where I bid you good night."

"You're not coming to dinner with us?" Sara asked me.

I caught Nikolas's eye and saw the subtle shake of his head.

"As much as I enjoy your company, Cousin, I think I'll see if Raoul wants to go for a steak. Then I'll probably head over to Buckhead."

She hugged Nikolas's arms. "I guess we'll see you later."

I smiled as I turned away. "Don't wait up."

Beth

I zipped up my weapons bag and set it on the floor next to my duffle. Straightening, I scanned the room I'd slept in since I was six. The pale-blue walls were covered in framed photos of my life here, and the shelves overflowed with books and treasures I'd collected over the years. A wave of nostalgia rushed over me. I'd had a good life here, and I was going to miss this place.

"Knock, knock."

I turned to smile at Mason as his muscled form filled my bedroom doorway. His black hair was artfully mussed, and his blue eyes gleamed with excitement.

"I didn't expect you until dinner. You packed already?"

He grinned and entered the room to throw his six-foot-one frame down on my pristine white bedspread. At a scowl from me, he kicked off his Chucks before he put his feet up.

"Unlike you, I don't have a hundred pairs of shoes to pack. I figured you'd need help lugging all your bags."

I let out a very unladylike snort. "For your information, I'm all packed, too."

It was true I liked shoes, but I'd probably have little need for most of them on this assignment. A thrill went through me. My first assignment away from home.

He glanced at the duffle bag, and his brows rose. "One bag?"

I shrugged. "Warriors travel light. And you'd be amazed how much I fit in that thing."

"Good, because we have a lot of traveling to do."

Our eyes met and grins split our faces. Before I knew what he was up to, he grabbed my hand and pulled me down on the bed. We lay side by side, hands clasped and faces turned toward each other.

"This is it," I said softly.

"This is it."

He exhaled loudly and stared up at the ceiling. "Did you ever think this day would come?"

"Yes." I studied his handsome face, which was as familiar to me as my own. "I always knew we'd get here, even if I had to drag your ass along with me."

"Yeah, right." He laughed and reached over with his free hand to tickle my ribs. "I seem to recall me kicking your little butt many times in training."

"With a sword, maybe. But you still can't best me in hand-to-hand."

"In your dreams."

I felt the slight tightening of his fingers on mine a second before he lunged. Bringing my legs and hands up against him, I twisted to the side, sending him flying over me. He hit the rug facedown, and I was on top of him before he could recover. My legs wound around his, and my hands twisted his arms to pin his larger body to the floor.

I leaned down to his ear. "Say 'Beth is the best warrior ever.'"

"Beth is the second-best warrior ever," said a muffled voice.

"Mason, Mason, when will you ever learn?" I let out a dramatic sigh.

"Beth, did you ask...? Oh, hello, Mason."

Mason squirmed, and I dug an elbow into his back, smirking at Rachel, who stood in the doorway.

"I assume Mason is staying for dinner." Her eyes sparkled, and her long red curls bobbed as she shook her head at us.

"Yes," he said in a sulky voice that made me grin harder.

"Okay then. Dinner is in an hour."

As soon as she left, I released Mason and rolled away from him, coming to my feet in a single motion. As expected, he grabbed for me, but I was already at a safe distance. I knew my best friend too well.

He sat up, glaring at me. I smiled back, and his lips twitched in response. He could never stay vexed with me for long.

I sank down on the edge of the bed and fingered the bedspread Rachel had given me years ago. Everything here was so familiar, and it felt strange to think that tomorrow night I'd be sleeping in a new room in a different state.

"It's not forever. You'll be back for a visit before you know it," said Mason, who knew me as well as I knew him.

"I know. It's just I've never lived anywhere else. Not since he...they found me. And I can't imagine going months without seeing Rachel."

I wasn't related to Rachel by blood, but she was a mother to me in every way that mattered. She'd taken me in when I was a frightened six-year-old orphan, loving me and helping me through my grief for my human grandmother. It was Rachel who had explained the voice in my head and taught me to control my demon. She had also given me my first knife and shown me how to use it.

Mason pulled his phone from his back pocket and waved it at me. "They have this amazing device now called a phone, and you can even do video calls."

I rolled my eyes at him.

"Besides, you'll have me watching your back. What more could you want?"

"Absolutely nothing." I chewed my lower lip. "You know, you can still go to Westhorne."

He drew his knees up and rested his arms on them. "Are you trying to get rid of me?"

"No. But I know how much you wanted to go there after training. You'd be there now if it wasn't for me."

"Every new warrior in the country wants to go to Westhorne. Well, except for you. By the way, have I told you lately how weird you are?" He gave me a lopsided smile. "There'll be plenty of opportunities to go to Westhorne, but we only get one first assignment, and we're doing it together like we always said we would."

"But –"

"But nothing. I want to do this, and the way I see it, you owe me."

My eyebrows shot up. "I owe you? For what?"

"For ruining me for other women."

I burst out laughing. I'd known Mason most of my life, but we hadn't become friends until we started training together at fourteen. He'd been a cocky thing and already a huge flirt, but back then, I'd had no interest in the boys at the stronghold. It wasn't until I was seventeen and I'd finally tossed away all my silly girlish dreams of *him*, that I'd agreed to date Mason.

By then, we were sparring partners and he was my best friend, and the romance was doomed before it had started. He'd been my first kiss, and though he was skilled in that area, I couldn't see past the friendship. He liked to joke that I'd broken his heart, even though he'd gone on a date with someone else two days later.

"I've lost count of the girls you've been with. If you're ruined, I wouldn't want to see you whole."

A self-satisfied smile curved his lips.

"And if anything, you've ruined me for other men. I can't talk to anyone like I do with you. So, the way I see it, you actually owe me."

"I knew it. You secretly want me."

I threw up my arms. "You're hopeless. You know that?"

His stomach growled in response. "And hungry. When are you going to feed me?"

I stood and held out a hand. He took it, and I pulled him to his feet.

"Come on. Let's go help Rachel. I'm sure we can find something to keep you alive until dinner."

***

"Did you remember your phone?"

"Yes." I pulled my cell from the inside pocket of my leather jacket and held it up to Rachel.

"Weapons?"

I pointed to the sword scabbard next to my seat and patted one of the large saddlebags on my bike. "All set."

"Cash? Credit card?"

I placed my hands on Rachel's shoulders and met her anxious gaze. "I'm good. Don't worry."

Her eyes misted. "How can I not worry? My little girl is going out into the world."

"I'm not little anymore, and I can take care of myself," I said in a soothing voice.

She sniffed softly. "I know you can, but that doesn't make it any easier. Now I know how my mother felt when I left home the first time."

I pulled her in and hugged her tightly. "I love you, Rachel."

"I love you, too," she said hoarsely.

We broke apart, both of us on the verge of tears. I looked at Mason, who stood with his parents a few feet away.

"Ready?" he asked, his eyes lit with anticipation.

I nodded, afraid my voice would crack if I spoke. This was no way for a warrior to behave.

Rachel handed me my helmet, and I donned it as I straddled the seat of my bike. When Mason and I had bought our motorcycles last year, he'd gotten a sleek black Ducati, the bike favored by most warriors. I'd gone for a more classic look and feel. I loved my dark-red Harley Davidson.

"Call me when you get there," Rachel ordered.

"I will."

I took a deep breath and started my bike, glad no one could see the tear that escaped and rolled down my cheek. I heard the Ducati rumble to life a few seconds before Mason pulled up beside me. We looked at each other, and I gave him a thumbs-up. And then we were off.

Side by side, we rode to the main gate that was already open for us. As we passed the gatehouse, I had a moment of panic, but it passed quickly. I stared at the road stretching out before us, and exhilaration replaced the butterflies in my stomach. This was it, the moment Mason and I had talked about for years. It felt almost surreal.

We reached the first bend in the road that would take us out of sight of home, and I slowed to look back at the sprawling stronghold behind the tall iron gates.

Mason's voice came over the speaker in my helmet. "You good?"

"Yes."

I sped up until I was beside him, and together, we rode away from Longstone.

2

Beth

"Beth, are you sure this is the right place?"

"I think so."

I slowed my bike and stared at the large one-story Spanish villa surrounded by tall trees and perfectly manicured grounds. It looked like something you'd see in a celebrity magazine, definitely not what I'd imagined a command center to look like. But then, this *was* Los Angeles, and the Council was generous when it came to outfitting and housing its warriors.

The arched front door opened, and a short, pretty brunette in jeans and a sweater came out. One look at her as she walked toward us told me she couldn't be a warrior. I glanced at the phone mounted to my dash. How could I have messed up the address?

"Hi," she called over the rumble of our motorcycles.

I turned off the Harley and removed my helmet, shaking out my long blonde hair.

"Hi. I'm sorry. I think we might have taken a wrong turn."

The girl smiled. "Not if your names are Beth and Mason. We heard you'd be arriving today."

"Oh." I stared at her for a moment, unsure of what to say. "Are you..." My voice lowered. "...a warrior?"

She laughed heartily. "I guess I am. Don't worry. I get that a lot."

Relieved, but still confused, I dismounted and held out my hand to her. "Beth Hansen."

"Sara Grey," she said as we shook hands.

I did a double take.

"*The* Sara Grey?"

I stared at the girl who was rumored to be half Fae, had single-handedly killed a Master, and was mated to the legendary Nikolas Danshov. She was as famous as her mate. Maybe more.

Her green eyes sparkled with amusement. "The one and only, but I prefer Sara." She turned to Mason. "And you must be Mason Young."

He took her hand, looking a little awed. I had to bite back a grin because I knew exactly what was going through his mind. Wherever Sara Grey went, so did her mate.

Lord Tristan wasn't the only reason Mason had wanted to go to Westhorne. It was also the home of Nikolas Danshov. *Every* new warrior, including me, dreamed of fighting alongside him. But I had my reasons for not wanting to go to Westhorne, and not even the chance to work with Nikolas could override those.

When we'd learned about the new command center in Los Angeles, Mason and I had immediately requested to be placed there. It was a great opportunity to work with seasoned warriors in the field, and the city was a hotbed of demon activity. We hadn't heard who would be running the center, and the last person either of us had expected to find here was Nikolas.

Sara waved at the house. "Come inside, and I'll give you the grand tour."

We grabbed our stuff and followed Sara into the house. The wide foyer opened into a spacious living area with floor-to-ceiling windows at the back that looked out over a courtyard and a large pool.

Leaving our bags near the door, we walked to the nearest end of the U-shaped house that had been converted into a busy control room. I looked around the room, taking in the computers and banks of monitors at the various workstations set up around the room. On the wall was the largest computer screen I'd ever seen, displaying a map of Los Angeles and the surrounding areas. Tiny colored dots moved on the screen, and it took me several seconds to realize they were locators for our warriors out in the city.

I'd been to the security center at Longstone a few times, but that was nothing compared to this. I was more than a little impressed by the size of it all as Sara walked us around, introducing us to the people there.

"This is the weapons room." Sara opened a door to a store room filled with shelves of weapons and other gear. "If you need anything, you'll probably find it in here. If not, let Raoul know, and he'll commission it for you."

She closed the door, and we moved on to the next one.

"And this is the gym."

We entered the room where two men were fighting, their movements so fast it was hard to follow them even when I used my demon sight. They stopped, and one of the men turned to smile at Sara. I didn't need to hear Mason's sharp intake of breath to know who we were about to meet.

"Beth and Mason, this is Nikolas and Raoul. Nikolas runs the command center, and Raoul is his second."

"Nice to meet you," I said, proud of how confident I sounded despite the nervous flutter in my stomach.

Mason muttered a hello.

The men walked over to shake our hands. They were the same height with black hair, but that was where the similarities ended. Raoul had an easy manner about him. Nikolas was friendly, but there was an edge to him, an aura of strength in every movement.

"This is your first field assignment?" Nikolas asked.

"Yes," I answered for both of us. "We've been assigned to Longstone since we finished training last year."

"I read your files. Top of your training class, and Teresa Fuller personally recommended you for this placement."

"Thanks," Mason and I said together.

I felt my face flush from the praise. I hadn't known the Longstone leader had spoken to Nikolas about us. This whole day had a surreal quality to it, and I was half expecting to wake up and find myself back in my old bedroom.

"Take today to settle in, and we'll meet tomorrow morning to discuss duties and team assignments," Nikolas said.

We nodded, and he and Raoul went back to sparring. I would have loved to stay and watch, but Sara was already leaving. Reluctantly, I followed, tugging Mason with me.

At the end of the hallway, Sara turned to us with a knowing smile.

"He has that effect on most people. It'll pass once you get to know him."

Mason smiled sheepishly. "I haven't acted that stupid since I was fourteen."

"Was it like that for you when you met him?" I asked Sara.

Sara laughed. "Not quite. But we'll save that story for another time. Let me show you the rest of the house."

Leading us into a gorgeous kitchen that was a perfect blend of old-world charm and modern appliances, she pointed to a door on the other side of the room.

"The previous owner must have had a big car collection because he added on a huge garage. You can get to it through here or through the control room."

We left the kitchen and walked through the rest of the house. Sara explained that most of the warriors working out of the command center lived at the three safe houses in the city. That way this place wasn't too crowded.

"We have four bedrooms in here, and there is a guesthouse with two bedrooms out back. One of you can take the last room, or you can both stay in the guesthouse. It's up to you."

"The guesthouse will work." I liked the idea of Mason and me having our own space.

Sara led us back to the living room and through a set of French doors to the backyard. The guesthouse was a much smaller one-story structure nestled in the trees a hundred or so feet from the house. It had a small living room, kitchen, and two bedrooms, each with their own bathroom.

Mason let me have the larger bedroom, and I set my things down on the queen-size bed, eager to unpack and settle in.

"Let me know if you need anything," Sara said from the bedroom doorway. "I'm the unofficial den mother until we get everything sorted out."

"You don't have to take care of us."

She waved a hand. "I like doing it, and the others don't complain unless I try to cook. Raoul says he's counting down the days until Chris gets here. Apparently, my omelet skills need some work."

The bottom fell out of my stomach. "Chris Kent?"

I mentally kicked myself for not putting it together sooner. Chris and Nikolas were best friends, and everyone knew they worked together. If Nikolas was here, then chances were Chris was around, too. My mind conjured an image of his green eyes and dimpled smile, and the old hurt pricked my chest.

"Yes. I figured you must know him since you're both from Longstone."

"It's been a while," I said a lot more casually than I felt. "So, he's coming here, too?"

She shrugged. "He's in Germany now, but I expect he'll turn up here eventually. Do you know him well?"

I swallowed. "I knew him when I was younger, but I haven't seen him in years."

Sara smiled. "Well, maybe you'll catch up again when he comes back."

"Maybe."

"Okay. I'll get out of your hair and let you unpack." She walked to the door and turned back to me. "Come inside when you're done, and we'll scrounge up some lunch."

As soon as the front door closed, Mason entered my bedroom. The concern in his eyes told me he'd overheard our conversation.

"We don't have to stay here."

I fingered the strap of my duffle bag. "We can't just pick up and leave. We asked to come here, and it'll look bad if we change our minds after one day."

"I don't care about that."

He was such a bad liar. Being a warrior meant everything to him, and like me, he wanted to make a good impression on his first assignment. And I'd seen the excitement in his eyes when he found out he'd be working with Nikolas. He'd already passed on Westhorne for me. No way was I letting him give up this opportunity.

"We're not leaving. He might never even show up here."

"And if he does?"

I lifted a shoulder. "Then I'll put on my big girl panties and deal with it. It's not the end of the world."

Mason scowled. "He hurt you."

"He didn't do anything to me. He just..." *Didn't want me.*

"He broke your heart."

"That was four years ago, and I'm over it. He's probably forgotten all about me anyway."

I bit my lip as my chest squeezed, hating that it hurt after all this time. Why did I still care? Chris didn't. He'd made that clear when he left and never came back.

I unzipped my duffle bag and pulled out my small toiletry case and a change of clothes.

"I'm going to shower before lunch," I said, putting an end to the conversation.

Mason stood. "Give me your keys, and I'll move our bikes. I want to check out the garage."

I tossed my keys to him. "Thanks."

Half an hour later, freshly showered and changed, I unpacked my things and hung my clothes in the closet. I smiled at my sparse wardrobe. I loved clothes, but there was only so much you could carry on a bike, and I'd give up my shoes before my Harley. Besides, now I had a good excuse to go shopping in LA.

I threw my empty bag into the closet, and a glint of silver on the bedspread caught my eye. Pressing my lips together, I stared at the silver chain for a long moment before I picked it up. I sat on the bed, letting the delicate chain wrap loosely around my fingers so the small silver dove pendant dangled from my hand.

I'd thrown the necklace into the back of my closet years ago, not wanting to look at it but unable to part with it. Seeing it now brought back memories of a time I wished I could forget – and the person who I'd thought had cared for me before he'd walked out of my life.

Of all the places in the world I could have gone, I'd chosen the command center run by Chris's best friend. I'd lied when I told Mason I could deal with it if Chris showed up here. The truth was my stomach clenched painfully at the mere thought of seeing him again. If I had any sense of self-preservation, I'd ride away from here today and not look back.

I flopped back on the bed with a groan. This was so stupid. Why was I still letting him get to me? It wasn't like we'd ever been together. All I'd been to Chris was the little girl he liked to indulge whenever he came to visit.

Until he never came again.

A knock came at my door, and I called for Mason to come in. His hair was damp, and he'd changed his clothes.

"Get the bikes moved?" I asked, sitting up.

He tossed me my keys. "Yeah. Wait'll you see the garage. You can fit two dozen bikes in there."

"I didn't expect you back so soon. I figured you'd be fawning over Nikolas's Ducati for at least half an hour."

"Ha-ha." He looked around my room. "You unpacked?"

"Yes."

"Good. Let's go get some lunch."

I grinned. "Yeah. I bet Nikolas eats around this time."

He snorted, but I noticed he didn't try to deny that was why he was eager to go to the main house. I was going to have so much fun watching my normally cool best friend get all tongue-tied around his hero.

I opened the drawer to the night table and dropped the chain inside. Then I waved at Mason.

"Lead the way."

I pulled into the parking spot next to Mason and shut off the Harley. Dismounting, I removed my helmet and watched as a black Jeep parked two spots away. The front doors of the Jeep opened, and Raoul and Brock got out.

My stomach fluttered, and I fought to keep the foolish grin off my face as the two men walked over to us. Mason and I had been in Los Angeles for three days, and most of that time had been spent being briefed on protocols and procedures and getting to know the other warriors. I was all for being prepared, but I was itching to get out and do what I'd been training for my whole life.

For the last two weeks, a tana demon had been at work in the city. Cousins to Incubi, tana demons lived on human energy, but unlike Incubi, they didn't feed off sexual energy only. A tana demon could be male or female, and they only fed from the opposite sex. And what they left behind was nothing more than a husk of dried skin and bones. Since all the victims had been women, we knew we were looking for a male demon.

Another team was hunting him, but Nikolas thought it would be good experience for Mason and me to ride along with Raoul and check out a tip from an informant. According to the informant, a succubus named Adele, the tana demon might hit one of two places tonight. The other team was checking out the first club a block away, and we got the second one, a club called Suave.

"When we get inside, spread out," Raoul said. "If you spot the target, keep him in sight and let the team know where you are. Any questions?"

He looked at Mason and me. We shook our heads, and the four of us walked toward the club, where a line of about fifty people stood outside the door. Instead of getting into line, Raoul headed for the door where a burly man stood guard. I didn't hear the exchange between them, but the bouncer smiled and waved us in amid complaints from the crowd.

Loud music and a wave of warm air hit me as we walked down the short hallway to the main section of the club. The interior was one big room with a round bar in the center, surrounded by a sea of undulating bodies. How did you find someone in all this, especially when you only had a vague description to go by? The only way to recognize a tana demon was by their unique odor, which could most aptly be described as rotting oranges. Humans couldn't smell it, but we could. The problem was that you had to get close enough to pick it up.

I waved to Mason and set off around the edge of the dancers, my eyes scanning every male face as my nose tried to detect the tana's presence. According to Adele, the demon was tall and blond, which wasn't a whole lot to go on and fit the description of half the men here. More than one of them caught me looking, prompting them to approach me and slowing my search. I brushed them off as politely as I could and continued on my way. Of course, there's always that one guy who is more persistent than the others.

"One drink," he called over the music.

"No, thanks. I'm looking for someone."

I continued to search the faces around us. When he spoke again, he was inches from me, and I could smell alcohol on his breath. I'd seen intoxicated humans in movies and on TV, but this was my first encounter with one. The alcohol fumes made me want to cover my nose and mouth. It was a good thing humans didn't have our sense of smell, or they'd probably never date.

"I'm someone," he drawled silkily.

I nudged away the hand he'd laid on my shoulder. He was good-looking, and I was sure any number of girls here would love him to be their *someone*. I wasn't one of them.

"Excuse me. I think I see my friend."

I plunged into the crowd, letting it swallow me up. My new direction took me toward the bar, and I had to push through the mass of bodies. A hand cupped my ass, and I swiped it away in annoyance. When a different hand groped my breast, I wasn't as forgiving. I squeezed the fingers until the face-less man yelped in pain.

My mood was darker by the time I reached the bar, and the excitement of my first job had dimmed. I wondered how Mason and the others were faring. I hadn't heard from them, so I assumed they weren't having any luck either.

A bartender stopped in front of me and asked what I wanted. I ordered a ginger ale and sipped it as I resumed my task of studying the face of every blond male around me. I soon came to the realization that hunting wasn't all chases and combat. It could be downright boring.

On the opposite side of the circular bar, a couple caught my eye. I'd seen them during my first scan of the people around the bar, but I'd dismissed the man because he was dark-haired, not blond. I noticed them this time because the girl, who had seemed alert a few minutes ago, now looked drunk. Or drugged, if her glassy eyes and slack mouth were any indication.

I looked at her companion and found him watching her with an expression that was more hunger than concern. I knew how easy it was for someone to slip you a drug in one of these places. I also knew predators didn't always come in demon form.

The girl got off her stool and would have fallen if the man hadn't grabbed her. She smiled at him with unfocused eyes as he led her away from the bar. I set my glass on the bar and followed.

I lost them in the crowd several times, but I managed to catch sight of them walking down a dark hallway toward the back exit of the club. I debated whether or not to alert my team and decided not to pull them away from the job for this. If it came down to it, I could easily handle a human male.

The metal door squeaked when I opened it and slipped outside into a loading area used for deliveries. At the bottom of a concrete ramp, I spotted the man carrying the girl, who appeared to be unconscious. He stopped walking and looked up at me.

"Well, this isn't the right door." I bit my lip, pretending to be embarrassed.

His gaze moved over my body before resting on my face. "You shouldn't be out here alone, sweetheart."

I jiggled the doorknob that had locked behind me. "Damn it. Now I'll have to walk all the way around to the front again."

"Come. I'll walk with you." He adjusted the girl's weight in his arms. "I was just leaving anyway. My girl had a bit too much to drink."

"Oh, thanks," I said with exaggerated relief as I started toward them. "Is she okay?"

"She just needs to sleep it off." He glanced down at the girl's face. When he looked up again, there was no mistaking the hungry gleam in his dark eyes.

I took another two steps, and my nose twitched as the unmistakable smell of rotten oranges filled my nostrils.

My mind raced as I evaluated the situation. Tana demons were strong, but so was I. I didn't have the speed or strength of a warrior like Raoul, but I could hold my own against a lone demon. My main concern was for the girl, who could be badly injured in a fight. And there was no way this guy was going down without one.

I had the element of surprise on my side. He wouldn't be this calm if he knew what I was. If I alerted the team, he'd know, and he could hurt the girl before backup arrived.

"You coming?"

I started when I realized I'd stopped halfway down the ramp. I gnawed the inside of my cheek as I began walking again. *What do I do?*

The decision was taken out of my hands when the demon suddenly stiffened and his eyes narrowed on me.

"Mohiri."

Crap. I'd forgotten that some demons – such as Incubi and tana demons – could recognize other demons. So much for the element of surprise.

"I only want the human," I said evenly.

I hoped he didn't see through my lie. This demon had already killed four women, and there was no way I was letting him go free so he could do it again.

His smile was more of a sneer. "You're young, and I bet you've never met one of my kind before now. I've been around longer than you, and I'm not someone you want to mess with."

A tendril of fear curled in my stomach, but I ignored it and spoke with confidence. "Leave the human and I won't mess with you."

He laughed.

Without taking my eyes from him, I reached down and pulled out one of the silver knives tucked inside my boots. I felt better with the familiar weapon in my hand.

The smile faded from his face, and he backed up several steps to lay the girl on the ground. He straightened and faced me, hatred churning in his dark, angry eyes.

I let my Mori come closer to the surface, relishing in its strength flowing through me. Now that the human was out of the equation, I was ready to fight.

"Report in."

Raoul's voice in my earpiece startled me. Before I could respond, the demon took advantage of the distraction and lunged at me, faster than I expected.

I moved to the side, but he managed to hit my right shoulder, throwing me off balance. I recovered in time to see him coming in for a second attack. This time, I was ready for him.

My knife sank into the flesh above his collarbone. He grunted in pain and spun away, pulling free of the blade. Black demon blood poured from the smoking wound.

"Beth, where are you?" Mason asked over the comm.

I hit the button on my earpiece. "Outside –"

It was all I managed to get out before the demon made a break for it. I guess he figured backup was coming, and he'd decided his meal wasn't worth dying for.

I let my knife fly, as I'd done a thousand times in practice, hitting him squarely between the shoulder blades. He stumbled, and I tackled him, taking him down to the ground. I wrenched his arms tightly behind his back, and he howled in pain. Yanking out the knife, I raised it to deliver the killing blow.

"You have got to be kidding me."

I paused mid-strike and stared at the blonde girl standing a dozen yards away. She wore dark jeans, red boots, and a red leather jacket I would kill for. In her hand was a long silver blade.

She scowled and strode toward us. "Do you know how long I've been after this bastard?"

The demon tried to buck me off, and I pulled his arms tighter. He let out a muffled scream and fell quiet again.

KAREN LYNCH

I looked at the girl. She wasn't close enough for me to sense her Mori, but I had a strong suspicion she was one of ours.

"You want him?" I asked her.

She huffed. "It's no fun once they're down."

A door opened, and I heard running feet.

The girl smirked. "Hello, boys. Come to watch?"

"Why am I not surprised to see you here?" Raoul sounded amused as he crouched beside me. "Nice work, rookie. You going to finish it, or sit on it for a while?"

I'd been about to take out the demon before everyone arrived. Now I felt self-conscious performing my first kill in front of an audience.

"Just taking a breather," I quipped, earning a snort of laughter from the blonde warrior.

Raoul chuckled and stood. "How's the human?"

"Out cold," Brock called. "But she'll make it. We should get her out of here, though."

That was all I needed to hear. I raised my knife again and plunged it into the tana demon's heart. He jerked, made a gasping sound, and went still.

I stood and brushed off my pants. Then I retrieved my knife, wiping it clean on the demon's shirt before I looked for Mason, who watched me with a mix of envy and pride.

He walked over and held up a hand for me to slap. "Niiiice."

"Thanks." I tried to be all cool about it, but I felt myself beaming. No one's praise meant more to me than his.

"Good kill." The blonde warrior nodded approvingly and came over to hold out her hand. "Jordan."

I shook her hand as recognition set in. "You're Sara's friend."

"That's me. And you must be Beth and Mason. She mentioned you last time we talked. Sorry I haven't been by to give you the LA welcome. Been busy looking for this guy."

"Guess this means we'll have the pleasure of your company tomorrow." Raoul smiled, putting his phone to his ear. As he walked past us, I heard him say, "We got him."

Jordan sheathed her knife at her thigh. "This was your first kill?"

"Yes."

"I saw you take him down. Those were some nice moves."

"Thanks."

She looked down at my tight black pants and red top.

"You can fight, and you have good fashion sense. I have a feeling you and I are going to be great friends, Beth."

26

Taking my arm, she led me away from the others toward the street.

"What about the girl and the body?" I asked her, tossing Mason a helpless look over my shoulder.

"There are enough big strong warriors left to take care of the girl and dispose of the demon."

"Oh."

She shot me a mischievous smile. "Besides, if we're going to be friends we need to get to know each other. Now tell me, have you been to Rodeo Drive yet?"

3
———

Chris

I walked into the control room and let out a low whistle at the setup. It was twice the size of the one we'd had in Santa Cruz, and Tristan had obviously spared no expense. I recognized the guys from Raoul's team manning some of the computers, and they all called greetings to me.

"Look who finally decided to visit us."

Raoul left a station and came toward me. "Great to see you, man."

"You, too." I waved a hand at the room. "Nice digs you have here."

Tactical operations had come a long way in the last few decades. I remembered when we didn't have cell phones or computers, and now we had surveillance equipment that would make the CIA wet its collective pants.

"You planning to stick around a while?" Raoul asked.

"Until I get bored with you guys."

He chuckled. "Plenty to keep you busy and entertained in LA."

I looked around. "Speaking of busy, where is the boss man?"

"I think he's in the garage, working on his bike. You know how he is with that thing."

"Yeah, I do."

We had service contracts with mechanics in every state, but Nikolas and I preferred to maintain our own motorcycles. Some of the places we'd ended up, you couldn't count on help if you had bike trouble.

My Ducati was being shipped from Westhorne and should be here tomorrow. Not soon enough. After a month away, I couldn't wait to have my own wheels under me again.

Raoul pointed me toward a door that led to the garage. As soon as the door closed behind me, I heard the clink of tools and saw Nikolas up to his elbows in grease.

"Need some help?" I called, walking toward him.

He stood, wearing a smile. "About time you got your lazy ass back here. How was Germany?"

"Too quiet." I leaned against the SUV closest to him. "Living here, it's easy to forget some countries don't have as much trouble as we do. I did a few jobs, but the trip was a little more relaxing than I'd hoped for."

Laughing, he reached for a rag to wipe his hands. "Well, we've got plenty for you to do here."

"That's what Raoul said. Trouble?"

He shook his head. "It's not as bad as it was last year, but I can see why this command center was needed. We manage everything from here to San Diego, and already we've seen a slight dip in vampire activity in the area. Tristan said the Council is planning to establish a center in New York City next and then Miami."

"Let me guess, he wants you to oversee the setup."

"Yes. Sara wants to see New York, so we'll probably go there."

I cocked an eyebrow. "You going to do the sightseeing thing now?"

"Sara heard there's a big demon community there, and she wants us to build relations with them."

A laugh burst from me at his pained expression. "Sara in the Big Apple. What could possibly go wrong?"

He made a sound that was suspiciously like a groan, and I laughed harder, earning a scowl from him.

"Has she transported again since that time in Atlanta?"

"No. Eldeorin thinks it's linked to her emotions. She was afraid for us, so she did it subconsciously. No telling when it will happen again."

His expression told me he'd be happy if it didn't happen for a long time.

"How much longer are you two staying in LA?" I asked.

"That depends on what your plans are."

Plans were something I didn't have. Nikolas and I had been partners for years, and there'd been no shortage of jobs to keep us on the road together. Now that he and Sara had mated, the three of us were a team. The dynamic was different, but I enjoyed working with them.

There was one place I'd been meaning to go for a while. I hadn't been home to Longstone in years, and on the long flight from Germany, I'd thought about driving up there for a few days. I wasn't sure what reception I'd get, but it was time to go back, to see her.

"I'll probably do a short trip to Oregon, and then I'm here as long as you need me."

"Good." He crouched beside the Ducati again. "I'll show you around when I finish up, and we'll talk about the setup here."

"Sounds good."

A rumble filled the air, and I turned to see two motorcycles pull up outside the open garage door. The first rider shut off her Ducati and removed her helmet to reveal short blonde hair and a face I knew all too well.

The other rider dismounted, facing away from us, and I couldn't help but admire the figure she cut in her jeans, boots, and black leather jacket. There weren't many things sexier in my book than a woman riding a Harley.

She removed her helmet, and I watched as she shook out long blonde hair that tumbled past her shoulders. Her hand came up to smooth down one side of her hair, and I found myself waiting for her to turn around so I could see her face.

Jordan said something to her companion as they removed shopping bags from their bikes' storage compartments. Feminine laughter floated toward me.

I frowned. I knew that laugh...

The women turned toward me, and a jolt of recognition stole my breath when I saw Jordan's friend's face. Shock rippled through me.

Beth.

It had been four years since I'd last seen her, but I'd know her face anywhere. I stared at her, unable to believe she was here and looking even more beautiful, if that was possible. At sixteen, her features had still borne the traces of youth, but at twenty, there was nothing childlike about her. She was curvier and a little taller now, and she walked with all the self-assurance of a young warrior.

I'd heard she had finished training, and so many times in the last two years I'd thought about going home to see her. But something had always seemed to get in the way. I'd assumed she was still at Longstone, and the last place I'd expected to see her was here in Los Angeles.

I knew the moment Beth saw me. Her eyes widened, and she faltered for a brief moment before her face took on a closed expression.

Jordan, who didn't seem to notice the change in Beth, smiled widely when she caught sight of me. "Blondie! I had no idea you were back in the country."

I returned her smile. "Got back today. I figured you guys were missing me, so I flew directly to LAX."

She chuckled. "You're so full of yourself. And I haven't missed you at all because I've been making new friends."

"So I see."

My eyes went to Beth, who met my gaze with the polite interest of a stranger, nothing that resembled the adoring looks from the girl I had known.

"Hello, Beth."

"Hello," she said. "It's nice to see you again."

Hearing her voice after all these years made warmth flood my chest. God, I'd missed her. The urge to hug her was strong, but her cool demeanor held me back. Regret filled me. We used to be so close, but she looked at me as if I was little more than an old acquaintance. And it was all my doing.

"What brings you to LA?" I asked.

She adjusted her hold on her shopping bags. "I work here now."

"At the command center?"

My eyes went to Jordan and then to Nikolas, who nodded. It was on the tip of my tongue to say Beth was too young for a place like LA, but I refrained when I remembered she had been a warrior longer than Jordan had.

"Yep!" Jordan gave Beth a one-armed hug. "Beth is the newest member of the Scooby gang."

"Scooby gang?"

Jordan laughed. "Sara has us watching reruns of *Buffy* with her."

"Ah." I had no idea what *Buffy* was, and I didn't ask.

Beth shifted on her feet, looking like she was about to leave. I wasn't ready for her to go, and I searched for something to say to keep her there a little longer.

"Have you been in LA long?" I asked her.

"We got here two weeks ago," she said in the same detached voice.

We? "Is Rachel here, too?"

Her brows drew together slightly, and she shook her head. "Mason and me."

"Mason?" I repeated, trying to ignore the sudden tightening in my gut.

"He's my friend from home." She took a step back. "I should go. I'm working tonight. It was nice seeing you again."

She turned toward the garage door, but Jordan snagged her arm.

"Wait. We have to show Sara what we got." Jordan looked at me. "Later, Blondie."

Without another glance in my direction, Beth followed Jordan into the house.

I stared after them, unable to take my eyes off Beth until the door closed behind her. I let out a long, slow breath as I recovered from the impact of seeing her again and the knowledge that she could still affect me after all this time.

"Do I want to know what that was about?"

I turned to find Nikolas crouched beside his bike again.

"What?"

"You and Beth. She's usually more talkative." He gave me a sideways glance. "You didn't...?"

The unfinished question hung in the air for a few seconds until the meaning sank in.

"Jesus, no."

His eyebrows shot up at the vehemence of my denial.

"It's Beth," I said.

He gave me a confused look, and I sighed. "You remember Beth. I found her at that fire in Seattle."

Recognition dawned in his eyes. "The one you were always buying gifts for?"

"Yes."

Beth's transition to her new life had been difficult, and I'd stayed at Longstone for a week to help her settle in. I'd never done that for another orphan, but there'd been something about the angel-faced waif that had stirred my protective instincts. Eventually, I'd had to get back to work, and she'd cried when I left. I'd made sure to pick up a little toy or trinket for her whenever I went on a job. I hadn't made it home every month, but she'd always been excited to see me. I'd loved watching her reaction when she opened the gifts I'd brought her.

Nikolas picked up a socket wrench. "I take it you haven't seen her in a while. How long has it been since you last went home?"

"Four years."

"Well, she's not a little girl anymore. And she doesn't look as happy to see you as she used to be."

"I know."

I stared at the door Beth and Jordan had gone through, but all I could see was sixteen-year-old Beth, her gray eyes filled with hurt. I didn't know how yet, but I was going to make things right with her again.

Fated

Beth

As soon as the door closed behind us, I sucked air into my lungs and eased up on the death grip I had on my shopping bags. I was grateful Jordan was ahead of me and couldn't see my face. I needed a moment to recover from seeing Chris so unexpectedly.

Ever since I'd realized he could show up here, I had told myself I was ready to face him again. God, I was such a fool. Coming face-to-face with him had sent me right back to that day, and it was all I could do not to run to my room and cry like I'd done back then.

I schooled my expression as we entered the kitchen. Jordan tossed her bags onto the table and went to the fridge for a bottle of water.

"Back already?" Sara walked into the kitchen. Her eyes fell on the bags, and she grinned. "Forget that last question. Did you leave anything for the other shoppers?"

"Only the stuff we didn't want," Jordan joked. "You should have come with us. We found the most amazing outfits."

Sara made a face. "I have more than enough clothes, thanks to you. I still haven't worn the stuff I bought the last time you dragged me with you."

Jordan's eyes took on a gleam I was starting to recognize. "That's exactly why we need to do a girls' night out."

"Define 'night out,'" Sara said with a hint of wariness. "Are we talking dinner or another one of those underground dance clubs you tricked me into last week?"

"What was wrong with Aro's?"

"Nothing, if you don't count the pixie who asked me to join him and his friends for a foursome," Sara said with a shudder.

Jordan laughed. "You should be used to faeries, as much as you hang around with Eldeorin."

"Eldeorin is my mentor, and he's like a cousin to me," Sara protested.

Jordan snorted. "If you weren't happily mated, he'd be trying his damnedest to get into your pants. Right, Beth?"

"I...can't say. I haven't met him yet."

Sara frowned. "You okay, Beth? You look a little flushed."

"Yes. I mean, I'm fine."

Jordan smirked at me. "Chris has that effect on most women."

Sara's mouth curved into a big smile. "Chris is here?"

"He's in the garage with Nikolas." Jordan finished off her water. "All we need are Emma and the wolf boys, and the whole gang will be here."

Sara chuckled. "Good luck getting any of them out of Maine these days,

33

especially Roland. If I hadn't seen it with my own eyes, I never would have believed he would settle down."

"Yep. Emma even has him housebroken."

"Jordan!" Sara shook her head and started for the garage.

"Hey," Jordan called after her. "Thursday night is girls' night, so don't make plans."

Sara mumbled something that sounded like "whatever." She reached for the door, but it opened before she could touch it. My stomach lurched when Nikolas entered, followed by Chris, who immediately pulled Sara into a hug.

"How was Germany?" Sara asked Chris when she pulled away from him.

He didn't answer immediately, and I looked up to find his eyes on me. My stomach fluttered despite the tightness in my chest, and I grew angry at myself for letting him have any effect on me.

"Germany was great, but I missed you guys," he said, still looking at me.

My jaw clenched. If Chris thought a few smiles and sweet words could undo the past, he was sadly mistaken. A few years ago, his charm would have worked on me, but I was no longer the naïve girl he used to know.

Sara said something, drawing his attention back to her, and I used that moment to make my escape. If anyone noticed me leaving, they said nothing.

Back in the guesthouse, I threw my shopping bags onto the couch and paced the living room, allowing my calm façade to slip.

I couldn't do this. I couldn't see him every day and pretend I felt nothing.

I'd told Mason I could deal with it if Chris showed up, but I'd been lying to both of us. I could leave, but it would raise questions I didn't want to answer. Plus, Mason would insist on going with me, and I would not let him give this up for me. He loved Los Angeles and working with Nikolas, and I'd never seen him so happy.

I sank down in a chair and put my head in my hands.

What am I going to do?

I yawned and rubbed my tired eyes as I walked into the kitchen. For the second night in a row, I'd done more staring at the ceiling and punching my pillow than sleeping. I needed coffee, stat, and I was grumpy enough to maim anyone who got in my way.

Some people liked a big breakfast to start the day. I was a coffee person, and I kept the cupboard stocked with my favorite French roast beans from New Guinea. Even Mason, who usually woke up with the appetite of a pack of ravenous bazerats, wouldn't dare touch my coffee beans.

He would, however, drink all the milk.

"Mason," I growled when I opened the fridge and saw nothing but bottled water and juice.

I looked longingly at the coffee pot then down at the camisole and short cotton pants I'd worn to bed. Coffee or shower?

It was no contest. Pulling my bed hair back into a messy bun, I left the house, not even bothering with shoes. It was still early and the sun hadn't yet risen above the trees, but there were lights on in the main house. Someone was always up here, manning the control room.

The house was quiet when I entered the living room through the French doors, except for the faint murmur of voices coming from the direction of the control room. I moved silently to the kitchen, not wanting to disturb anyone still sleeping, and I let out a happy sound when I opened the fridge and saw four large cartons of milk. Jackpot.

I was grabbing one of the cartons when I heard voices coming toward the kitchen. I grimaced at what I must look like, and then shrugged it off. No one could possibly expect me to look civilized before my first cup of coffee.

Raoul's voice drifted toward me. "I'm going to recon the place for the next day or so."

"Sounds good," Nikolas replied. "Who are you taking with you?"

"Whoever is available."

I turned as the two men walked into the kitchen. Raoul smiled when he saw me with the milk carton.

"Did your roommate drink all the milk again?"

I made a face. "Yes."

He chuckled. "I have something that might cheer you up. How would you like to go on a stakeout with me today?"

"A stakeout?" I asked a little breathlessly, because that could only mean one thing. Vampires. My stomach fluttered in anticipation.

"We have reason to believe there's a new vampire nest in Long Beach. If you're –"

"Yes!"

Raoul and Nikolas laughed. Okay, maybe I was more than a little excited, but they were talking about a *real* vampire nest. New warriors never got to see a nest. This was exactly the reason I'd wanted to come to Los Angeles, to have opportunities like this one.

"When do you want to leave?" I asked, my coffee all but forgotten.

One corner of Raoul's mouth lifted. "Can you be ready in an hour?"

"Ready for what?"

My body stiffened at Chris's voice. Since his arrival two days ago, I'd managed to keep my distance from him, mostly thanks to Mason. My best friend had not been happy to see Chris, and the first thing he'd asked me was if I wanted to leave. When I said no, he'd stuck by my side whenever we were at the house, blocking Chris's attempts to talk to me. The last thing I wanted was to dredge up the past, so I was grateful to Mason for running interference. I wasn't too proud to hide behind my best friend, and I really wished he was here now.

I comforted myself with the reminder that Chris would leave again soon and my life could go back to normal. In a month or so, Sara and Nikolas were heading to New York City to oversee a new command center there. I fully expected Chris to go with them. Until then, I had to bide my time and do my best to avoid him. As far as I was concerned, we had nothing to talk about.

"Beth and I are going to recon a nest," Raoul told Chris.

"How big a nest?" Chris asked.

"Small, maybe three or four vampires."

I felt Chris's eyes move to me, but I kept my gaze fixed squarely on Raoul until Chris spoke again.

"I can go with you if you need a backup."

What? No. Anger and dismay flooded me, and I glared at Chris, only to find him looking at Raoul again. I opened my mouth to protest, but Nikolas spoke first.

"I think this would be a good learning experience for Beth, and she'll be safe with Raoul."

I could have hugged Nikolas at that moment. I turned hopeful eyes on Raoul, who gave me one of his familiar smirks.

"Beth and I can handle it. I'll just have to make sure to get her some coffee on the way."

I could barely contain my excitement. "I'll be ready to go whenever you are."

He came over and took two wrapped muffins from the basket on the counter. "See you back here in an hour."

He and Nikolas headed back toward the control room, and I almost did a happy dance until I remembered I wasn't alone. Chris was still there, and the look on his face said he was going to try to talk to me again.

Dread twisted my stomach. The logical part of my brain said I should just be an adult and get it over with. Let him have his say and move on. But the hurt sixteen-year-old in me wanted to run away and cry every time I saw his face. That part of me was frantically trying to think of a way to escape now.

"Beth, I –"

The door to the garage swung open, and Mason entered, followed by a laughing Brock. Mason came up short when he saw me alone with Chris, and my expression must have told him all he needed to know. He headed straight for me and wrapped me in a one-armed hug.

I immediately ducked out of his hold. "Ew! You stink of fish and seaweed."

The two of them laughed. Mason and Brock had hit it off since we got here, and Brock had introduced Mason to his first love: surfing. Mason had taken to the sport like a...well, like a fish to water. If he wasn't talking about watching Nikolas spar, he was telling me about the perfect wave he'd caught that morning.

I didn't mind. I liked seeing his face light up when he talked about the things that made him happy. And it wasn't as if I hadn't made new friends here, too. I spent half my free time with Sara or Jordan, sometimes both. Mason and I would always be close, but we were getting to know new people, and that was a good thing.

His eyes lit up. "We caught some great waves this morning. Brock knows all the best places to go."

"You should come with us. Give it a try," Brock said.

I made a face, and he chuckled. I liked the ocean, but my idea of communing with nature involved a mountain trail and a sturdy pair of hiking boots. At home, I used to drag Mason along with me, before he'd discovered his love of surfing. Now I either went alone, or Sara joined me if she was free.

"No, thanks. I'll stick to dry land, if you don't mind."

Brock looked behind me. "How about you, Chris? You still surf?"

"Not in a few years."

Suddenly, I had an image of Chris's wet muscled body walking out of the ocean, and warmth infused me. I swallowed and pushed the thought to the farthest recesses of my mind. So, I was still attracted to him. What female wouldn't be? It didn't change anything.

I clutched the milk carton I still held. "I'd love to stay and talk surfing with you boys, but I have to run. I'm going on a job with Raoul today."

Mason's eyes widened with interest. "Oh, yeah? What kind of job?"

I could barely contain my excitement. "We're staking out a vampire nest."

"No way. Are you messing with me?"

"Nope. He asked me right before you got here."

"Ah, man."

I shrugged, deciding a little payback was in order. "Just think. If you hadn't drunk all the milk *again*, I'd be over at our place right now, enjoying my coffee in blissful ignorance, and Raoul might have asked you to go with him instead."

Brock snorted, and I thought I heard Chris chuckle behind me. Mason looked like someone had taken away his surfboard.

"Later, boys."

Smiling, I headed for the door to the garage to avoid walking past Chris. I heard footsteps behind me, and for a second, I thought he'd followed me. Then I caught the smell of salt water and knew it was Mason. I should have known he'd have my back, no matter what.

I slowed to let him catch up, smiling my thanks at him.

He gave me a devilish grin and laid an arm across my shoulders again. This time, I didn't push him away. It was a small price to pay.

4

Chris

I placed the tablet on the desk and sat back in my chair, rubbing the back of my neck. It had taken me several minutes to realize I'd read the same paragraph at least a dozen times. At this rate, I'd never get through these reports.

Closing my eyes, I saw the same image that had occupied my mind since yesterday morning – Beth standing barefoot in the kitchen and looking like she'd just crawled out of bed. The sight of her had sent heat through me, and my hands had itched to release her hair from the bun and run my fingers through its softness.

"Argh." I got up to pace the office. I had to stop thinking about her like this.

A groan slipped out because I knew that was wishful thinking. I'd thought I had dealt with this, until coming here and seeing Beth again. The moment I saw her in the garage, I knew I'd been deluding myself.

Since the day I'd arrived, she'd gone out of her way not to talk to me, and the more she avoided me, the stronger my need to see her became. I kept telling myself I just wanted to clear the air between us and to repair the damage I'd done to our friendship. I was lying to myself. I wanted more than her forgiveness, but I knew that was all I could ask for.

A phone rang in the control room, yanking me from my thoughts, and I heard Will answer it. Before I could walk to the door of the office, he called out to me. My gut hardened instinctively. Beth was out with Raoul again, staking out the nest, and my first thought was that she was in trouble. Raoul would never allow her to enter a dangerous situation without backup, but vampires were unpredictable and anything could happen on a job.

"What's up?" I asked, keeping my inner turmoil out of my voice.

Will hit the intercom button, and Raoul's voice filled the speaker.

"We've got trouble here."

My heart began to pound. "Is Beth okay?"

"Yes. She's here beside me. A van pulled up behind the house a few minutes ago, and I just heard a human scream inside the house. We need to go in."

"I'm on my way." I looked at Will. "Call in one of the other teams."

"On it."

I pulled out my phone as I ran for my bike and called Brock, who was patrolling Newport Beach with Mason tonight. I gave him the address, and he said they'd meet us there. Raoul and I could handle a small nest, but I preferred to have backup with humans involved. I had no idea how long it would take another team to respond if they were busy.

The house was an old Queen Anne Victorian surrounded by a short iron fence and well-maintained rose bushes. It didn't look anything like what you'd expect for a vampire nest, which made it the perfect hideaway for them. Vampires looking to set up house liked to prey on older people who lived alone. They killed the house's owner and moved in with no one the wiser.

Beth and Raoul were camped out on the roof of a small convenience store across the street from the house. They met me in the parking lot behind the store, which was closed for the night, and Raoul filled me in.

"We've spotted four different vampires coming and going since yesterday. I couldn't see how many arrived in the van though, so I have no idea how many are in there now."

"Young vampires?" I asked.

"Couldn't tell from here."

I studied the house. When Nikolas and I had worked as a team, we'd thought nothing of entering a small nest without backup. I'd worked with him so long we could practically read each other's minds. Raoul was a seasoned warrior, but we'd never raided a nest together. We could wait for Brock, but we had no idea of the condition of the humans in the house.

"Raoul, you climb up to the roof of the porch and see if you can get in that way. I'll take one of the downstairs windows. Beth, you stay here."

She nodded, though I could see the disappointment in her eyes. No warrior wanted to stand by and watch the action, but new warriors did not enter a nest, at least not until after it had been cleared out.

Raoul and I approached the house carefully, splitting up after we'd hopped the fence. He went toward the porch, and I walked around the house, stopping at each window to listen for movement or voices inside. I peered into a small laundry room and knew this was the best entry point for me. The odds of a vampire using a laundry room were slim, so I could enter undetected.

I wasn't surprised to find the window unlatched. Vampires were careless when it came to security, too sure of their own strength to worry about an attack. I eased the window up and slipped in, listening for sounds from the rest of the house.

Raised voices came from another room, and it didn't take long to figure out they were arguing over what to do with the humans. A male vampire wanted to make them last a few days, and a female argued that there were plenty of humans in the city when these were gone.

I smiled. New vampires.

I left the laundry room and moved stealthily down a hallway toward the voices. Peering through an open door, I saw the two vampires facing off against each other in the middle of the living room. On the couch, two women and a man huddled together. The man had blood on the collar of his white shirt, and the dazed look on his face told me he'd been fed upon. But the three of them were alive, and that was all that mattered.

A loud thump upstairs silenced the two vampires, and I ducked out of sight as they turned to the doorway.

"He'd better not be messing with her," the male growled. "I told him that one was mine."

Footsteps approached the doorway, and I prepared to strike. The male ran into the hall, his eyes going wide when he saw me. Before he could yell a warning, I drove my sword into his chest. He gasped and sank to the floor.

"Jack," the female called.

I didn't wait for her to come check on her friend. I sped into the living room, moving too fast for her eyes to track. She barely got out a scream before my blade silenced her.

One of the human women cried out, and I lowered my sword to appear less threatening.

"How many are there?" I asked them.

"F-four," the other woman croaked.

"Stay here," I ordered them.

I left the room, and I was at the bottom of the stairs when Raoul shouted from above. "We have a runner."

Fear shot through me. Beth was out there alone.

I tore open the front door and raced outside in time to see a figure running across the dark street. He was headed straight for Beth, who still stood in front of the convenience store.

Beth moved. Metal flashed and the vampire staggered, grabbing at the knife buried in his chest.

I sped down the steps and sailed over the fence – and came up short when I saw Beth run out to intercept the injured vampire. Her face was a mask of determination as she swung her sword, slicing cleanly through his neck. He dropped, and she stared at the body with an expression of disbelief on her face. I knew that look. I'd seen it enough times on warriors making their first vampire kill.

My chest expanded with pride and the knowledge that I'd been here for her first kill. I walked toward her as she pulled her knife from the vampire's chest and wiped it clean on his pants.

"Good work," I said.

I meant it. She had great aim with her throw, and she'd finished the job quickly. A more experienced warrior would have gone for the chest instead of the throat because the vampire was already half-dead. But I wasn't going to correct her technique and ruin this moment for her.

"Thanks."

She swallowed and took a step back. It was clear she was flattered by the praise but not comfortable with the person delivering it. I needed to change that.

Running feet alerted us to the fact we were not alone, and the two of us looked down the street as Brock and Mason approached, swords drawn. They slowed when they got close, and Mason's eyes widened at the sight of Beth's bloody sword.

"Way to go, Beth."

Brock walked over to her and gave her a fist bump. She smiled, and I felt a pang of envy that she was so at ease with the other warrior.

"You guys going to stand out there all night?" Raoul called from the front step of the house.

I looked at Beth. "Ready to see the inside of a vampire nest?"

"Yes!" she and Mason said in unison.

I smiled at their excitement as I grabbed the dead vampire by the foot and dragged him to the house. Brock made a sound of disgust and picked up the head.

I left the corpse near the bushes lining the fence where it was out of sight of passersby. Then I followed the others into the house. When I entered the living room, I found Beth already tending to the humans, talking to them in a gentle, reassuring voice.

Raoul came to stand beside me in the doorway. "We have another girl upstairs. She's in shock but uninjured."

"Laurie!" One of the women leaped to her feet. "My sister. Where is she?"

Raoul held out a hand to her. "I'll take you to her."

"Should we call in a cleanup crew?" Mason asked me.

"They're on the way."

I stepped over one of the bodies to do a final sweep of the house, something I should have done before allowing Beth and Mason to come in.

The other team arrived a few minutes later and quickly got to work, disposing of the four bodies. The humans were treated and taken home since none of them had sustained serious injury. The man had been bitten, but he improved once we administered gunna paste.

While the others handled cleanup, Raoul and I went through the house and yard to look for clues to the fate of the homeowner. We both knew the elderly woman was dead, but it was part of our job to make sure. In the backyard, we found a mound of freshly turned soil, but we didn't dig it up. Once we cleared out of here, one of us would call the human authorities to report a disturbance. They would investigate and discover the grave. It was all we could do for her.

It was after midnight when we finished up. I walked outside, looking for Beth, and saw her walking down the street to where she and Raoul had parked their bikes. Mason was nowhere to be seen. For once, she was alone.

Beth

I smiled to myself as I walked to my Harley. I'd killed my first vampire, and I'd been inside an actual vampire nest. The fact that Chris had been here didn't even dim my excitement. I'd have to work with him eventually, so I might as well get used to it. As long as we kept our conversations about work, I could do this. I would.

Yeah, that's why you're sneaking away while he's busy.

I was pulling on my helmet when I felt a small gust of air and Chris appeared in front of me. Startled, I dropped the helmet, and it rolled noisily across the pavement.

I scowled at him. "It's not nice to sneak up on people."

Chris smiled, not looking the least bit sorry as he retrieved my helmet. "You used to love it when I did that, Dove."

I ignored the little thrill that went through me at hearing his old pet name for me. "No one calls me that anymore, and I haven't played games since... in a long time."

His smile dimmed, and regret filled his eyes. "Dove – Beth, I'm sorry."

I said nothing.

"I'm sorry for everything, for hurting you, for the way I left. At the time, I thought it was the right thing to do. I never meant to hurt you, but you were so young and I was –"

"You don't have to explain," I said in a tight voice. "I was a silly girl, and it hurt for a little while, but I got over it. There's nothing to apologize for."

I looked away, swallowing around the lump forming in my throat. I was a warrior, damn it. I would not cry.

"If that were true, you wouldn't be avoiding me and you'd be able to look at me now." He came closer and rested a hand on the handlebar. "I've missed you, Dove. Tell me how to fix this and how we can be friends again."

"I..." I wanted to say he'd known where to find me all these years if he'd missed me, but I was afraid my voice would crack before I got the words out.

"Look at me," he ordered in a tender voice I was unable to refuse.

I lifted my eyes and instantly regretted it when I saw the sadness in his. No fair. He'd hurt *me*, not the other way around. He didn't get to be the injured one here.

"I left because I thought it was best for you. It didn't mean I stopped caring about you." He ran a hand through his blond hair. "It just got...complicated. One day you were a little girl, and the next you were a young woman, and everything changed."

I nodded mutely. He didn't need to remind me of how things had changed between us. I'd wasted too many hours trying to figure out what I'd done wrong and how I'd driven him away. It had taken me a long time to admit it wasn't my fault and to accept I couldn't have done anything to make him stay.

"Did you get the things I sent you?" he asked.

"Yes. Thank you."

Every birthday and Christmas, a package had arrived from Chris without fail. But it was hard to feel happy about gifts from someone who couldn't be bothered to deliver them himself. As much as I'd wanted to get rid of them, I couldn't, so they'd ended up in the back of my closet, along with every other gift he'd given me since I'd known him.

An uncomfortable silence fell between us, broken after a long moment by Chris's barely perceptible sigh.

"I know we can't go back to the way things were. Too much time has passed, and you're not a little girl anymore. But I hope we can be friends."

I should have avoided his gaze. One look into his beseeching green eyes and I couldn't come right out and tell him no, even if the ache in my chest warned me against letting him in again.

As if he knew I was weakening, his smile returned, and my traitorous stomach fluttered. I needed to get away from him before I reverted to that naïve girl of four years ago. Like he'd said, there was no going back.

"Beth," Mason called.

I caught the frustration in Chris's eyes before I looked over my shoulder at Mason, who was walking toward us.

"You heading back to the house?" Mason asked, standing so close to me that our arms touched.

I had to stifle a laugh. I loved that Mason always had my back, but no one could ever accuse him of being ambiguous.

"Hey, Chris," Mason said.

Mason wouldn't admit it out of loyalty to me, but I knew he was conflicted about Chris. His anger at Chris for hurting me was tempered by Chris's easy manner and a little bit of hero worship on Mason's part. Chris was almost as well-known as Nikolas, and his fighting skills had been talked about just as much among the trainees back home.

Chris smiled. "Mason, how'd you like your first nest?"

"It was cleaner than I expected, except for the blood from your kills."

Chris laughed. "That was a new nest, no more than a few weeks old by the look of it. I've seen some that would make you not want to eat for a week."

Mason made a face. "I bet you've seen some crazy stuff."

"You have no idea." Chris's gaze moved between Mason and me. "Remind me to tell you about it sometime."

"That'd be great."

My sigh was inaudible. It was like Chris knew exactly what to say to win over my best friend. Not that I didn't want the two of them to be friends. Did I?

Mason looked at me. "Brock and I are heading back to Newport Beach. You want to patrol with us?"

"Raoul's going to show me how to write up our recon report, so I have to go back to the house." And then I was going to have a long shower and crawl into my very soft bed.

I extended my hand toward the helmet Chris was still holding, and he passed it to me. I donned it and started the Harley, raising a hand to Chris as he stepped aside to let me out.

I let out a long breath when I rounded the corner and headed down the next street. Okay, that wasn't as bad as I'd expected. He'd said his piece, and I'd managed not to embarrass myself by crying. Now he could go about his business, and I could stop worrying about talking to him.

I hadn't replied to his comment about us being friends because I didn't think I could open myself up to him that way again. I'd work with him as long as he was here, but that was as far as I was willing to go. I'd let Chris in once, and he'd hurt me deeply. I wouldn't give him the chance to do that a second time.

Chris

"Vampires?"

I nodded grimly at Nikolas. "That's my first guess."

We entered the living room where Sara, Jordan, Raoul, and several of the other warriors milled around. Upon our arrival, everyone found seats and waited for Nikolas to speak.

The door to the back terrace opened, and Beth and Mason hurried in.

"Are we late?" Beth asked.

Her gaze flicked to mine for a brief moment before going to Nikolas. It was like that every time she and I were in the same room. Since our talk two nights ago, she had stopped avoiding me, but little else had changed between us. I missed the easy relationship we used to have, but I couldn't push her. I'd hurt her badly, and it would take time to earn her trust again.

It was because of Beth that I'd agreed to take command of the center from Nikolas when he left for New York. If she hadn't been here, I probably would have decided to go with Nikolas and Sara. But Los Angeles had the most demon and vampire activity in the country, and Beth, though well-trained, was a new warrior on her first field assignment. She didn't know yet that I was taking over for Nikolas, and I wasn't sure how she'd react to the news. We planned to announce it once we got final approval from the Council.

"We're just about to start." Nikolas looked at me, and I glanced down at the report displayed on the tablet in my hand.

"In the last ten days, there have been eight missing person reports filed with the LAPD. That's not unusual in a city like Los Angeles, but we've detected a pattern in three of the cases that suggests they are connected."

"What kind of pattern?" Jordan asked.

"Three of the missing people are young women between the ages of seventeen and twenty-one. Two of the girls are seniors at Catholic schools in the area, and the third is a novice from a convent in New York who was visiting her family."

Sara's brows drew together. "Who would target Catholic girls?"

"The most likely answer is a vampire," Nikolas said. "Some of them have been known to have such fetishes. No bodies have turned up yet, so if it is the work of a vampire, they're being careful to hide their tracks."

I nodded. "It could also be the work of slave traffickers. Healthy young women would fetch a high price on the black market. Their religion might be a coincidence."

Sara's mouth formed a thin, angry line. "I'll work with Kelvan to reach out to the demon community and find out if we have another gulak setting up shop here. They like to run slaves, and as soon as we shut down one operation, another pops up."

Sara's friend Kelvan was a vrell demon who also happened to be an elite computer hacker skilled enough to outmaneuver our own security guys. Thanks to their friendship, we had access to Kelvan's unique talents and an inside connection to the vast demon network across the country.

"Do we know where the girls disappeared?" Raoul asked.

I looked at the tablet again. "Alice Carney – the novice – was the first to go missing. She went to mass at St. Vincent's a week and a half ago, and her family said she never came home. We don't know if she even made it to the church."

Raoul nodded. "I'll start there."

"What about the other girls?" Jordan asked me.

"Jessica Ryan left Our Lady of Mercy Academy alone last Saturday to go to a movie in Pasadena. She never returned to the school.

"Tracy Levine went to St. Teresa's Preparatory School. She left school on Monday afternoon, and that was the last anyone's seen of her. Her car was found in the student parking lot, and there were no signs of a struggle."

"A vampire wouldn't take her from a school parking lot in the middle of the afternoon," Beth said almost to herself. "Do they have outside security cameras?"

"Yes, but they only cover the exits, not the parking lot."

"Beth and I will check out the high schools," Jordan said.

Beth gave her a look of surprise. "We will?"

"Yeah. Who better to talk to a bunch of girls than us. We can fit in there, and no one will know the difference."

I let out a short burst of laughter, earning a glare from Jordan.

"What?" she demanded.

It was Sara who answered her. "Sorry, Jordan, but the idea of you posing as a Catholic school girl is hilarious."

Jordan glowered at us. "Are you guys saying I can't blend in?"

Sara grinned. "You'd blend into a high school about as well as I would at a Paris fashion show."

That got a snort from Jordan, who looked slightly appeased.

"I'll go with Beth to the schools," Sara offered. "I'm the only one here who's actually been to high school, so I'm the best one to go."

"Well, when you put it that way," Jordan drawled.

"Good." Nikolas stood. "We'll send word to our local informants and see if anyone's heard something about the missing girls."

Jordan jumped up from her seat. "I guess that's a wrap. Come on, ladies."

Sara groaned. "Do I have to?"

"Yes, you have to. We made plans." Jordan reached for Sara's hand and pulled her to her feet. "It'll be fun. I promise."

Sara gave Nikolas a helpless look before Jordan tugged her toward the bedrooms on the other side of the house. Beth followed them, laughing at their antics. Seeing her smile brought one to my own lips. I hoped someday she'd be like that with me again.

"Where are they off to?" I asked Nikolas.

"Jordan planned a girls' night. Dinner and then dancing at Lure."

I shot him a disbelieving look as we walked back to the control room. There'd been a time when Nikolas wouldn't let Sara out of his sight in this city, and now she was going to a nightclub without him after we'd just had a meeting about missing girls.

We entered the control room, and he smiled as if he'd read my mind.

"Sara lets me know where they're going, and she carries a tracker whenever she leaves the house."

"How did you get her to agree to that?" I laughed, remembering how much Sara had detested our tracking devices when we met her.

"It was her idea. She thought it would give me peace of mind."

"Does it?"

"No, but she won't have a good time if she thinks I'm worrying."

He led the way to the room we were sharing as an office, and we sat on either side of the desk. Leaning back in his chair, he ran his hands through his hair in agitation.

I rested my elbows on my knees. "Nikolas, you do remember Sara can sense a vampire a block away, and she has enough Fae power in her pinky to take down an army of demons. I'd be more worried about what damage she and Jordan could cause together."

"You're right, I know." He rubbed his jaw. "My parents told me it'll be like this for the first few years."

"Years?" I grimaced.

The thought of always worrying about another person's wellbeing sounded exhausting. Beth's face immediately filled my mind, and I dismissed it. Being protective of someone you cared about was nothing like what a bonded male felt for his mate.

Nikolas opened his laptop. "Keeping busy helps. It's that or follow her, and we both know how well that would go over if she found out."

I didn't try to hold back my laughter. "By all means then, let's get to work."

We spent the next three hours reaching out to every informant and contact we had in southern California. There were no leads on the missing girls, but we put out enough feelers that we were bound to get a hit if a vampire or demon was involved.

Raoul filled the doorway as we were finishing up.

"Spoke to some of the parishioners at St. Vincent's, and two of them remember seeing Alice Carney at mass the night she disappeared. They didn't notice anything out of the ordinary, though."

I leaned back in my chair. "That means she was taken on the way back to her parents' house."

Raoul nodded. "Looks that way. I'll pick it up there tomorrow. Right now, I'm heading out for a steak. Either of you want to join me?"

"Yeah." I stood and gave Nikolas a questioning look.

He closed the laptop. "Sounds good."

We went through the door to the garage, and Nikolas grabbed a set of keys for one of the SUVs. He was backing us out of the garage when the door to the kitchen opened and Jordan emerged in a short red dress and heels. She was followed by Sara, who was dressed more demurely in pants and an off the shoulder top.

Nikolas put the SUV in park, and Raoul and I rolled down our windows to make catcalls at the girls. Jordan gave us a sexy pose. Sara rolled her eyes and walked over to Nikolas, who had gotten out of the vehicle.

I was about to ask if Beth was going with them when movement in the corner of my eye brought my gaze around to the front of the SUV. Through the windshield, I saw Beth exit the guesthouse. My jaw literally dropped at the sight of her in a tiny pale-blue dress and strappy high heels that showed off her feminine curves and long, toned legs. It was such a change from the jeans and boots she normally wore that I forgot for a moment who I was staring at.

A sharp whistle from Raoul brought me to my senses, and I fought the urge to scowl at him as I opened my door and got out. I wasn't sure if I was more annoyed at him for looking at Beth with such open appreciation, or at myself for having done the same thing.

"Whatcha think, Blondie?" Jordan called over her shoulder as she walked out to meet Beth.

"Gorgeous."

My gaze went to Beth, who looked away with pink tingeing her cheeks. She was stunning and sexy as hell in that dress – and I had the sudden urge to strip off my shirt and cover her up.

"Smooth." Jordan grinned and hooked her arm around Beth's. "But you're right. We do look hot."

Raoul came up and slapped me on the shoulder. "I'm thinking we should skip the steak and go with the ladies instead."

Jordan held up a hand. "Oh, no. It's called 'girls' night' for a reason." Her voice grew louder. "And as soon as we can surgically separate Sara from her mate, we'll bid you gentlemen good night."

I glanced over at Sara and Nikolas, who were standing beside the SUV, kissing. At Jordan's words, they broke apart, smiling at each other.

Jordan and Beth walked over to a silver Porsche parked outside. My eyes followed the sway of Beth's hips until I forced my gaze elsewhere.

Off-limits. Don't even think about going there.

"Nice ride, Jordan," Raoul called.

She patted the roof. "It's a loaner. I'm thinking about getting one for myself."

Beth went around to the passenger side and climbed into the back. Jordan and Sara took the front seats.

"Don't wait up," Jordan called as they drove away.

I turned back to the SUV to find Nikolas watching me curiously. No doubt he'd noticed me staring at Beth, but he wasn't the type to mention it. That was a good thing because I had no idea what to say.

"Do you think it's safe to let the three of them out in the city like that?" Raoul asked as we climbed back into the SUV.

"They can take care of themselves," I said. Then I thought about a club full of men staring at Beth in that dress, and an unpleasant burn started in my stomach.

Raoul scoffed. "I'm worried about the city, not the girls."

We laughed, and Nikolas and I shared a look.

"You have the receiver for that tracker?" I asked him.

He patted his front pocket. "Right here."

5

Beth

I was quiet when we drove away from the house, happy to let Jordan and Sara carry the conversation. Thoughts and images tumbled through my mind as I replayed that moment outside the garage over and over. Even now, my stomach fluttered when I remembered the heat in Chris's eyes when he'd looked at me.

Since our talk, I'd caught him watching me a few times, but his expression was always one of regret. He'd seemed sincere when he'd apologized and asked to be friends, and I'd been trying to get my head in a place where I could at least live in the same house with him.

But that look.

"Earth to Beth."

Jordan's teasing voice pulled me from my thoughts, and I looked up to meet her laughing eyes in the rearview mirror.

"Sorry. What were you saying?"

Her gaze held mine for a second before it flicked back to the road. "I asked if you are going to tell us what's up with you and Chris."

I frowned. "Nothing."

"Nothing? Right." She exchanged a look with Sara. "Remember when you told me there was nothing between you and Nikolas?"

Sara nodded. "I believe you said I was clueless."

"Yeah, well, I thought saying you were full of shit was a bit much at that point in our friendship." Jordan snickered. "And I was so right about you guys." Her eyes met mine again in the mirror. "I think our friend Beth's been holding out on us."

"I think you may be right," Sara said.

I let out a strangled laugh. "Are you seriously comparing me and Chris to Sara and Nikolas?"

Sara and I had gotten close in the weeks since I'd arrived in Los Angeles, and she'd shared some of how she and Nikolas had met, bonded, and eventually fallen in love and mated. It was an incredibly romantic story and so far removed from Chris and me that it was laughable.

Jordan lifted a shoulder. "I'm saying you guys have more than a casual friendship."

"No," I blurted. "Why would you think that?"

"I don't know," Jordan said slowly. "Maybe because of the obvious tension between you two."

"There's no –"

"Or the way he looks at you whenever you're in the same room," Sara added.

Jordan snorted. "You mean the way he practically devoured her with his eyes back there?"

"He did not." Heat crept up my neck. "It's not what you think."

"But it is something." Jordan smirked at Sara. "Told you."

Sara turned halfway in her seat to look at me. "You don't have to talk about it if you don't want to, but you can tell us anything and we'll never break your trust."

I clenched my hands in my lap. "I know."

"The thing is," she continued, "as long as I've known Chris, he's never shown any interest in Mohiri women. But it's clear he cares about you from the way he acts around you."

I stared at her, not sure how to respond to hearing Chris didn't date Mohiri women. I'd gone out of my way not to hear about his extracurricular activities in the last four years, so I had no idea about his love life.

"He's not interested in me, at least not that way. Trust me on that."

Jordan turned the wheel, and the Porsche suddenly swerved into the parking lot of the French restaurant where we had reservations. A few minutes later, we were seated at a corner table, ordering appetizers.

As soon as our waitress left us, Jordan leaned in, giving me an expectant look.

I sighed in defeat. "I told you guys I was an orphan and that I lived at

Longstone since I was six. What I didn't tell you was I nearly died in an apartment fire. A warrior saved me and brought me to Longstone."

Jordan's eyes widened. "Chris?"

"Yes. I don't remember much about my first days at Longstone, except him. Rachel, my guardian, told me I was traumatized when I came in and I wouldn't let anyone near me but Chris. She took me to her home, and Chris stayed with us until I felt safe with her. He even slept in a chair in my room for the first few nights."

Sara put a hand over her heart. "That's so sweet."

Jordan nodded in agreement.

"Eventually, Chris had to go back to work. He'd come home every few months, but he didn't stay with Rachel and me. I used to get so excited when I heard he was coming for a visit, and he'd always spend a whole day with me. When I was a kid, we'd play games and do fun things. I grew out of that, and he showed me how to fight and let me hang out with him when he trained. Those were some of the best days of my life."

The waitress returned with our beverages, and we ordered our meals, so it was a few minutes before I could continue my story. Now that I'd begun, I wanted to tell Sara and Jordan the rest of it so they'd understand why there would never be anything romantic between Chris and me.

I took a sip of water and set down my glass.

"I think I was thirteen when things changed for me. Chris came home one day, and the next thing I knew, I was crushing on him. He had no idea, of course. By the time I was sixteen, I was head over heels in love with him. I thought all I had to do was wait until he noticed I was no longer a little girl."

"Did he?" Jordan asked.

I pressed my lips together and shook my head.

Sara laid a warm hand over one of mine. "What happened?"

"I told him how I felt." I winced. "It didn't go well."

I looked down at my hands as I remembered that day. Had it really been only four years ago? It felt like a decade had passed since then.

I smoothed down my hair for the last time and knocked on Chris's door. I couldn't believe he was finally home after an eight-month job in South America. He'd missed my sixteenth birthday by one day, but having him home was the best gift I could have asked for.

The door opened and Chris stood there, his hair damp like he'd just gotten out of the shower. He stared at me in surprise for a moment before he smiled and reached out to pull me into a hug. I was so happy to see him I didn't make much of the fact that the hug was quicker than usual.

"Look at you," he said when he let me go. "You grew up on me. When did this happen?"

I beamed at him, my heart near to bursting. "While you were running around the Amazon."

He moved back to let me into the small apartment he used when he was home. I sat on the couch, and he disappeared into his bedroom for a few minutes, returning with a small box wrapped in tissue paper, which he handed to me.

"Happy birthday, Dove."

I smiled and accepted the gift from him, trying to quell my disappointment when he took the chair across from me instead of sitting beside me like he always did.

"I'm sorry I missed your birthday," he said as I unwrapped the box. "But I hope this makes up for it. As soon as I saw it, I thought of you."

I lifted the lid on the white box, and my breath caught at the sight of the dainty silver necklace inside. He'd never brought me jewelry before. I swallowed at the thought of what this could mean.

With trembling fingers, I lifted the necklace from the box and gazed at the silver pendant in the shape of a dove taking flight.

"It's perfect!" I held the necklace to my chest. "I love it."

He smiled, showing his dimples. "I thought you might. Put it on, and let's see it."

I stood and held up the necklace. "Will you help me?"

He hesitated for a moment before he got up and came over to take the necklace from me. I turned, and he lifted the chain over my head, his warm fingers brushing the back of my neck as he secured the clasp and sent a delicious shiver through me.

I looked down, admiring the pendant lying just above my breasts, before I turned to face Chris.

"How does it look?" I asked him.

For a second, he wore an indecipherable expression. Then it was gone, and he smiled at me again as he took a step back. "Beautiful, just like the girl wearing it."

Joy radiated through my body. Chris thought I was beautiful and grown-up, and he'd brought me jewelry. I threw my arms around his neck and hugged him tightly.

"I love you, Chris."

"Love you, too, Dove."

Taking a deep breath, I leaned back to look up into his green eyes. "No, I mean I really love you."

The smile faded from his eyes, and his face took on an almost pained expression.

His hands came up to my shoulders, and he gently set me away from him before letting his arms fall to his sides.

"Beth," he began slowly. "You don't mean that."

"Yes, I do," I said in a quieter voice.

His expression softened. "You're only sixteen —"

"I'll be eighteen in two years," I pressed.

At eighteen, you were an adult and you could become a warrior. Age difference no longer mattered once you reached eighteen.

"I know. But so much can happen in two years, and things you like now might not matter to you by then."

My chest constricted, making it hard to breathe. "It won't change how I feel about you."

He looked away, as if searching for what to say. When his gaze returned to mine, the anguish in his eyes told me his answer before he spoke.

"I'm sorry, Dove. I love you but not in that way."

Tears scalded my eyes, blurring my vision as I backed away from him. His hand reached for me, but I turned and ran for the door.

"Beth, please understand," he called after me in a voice laced with regret.

I didn't look back. I ran home, trying to hold together the edges of my broken heart.

I watched Sara's and Jordan's faces as I finished my story. My telling was less detailed than the actual events of that day, but it was enough to paint a clear picture for them.

Understanding filled Jordan's eyes. "You can't forgive him for breaking your heart."

I shook my head. "I would have forgiven him for that eventually."

"Then what is it?" Sara pressed gently.

"He left, and I never saw him again after that day. He walked out of my life and didn't come back." I swallowed painfully. "That hurt more than anything else he could have done."

"So that day he showed up here..." Jordan began.

"That was the first I'd seen him since my sixteenth birthday."

"Well shit." She sat back heavily. "No wonder you're giving him the cold shoulder."

Sara's brow furrowed. "Why would Chris do something like that? Has he said anything about it since he got here?"

"He said he's sorry for the way he left and that he thought he was doing what was best for me, but now he realizes he handled it wrong." I toyed with the stem of my glass. "He asked if we could be friends again, but I don't know if we can after all that's happened."

Sara smiled kindly. "Maybe just give it time."

I wished it was that easy. Sometimes when Chris smiled, I remembered the man I'd adored before that day in his apartment. But it was always followed by the memories of the pain after he'd left, the feeling of abandonment and betrayal when he never returned. He might be sincere in his wish to rekindle our friendship, but he also had the power to hurt me deeply. I couldn't let him do that to me again.

Jordan let out a deep breath. "I think that's enough serious talk for tonight. We're supposed to be having our wild girls' night, and you two are depressing me."

Sara's eyebrows shot up. "When did this become a *wild* girls' night?"

Jordan made a *pfft* sound and lifted her glass. "Is there any other kind?"

Sara frowned.

"Come on, bestie. I promise it'll be fun," Jordan said with a playful pout.

I hid my grin behind my own glass. It was impossible to stay sad for long with these two.

"Just dancing. No crazy stuff." Sara fixed Jordan with a hard look.

Jordan held up a hand. "No crazy stuff. Scout's honor."

***

"Son of a bitch!"

I looked up from the first aid kit I was rummaging through to see Jordan throw her shoes down in disgust.

"What's wrong?"

"I broke a heel on my new Jimmy Choos." She stomped barefoot over to where I sat on the couch beside my bleeding patient. "He going to live?"

I pressed a wad of gauze to the shallow cut near the man's hairline. "Just a flesh wound. He won't even need stitches."

"This one might need a doctor," Sara called from the other side of the room.

I took the man's hand and pressed it to the gauze. "Hold this here."

Standing, I made my way across the room to Sara, skirting an upended side table and stepping over two bodies. She was kneeling behind a white grand piano that listed to one side, its polished surface marred by blood splatter.

I crouched beside Sara and the red-haired woman she was tending to.

The woman's eyes were closed, and her skin was almost pasty white, except for a bruise forming on her right cheek.

"Cecelia," I called, remembering her name from earlier in the night. "Can you hear me?"

The woman's face twitched, but she didn't open her eyes.

"What the hell?" A loud male voice filled the room. "Sara?"

"Over here," Sara called.

I stood to see Nikolas striding toward us, his expression a mix of anger and relief.

Raoul stood on the other side of the spacious living room, and I could only guess what he was thinking as he took in the scene before him. Almost every one of the windows was broken, and there were blood sprays on the white walls along with a person-shaped scorch mark – Sara's handiwork. Any piece of the expensive furniture not overturned had an injured or drunken human draped across it.

Nikolas reached us and crouched beside Sara. "Are you okay?"

"I'm good. But we have people here who need medical help." She gave him a wry smile. "Or a good dose of gunna paste."

His face softened, and he smiled as he reached inside his jacket, producing a can of paste, which he handed to her. Then he stood and assessed the situation before looking from me to Jordan. "How many?"

"Six," Jordan answered. She walked over to check on a blonde girl who was retching behind a potted plant that had miraculously survived the carnage.

I heard running feet, and Chris appeared in the doorway, his hair wind-blown like he'd ridden without a helmet. His gaze searched the room until he found me, and my breath caught at the intensity of his stare as he took in my torn dress and bare feet. The blood on my legs wasn't mine, but it probably made for a pretty gruesome picture.

"Are you hurt?"

The edge in his voice surprised me. I'd never heard him speak that way, and it took me a few seconds to respond.

"No."

Something unreadable flashed in his eyes before he looked at Nikolas. "Our guys are a few minutes out. No one's called the police yet, but there are two men with cameras by the main gate."

Nikolas nodded grimly. "Paparazzi. Just what we need."

He turned to Jordan, who was coming toward us. "Sara texted me an hour ago to let me know you were going to a party at some celebrity's house. Next thing I know, she's calling for a cleanup crew. What the hell happened tonight?"

Jordan rolled her shoulders. "We were at Lure, and Brent Lassiter invited us to join him in the VIP section."

"Who is Brent Lassiter?" Chris asked, his brows drawn together.

"He would be Hollywood's newest golden boy." Jordan waggled her eyebrows at me. "Who totally has the hots for our girl Beth."

As if on cue, the blond man I'd been tending to on the couch pulled himself into a sitting position and looked around in confusion. "Beth?" he said groggily and grimaced. "Who are these people? Why does my head hurt?"

Raoul headed toward him with a can of gunna paste in hand. I turned back to Nikolas, deliberately not looking at Chris, who had come to stand beside him.

"Brent invited us back to his place for a party," I said. "We were here about twenty minutes when some of his friends showed up with the vampires. I don't think his friends knew what the vampires were. And the vampires were not expecting to find us here."

Jordan grinned. "Sara felt them coming, so we were ready for them. You should have seen those vampires' faces when they realized what we were. Priceless. We took care of them, but it was a little messy, as you can see."

Nikolas rubbed his jaw. "Yes, I can see that. Did we lose any humans?"

"No," I said proudly. "But some of them might need medical care."

I felt Chris's eyes on me again, and I had to resist the urge to look at him. There was something different about him tonight, and I could almost feel the tension rolling off him. Was he angry at me? Did he think we could have handled the situation better?

Uncertainty gnawed at me as I waited for him to say something. In spite of everything, the thought of him being disappointed in me caused a tiny knot to form in my stomach. Damn him. Why did I care what he thought of me?

The door opened again, and eight warriors filed into the room. Chris and Nikolas started issuing orders, and I put thoughts of Chris out of my mind as we set about taking care of the humans and removing all traces of the vampires. Disposing of vampires wasn't nearly as much fun as killing them.

Everyone worked with quiet efficiency, and two hours later, the house looked like it had been vandalized instead of having been a battleground. The humans were tended to and given a dose of gorum, the drug we used to modify short-term memory. Most people weren't ready to learn about the real world, so part of our job was to keep it hidden. The humans here would think they were the victims of a home invasion and never know how close they'd come to a gruesome death.

Even the two paparazzi at the gate were given gorum to make them forget the large vans coming and going in the wee hours of the morning. No one liked drugging humans, but it was a necessary part of our job if we were to remain hidden. That wasn't to say no humans knew of our existence. The Council worked with the highest levels of government and law enforcement in every state, and the humans knew it was to their benefit to keep us a secret.

The vans left, and I walked into the living room to retrieve my shoes. I'd kicked them off in the fight and left them off during the cleanup. I picked them up as Jordan and Sara walked into the room.

"I'd say that was a good night's work," Jordan declared.

Sara gave her an eye roll. "That had to be wild enough, even for you."

I nodded in agreement. From partying with celebrities to saving a houseful of humans from vampires, this, by far, had been the craziest night of my life. Not to mention Chris's odd behavior. We hadn't spoken during the cleanup, but I'd sensed his eyes on me more than once. I had no idea what his deal was, and I didn't want to know.

I glanced down at my ruined dress. "I don't know about you girls, but I'm ready for a long hot shower and a soft bed."

"I bet Brent has a very soft bed," Jordan said.

I laughed at her suggestive smile. I'd flirted with Brent at the club because it was fun and harmless, and really, how often do you get to party with a hot young movie star? But I'd had no intention of taking it beyond that, even before things had gone to hell.

"Are you girls ready to leave?"

The three of us turned to face Chris, who stood by the door, his brows pulled down in a scowl that looked out of character for him. I wasn't the only one surprised by his expression or his brusque tone.

"Whoa, Blondie. We keeping you up past your bedtime or something?" Jordan quipped.

"We need to clear out so we can alert the authorities." Chris's green gaze locked with mine. "And I think you've had enough fun for tonight."

My lips parted, and I'm pretty sure my eyebrows touched my hairline. *Oh, no. He did not just say that.* He'd given up the right to have any say in my life a long time ago.

"I'm a big girl now, and I can decide when I've had enough."

He crossed his arms. "Judging by what's left of your dress, I don't think you can."

I gaped at him, at a loss for words.

"What the...? Does he remind you of someone we know?" Jordan asked Sara in a stage whisper.

"Uh-huh," Sara murmured.

I turned my head to ask what they were talking about and found them staring at Chris like he was about to sprout wings any second. What was up with all of them? They were acting crazy.

I heaved an angry sigh. "I need some fresh air. I'll wait for you girls outside."

Chris stepped into my path as I walked to the door. His scowl was gone, and he looked as confused as I was. He opened his mouth to speak, but I was done talking.

I moved to go around him.

"Beth, wait."

Warm fingers wrapped around my wrist, and I gasped as a tingle shot up my arm and straight to my chest. My heart began to pound as if it had been hit with a jolt of electricity. Then a storm of emotions erupted inside me – longing, love, joy – until I was almost dizzy from them.

The strange tingling sensation faded, but the emotions in my chest only intensified until my heart was ready to punch through my ribs.

I put a trembling hand to my face. *What's wrong with me?*

I turned my head toward Chris. Our eyes met, and his darkened to a bottle-green, the heat in them sending a thrill of fear and excitement through me. His hand tugged me toward him, and I took a step in his direction.

And then, amidst the clamor in my head, a small desperate voice cried out.

Solmi!

6

Chris

Mine.

My Mori's growl filled my head as a fierce surge of joy and possessiveness swept over me, almost rocking me back on my heels. Deep inside, something shifted and clicked into place, and a new awareness blossomed as my Mori tethered itself to its mate.

My mate.

Beth turned her head, and the sight of her pale cheeks and confused eyes made me forget everything but the need to comfort and reassure her. I gently drew her toward me as I fought an internal battle with my demon that strained to get to her.

"No."

Beth's choked cry came a second before she yanked out of my grasp. I saw the panic in her eyes as she spun and ran outside.

Stunned, I stood unable to move as the reality of what had just happened settled over me. I had bonded...with Beth. My Beth.

I looked at Sara and Jordan, who stared back at me with wide eyes and slack jaws. I opened my mouth to speak, but no words came out.

The rumble of an engine coming to life shook me from my stupor. I raced outside, nearly running over Nikolas as he entered the house. I was in time to see the taillight of a motorcycle as it passed through the open gates and disappeared from sight.

I ran for my bike, only to come up short when I saw it wasn't where I'd left it. When I'd arrived, I'd been in such a rush to make sure Beth was okay that I must have left my keys in the ignition.

"She took my bike," I said in disbelief.

Nikolas came up behind me. "What happened? She looked upset."

Instead of answering him, I said, "I need your bike."

He pulled out his keys and handed them to me without question. I muttered "Thanks" and ran to his Ducati. Pulling on his helmet, I started the bike and took off after Beth.

In a city this big, she could be anywhere, and the thought of her out there alone made a knot form in my gut. I had weapons on my bike so she wasn't unarmed, but in her current state of mind, she might be too distracted to handle a threat. I sent up a silent prayer that she'd gone back to the command center, and I headed in that direction.

Her single word of denial replayed in my head, along with the image of her distraught face. Not that I could fault her for reacting like that with the way things were between us. Since the night we'd spoken, I'd been trying to think of how to earn back her friendship and her trust, but she'd blocked any attempt to talk about that again.

And now this.

I had nearly destroyed the grips on Nikolas's bike by the time I reached the command center. When I rounded the back of the house and saw my Ducati sitting outside the garage, I let out the breath I'd been holding since I hit the driveway.

I parked and walked toward the guesthouse where a light shone from one of the windows. My Mori fluttered wildly when I got within a few feet of the front door, stopping me in my tracks for a long moment. Being able to sense her drove home the fact that we were bonded. I had to take a few steadying breaths before I stepped up and knocked on the door.

When no one answered, I enhanced my hearing and picked up muted voices at the back of the house. Beth shared the house with Mason, so it had to be him she was talking to. It made sense for her to confide in her best friend, but the thought of her in there with another male did not sit well with my Mori.

Solmi.

I raised my hand to knock again when I heard footsteps approaching the door. It swung open to reveal Mason's scowling face.

He spoke in a low voice, not bothering to hide his displeasure at my presence. "She doesn't want to see you."

I wasn't surprised she didn't want to talk to me yet, but I hadn't expected the stab of pain in my chest at her rejection.

"Is she okay?"

"I don't know. She came home crying and won't tell me anything."

My gut clenched. "She's crying?"

"Yeah. What did you do to her?" he asked harshly. "Haven't you made her cry enough?"

"Fuck." I raked a hand through my hair.

Mason's scowl deepened. "You going to tell me what happened?"

It wasn't like he wouldn't know in a few hours, so I just came out with it. "Beth and I bonded."

He blinked several times, and I watched his expression change from anger to shock to understanding. "Shit." He glanced over his shoulder and looked at me again. "I don't know what to say. You and Beth..."

I nodded. "Can you tell her I'm here when she's ready to talk?"

He looked like he was about to say something and changed his mind. "I'll let her know. I better go to her."

The thought of him offering Beth comfort made me bristle with jealousy. We hadn't been bonded an hour, and already I couldn't stand the idea of another male with her, even her best friend.

I took a step back so he could shut the door. Instead of going to the main house, I walked over to the pool and sank down on one of the cushioned chairs. I held my head in my hands as I tried to process the enormity of what had happened.

For most of my adult life, I'd avoided intimacy with Mohiri women to lessen the odds of me bonding with one of them. It wasn't that I was against mating. My parents were devoted to each other. I just hadn't seen it as something for me. I'd figured if I ever met a potential mate, we would both go our separate ways and be done with it.

What I hadn't counted on was Beth. Of all the Mohiri females in the world, I'd bonded with the only one I couldn't walk away from.

My mind went back to that day at Longstone four years ago. I'd just come home after being away for the better part of a year. My parents had already moved to Germany, but I'd wanted to bring Beth the necklace I'd gotten her for her birthday. I'd promised her I'd be there for her sixteenth birthday, and I always kept my promises to her.

The knock came as I was toweling my hair dry from my shower. Entering the bedroom, I grabbed a T-shirt and pulled it on as I walked out to get the door.

I swung the door open and stared in confusion at the young blonde woman standing there with a smile lighting up her beautiful face. My eyes met her gray ones, and my breath caught as recognition hit me.

Recovering from my surprise, I pulled her into a hug, only to discover what else had changed about her. Gone was the lanky girl, and in her place was a young woman with lush curves and a delicate floral scent that made me want to bury my face in her silky hair. Never had holding a woman felt so right – and so wrong.

Shame slammed into me, and I ended the hug abruptly. Christ, what was wrong with me? This was Beth, not some woman I'd met in a bar.

"Look at you," I said as I fought to compose myself. "You grew up on me. When did this happen?"

Her smile was radiant. "While you were running around the Amazon."

I waved her in and escaped to the bedroom, where I spent the next few minutes mentally castigating myself for having a single impure thought about her. Sixteen was almost an adult, but this was Beth. My Beth. She was young and innocent, and no male should be thinking of her as anything else, least of all me.

Schooling my expression, I picked up the small tissue-wrapped box that contained the birthday present I'd bought Beth in Venezuela.

Beth was sitting on the couch when I went back to her. I smiled and held the box out to her.

"Happy birthday, Dove."

I took the farthest seat from her as she opened her present. In the past, I'd think nothing of sitting beside her, but things had changed between us. No matter how much I willed it otherwise, I no longer saw Beth as a little girl, and it felt inappropriate to sit close to her now.

"I'm sorry I missed your birthday. But I hope this makes up for it. As soon as I saw it, I thought of you."

I'd been walking through an outdoor market when I'd come upon a vendor selling handmade silver jewelry. I'd always picked up toys and souvenirs for Beth, but the moment I spotted a dove pendant on a thin silver chain, I knew I had to buy it for her.

Beth's face flushed with pleasure as she lifted the chain from the box. "It's perfect! I love it."

"I thought you might. Put it on, and let's see it."

She stood and smiled sweetly, holding the necklace out to me. "Will you help me?"

I froze for several seconds at her request. I didn't want to get that close to her, but to refuse her would only make her realize something was off. I went to her and clasped the chain around her throat, trying to minimize contact with her skin. I hated that the little touches that had been so innocent the last time I saw her now felt wrong.

Beth faced me, and I became all too aware of her proximity.

"How does it look?" she asked, glowing with happiness.

I backed up a step as if to get a better look. "Beautiful, just like the girl wearing it."

I wasn't expecting her reaction, and I could only stand there as she hugged me tightly around the neck.

"I love you, Chris," she said breathlessly.

I closed my eyes against the sudden tightness in my chest. "Love you too, Dove."

She gazed up at me, her eyes wide and guileless. "No, I mean I really love you."

It took several seconds for the meaning of her words to sink in. I broke the hug as gently as I could and backed up a step, trying to figure out how to respond to her declaration.

"Beth, you don't mean that."

She frowned uncertainly, looking more like the young girl I knew. "Yes, I do."

"You're only sixteen –"

"I'll be eighteen in two years," she argued weakly.

I'd had a similar thought a few minutes ago, but hearing her say it drove home just how young she was and how much she had yet to experience.

"I know. But so much can happen in two years, and things you like now might not matter to you by then."

Her chin trembled. "It won't change how I feel about you."

The hurt in her eyes was almost my undoing, and I had to refrain from pulling her into my arms and comforting her. It would only send her false signals, and I wouldn't do that to her. It was hard enough to say what had to be said, knowing it would cause her more pain.

"I'm sorry, Dove. I love you but not in that way."

Pain pricked my chest at the sight of the tears spilling down her cheeks and the knowledge that I'd hurt the one person I'd vowed to always protect. I reached for her, but she spun away.

"Beth, please understand," I called as she flung open the door and ran out.

I'd planned to give Beth a day or two before I went to talk to her. But lying in bed that night, I couldn't stop thinking about how she'd felt in my arms, and how much I wanted to hold her again. Disturbed by my thoughts, I'd gotten very little sleep.

The next day, Rachel had come by, wanting to know why Beth had been in her room crying all night. In as few words as possible, I filled her in. I was surprised when she'd admitted she had known about Beth's crush on me. I couldn't believe I'd been oblivious to Beth's feelings, and I'd wondered if maybe I'd said or done something to lead her on.

It was Rachel who'd suggested I shouldn't try to talk to Beth right away. She'd told me a girl needed time to get over her first heartbreak, and Beth would be embarrassed to see me. I'd agreed because it was in Beth's best interest for us to not see each other. I couldn't be around her until I'd rid myself of this attraction I felt for her.

I'd left that day with the intention of returning in a month or two. Rachel had kept me updated on Beth, letting me know how she was doing and when she'd gotten over her crush. But while Beth's feelings for me had faded over time, mine for her had not. Shame and guilt followed every thought of her, even though I told myself I would never have acted upon my feelings. In my mind, no male was good enough for Beth, including me.

One month became six, and six became a year. I'd missed Beth, but I'd feared I would do or say something to give myself away if I saw her. Rachel had told me she was happy and doing well in her training, and I hadn't wanted to disrupt her life. So, I'd stayed away from her, and I'd immersed myself in work and the company of beautiful women, trying to forget the girl I couldn't have.

After all of that, after the years of keeping my distance from Beth, one touch had changed everything.

How was it possible that we had shared this house and worked together for a week, and we hadn't touched once until now? What if I hadn't touched her tonight? How long would we have gone on without knowing what we really were to each other?

Headlights splashed across the lawn as an SUV pulled up and parked outside the garage. Three people got out, two of them going into the house while the third headed in my direction.

Nikolas sat on one of the chairs with his arms resting on his knees. Neither of us spoke for a long moment.

"You look like hell," he said at last.

"I've been better."

Another short silence followed.

"You know?" I asked him.

"Sara and Jordan said they thought you and Beth bonded, but they weren't sure."

"We did."

"You want to talk about it?" he asked.

If I didn't talk to someone about it, my head was going to explode. "I can't believe it's Beth, of all people. I've known her for most of her life."

"It happens. Remember the Council member who found his mate a year ago?"

I nodded. The Council member's mate had grown up in the stronghold he led. He'd seen the girl around, but it wasn't until her induction ceremony when they'd shaken hands that they bonded.

"That's not the same. He didn't know the girl like I know Beth. I watched her grow up."

"You're right. I've wondered how different it would have been for Sara and me if she'd been raised at Westhorne."

I managed a weak smile. "Tristan probably would have banished you the first time you looked at her."

He chuckled. "I think you're right about that."

I blew out a harsh breath. "How could I have been so close to her and never known?"

"Maybe you two were so close because you did know on a subconscious level, or your Mori did, but she was too young to bond. Until now."

Until now. His words resonated with me. Was it possible my Mori had recognized Beth as my mate from the very beginning? Could that be why I'd always felt so protective of her and why I suddenly began to want her when she'd become a young woman? Was that why my attraction to her hadn't faded away in the years since?

I'd beaten myself up for years over my feelings for Beth, and I'd stayed away from her because of them. If I'd gone back to see her, we would have bonded when she was old enough, and it could have saved us so much pain. God, I was such a fool.

"And now she hates me," I said almost to myself.

"I don't believe that."

"You don't know the whole story. She has good reason to."

He waited patiently for me to elaborate. With a deep exhale, I told him the truth about why I hadn't been back to Longstone or seen Beth in four years. It felt good to unburden myself to someone who listened without judgement.

I grimaced. "I felt like a pervert, thinking about her that way."

Nikolas's next question took me by surprise.

"Do you think you would have thought your attraction to her was wrong if you'd just met her when she was sixteen? If you hadn't known her since she was a little girl?"

"I would have wondered what had gotten into me, but it wouldn't have felt so wrong."

He nodded knowingly. "Sara was seventeen when we bonded, and I felt conflicted, too. One minute, all I saw was her youth and how much she needed my protection. In the next, I would see my mate. It was not easy at times."

"That's putting it mildly."

The two of us smiled at the mention of his turbulent months with Sara before they'd mated. It hit me then that I was in for the same stormy ride with Beth. Maybe worse.

I groaned. "I'm screwed, aren't I?"

"That depends. Are you going to break the bond?"

"No," I replied vehemently.

"Then yes, you're completely screwed."

"Thanks for sugarcoating it." I leaned forward to rest my head in my hands.

He laughed and stood. "Get some rest. You're going to need it."

My gaze moved to the guesthouse.

"She's not going to talk to you tonight, and you'll drive yourself crazy sitting out here. Trust me on that."

He went into the house, and I stayed where I was. Nikolas was right, but it was hard to leave Beth when she was so upset. Even without the bond, I could never stand to see her cry. But I also knew my presence would cause her more distress. As much as I needed to be near her, I couldn't do that to her.

I entered the house and went to my room to shower and stretch out on my bed. But after an hour of staring at the ceiling, I dressed and made my way to the control room. I might as well get some work done as long as I was up. Brock was the only one there, and he shot me a look of surprise when I walked in at 4:00 a.m.

"Something up?" he asked.

"No. Couldn't sleep."

I sat at one of the work stations and started the report for tonight's incident. Technically, the warriors at the scene were supposed to do the report, but I had a feeling none of them would mind me doing the tedious work. Jordan hated reports, and Beth had enough to deal with. Sara didn't mind reports, but she wouldn't say no to some help.

I'd thought the work would help take my mind off Beth, but all I could think of was her in that dress, dancing with other men and going back to Brent Lassiter's place. It didn't matter that she hadn't been alone with him and nothing had happened. Just the thought of what might have happened made my heart pound and my nostrils flare.

"You okay, man?"

I looked up to find Brock watching me with his eyebrows raised in question.

"Yes." I went back to my report, only to discover the mangled remains of my computer mouse.

Groaning inwardly, I tossed the lump of plastic in the trash and stole the mouse from the nearest computer, aware that Brock was watching me with undisguised curiosity. It was clear he hadn't heard about Beth and me, and I was in no mood to fill him in. By noon today, everyone living here would know Beth and I had bonded.

Not that I cared who knew. The shock was wearing off, and in its place was a lightness I'd never experienced before. Beneath the turmoil and uncertainty, I was elated because I could finally acknowledge what my heart – and my Mori – had been telling me for years. Beth and I belonged together.

Now, I had to convince her of that.

Beth

I shouldn't have come back here. I wasn't ready to see him or to face what had happened. The last hour felt almost like a dream. A bad dream where I'd bonded to the man who'd broken my heart and had made it abundantly clear he didn't want me. He'd stayed away from his home for four years to avoid me. If that hadn't driven the message home, nothing would.

I rolled over and buried my face in the pillow. God, how could this have happened? How could I have bonded to *him* of all people?

No one knew what made someone a potential mate. Most people believed it had to do with the compatibility between two Mori. But some people thought it was because of an even deeper connection. They believed two people who were destined to be together would eventually find each other. Neither of these beliefs was helpful or comforting to me now, not when it was Chris I'd bonded to.

I believed Chris when he said he hadn't meant to hurt me, but his apologies couldn't erase the past. His abandonment had cut me deeply and had changed me, hardening me against being that trusting and open with my heart again. I loved Mason, but it was a different kind of love, a safe love, and nothing like what I'd felt for Chris. It was the only kind of love I could trust.

I jumped when someone lifted the pillow covering my face, but it was only Mason, his eyes dark with concern. Fresh tears blurred my vision, and he sat with his back against the headboard, pulling me into his arms. With him I didn't have to be strong, and I gave into my tears as he held me.

"Why didn't you tell me?" he asked after I'd finally stopped crying.

I hiccupped. "I didn't want to believe it."

He hugged me tighter for a few seconds. "And now?"

"Do you even need to ask?"

"Guess not."

We were silent for a few minutes before he spoke again.

"Chris said to tell you he's there when you're ready to talk. If it makes you feel any better, he's pretty upset, too."

"He can't be too happy about this either."

Chris was probably out there figuring out the best way to get out of this, although there was only one solution to our dilemma. The question was, which one of us would do it first.

Mason sighed. "I have to admit he seems more worried about you than anything else. All he cared about was how you were doing. I thought he was going to go through me to get to you when I told him you were crying."

I leaned away to glower at him. "You told him I was crying?"

All I needed was for Chris to know how deeply this affected me. Bonded males were known to act irrationally, and he might think he had to complete the bond out of some misguided sense of chivalry. No, thank you. If I took a mate, it would be out of mutual love, not out of obligation.

Mason's brows drew together. "I was angry because you came home bawling your eyes out, and he's the only one who can make you cry like that."

I let out a ragged breath. "I'm sorry. I shouldn't be taking this out on you."

"That's what best friends are for."

He pulled me back so I was propped up against the pillows next to him. I rested my head on his shoulder, and he clasped our hands together.

I'm bonded to Chris.

It sounded unreal no matter how many times I said it in my head. How often had I dreamed of this when I was younger? There'd been a time when I would have given anything to be Chris's mate. Now I only wanted to come out of this with my heart intact.

"What do I do?" I said more to myself than to Mason.

His fingers flexed around mine. "What do you want to do?"

"A part of me wants to walk out there right now and break the bond."

"And the rest of you?"

A painful knot formed in my throat. "The rest of me wants to curl up in a ball and cry some more."

"Then cry if that's what you need to do. I'll make sure your room is stocked with Kleenex until you're done. Just promise me you'll shower. I still have to share this house with you."

I let out a choked laugh. "Thanks."

"Anytime."

The room grew quiet for a long moment.

Mason cleared his throat. "Can I ask you...? What does it feel like?"

If the question had come from anyone else, I wouldn't have answered it. It wasn't a taboo subject, but bonding was a deeply personal experience and people generally didn't go into the details. I'd always been curious about it, too, and I knew Mason would share it with me if he were in my shoes.

"It's hard to describe. It's like finding out I'm no longer alone, only I never realized I was alone until now. I can sense him when he's near, but even when he's not, I'm aware of him."

"Wow. It sounds intense."

"It is."

Longing poured from my Mori as it tried to reach across the new bond to Chris's Mori. I couldn't imagine what it would be like in a few days or weeks. I'd thought it strange when Sara told me she hadn't really felt her bond with Nikolas until they completed it. Now, I was envious of her. There was something to be said for blissful ignorance.

Mason released my hand. "You should get some sleep."

I nodded and sat up, my eyes going to the front door, which was visible from my bedroom.

"Do you think he's still out there?"

"Probably. I can ask him to leave if it bothers you," Mason said.

"No. It's okay."

I wasn't the only one affected by this. If Chris felt half of what I did, he couldn't be doing too well either. If it made him feel better to stay near tonight, who was I to send him away? Tomorrow, we'd sort this out and decide the best way to handle it.

Mason got off the bed. "Okay. I'll see you in the morning."

"Night."

I slid down into the bed, burrowing beneath the covers. I should have showered, but with everything else that had happened tonight, I couldn't bring myself to care about much of anything.

I tried to clear my mind to help me sleep, but every time I closed my eyes, I saw Chris's face. I let out a shuddering breath. It was going to be a long night.

Solmi, whispered a mournful voice in my head.

7

Beth

"How do people study in a place like this?" I asked Sara as we exited Our Lady of Mercy Academy. It was lunchtime, and the halls were full of girls rushing to the cafeteria. The school was so noisy and crowded, nothing like the quiet classrooms at home.

Sara laughed. "You don't get much studying done at school unless you go to the library. I spent a lot of time in the library at my old school."

I watched three girls run past us down the steps. "Was your school like this?"

"Pretty much, except mine was smaller and we had boys and girls."

We headed for the parking lot where we'd left the SUV. Our visit to Jessica Ryan's school had turned up no clues about her disappearance, and nothing we'd learned about the missing girl was out of the ordinary. Jessica was well-liked, a straight-A student, and she sang in the choir. She didn't have a boyfriend, and she'd rarely missed a day of school.

It was similar to what we'd found out about Tracy Levine at St. Teresa's Preparatory School this morning. Tracy's friends said she was fun and loved music. She went to parties, but she never did anything reckless. Her friends said they'd all gone to a rave a few days before Tracy disappeared, but nothing out of the ordinary had happened at the rave.

I climbed into the SUV and looked over at Sara. "I feel like there's something we're missing here. Some link between Jessica and Tracy."

"I know what you mean." She looked thoughtful as she clicked her seat belt. "For two Catholic school girls to disappear within days of each other, there has to be a connection."

Starting the vehicle, I glanced at the clock on the dash and bit my lip. I'd been hoping it would take us longer to check out the schools because I had no desire to go back to the house. I knew I was being a coward, but I wasn't ready to face Chris yet.

Mason and Sara had suggested I stay home today after my emotional night, but I couldn't do it. I'd gotten up at dawn and snuck out for a two-hour run, hoping the fresh air would clear my head. It hadn't.

"Hey, you feel like grabbing a coffee?" Sara asked as if she'd read my mind. "I could really go for a mocha."

"I'd love one."

There was a coffee shop less than a block from the school, so we headed for that one. We went inside, and I wasn't surprised to see girls in school uniforms. The place was bustling, so Sara grabbed us a table while I went up to order our coffees.

A tall blonde girl ahead of me in line turned to smile at me. "Hey. Didn't I see you at my school a little while ago?"

I smiled back and gave her the cover story we'd made up to explain our presence at the school.

"Yes. My sister and I might go there, and I wanted to check out the school."

"Oh. It's a good school but kind of boring." She rolled her eyes. "I wanted to go to public school this year, but Mom and Dad wouldn't hear of it."

The line moved, and we both took two steps forward. Then the girl turned back to me. "I'm Alicia, by the way."

"Beth."

"Are you a senior?" she asked.

"Yes."

Her smile brightened. "Me, too. We'll be in the same class."

I lifted a shoulder. "I haven't even started there, and I've already made a friend."

Looking pleased, she went up to the counter to order her drink. I went next, and ended up beside Alicia again as we waited for our coffee. We talked for a few minutes, and I found her to be nice and very chatty.

We got our drinks at the same time, and I wasn't surprised when she walked with me to the table where Sara waited for me.

"Sara, this is Alicia," I said as we sat. "Alicia's a senior at Our Lady of Mercy, and she's been telling me all about the school."

"Are you Beth's sister?" Alicia asked Sara.

"Just a friend who tagged along."

Alicia was easy to talk to and eager to tell us all about the school and what she and her friends liked to do for fun. I listened to her with half an ear because my mind was occupied with thoughts about last night. It wasn't until I heard her say the word "rave" that I snapped back to the present.

"Rave?" I asked. "Where?"

"At this cool new club called Luna. It's an all-ages club, and they have the best music. I went to a rave there with some friends last Friday and had a total blast. They're having another one Saturday night, and a bunch of us are going. You should come."

She opened her messenger bag and pulled out what looked like two concert passes. "A guy I know from the club asked me to give out these passes at school. I have two left if you want them."

"Don't you want to give the passes to your friends?" Sara asked her.

"We all have passes for Saturday, and they're only good for one night."

I sipped my coffee. "We heard about that girl Jessica who went missing. You're not nervous about going out after that?"

Alicia shook her head. "Jessica went off alone to a movie. I only go out with friends. Besides, we were all at Luna last week, and nothing happened. Jessica was there, too."

My chest fluttered with excitement. Jessica and Tracy had both gone to a rave before they disappeared. No way this was a coincidence. I shot Sara a glance and saw she'd come to the same conclusion.

Alicia looked from Sara to me. "What do you say? I promised the guy who gave them to me that I'd give them all out."

I didn't wait for Sara to answer. My gut told me this was the connection we'd been looking for between the two missing girls. "Sounds like fun," I said. "Count us in."

"Yay!" She handed us the passes. "The address is on the back." She stood. "I have to get back to school. See you Saturday night."

"We'll see you there."

She started to leave and stopped. "Oh, and those passes are for girls only, in case one of your boyfriends wants to come."

I turned my pass over in my hands. "Girls only?"

"Yeah." Alicia pointed to a pink stripe along the bottom of the pass. "See that there? That means it's a girl's pass. The boys' passes have a blue stripe. They give out an equal number for each rave."

"Smart," I murmured.

I looked at Sara as soon as Alicia left. "What are the odds of Jessica and Tracy both going to a rave the week before they disappeared?"

Sara laid her pass on the table. "I don't believe in coincidences."

"Me either."

Sara was quiet for a moment. "About the rave, I can ask Jordan to go to Luna with me if you're not up to going out after... you know."

"You can say it." I smiled to hide the anxiety that had been simmering in my gut since I woke up.

The kindness in her eyes made my throat tighten. I knew how close she was to Chris, and I waited for her to tell me what a great mate he would be. Or to say something about me running out last night. I was not expecting her next words.

"When I found out about my bond with Nikolas, I wouldn't even talk to him about it for a week. Then I got drunk, threw up in front of him, and told him I was breaking the bond."

I gaped at her. "You did not."

"Yep." She nodded, amusement flashing in her eyes. "Trust me, your reaction last night was nothing compared to some of the stuff I've done. Oh, and stealing his bike was a nice touch. Jordan and I agreed you get points for style."

"You really tried to break the bond?"

Seeing Sara and Nikolas together every day, it was impossible to imagine them not being crazy in love with each other. I knew they'd been bonded a while before they mated and that it had been stormy at times, but she'd never mentioned trying to break it off.

"I told him I was going to break it because I thought he didn't want it." She laughed when my eyes widened. "I know, I know. I was totally clueless. Nikolas was happy to set me straight."

"I had no idea."

"I told you we had a rocky start. I didn't trust a lot of people back then, and I tried to push him away so many times." She grinned over her cup. "Lucky for me, he's a very determined man."

"Are you saying I shouldn't break the bond with Chris?"

For a brief moment, I allowed myself to imagine being mated to Chris. My stomach did flips at the thought of having that kind of intimacy with him.

Sara set down her cup. "No. I'm saying you should break it only if you know in your heart that he's not the one you want to spend your life with. If you have a single doubt, don't rush into something you might regret. I loved Nikolas, but I almost let my fear and mistrust come between us. I can see you still care about Chris even after he hurt you. I'm not telling you to run into his arms, but don't let the past dictate your future."

I swallowed painfully, not sure what to say.

"I'm sorry. I didn't mean to upset you."

"I know." I gave her a small smile. "And I appreciate you caring enough to tell me about you and Nikolas."

She reached across the table to lay a hand on mine. "I do care about you, and no matter what happens between you and Chris, it won't change our friendship."

"Thanks." I looked down, blinking away tears. "I'm sorry. I don't usually cry this much."

Sara chuckled. "Been there. The bond makes you more emotional. It'll pass after you..."

Her words trailed off, and I looked up to see her pressing her lips together. She didn't need to finish the sentence because I knew what she'd been about to say. Once you completed the bond, things settled down. But what if you broke the bond? Did your heart recover from that?

We finished our coffee, and I reluctantly drove us back to the house. The faint flutter from my Mori told me Chris was there before I rounded the garage and saw him sitting on the front step of the guesthouse. There was no mistaking the relief that passed over his face as he watched me park the SUV and shut off the engine. Was he afraid I'd run before he could break the bond?

I sat there with my hands on the steering wheel, until Sara's voice jolted me from my thoughts.

"Talk to him," she said softly. "You'll have to do it sooner or later, and sooner is better in this case."

I nodded and took a deep breath before I opened the door and got out.

Chris

I stood when Beth exited the SUV, and my body tensed, half expecting her to run away again. I understood her hesitation to talk to me with the way things had been between us before last night. But we had bonded, and there were things that needed to be said, like the fact that I had no intention of walking away from her this time.

When I'd come to the guesthouse earlier and discovered she was gone, I'd been afraid she'd left for good. Nikolas told me she and Sara had gone to check out the schools, and I'd been relieved but also disappointed because

I'd wanted to see her and to know she was nearby. As the hours had passed, I'd used the time to think about what I would say to her when we talked and how I would convince her to give us a chance.

The way I saw it, there were two ways to approach this. I could wait until Beth decided that being bonded to me wasn't awful after all, forgave me, and fell in love with me again. Or I could come right out and make my intentions toward her clear from the start – and then get her to forgive me and fall in love with me again. Both would have the same final outcome, but I'd always preferred the direct approach.

I watched Beth walk toward me, and my chest tightened as it hit me again that I was bonded to this beautiful woman.

"Hi," I said when she reached the step. I smiled, hoping to dispel the apprehension in her eyes.

Her fingers twisted in the bottom of her top, and she looked ready to flee.

"Hi."

"Can we talk?" I asked.

For a moment, I thought she was going to say no. When she nodded, some of the tension left me. I opened the door for her, and she walked past me into the house. There was no mistaking the stiff set of her shoulders or the way she leaned slightly away as she passed me. I smiled at her back as I followed her inside. I had my work cut out for me.

Beth went into the small open kitchen and took a bottle of water from the fridge. She offered me one, and I accepted it. I expected her to go to the living room, but she stayed where she was, keeping the breakfast bar between us.

She took a drink of water and wiped her mouth with the back of her hand, looking around uneasily before finally settling her gaze on me. Her voice sounded small and uncertain when she spoke.

"How do we do this?"

I hadn't expected her to jump right in, but I was happy she was willing to talk.

"I think we should talk about the past first."

She frowned. "What does that have to do with anything?"

"It has everything to do with this. I hurt you, and I deserve the anger you're feeling toward me. We can't move on until we get it all out there and you can forgive me."

"Why does it matter if I forgive you?" Her lower lip quivered, and she trapped it between her teeth.

I set my water bottle down on the counter and braced my hands on the edge of the granite.

"It matters because your happiness is all I care about. I know you're not happy with any of this or me, and I'll do whatever it takes to change that."

Her brows drew together. "I don't understand. You need me to be happy before we break the bond?"

My Mori growled, and my voice deepened.

"We're not breaking the bond."

Water sprayed everywhere, drops of it hitting my face. Beth gasped and stared at the crumpled plastic bottle in her hand as if she had no idea how it had gotten there.

I grabbed the paper towels, handing several to Beth, who still stood there frozen. She began drying her face and hands as if she was on autopilot, while I wiped down the counter and floor.

I took the crushed bottle and sodden towels from her, and she looked at me in confusion and disbelief until she finally found her voice.

"What do you mean we're not breaking the bond?"

"I mean exactly that. I don't want to end it, and I don't think you do either."

"Yes, I do," she blurted.

The lack of conviction in her words told me she was lying, probably to herself as well. I felt lighter at the knowledge, and it was all I could do not to smile. Something told me that would only damage my cause.

"No, you don't," I said softly.

"Don't tell me what I want."

Her chest heaved, and color rose in her cheeks. My body stirred in response. I wanted nothing more than to pull her to me and kiss those lips I'd spent too many hours thinking about.

"Okay. Then I'll tell you what I want."

I walked toward her, and she backed up until she was in a corner with no escape. Her gray eyes were wide as I reached up to graze her jaw with my fingers. The contact with her skin sent heat surging through me, and I almost groaned when her lips parted slightly as if in invitation.

Instead of claiming her mouth, I leaned in until my lips brushed against her ear. I smiled at the shiver that went through her.

"What I want is you, Beth."

"No. It's the bond," she said breathlessly. "It makes you feel things you normally wouldn't. You think you want me, but you don't."

All I had to do was press my body against hers, and she'd know exactly how much I wanted her. But she'd only claim it was a physical reaction to the bond, and I needed to prove to her that what I felt for her went far beyond desire.

78

I leaned back so I could look into her eyes. "You don't sound convinced. You feel it, too, and you're lying if you say you don't."

Her throat worked as she swallowed. "The bond –"

"The bond doesn't make you love someone."

She moved her head back and forth. "I don't love you. I might have once but not anymore."

"Liar."

She opened her mouth to speak, but I placed a finger against her lips. Her breath tickled my skin, sending a fresh wave of heat through me. If I didn't leave soon, I was going to lose all control and kiss her.

"I won't push you, but I'm not backing off either. I'm going to prove to you that we belong together."

I heard the catch of her breath as I closed the distance between us. But all I did was press a brief kiss to the corner of her mouth. Then I turned and walked away from her and out of the house.

Beth

"Want to dance?"

"Huh?"

I blinked at the blond boy standing in front of me, wearing a hopeful smile. I'd been so distracted by my thoughts I hadn't seen him approach. Some warrior I was if a human could sneak up on me in plain sight.

"Uh, sure."

I gave him a smile and followed him out onto the dance floor. Around us, at least a hundred people moved beneath the flashing lights to the music coming from the DJ on a platform in the corner of the club.

My body swayed with the music, but my mind was soon far away again, replaying Chris's words from yesterday. I couldn't block them out, just as I couldn't forget the warmth of his touch that made my stomach do flips every time I thought about it.

We belong together.

What I want is you.

I put a hand to my mouth and touched the place where his lips had been right before he'd walked out. If his plan had been to unsettle me, then mission accomplished. My emotions had been in a tailspin ever since.

He couldn't be serious about not breaking the bond. Four years had gone by without a word from him. Four years. And now because our Mori liked each other, he suddenly wanted me?

I swallowed, remembering how my body had reacted to him, how I'd stood there breathlessly, waiting for him to kiss me. Wanting him to kiss me. I couldn't even try to blame the bond for my desire for him. It might have heightened my emotions, but my physical attraction to him had always been there. Apparently, neither heartbreak nor time could change that.

"You might want to tone it down a notch."

I turned my head to find Jordan dancing beside me. When she'd heard about the rave, she'd volunteered to come with me, and Sara had been only too happy to relinquish her pass.

"Tone what down?"

She arched an eyebrow. "That sexy vibe. If you don't want every male in here lusting after you, stop thinking about him."

"I'm not..."

My gaze went to my dance partner, who was watching me with undisguised interest. When our eyes met, he smiled and closed the gap between us.

"What school do you girls go to?" he said over the music. "I haven't seen you here before."

"Not from around here," Jordan said before she began to dance provocatively against my back. The boy's eyes bugged, and I had to fight not to laugh. Jordan was incorrigible.

Discretely, I elbowed her to tell her to behave. She let out a throaty laugh and danced beside me until the song ended. Then she waved at the boy and herded me off the dance floor, where we ran into Alicia and another girl.

"Beth, you made it!" Alicia squealed. "Is Sara here, too?"

"Sara couldn't come. My friend Jordan used her pass."

I introduced Jordan, and Alicia introduced us to her friend Mei, who smiled shyly at us. Mei was petite and pretty, and she reminded me of a doll Chris had once brought me from China. And I was thinking about him *again*.

Alicia beamed. "Isn't this amazing? I don't think I've ever seen this many hot boys together in one place."

I glanced around the room and realized she was right. Most of the people in this room – male and female – were attractive. And except for one or two, everyone looked to be in their late teens. Who opened a club and invited only people too young to drink alcohol?

Jordan nodded. "How often do you girls come here?"

"It's my third time," Alicia said. "I had to work to convince Mei to come tonight."

I looked at Mei. "Not into raves?"

"Not really, but Alicia promised we'd only stay an hour."

Alicia gave us a pained look, as if her friend had asked for a kidney instead of cutting their night short. She looped her arm through Mei's. "We're going to get something to drink. Want to come with us?"

"I'm good," Jordan and I said together and laughed.

I leaned against the wall and watched the two girls disappear into the crowd. Jordan and I had been here for an hour already, and I hadn't seen anything out of place. It looked like a bunch of high school and college kids letting loose. But nothing too wild.

"You didn't have to come tonight," Jordan said. "I could have handled this on my own. Or I could have dragged Sara with me."

I gave her a sideways look. "Why wouldn't I want to be here?"

"Oh, I don't know. Maybe because you *bonded* to someone less than two days ago." She frowned. "I'd still be freaking out."

"Nothing freaks you out."

"That's true," she said with a smirk. "Still, this *is* Chris we're talking about. The love of your life."

I huffed loudly. "He is *not* the love of my life. I don't even like him that much anymore."

Her eyes widened. "Wow, you said that with a straight face. Have you considered acting?"

"Shut up. I'm serious."

"No, you're angry with him, and you're hurt about what he did. Totally understandable. But be honest. Would you be hurt after all this time if you didn't still care for him?"

"Yes... I don't know." I sighed. "I admit I do feel something for him, but it's not enough. I can't trust him. He'll only hurt me again."

Her face softened. "Have you told him that?"

"No, because it doesn't matter. I'm going to break the bond soon. He and I both know it's for the best."

She moved to stand in front of me so I couldn't avoid her gaze. "He's not behaving like a male who doesn't want to be bonded. In fact, I'd say it's just the opposite. He argued against you coming tonight, and then he insisted on being our backup. If he could have used one of those passes, he'd be standing here with you now instead of waiting outside."

"It's the bond. It makes males overprotective."

"It hasn't even been two days." Her brows drew together thoughtfully. "From what I hear, Nikolas was super protective of Sara early in their bonding, too. He was a total bear by the time they completed the bond."

I shrugged. "Nikolas is an intense guy."

She pursed her lips and studied me.

"What?" I demanded nervously.

Leaning closer, she lowered her voice. "You know what they say about bonded males going a little haywire if the female is a virgin."

My mouth went dry. "Um, yes."

"Nikolas was downright scary at times."

"Can we please talk about something else now?" I pleaded. "What do you think of the club?"

She gave me a knowing look and turned to face the room. "It looks normal. Boring, really."

My gaze swept the room again, taking in the smiling, dancing teenagers. Everyone looked happy, and I could almost feel the positive energy filling the air. If there was something wrong with this place, I couldn't see it. Our people had checked into the club, and the owner was a local businessman with several restaurants in the area. Nothing unusual there.

"Let's split up again," I said. "I don't think we're going to find anything, but it's better to be sure."

She nodded. "I'll hang out by the bar."

"I'll cover this side of the room. We'll meet up again in an hour."

As soon as Jordan left me, a boy approached and asked me to dance. Figuring I'd look less conspicuous if I was interacting with others, I said yes. I spent the next twenty minutes dancing with several guys and pretending not to notice their attempts to flirt with me.

Finally, I excused myself and headed toward a seating area where a few people sat and talked. The place was decorated with white leather couches and small lamps that cast an intimate glow. It seemed more fitting for an adult nightclub than for a teenage hangout.

"You look like you'd rather be somewhere else," said a male voice beside me.

I turned my head to find a tall man with short blond hair and blue eyes behind dark-framed glasses. His mouth was curved into a wry smile. I would have guessed him to be around twenty-one.

"Why do you say that?" I asked him.

His smile widened, revealing a dimple in his left cheek. I immediately thought of Chris and then cursed him for invading my head again.

"Maybe it's just wishful thinking so I don't feel like the only one. This isn't my usual scene."

"What's your usual scene?"

"I prefer a party with friends over a large crowd."

I smiled. "Then why did you come?"

"I lost a bet, so my friend dragged me to this thing."

He made a face and pointed to a dark-haired man on the dance floor who looked to be his age. His friend was slow dancing with a girl who couldn't have been older than sixteen and who appeared to be totally enamored with him.

"I guess I shouldn't be too hard on Wes," my companion said. "He got me out of my dorm room for a few hours."

"You go to UCLA?" I asked him.

"Yes. You?"

"I just moved here from Oregon, and I'm still trying to decide what I want to do with my life."

"Aren't we all?" He held out a hand. "Adam."

"Beth."

I gave him my hand, and he surprised me by lifting it to his lips and kissing the back of it.

"I'm delighted to meet you, Beth. I'll have to thank Wes for making me come with him."

I smiled as I eased my hand from his. The college boy had moves.

"What are you studying at UCLA?"

"Finance. I promise not to bore you with the details. I'd much rather hear about what you do."

Adam wasn't overly flirtatious, but he didn't hide his interest in me either. He seemed like a nice guy, so I made sure I didn't send him any mixed signals as I gave him a story about me staying at my friend's place while I decided what I wanted to do.

"Leave it to you to find the prettiest girl in the room," said a silky voice.

Adam and I turned our heads toward his friend Wes, who had left his dance partner to join us. Wes was taller than Adam by at least two inches, with olive skin, dark eyes, and a smile that could melt the heart of every girl in this place. Well, almost every girl. I was most decidedly off men at the moment.

"Beth, this is Wes," Adam said.

"Pleasure to meet you, Beth."

Wes shook my hand, and I couldn't help but notice the Cartier watch that peeked from beneath the cuff of his Armani shirt. Adam dressed like a hip college student, but his friend had money and liked to show it off.

"Do you go to UCLA with Adam?" I asked him.

"No. I live in New York. I'm just visiting for a few weeks and trying to make the rounds with all my friends here." He glanced at his watch. "Speaking of, we're supposed to be meeting up with some people in thirty minutes." He looked at Adam. "I'll get the car and meet you out front in five minutes."

"Okay," Adam replied, looking like he'd rather stay here.

Wes said goodbye to me and left. I watched him go and turned back to Adam, who gave me a hopeful smile.

"Would you have dinner with me tomorrow?"

"I can't. I'm sorry."

"Coffee then?" he pressed.

"I would, but I'm kind of involved with someone."

I almost laughed at my choice of words. *Involved.* That was putting it mildly.

Adam's face fell. "He is a very lucky man."

"Thank you," I said, hating the way my heart constricted.

Alicia ran up to us. "Beth, have you seen Mei?"

"Not since I saw her with you. How long have you been looking for her?"

"Ten minutes." Alicia craned her neck, searching the crowd. "She went to the restroom and never came back. I checked, and she's not in there."

"It's a bit warm in here. Maybe she went outside," Adam suggested.

Alicia shook her head. "No. Mei wouldn't do that, not without me."

Warning bells started to go off in my head, but I didn't want to scare Alicia. Not yet.

"Come on. I'll help you look for her. Jordan's over by the bar. Maybe she's seen her."

I said a hurried goodbye to Adam, then Alicia and I went in search of Jordan. She hadn't seen Mei either, and the look she shot me said she and I were thinking the same thing. We had another missing girl, and this one had disappeared right beneath our noses.

There was no sign of Mei in the club, and the man at the door said he didn't remember a Chinese girl leaving. Jordan and I went outside to be sure. Across the street from the front entrance of the club, Chris stood, leaning against his bike, and he straightened when he saw us. I didn't want to talk to him, but a girl was missing and time was of the essence.

"What's wrong?" he asked when we ran over to him.

"A girl's gone missing from the club," I said in a rush. "Have you seen a Chinese girl come out in the last twenty minutes?"

"No." He pulled out his phone and made a call. "Brock, anyone leave by the back door in the last half hour?"

He shook his head at us as he continued talking to Brock. "Not sure yet. No, stay there for now."

"If she didn't come out through either door, she has to be in there somewhere," Jordan said. "Beth and I will go in and find her."

Chris held up a hand, and I thought he was going to argue against me going back to the club. He surprised me when he said, "Are you girls armed?"

"Did you really just ask me that?" Jordan scoffed and showed us the blade tucked into her long boot.

"Beth?" he asked.

"I have a knife."

"Okay. Be careful in there, and stick together. Call me if you get into trouble."

Jordan and I went inside the club and worked our way from one end of the building to the other. Near the back door were an office and a locked door that read "Staff Only." I made short work of the lock and discovered a flight of stairs to the basement. We listened, but no sounds came from below.

Jordan waved at the stairs. "After you."

The stairs led us to what was obviously a storage area. Past that was the furnace room and one with nothing but wiring and electrical boxes. It was in the last room that we found what we were looking for. Dread coiled in my gut at the sight of the low-heeled shoe lying next to an open grate in the floor.

I looked at Jordan. "You want to go first?"

She grinned wickedly and pulled out her knife. "*This* is what I live for."

And then she jumped into the hole.

8

Beth

I landed lightly beside Jordan in a tunnel lit by a single light bulb. The tunnel disappeared into the darkness in either direction, and I looked at Jordan for guidance.

She looked in one direction and then the other, her mouth pressed together in concentration.

"If we knew what we were dealing with, I'd suggest we split up. But we'd better stay together for this one."

"Which way do we go?"

A shuffling sound echoed down the tunnel, but I couldn't tell what direction it had come from. Jordan cocked her head and nodded to her right.

"This way. Stay close."

We ran down the tunnel, our demon sight allowing us to see in the dark stretches between the lights, and our enhanced hearing picking up the faint sounds of footsteps in the distance. Whoever was up ahead, they were walking at a steady pace, so they had no idea they were being followed. Or they didn't care.

We slowed when we came to another tunnel. Jordan put a finger to her lips then pointed to the left to let me know we were close.

I nodded, my heart racing as adrenaline surged through me. A voice in my head told me we should have called Chris and waited for him, but the thought of Mei down here, frightened and helpless, spurred me on. Gripping my knife tighter, I followed Jordan down the new tunnel.

It wasn't long before we sighted our prey. Anger and relief made my blood roar in my ears when I saw the man with Mei draped over his shoulder, her long black hair swaying as he walked. From here, I couldn't tell if she was hurt, but her lack of movement said she was probably unconscious.

My foot kicked a loose piece of concrete, and I swore silently as the man spun to face us. He was young, no older than twenty, with dark hair pulled back in a short ponytail and a small goatee.

His eyes widened at the sight of us. I waited for him to open his mouth and show us a pair of fangs. If he was a young vampire, we could take him easily. If he was older, we might have trouble. But there were two of us, and we were highly trained.

We stared at each other for a few heartbeats, none of us moving. He sized us up, and then he turned and ran.

He didn't get far. Carrying the girl slowed him down, and Jordan tackled him before he made it ten yards. I reached them as they went down, and I was able to catch Mei before her head slammed into the concrete floor of the tunnel.

Her captor, moving too quickly to be human, rolled and threw Jordan off him. He came to his feet and took a step toward Mei and me, his hand covering a spreading black spot on his stomach.

I reached for the knife beside me, and his eyes flitted to the weapon. In the dim light, I saw the gleam of silver around his pupils. Incubus.

He must have decided Mei wasn't worth the risk because he ran off down the tunnel.

"Stay with her," Jordan ordered as she gave chase.

I gently laid Mei on the floor. Her eyelids twitched, and she moved her mouth, but no sounds came out. I lifted one of her eyelids and found dilated pupils. She looked like she'd been drugged. Or worse.

Standing guard over the girl, I took out my phone and called Chris. The signal was bad down here, and I heard him say my name several times before I was able to tell him where I was. He ordered me not to move and said he was on the way.

From deeper in the tunnel, I heard a yell. I sent up a silent prayer that Jordan was okay. She was tough and a skilled warrior, and Incubi hunted alone. At least he'd have no friends waiting down here for him.

The air moved a second before Chris arrived in front of me. If I hadn't been expecting him, I would have screamed at his sudden appearance.

"You okay?" he asked, not even winded. His gaze moved over me as if he needed to see for himself that I was unhurt.

"Yes. Mei is unconscious, though. I think it's an Incubus trance."

He crouched beside the girl, checking her eyes and breathing. "You're right. She's in a trance."

A shudder went through me when I thought of what would have happened to Mei if we hadn't found her. "Do you think all those girls were taken by an Incubus?"

"It's possible but unlikely. Incubi only have to feed once a week, less when they get older. One Incubus wouldn't need that many females at once."

He frowned as if he'd thought of something. I opened my mouth to ask him about it when running feet announced Jordan's return. She entered the circle of light, and I jumped to my feet when I saw black stains on her top.

"Did you get him?" I asked her.

Anger flashed in her eyes. "He got away, but it'll take him a few days to recover from that gut wound."

Chris stood. The set of his jaw told me he was unhappy before he spoke.

"You should not have come down here without backup. You had no idea what you were walking into, and you're lucky it was a single Incubi."

He was right, but his condescending tone irked me. It was clear from Jordan's raised eyebrows that Chris had never spoken this way to her. I knew it was because of me and the bond.

I had to end this before it got worse and caused problems between Chris and his friends. It would mean leaving Los Angeles, and I hated the thought of leaving the friends I'd made here. But I couldn't ask them to choose between me and Chris.

I opened my mouth, but nothing came out.

"We did what we had to in the moment," Jordan said unapologetically. "How's the girl?"

"Entranced. She'll be fine in an hour or so." He stood, lifting Mei as if she weighed nothing. "Let's get her out of here."

"What happens now?" I asked Chris, walking behind him.

"Now we bring in a team to go over this place. If either of you got a good look at the Incubus, we'll pass the description along to Adele and see if she can identify him."

"I saw him," I said.

Jordan sheathed her blade. "I did, too. I also saw a tattoo on his arm."

"Tattoo?" Chris asked. I detected an edge in his voice that hadn't been there a moment ago.

"On the inside of his wrist. It looked like flames with writing underneath. I couldn't make out the words."

Chris sped up. "Come on. We need to get Mei back to her friend."

Jordan and I exchanged a confused look.

"You going to let us in on the secret?" Jordan pressed him.

"Not here. We'll talk at the house."

There was an urgency in his tone I'd never heard before. I couldn't help but wonder what worried a seasoned warrior like him.

Something told me it was nothing good.

Chris

The team I'd called in when Beth and Jordan had told me about the missing girl was outside by the time we reached the street. I sent them in to search the club and the tunnels for more Incubi.

When Beth had called me to tell me she was in a tunnel beneath the building, fear had twisted my gut in knots. The fact that she was a trained warrior and a skilled fighter should have reassured me, but I was finding it hard to think logically where she was concerned.

Beth went to find Mei's friend Alicia, and I went with her. If my suspicions were right about what was taking these girls, I wasn't letting Beth out of my sight until we were back at the command center.

Mei was awake when we returned, and I wasn't surprised that she had no memory of the attack. As far as she and her friend knew, a human man had tried to take her away. I sent them home with a stern warning to stay away from clubs, and their frightened expressions told me they weren't going to party again anytime soon. They left in Alicia's car, and I sent Brock to follow them and make sure they got home safely.

Beth and Jordan had driven here in one of the SUVs, so I followed them back to the house on my bike. I called Nikolas on the way to tell him what Jordan had said about the Incubus's tattoo. He hung up to make a few calls before we got there.

We parked our bikes outside the garage, and Beth and Jordan gave me expectant looks.

"We'll talk inside," I said.

Nikolas and Sara were waiting for us in the living room, wearing grim expressions.

Jordan looked between us and threw up her hands. "Will someone please tell us what the hell is going on?"

I waved for everyone to sit while I remained standing. I was a little too worked up to sit still.

"We assumed a vampire took the missing girls, but the attack at Luna points at something a lot more dangerous."

Jordan's eyebrows shot up, and Beth's eyes widened. I knew they were both wondering what was more dangerous than a vampire.

"I thought this was a random Incubus attack until Jordan described the tattoo on the Incubus's wrist. That tattoo is the mark of a Lilin."

Jordan made a sound, but my eyes were on Beth, who sucked in a sharp breath as realization dawned. She'd studied demonology so she knew what a Lilin was, but reading about it in a book and facing it in person were two entirely different things.

Incubi were among the more powerful demons that lived among us. By the time an Incubus reached adulthood, he was already stronger than a new vampire. But unlike vampires, most Incubi did not kill the people they fed off, which was why they were not at the top of our kill list. That and the fact that they were solitary and territorial and usually killed each other off. Old age was something very few Incubi experienced.

An Incubus reached his first fertile cycle at age thirty, and every thirty years after that, he was consumed with the need to reproduce. It was only during this fertile period that he could breed. There were no female Incubi, so he chose a human woman to bear him a son. Gestation took six months, and as the fetus grew, it fed off the mother's energy, draining her strength. The Incubus would carefully tend to the woman, feeding her his own energy daily to help her make it through the difficult pregnancy. Even then, many women did not survive the birth and the infant mortality rate for Incubi was high.

The Incubus raised his son until the child reached adulthood at twenty. By then, the younger Incubus's territorial instincts kicked in, and he went off on his own.

The rare Incubus that lived past two hundred years was driven by more than the need to produce offspring. He became obsessed with creating a family, and he bound his children to him before puberty, in a special cere-mony. During the ceremony, the child received his sire's mark on his wrist, a mark that only a very powerful Incubus could bestow. When the son hit adulthood, he did not feel the urge to leave, and he stayed with his sire for the rest of his life.

An Incubus that bound his children to him was called a Lilin, and they were as reclusive and as powerful as a vampire Master. When they entered their fertile cycle, their need to reproduce made them one of the most dangerous demons on earth.

"A Lilin?" Beth echoed incredulously. "But I read that they hate cities."

I nodded. "That's true. The only reason one would come to a city this big is to breed."

Sara held up a hand. "Wait. Don't Incubi have one baby at a time? Why would he take more than one girl?"

"A Lilin is not like a normal Incubus," I told her. "The older they get, the more offspring they want, and some are said to sire as many as twenty in one cycle."

"Twenty?" Sara choked out.

Beth put a hand to her mouth, her eyes rounded in horror. "But those girls are so young. Jessica and Tracy are only seventeen. So is Mei."

I rubbed the back of my neck. "A Lilin will only breed with strong, healthy females between the age of sixteen and twenty-one. Incubi can sense if a human is diseased or sick, so they know which ones to take."

"Now we know why there were only teenagers at the club," Jordan said. "The rave was a perfect cover for them to check out the girls and choose the ones they wanted."

Sara looked ill. "Those poor girls. We have to find them before he…"

Nikolas took her hand in his. "The Lilin will wait until the peak of his cycle, when he's most fertile, to breed. He has to prepare the females first by feeding them his energy. And he won't breed until he has all the females he needs. As far as we know, only three girls have been taken. The attack at Luna tells us he's still looking."

"And now we know what we're looking for," I said.

Beth frowned. "But there are thousands of girls that age in Los Angeles. How will we know who he'll go after next?"

I sat on the arm of a chair. "We don't. But a Lilin won't go unnoticed long by other demons in this city, especially by other Incubi and Succubi. Lilin are like royalty among their kind, and their mark is easily identifiable to anyone who knows what to look for."

Jordan tapped her chin. "He'd need somewhere to keep the girls. Or would he take them back to his lair?"

"He'd have to keep them near him so he can feed them every day," I said. "And a Lilin never takes females from his own territory, so we know his permanent lair is not close to Los Angeles."

"Then they're still in the city," Beth said.

She wore a determined look that made my stomach clench. I didn't want her anywhere near this one, and if I had my way, she'd be leaving Los

Angeles tonight. Once this Lilin figured out we were onto him, he was going to feel threatened, and a cornered Lilin was unpredictable and deadly.

"Okay then." Jordan looked from me to Nikolas. "Where do we start?"

"The first thing we do is reach out to our most trusted contacts in the demon community." I looked at Sara. "Can you work with Kelvan and David to see if you can find where the Lilin is staying? It will be a large, secure property, most likely rented within the last six months. And tell them we have to be discreet so we don't tip off the Lilin."

"I'll call them as soon as we're done here."

"Good."

"What about us?" Jordan asked.

"You work with Raoul. Find out everything there is to know about Luna and whether or not there are similar places we haven't heard about. If anyone can find a party, it's you."

"Sounds good." She smirked at Beth. "Let's party."

"Beth won't be working with you on this one," I said, earning startled looks from them.

Beth opened her mouth to protest, but I cut her off.

"New warriors pair with experienced warriors for this job. You will work with me, and Sara will be with Nikolas. Mason will work with Brock. If we need to switch it out for any reason, we will, but this is how it will be for now."

Beth's lips pressed into a mutinous line, but it had been ingrained in her to follow the orders of the senior warrior in the field. It would take a few years for her to start breaking free of those restraints – unless Jordan's rebelliousness had rubbed off on her. I sent up a silent prayer that wasn't the case. I didn't think I could concentrate on my job, knowing she was out there with a Lilin loose in the city.

And I wouldn't pretend I wasn't happy with this arrangement for other reasons. Working together would give me time with Beth, to talk and to get to know each other again. She'd done her best to avoid being alone with me since I'd declared my intentions toward her, but she also hadn't tried to break the bond. She might say she didn't want me, but until she made it official, I'd do everything in my power to win back her trust.

"What will you and I be working on?" Beth asked in a tight voice.

"Tomorrow, we'll pay a visit to one of our informants. If anyone knows about a Lilin in Los Angeles, Adele will, and this is not something I want to talk to her about over the phone."

"You need me with you to talk to her?" Beth asked skeptically.

Sara scoffed. "More likely he needs you to protect him from that she-demon."

"That, too." I smiled at Sara, who did not try to hide her dislike of the succubus. I turned back to Beth. "Talking to informants is an important part of our job, and I think this would be good practice for you."

She looked only slightly appeased by my answer. "Okay."

Nikolas leaned forward with his arms resting on his knees. "We don't have to tell any of you how serious this situation is. A Lilin is single-minded when it comes to breeding, and he will let nothing get in his way. If by some chance you encounter him, do not engage him. Chris or I might take him in a fight, but he is stronger than the rest of you combined."

"Hey!" Sara poked Nikolas in the ribs.

"Except for Sara," he amended, capturing her hand. "But I don't want you anywhere near him either."

"This is not like any demon you've met so far," I told Sara. "He is highly intelligent and ruthless. His offspring are fanatics when it comes to serving him, and they will gladly give up their lives for him. Plus, their bond with him makes them stronger than the average Incubi."

Jordan grimaced. "I can attest to that."

"You sound like you know him," Sara said to me.

I shook my head. "This isn't the first Lilin Nikolas and I have hunted. They all share certain characteristics that help them survive so long."

Sara frowned. "They must have some weaknesses."

Nikolas nodded. "Like all demons, a Lilin can be killed with a silver blade to the heart, beheading, or fire. But they are stronger and faster than most demons, which is why it would take an older warrior to match them in strength and speed. The only time a Lilin is weak is at the peak of their cycle right before they breed and during the pregnancy. They drain their power by feeding it to the females to help them through the pregnancies. But by then, they are safe inside their lair."

"Great," Jordan muttered.

Sara got to her feet. "If you guys don't mind, I'm going to call David and Kelvan. The sooner we get working on this, the better."

I nodded, and she pulled her phone from her pocket, dialing a number as she walked toward the control room.

"And I'm going to find Raoul and give him the great news about his new partner." Jordan stood, wearing a Cheshire grin. "You coming, Beth?"

Beth darted a glance at me then back to Jordan. "Might as well."

She got up, and the two of them followed Sara. I watched Beth until she was out of sight. All I could think of was her in that tunnel and what could have happened if the Incubus hadn't been alone, or if he'd chosen to fight instead of run.

"I know what's going through your head," Nikolas said, pulling my gaze back to him. He smiled sympathetically. "I wish I could tell you it gets easier, but you'd know I was lying. You saw what I went through with Sara."

I gave him a pained look. "Don't remind me."

"All you want to do is take her and get as far from Los Angeles and the Lilin as possible. If Sara wasn't as powerful as she is, I'd try to take her away, too."

"I'm sure she'd have something to say about that."

He chuckled. "She already did. When I told her about the Lilin, she told me in no uncertain terms that she is not leaving."

I sighed heavily. "As much as I want Beth away from this, I know she'd hate me if I tried to get her to leave. I'm already on thin ice with her."

"She hasn't broken the bond, so the ice can't be that thin."

My heart constricted at the mention of breaking the bond. Even though Beth had stayed away from me since yesterday, I could feel the connection between us every time I saw her or felt her nearby. The furtive looks she shot me when she thought I wasn't paying attention said she felt it, too.

"We're not breaking it," I said gruffly.

His brows rose in question.

"We have things to work out, but it's nothing I can't handle." I gave him a sheepish smile. "There may be some groveling involved."

Nikolas burst out laughing.

I scowled. "You're going to enjoy this, aren't you?"

He leaned back into the couch, wearing a devilish smile. "Immensely."

9

Beth

"Mr. Kent, it's good to see you again," said the blond half-ogre male who admitted us to Blue Nyx.

Chris smiled and ushered me in ahead of him. "Dolph, it's been a while."

"It has. Mistress Adele is expecting you. You can go on up."

I'd been in a few underground clubs in Los Angeles, but one look at the interior of this one told me it was vastly different from the other clubs. Most places catered to a specific nonhuman species such as weres, demons, or Fae. Blue Nyx's patrons were an odd mix of people I never would have expected to see together in one building.

As we entered the main room and walked past the dance floor, I saw several species of demons, some of whom I'd only read about. Mox, vrell, and taag demons danced together away from a group of tall, blond, and exquisitely beautiful people who had to be faeries. A human male ground against a female pixie, and beside them an elfin male was practically undressing a human woman.

The air in the club was thick with lust and something else that made me think of pressing my body against Chris's and...

Whoa. I blinked and mentally shook off the naughty images flooding my mind. I resisted the urge to place my hands against my heated cheeks, and I prayed Chris had no idea what had been going through my head. Sneaking a glance his way, I let out a sigh of relief when he seemed unaware of my frazzled state.

I should have been more guarded. I knew Adele was a succubus, and she fed off the sexual energy in the club. Her magic drove people to a higher state of arousal, and apparently, I was not immune to it.

I couldn't tell if it affected Chris at all or if he was just used to it. Either way, he ignored the dancers and headed straight for a flight of stairs to the second floor. He checked to make sure I was beside him, and then we ascended the stairs together.

At the top of the stairs, Chris turned toward another half-ogre standing in front of a door. The guard tipped his chin in recognition and stepped aside to allow us entry. Chris opened the door and waved me into what must be Adele's office. There was no sign of the succubus, but Chris looked unconcerned as he took a seat on one of the two couches. I sat on the other end of the same couch, keeping two feet of space between us.

A door at the far end of the room opened, and a tall, gorgeous woman with long blonde hair and violet eyes emerged. She wore a floor-length gown of midnight blue with a deep V neckline that plunged to her naval, where a diamond piercing winked at us.

She gave me a brief assessing look before her gaze settled on Chris. Her red lips curved into a sensual smile. "Chris. It's good to have you back in LA. Why have you waited so long to come see me?" She pouted as she walked toward him. "You know how much I enjoy your company."

I felt my brows shoot up at her suggestive tone. When Chris stood and Adele pressed against him in what was definitely not a friendly hug, something dark and ugly stirred in my gut.

Mine, my Mori growled.

Not ours, I thought as my hands curled into fists. I had to fight the stupid urge to tear Adele away from Chris and throw her through the window overlooking the club. I gritted my teeth and looked away from them. If he wanted to get cozy with her, it meant nothing to me, even if my Mori wanted to rip her limb from limb.

"Good to see you, Adele," Chris said amiably. "I'd like you to meet my new partner, Beth."

Partner?

Adele echoed my thoughts. "Partner? But what about Nikolas? You two have worked together so long."

"We still do, but it was time for a change." Chris smiled down at me. "Beth and I go way back, and I think she'd make the perfect partner for me."

My stomach fluttered at the dual meaning of his words.

"I see." Adele looked at me with new interest. "It's nice to meet you, Beth. Any friend of Chris is welcome at my establishment."

"Thank you. It's nice to meet you, too." *Liar, liar.*

Adele trailed a hand down Chris's arm before she sauntered over and reclined on the other couch in a provocative pose. Now I saw why Sara couldn't stand the succubus. If she'd behaved like this around Nikolas, it was a wonder Sara hadn't fried her ass. I wasn't even mated to Chris, and I wanted to gouge Adele's eyes out to stop her from looking at him like he was her next meal.

"So, what brings you here tonight?" Adele asked as Chris sat again. "You were very mysterious on the phone."

"This is not something either of us wants to discuss on the phone," he replied soberly.

Adele sat up straighter, suddenly all business. "It sounds serious."

"A fertile Lilin always is."

The succubus drew in a sharp breath, but her eyes betrayed her. She knew something.

"Who is he?" Chris asked, coming to the same conclusion.

"I don't know."

I had planned to let Chris ask all the questions since he knew Adele, but I couldn't resist saying, "I thought you knew everything that happened in this city."

Her lips pressed together in annoyance. "There are some things even I don't know."

"Tell us what you do know," Chris said.

Adele smoothed the fabric of her dress over her thighs. "Two weeks ago, there were twenty-three Incubi in the greater Los Angeles area. To my knowledge, there are none left as of today. They were either killed or scared off. There is only one thing I know of that could drive every Incubus out of a city."

Chris nodded. "Did you ask around to see what was going on?"

"I did when the Incubi first started disappearing, and an Incubus friend told me he believed a Lilin had arrived in town. He was planning to leave the city because we all know a Lilin will not tolerate other Incubi except his sons in his breeding ground."

"Do you know where your friend went?" Chris asked her. "I'd like to contact him."

Fear flashed in her eyes. "That would be difficult because he was killed last week. Since then, I've stopped asking questions."

"I'm sorry," I said. I had no love for Incubi or Succubi, but it felt like the right thing to say. She had lost a friend.

Adele gave me a surprised look. "Thank you."

Chris leaned forward with his arms resting on his knees. "Can you tell us anything else?"

"I can tell you that it takes a very old and powerful Lilin to clear a city of Incubi this fast, and there are about to be a lot of disappearances in this area."

"It's already started," Chris said. "Three girls so far, that we know of."

She nodded gravely. "If he is as old as I suspect, he'll want to sire at least ten to fifteen young, maybe more. He'll take twice that many girls."

I gasped loudly. "Thirty girls?"

Her violet eyes met mine. "I don't know how much you know about Lilin. They will breed with as many females as possible to ensure viable pregnancies."

"Oh my God." I felt ill thinking about what those girls would suffer if we didn't find them.

"What made you suspect a Lilin?" Adele asked Chris. "There are many reasons why human girls go missing."

"Last night, Jordan fought an Incubus who was trying to abduct a teenage girl. He had the mark of a Lilin."

"Did the Incubus escape?"

"Unfortunately."

Adele wore a troubled expression. "The Lilin will know you are onto him, and that will make him a very dangerous adversary."

Chris rubbed his jaw. "I know. Can you tell us anything else?"

She thought for a moment. "A Lilin spends a lot of time searching for acceptable females, but he doesn't start collecting them until he is less than a month from the peak of his fertile cycle. You have four weeks, maybe less, to find them before he begins breeding. And he'll guard them like they are the crown jewels, so the lair will not be easy to find."

"We already have our people on that."

"Good."

She tucked her hair behind her ear, and I could have sworn her hand shook.

"I appreciate your discretion in this," she said to Chris. "I like my life here, and I'd hate to have to leave it because I made an enemy of a Lilin."

Chris stood, and I followed suit.

"You have my word that we'll tell no one outside our own people about your involvement," he told her.

We said our goodbyes and left the office. On the main floor, I started for the exit, not wanting to linger here longer than I had to. I was inexperienced, but wasn't a prude by any means, and I had no problem with the risqué action taking place everywhere I looked. To each his own.

What I didn't like was the effect Adele's magic had on me, and it had hit me full force again the second we left her office. The slightest brush of Chris's hand against my arm as we descended the stairs had sent heat unfurling in my belly. How much of it was the bond and how much was Adele's magic, I didn't know, but the intensity of it scared me. Even during my girlish crush on Chris, I'd never experienced anything like this sudden desire for him.

"In a hurry?"

I stopped just past the dance floor and looked back at Chris, who gave me a smile that did funny things to my stomach.

"We're finished here, aren't we?" I asked as nonchalantly as I could.

He closed the distance between us. "Business, yes, but it would be a shame to leave without having at least one dance."

I glanced sideways at the gyrating couples on the floor and found it suddenly hard to swallow. "I don't feel like dancing."

The corner of his mouth lifted, making one of his dimples appear. "Afraid you'll like it?"

"No," I shot back as a little thrill went through me.

"Liar."

I scowled at him and turned back to the exit.

"Coward."

I stopped walking and closed my eyes, gritting my teeth at the amusement lacing that single word. If I left now, he'd think it was because I couldn't handle being that close to him. It was true, but I didn't want him knowing that.

"Fine." I spun to face him again. "One dance, that's it."

"One is all I need," he murmured as he took my hand in his and led me onto the dance floor.

Heat emanated from his touch, and my body felt warm even before he stopped and tugged me toward him. My breath hitched, and I could hear my own heartbeat above the music as his arms came around my waist.

I put my hands on his shoulders, feeling the muscles ripple beneath his shirt as we began to move to the slow, sensual music. Unable to meet his eyes, I looked over his shoulder and tried not to think about the way his hips brushed against mine or the tickle of his breath on the side of my neck. When one of his hands slid lower, almost touching my backside, every nerve ending in my body tingled and I smothered a gasp.

"Breathe, Beth." Chris's lips grazed the shell of my ear, sending a delicious shiver through me. "Although, I wouldn't mind having to do CPR if necessary."

I huffed and leaned back to look at him. Big mistake. Heat blazed in his eyes, and his full lips were curved into a heart-melting smile that left me breathless. I'd never been immune to his smiles, but the combination of his closeness and the succubus's magic pulsing around us made it impossible to think of anything else but tasting his lips.

"So, have you known Adele long?" I asked in an attempt to distract myself.

Chris's mouth twitched as if he'd read my mind. "About twenty years or so. She's one of our most reliable contacts here."

"She's beautiful."

"All Succubi are."

Without warning, he dipped me. When we came back up, our faces were mere inches apart.

Moisture flooded my mouth, and I swallowed. Oh, God. If this dance didn't end soon, I *was* going to kiss him. Or worse, jump him.

No, no, no. I can't give in. It's exactly what he wants.

"You've been spending a lot of time with Sara and Jordan since you came to LA," he said casually, as if he had no clue about the turmoil inside of me.

"Yes, I like them a lot," I managed to say, hating the breathy way my voice came out.

"I'm happy to hear that. You couldn't ask for better friends."

I smiled. "I have Mason, too."

The muscles of his jaw tightened, and I felt his fingers flex on my waist. His voice was gruffer when he spoke.

"How long have you and he been friends?"

"Since we started training together, about six years. I had other friends at Longstone, but I was always closest to Mason."

"How close?"

The possessiveness in his tone should have angered me, but it only made my stomach flutter wildly.

I met his gaze squarely. "He's my best friend. We tried dating once, but we decided we were better off as friends."

"Good." He pulled me closer until my chest was pressed against his harder one. His forehead touched mine as we swayed to the hypnotic beat, and I could feel his breath mingling with mine. If I moved my face a little closer, our lips would meet.

The music changed, jolting me from the spell Chris had woven around me. I stepped back, and he hesitated a moment before he released me. My knees wobbled slightly, and I was sure my face bore a telltale flush as I moved to put much needed distance between us.

"Thanks for the dance," I said, surprised that my voice sounded normal.

He gave me a satisfied smile. "My pleasure. We'll have to do that again."

His expression was cocky, but the tenderness in his eyes silenced the little retort on the tip of my tongue.

"Ready to go?" he asked.

I nodded and started for the door again, jerking in surprise when Chris clasped my hand in his. I tried to tug free, but he was having none of it. Expelling a sigh of resignation, I left the club hand in hand with him. I'd let him have this one, but that was it.

Chris

I sighed loudly and laid down the wrench I'd been holding for at least five minutes while I'd stared off into nothing. It had been like this all day, and I'd had to leave the house to get away from Nikolas's knowing smirk.

I couldn't stop thinking about that dance with Beth last night, and my thoughts were bordering on obsessive. Even now, my body warmed at the memory of holding her and feeling her resistance to me slowly crumble. She'd held back at first, but I'd felt her relax against me after a few minutes, and I'd caught her looking at my mouth. It had taken all my willpower not to close that tiny gap between us and finally taste her lips.

I let out a sound of frustration and began to gather my tools since it was useless trying to work on my bike now. Was it normal for bonded males to lose the ability to focus on anything but their mate? I had a whole new level of respect for Nikolas, who'd managed it for months. *Months.* Christ, I would lose my damn mind if I had to wait that long.

My phone rang as I cleaned my hands with a rag. Glad for a reprieve, I picked up the phone and smiled when I saw my mother's name on the screen. I hadn't spoken to either of my parents since I'd left Germany weeks ago. I'd wanted to call and tell them about Beth, but I'd held out because I didn't know where I stood with her.

After last night, I knew without a doubt that Beth was as into me as I was into her. And it wasn't only because of the bond. We had a history, and we cared for each other. I just had to keep reminding her of that.

"You miss me already?" I teased when I answered the call.

"You know I always miss you," my mother chided lightly. "How are things in Los Angeles?"

"You heard about the Lilin?"

"Tristan told me last night. It's not often you see an active Lilin in the US. Everyone is talking about it."

Between Beth and the situation here, I'd been too busy the last few days to pay attention to anything else. I could understand why the Lilin would interest everyone, and I'd bet there were a lot of warriors who wished they were on this job. I'd gladly give it to them if it meant getting Beth away from here. But she wouldn't go willingly, and I couldn't abandon my duty, not unless her life was in immediate danger.

"Your father and I told Tristan we'll go home if we're needed there," my mother said.

"Let's hope it doesn't come to that."

"I'm sure it won't with you and Nikolas on the job," she replied with pride in her voice.

I walked outside and sat on one of the chairs by the pool. "I've been meaning to call you and Dad about something. Is he there?"

"He's gone for the day. Is everything well with you?"

"Nothing's wrong," I said quickly to reassure her. "It's great news, actually."

"Are you planning to move to Germany? That would make me very happy."

"No, but another visit might be in order."

She laughed. "Are you being cryptic on purpose? Tell me your news."

"I bonded." I grinned, wishing I could see her face.

There was silence on the line for a moment before she cried, "Bonded? Who? When?"

"It happened last week."

"Last week? Christian Kent, are you telling me you've been bonded for a whole week and you're only telling me now?"

I rubbed my jaw. "A week's not that long, Mom, and this blindsided me. I've been trying to wrap my head around it."

"Bonding will do that to you," she said in a softer voice. "Do I know her? More importantly, are you happy?"

"You do know her, and she's perfect for me. I just have to convince her of that."

"She doesn't want it?"

The incredulity in my mother's voice made me smile again.

"She has doubts, for good reason. We have a history, and I hurt her. She hasn't forgiven me for that."

"I don't remember you being involved with a Mohiri female, not since you were young."

"I haven't been, not romantically. But I used to be very close to this one up until a few years ago." I took a deep breath. "It's Beth."

My mother's gasp was loud in my ear. "Beth? Our little Beth?"

I remembered the feel of Beth in my arms last night and smiled to myself. "She's not little anymore. She's twenty now, and a warrior."

"Oh, my," my mother murmured. "Who would have thought that the little girl who followed you everywhere would one day be your mate?"

She paused, but before I could speak, she continued. "What do you mean you *used* to be close? You love Beth, and you'd never hurt her."

"Never intentionally."

I dragged a hand through my hair and told her everything that had happened between Beth and me four years ago. Guilt and shame washed over me again when I related how I'd left Longstone and hadn't seen or spoken to Beth again until a few weeks ago.

"Do you mean to tell me you left and cut off all contact with her because you were afraid of the feelings you had for her?" my mother asked in an admonishing tone I remembered all too well from my childhood. "Christian, how could you? That girl loved you, and you abandoned her."

"I meant to go back," I said in a weak defense of my actions.

"You know what they say about good intentions. And you could have called her to let her know you still cared."

"I know."

I stood and paced around the pool. Knowing I'd handled things poorly was one thing. Hearing my mother lay my mistakes out for me drove home how badly I'd screwed up, and it made me wonder if Beth could ever forgive me.

"Now you know why she's not happy about the bonding," I said thickly. "I can tell she still cares for me, but she's angry and hurt about the past."

"You've been bonded a week, and she hasn't broken it off. That tells me she might be more willing to forgive you than you think. The big question is, what will you do to win back her affection?"

"Be my usual charming self," I quipped without humor.

My mother snorted delicately. "Charm only carries you so far. You'll have to do better than that."

"I'll do whatever it takes."

"So, she's the one?"

I pictured Beth's face and smiled. "I think she always has been."

Beth

I sank down on a chair at the outdoor café and watched Jordan arrange shopping bags around her feet. I liked to shop, but she took it to a whole new level.

"Do you really need two new leather jackets?" I asked, shoving my sunglasses to the top of my head.

Jordan rolled her eyes at me. "You sound like Sara. And I didn't see you saying no to those suede boots you found. How many pairs of boots do you own now?"

"Touché."

I caught the eye of a waiter and waved him over. We ordered sandwiches and soda, and he hurried away to get our food.

Leaning back in my chair, I watched people walking past on Rodeo Drive until Jordan waved a hand to get my attention.

"You haven't said how it went at Club Nyx," she said. "What did you think of the lovely Adele?"

I shrugged. "I can see why Sara doesn't like her. She's a bit much."

Jordan grinned. "Did she try to move in on your man?"

A snort slipped from me. "He's not my man."

Even as the words left my lips, my stomach quivered at the memory of dancing in Chris's arms. I'd lain awake for a long time in bed remembering the feel of his body against mine. As a girl, I'd dreamed so many times of him holding me that way, but the dream had been only a shadow of the real thing.

"True. He's your mate. That's even better. Speaking of that, have you told your family?"

I lowered my voice even though there was no one sitting nearby. "Bonding with someone doesn't mean you'll mate them. And no, I haven't told Rachel yet."

I didn't know why I hadn't told Rachel about me bonding with Chris. Maybe because telling her would make it real. Or maybe I was afraid she'd ask what I intended to do about it, and I had no answer for her.

Jordan chuckled. "You don't continue to live in the same house with someone you don't plan to stay with. It's clear Chris isn't leaving. If you didn't want him, you would have gone already. Not that I want you to go," she added quickly.

"It's not that simple." I wrung my hands in my lap. "I admit I feel something for him, but I don't trust him not to hurt me again."

She nodded thoughtfully. "Trust is important. So, you do plan to break the bond?"

"I tried to, but he wouldn't let me."

She quirked an eyebrow. "He wouldn't let you? I don't think you need his permission."

I chewed my bottom lip. "He was so insistent, and he said he's going to prove we should be together. It was impossible to say no to him. I'd feel like a total jerk if I up and broke the bond right after that."

"Oh, girl." She shook her head sorrowfully. "You're a goner. Of course, I can think of a lot worse ways to go."

"I didn't say I wasn't going to break it. I just need a few days. That's all. Maybe a week. I mean, how much can a bond grow in a week?"

God, I sounded weak even to me.

The waiter returned with our order before Jordan could answer me. She took a drink of soda and thankfully changed the subject.

"Did you hear the Council is sending two more teams here to help with the hunt for the Lilin?"

I nodded. "Sara told me Nikolas called Lord Tristan last night to request them. They're taking this demon very seriously."

"When Nikolas Danshov asks for backup, you know it's bad," Jordan said wryly. "And you don't have to call him Lord Tristan. He hates that."

"I'll remember that if I ever meet him."

She picked up her sandwich. "What I'd like to know is where they are planning to put all these warriors. The safe houses are already full."

"I guess some of them can bunk at the command center for now."

We had one free bedroom at the main house, plus the large couches in the living room. And Mason and I had a comfortable couch in the guest-house someone could use. Warriors were used to less than ideal sleeping conditions. They'd make do until something better could be arranged.

Jordan smirked. "If any of them are super hot, I might volunteer to share my room. You know how much I like to help out."

"Such a giving person." I grinned and sipped my soda.

"Beth?"

I looked over my shoulder at the sound of the male voice calling my name, and it took me a few seconds to put a name to the face of the blond man walking toward us on the sidewalk.

"Adam, hi."

He stopped outside the iron fence that encircled the tables. "I didn't expect to see you again after you broke my heart the other night."

I laughed softly. "Jordan this is Adam... I don't believe I know your last name," I told him apologetically.

"It's Woodward." Adam smiled at Jordan. "It's a pleasure to meet you."

"You, too," she said, shooting me a look that said I had some explaining to do.

"I met Adam at Luna," I told her.

Jordan unabashedly gave him the once-over, taking in his lean physique, artfully messed hair, and glasses.

"What do you do, Adam?" she asked when she'd finished sizing him up.

"I'm a finance major at UCLA."

"Smart guy, huh?"

One corner of his mouth lifted. "I like to think so." He looked at me. "Did you hear Luna got shut down after we were there?"

I feigned surprise. "No. Why?"

"I heard it was because of all the underage teenagers, but I don't know for sure."

He looked like he was about to say something else, but he faltered, his hand gripping the top of the fence for support.

"Are you okay?" Jordan and I asked at the same time.

Adam waved off our concern. "It's nothing that a good night's sleep won't fix. I think I've been partying a bit too much since Wes came to visit."

A dark-blue Mercedes stopped on the street behind Adam. The passenger window rolled down, and I could see Adam's friend Wes behind the wheel. His eyes met mine, and he smiled.

"Beth, right? Fancy meeting you here."

I nodded. "Small world."

"Indeed." Wes looked at Adam. "You ready?"

"Yes," Adam replied. He stepped closer to where I sat, his expression hopeful. "I can't leave without asking you to have coffee with me this week. As friends," he added when I opened my mouth to answer.

I smiled apologetically. "I wish I could, but..."

"But you are involved with someone." He didn't try to hide his disappointment.

"Yes."

He looked at the waiting car then turned back to us. "It was nice to see you again. And to meet you, Jordan."

"Nice meeting you, too," she said.

I had my hand resting on the fence. Before I could react, he lifted it to his mouth and kissed it. "Until next time."

"Wowsers." Jordan waggled her eyebrows at me after Adam had gotten into the car. "I might need to consider higher education if all the college boys look like those two."

"Adam does seem to have it all. Good looks, personality, and intelligence."

"Not everything. He can't have you because you're *involved*."

I made a face at her, and she snickered.

"Sorry. My bad. You're *temporarily* involved with a sexy-as-hell warrior who makes mere mortals swoon. And whom you've been in love with since you hit puberty. Did I forget anything?"

I crossed my arms. "Just eat your lunch."

I walked into the guesthouse and came up short at the sight of the person sitting on the couch, reading a book.

"What are you doing in here?" I demanded.

"Hello to you, too, roomie."

"Roomie?" I croaked.

Chris took his sweet time setting the book down on the coffee table. Following his movements, I spied the duffle bag sitting on the floor beside the couch.

He smiled, looking completely at home. "One of the Las Vegas teams is staying at the command center until we set up some extra safe houses in the city. I offered up my room to Abigail. It was the least I could do."

"Why didn't you take one of the couches in the main house?" I asked, trying to keep the panic out of my voice. This place was my refuge. How was I supposed to relax – or sleep – with him in the next room?

"Those are taken." He patted the armrest. "And I like this one."

The door opened behind me, and I turned to see Mason enter the house. He looked from me to Chris.

"What's going on?"

Laying my shopping bag on the table, I said, "Chris is going to crash on our couch for a few days because the main house is full."

I expected Mason to ask why Chris couldn't stay somewhere else, but he only nodded.

"That explains the extra bikes parked by the garage. Guess it's going to be crowded here for a while."

He walked past me toward his bedroom. Before he went inside, he looked at Chris. "Just try to leave some hot water for me in the morning. And for God's sake, don't touch her milk or coffee if you value your life."

I stared at him as he entered the room and shut the door. Since when was he okay with Chris moving in? Where was my best friend who always had my back, especially when it came to Chris?

Chris chuckled, drawing my attention back to him.

"What?" I snapped, feeling like I'd been ganged up on.

He stood, holding his hands up as if to ward me off, a small smile playing around his mouth. "If it really bothers you, I can find a spot in the house somewhere. I don't want you to be uncomfortable."

His offer deflated my anger, and I was suddenly ashamed of my rudeness. "No, it's okay. You can stay."

"It's not like we'll be here that much anyway," he said, looking far too pleased by my concession. "And being work partners, this will be more convenient for us."

"Great," I muttered, trying not to think about being around him night and day.

I started toward my room and stopped when a new thought occurred to me. "I was supposed to go on patrol tonight with Raoul. Does our new working arrangement mean I can't do that anymore?"

"For now, Jordan is taking your place on his team. We'll go back to regular patrols once the Lilin threat is gone."

"What will we do tonight then?" I asked, and regretted it immediately when he gave me a slow smile.

"I'm sure we can think of something to occupy us."

I sighed because I'd walked right into that one.

This was going to be a long few days.

10

Chris

I pulled on a pair of jeans and combed my fingers through my damp hair one more time before I opened the bathroom door. Walking into the living room, I went to find a fresh T-shirt, and I grinned when I saw the wrinkled contents of my duffle bag.

When Sara had told me Geoffrey's team would be staying at the house for a day or two, I'd immediately offered up my room to Abigail and threw my things in the bag to move to the guesthouse. I wasn't above using any excuse to spend more time with Beth.

A small sound made me straighten and turn to the kitchen where Beth stood with a coffee cup halfway to her mouth. She wore a camisole and sleep shorts, and her hair was still messy from sleep. I'd seen her all dressed up to go out, but this was by far my favorite of her outfits.

"Morning."

She blinked, and her eyes lifted from where they had been staring somewhere below my chin.

"Hi."

Fighting back the smirk tugging at my lips, I donned the shirt in my hand and walked into the kitchen.

"Coffee smells great. You make enough for two?"

"Yeah, um...help yourself."

She stepped back to let me through and then walked around to sit on one of the barstools at the breakfast bar.

I hid my smile as I poured a cup for myself and turned to her. Suddenly, I had an image of the two of us living together and doing this every day. I'd never considered myself a domestic person, having spent most of my adult life on the road, but I'd never known a woman I wanted to make a home with. Until now.

"Did you sleep well on the couch?" she asked shyly.

"Like a rock," I lied.

I'd gone to bed late, weary after a long call with Tristan and the rest of the Council. Instead of falling asleep, I'd lain awake thinking about Beth sleeping in the other room. It was a good thing I was used to functioning on a few hours of sleep, because I had a feeling I was going to suffer from insomnia for the foreseeable future.

She fidgeted with the handle of her cup. "Good."

I took a sip of the rich brew and set my cup on the counter. "Sara's friend Kelvan gave her the names of some local vrell demons who might know something about the Lilin's whereabouts. I'm planning to visit them today, and I'd like you to come along."

"Okay." She gave me a small smile, looking relieved to be discussing work. "What time do you want to go?"

"We'll leave at ten and –"

A ringing cut me off, and I went to the living room to find my phone beneath one of the couch cushions. Nikolas's name flashed on the screen.

"What's up?"

"We just got word on two missing girls in San Francisco. Eighteen-year-old twins. The parents were out of town for three days and got back yesterday to discover them gone. We don't know yet how long the girls have been missing, but they match the profile of the other missing girls."

I swore softly. "If this is him then he's gone statewide. Going to be a lot harder to find him."

"I know," Nikolas said. "One of us needs to go to San Francisco."

"You deal with the Council. I'll take a team and check it out."

"Thanks. Keep me posted."

I ended the call and looked up to find Beth standing a few feet away, watching me with a worried frown.

"He took another girl, didn't he?"

I shook my head. "We don't know yet if it was him. That's what we need to find out." I glanced at the time on my phone. "Get ready to leave in an hour."

"Where are we going?"

"San Francisco."

Less than three hours later, Beth, Mason, Brock, and I left a private hangar at the San Francisco airport and drove to the home of Natalie and Nicole Thomas. The front yard of the upscale suburban house was crowded with people who looked like they were planning a search for the missing girls. The police had already come and gone, making it easy for us to enter the place without arousing suspicion.

I parked the SUV in the closest spot on the street and turned in my seat to look at Beth and Mason, who had never worked a scene like this before. Both wore expressions of barely-concealed excitement.

"Brock, you and Mason stay outside and question the people out here. Beth, you're with me. Just follow my lead."

"Okay."

We entered the house, which was just as crowded inside, and found Mr. and Mrs. Thomas in the kitchen with an older black man who resembled the girls' mother. I introduced Beth and myself as detectives, and we showed them our fake badges and IDs.

The older man gave us a wary look. "You two don't look old enough to be detectives."

I smiled. "We get that a lot."

"Dad, not now," Mrs. Thomas said hoarsely, her eyes red-rimmed.

"How can we help you?" her husband asked me.

"We know someone's been here already, but we'd like to ask you a few questions and take another look around."

Mrs. Thomas gave us a hopeful look. "What do you need to know?"

"Tell us what you told the other officers you spoke to," I said. I'd studied the police report on the plane, but it was always better to get a firsthand account.

The couple took turns telling about how they'd gone to a bed and breakfast in Monterey to celebrate their anniversary, and the last time they'd spoken to their daughters was the day they'd gotten there."

"I called them to let them know we'd arrived," their mother said between sniffles. "They told me to have a great time and not to worry about them. I tried calling them again before we left to drive back, but no one answered."

"And when you arrived home?" I asked calmly.

Mr. Thomas put an arm around his wife's shoulders. "The back door was unlocked and no one was home. Natalie and Nicole are responsible girls. They'd never leave the house unlocked or go off without telling us."

"Was anything disturbed?"

"Not that we can see." He ran a shaky hand through his hair. "Where could they be?"

"Mrs. Thomas, may I see the girls' bedrooms?" Beth asked.

The woman nodded jerkily. "Of course. I'll show you where they are."

The two of them left the kitchen, and I heard their steps on the stairs. I stayed with Mr. Thomas, asking him questions about his daughters' friends and whether or not they had boyfriends. I wanted to rule out the possibility that the girls might be off with someone they knew.

Ten minutes later, when Beth and Mrs. Thomas still hadn't returned, I went upstairs to look for them. I found Beth in one of the girls' bedrooms, studying photos of the Thomas twins. Tall and slender with creamy dark skin, hazel eyes, and long braided hair, they were a stunning pair, and exactly what a Lilin would find appealing.

"Find anything?"

"Yes." She plucked something from the mirror and turned to face me, holding a piece of paper.

"What is it?"

She passed it to me, and I turned it over. It was a ticket stub for a night-club, and when I saw the name, my eyes lifted to meet hers.

"Luna," I said.

She nodded. "It looks like the pass I had to the club in Los Angeles. Only this club is in San Francisco." She held up her other hand, revealing a second stub. "I found this in Natalie's room. They're both from two nights ago."

I exhaled harshly. I'd held out a small hope that the Lilin hadn't taken the sisters. But to discover he'd set up a second club here to draw in prospects told me this was bigger than we'd feared. A lot of money went into this kind of setup, and it had to have been planned months in advance, maybe longer. The most troubling fact was that this demon wasn't keeping to one city, which didn't match the behavior for a breeding Lilin. What else was he doing that we hadn't accounted for?

"Good work, Beth." I stuck the club pass in my back pocket. "Let's go check this out."

The address on the pass took us to SoMa, which was the perfect location to set up a trendy underground nightclub. The building was small and nondescript with no signage to indicate what type of business it housed.

My first instinct was to tell Beth to stay outside, but I stopped myself before I opened my mouth. I had no good reason to exclude her except for my strong need to protect her. Singling her out would only anger her.

I picked the lock, and the four of us entered what had obviously been a nightclub, but it looked like it had been deserted in a hurry. The furniture remained, but the bar area was empty, and there were passes and plastic cups littering the floor. The smell of stale alcohol was no more than a few days old.

"I'm going to bet this place closed the same night we raided the club in Los Angeles," I said as I walked around the main room. I bent and picked up one of the passes, confirming my suspicions. The date was two days ago.

"You think he took Natalie and Nicole from here?" Beth asked.

"The unlocked door at their house suggests his Incubi followed them home and took them from there. But I believe he discovered them here."

She pressed her lips together, her expressive eyes showing her revulsion for this place and what it stood for. "He's probably taken more girls," she said.

"I know. We had our guys start looking at other missing persons reports here as soon as we heard about the Thomas sisters."

Her eyes grew troubled. "We have no idea how many girls he has now or how long he's been taking them, which means he could be ready to breed any day. We have to help them, Chris."

"We will."

I resisted the urge to go to her and wrap her in my arms, knowing how well that would be received. Instead, I pulled out my phone and called Nikolas to let him know what we'd found. As expected, he was not happy about the discovery, and he said he'd asked our guys to search for more of the clubs.

"I don't like this," I said in a low voice as I watched Beth walk over to talk to Mason. "I'm already afraid to let Beth out of my sight."

"I know," Nikolas growled. "I tried to get Sara to go home for a visit, and she's a little upset with me now."

I would have laughed at his morose tone if I wasn't in the same situation with Beth. I raked a hand through my hair. This was going to get a lot worse before it got better; I could feel it in my gut.

"It looks like they cleared out of this place in a hurry. I'm going to go over it, see if I can find anything they might have forgotten."

"Are you coming back today?" he asked.

I looked at Beth again, weighing whether she'd be safer here or in Los Angeles. The command center was protected by a state-of-the-art security system that included perimeter alerts and cameras. On top of that, Eldeorin had warded the place with his powerful Fae magic as a favor to Sara. The only demons that could pass through the ward were Mori demons, making the place impervious to vampire and demon attacks.

But the Lilin was in Los Angeles. He would not have driven off and killed all other Incubi there otherwise. The need to be near his captives would keep him mostly to his lair, but his sons' fanatic loyalty to him made them a serious threat. The longer I kept Beth away from that, the better.

"I think we'll stay here tonight, unless you need me there."

"No, we're good here. Let me know if you find anything."

I hung up and called the others over to me. "The place looks empty, but I'm not taking any chances. We'll split up into pairs and search for anything that might tell us who was here and where they could have gone. Beth, you're with me."

She frowned but didn't argue, quietly following me down a short hallway to what had been the office. The two of us went over every inch of the room until I admitted there was nothing to find. The club owner had been very careful not to leave a scrap of paper behind, more proof that we were dealing with a meticulous adversary.

"Back to the airport?" Brock asked as we left the club half an hour later.

"No, we're staying in San Francisco tonight."

Ignoring their inquisitive looks, I called the two local safe houses to see if one of them could put us up for the night. I'd stayed at both places in the past and knew all the warriors stationed at them.

We worked it out that two of us would stay at each house. Beth was not happy when I told her she was coming with me.

She crossed her arms. "Why can't I go with Mason?"

I ignored the prick of pain in my chest at her wanting to be with her friend over me. I knew she was afraid of her feelings for me, but as much as I hated causing her discomfort, I would not even entertain the idea of her and me in separate houses.

Mason surprised me by stepping in. "We're just sleeping at the other house. We'll all be together until then."

Her shoulders relaxed, and relief flashed in her eyes before she nodded.

I wasn't sure what had changed with Mason, but he seemed to have softened toward me in the last few days. Maybe he saw that I truly cared for Beth, or maybe he knew she still loved me. Whatever the reason, I was grateful, and I shot him a look to let him know that.

The closest safe house was in Pacific Heights, so we headed there to check in before we made plans for the evening. The previous owner of the three-story building had been a classic car collector, and he'd converted the entire first floor into a garage. The second floor was the kitchen, living area, and control room, and on the top floor were three bedrooms.

We parked in the garage and climbed the stairs to the second floor where Charles, the ginger-haired leader of the two San Francisco teams, greeted us.

"Chris, good to have you back with us." Charles thumped me on the back before turning to the others.

I saw his eyes light with interest when they fell on Beth, and I moved closer to her before I made the introductions. I didn't mention our bond, but Charles's smile of acknowledgement told me he knew she was off-limits.

"Mike and Keith are out on an overnight stakeout, and you're welcome to crash in their room," Charles said. "Top of the stairs, second door on the right."

"Oh...thank you," Beth stammered. She turned to the stairs but not before I saw the blush creeping up her cheeks.

It wasn't unusual for male and female warriors to share rooms when a safe house got crowded. Most bedrooms had two single beds, so it wasn't as if they slept in the same one. This was one time when I wouldn't have minded sharing a bed. I imagined sleeping next to Beth, holding her, and warmth spread through me.

"Thanks," I replied a little too gruffly. Jesus, I was acting like a horny teenage boy who'd never been with a girl. I had to pull myself together before I embarrassed us both.

Charles led us into the control room where another warrior named Juan was manning the monitoring stations. The room seemed small and cramped after getting used to the much larger one at the command center.

"Tell us about the Lilin situation in Los Angeles," Charles said.

"It's not just Los Angeles," I said, bringing them up to date on everything we'd learned so far.

Juan let out a whistle. "I've never heard of one of them hunting in such a large area. They usually stick to one city."

"That's what has us worried. This one is not behaving like other Lilin."

We talked about the Lilin and then what we'd both been up to since we last saw each other a few months ago. Beth rejoined us as I was telling Charles about my trip to Germany and my visit with my parents.

"You guys have dinner plans?" Charles asked after we'd been talking a few hours.

"Not yet," I said.

"We have a bunch of steaks in the fridge. How about we grill them?"

I looked at Beth, Mason, and Brock, who nodded in agreement.

"Great." Charles stood and went into the kitchen. "Let me see what I have to go with them."

While Charles prepared dinner, I called Nikolas again to see if they'd learned more. The news was not good. In the last two weeks, five young women between the ages of seventeen and twenty-one had been reported missing in San Francisco, in addition to the Thomas sisters. There were four missing in San Diego, two in Sacramento, two in San Jose, and another one went missing in Los Angeles last night. Those were the ones we knew about. If the Lilin had taken all of them, he had at least seventeen girls in captivity. And if Adele was right about the numbers, he needed a lot more before he started breeding with them.

The mood at dinner was somber. Beth picked at her food and only spoke when someone addressed her. Jobs like this one were especially difficult for inexperienced warriors, and I worried it might be too much for her to deal with on top of everything else she was going through. I tried to get her to open up to me as we washed dishes together after the meal, but she gave only minimal answers to my questions.

When all else failed, I did the only thing I could. I pulled Mason aside and asked him to talk to her. It stung to know she felt more comfortable talking to another male, but I'd do whatever it took to ease her mind. They spent over an hour together out on the back deck. When they came in, she was smiling, and he shot me a look to let me know she was okay.

I was trying to find a way to get Mason alone and ask him about what had been troubling Beth when Juan called to Charles from the control room. I followed Charles into the room.

"What's up?" Charles asked him.

"Soren's on the phone. He saw an Incubus carrying a human girl onto a boat."

The small gasp behind me told me Beth had followed us and she'd heard what Juan had said.

My whole body tensed. "What boat? And who is Soren?"

"Soren is a vrell demon who works at the marina," Charles said. "Sara and her friends put us in touch with him a few months ago, and he lets us know if he sees anything suspicious."

Charles nodded at Juan, who hit the speaker button on the phone. "We're listening, Soren. Tell us about the girl."

"She's dark-skinned, and she has those long braids. She tried to fight him, and he used his power to subdue her."

My eyes met Beth's wide ones. The girl matched the description of the Thomas sisters.

I moved closer to the phone. "You're sure it was an Incubus?"

"Yes, sir," Soren said. "I was close enough to feel his power."

"It's them. I know it is," Beth blurted, and the air in the control room suddenly seemed to crackle with excitement and a sense of urgency.

"What boat are they on?" Charles asked. "Is it still there?"

"It's a Sea Ray at one of the guest slips." Soren paused for a moment. "I can see him on the boat, talking to another one of them. It looks like they're waiting for someone."

"This is good. Thank you, Soren," Charles told him. "Can you keep an eye on things until we get there?"

"Sure, but hurry. They look like they're getting the boat ready to leave."

Charles smiled at me. "Feel like going for a ride?"

"You bet," Beth said for us, already headed for the door.

The last place I wanted her was near an Incubus, but I had no good reason to ask her to stay behind. I followed her, already trying to figure out how to do this while keeping her out of danger.

The four of us and Charles piled into our SUV, and a minute later, we were speeding toward the marina. On the way, we discussed the best way to approach the situation. It was Charles who suggested Beth and Mason stay with the SUV while he, Brock, and I entered the marina.

"If these are the Lilin's sons, we'll need the strongest warriors in there," Charles explained when Beth and Mason protested. "We'll call you in after we neutralize the threat."

I parked the SUV across the street from the marina, tossing the keys to Beth before I got out.

"This shouldn't take long," I told her as I checked my comm and made sure she and Mason were wearing theirs. "We'll stay in touch the whole time to keep you updated."

"Okay," she said unhappily, and I wanted to kiss the little pout off her lips.

I understood her disappointment, but there'd be many more opportunities for her to see action. Capturing these Incubi could be the break we needed to find the Lilin, and I needed to go in there undistracted.

Charles's phone rang as we were about to enter the marina. It was Juan calling to let him know he had Soren on the phone again. Two more Incubi had shown up with another girl, and they were all on the boat now.

"Oh, shit," Juan said so loudly I could hear him. "The boat's leaving."

Charles, Brock, and I sped across the street and into the marina, where we met up with an agitated vrell demon by the harbormaster's office. He pointed to the fifty-foot yacht easing out of its slip on the other side of the marina.

I engaged my Mori speed and raced along the docks with Charles and Brock at my heels. Reaching the slip, I moved to jump aboard the boat, but I flew backward when someone leaped off the boat, tackling me. We hit the water together and sank below the surface.

The Incubus wrapped his arms around me in a choke hold, and his strength surprised me. I had to fight harder than I would have expected to break his hold, and my punches did little to slow him down. My first thought was of Beth and how glad I was we'd made her and Mason stay with the SUV. There was no way either of them could have gone up against this demon.

My feet hit bottom, and the Incubus lunged for me again. It became clear when he tried to get me in another hold that his aim was to restrain me, not kill me. Both of us could hold our breath longer than a human, so we were in no danger of drowning, but he had to know by now he wouldn't win this fight.

He was a strong bastard all the same, and it took several minutes and well-aimed strikes to subdue him. I could have used the knife at my hip to end him, but I wanted him alive.

I kicked off from the bottom, dragging the limp body of the Incubus with me, and sucked in a lungful of air when I broke the surface.

Brock shouted my name, and I swam toward the dock that was a few yards away. He grabbed the unconscious Incubus by the arms and pulled him up onto the dock, where two more lay. One was dead, but the other appeared to have been knocked out. Brock sported a cut on his cheek and another on his leg.

I hoisted myself up to the dock and looked at Charles, who was binding a bloody gash on his stomach.

"You okay?" I asked him.

He grimaced. "Yeah. Bastard blindsided me and nearly gutted me."

"I've never seen Incubi fight like that," Brock said from behind me. "They came at us with blades and fought like warriors."

"Did we get them all?" I turned to see an empty slip. In the distance, I could hear the fading sound of a motor.

I jumped from the dock and ran along the jetty in time to see the boat speeding north toward the strait. Once it passed the Golden Gate bridge, they'd be in open water and those girls would be lost.

Racing back to the others, I jumped aboard a small runabout and had it hotwired in less than a minute. It wasn't as fast as the Sea Ray, but I only needed to keep them in sight until we could call in reinforcements.

Brock leaped into the boat as I cast off, leaving Charles to deal with our captures. He was on the phone, calling in his team as we pulled away from the dock.

I reached for my radio and came up empty. It was probably at the bottom of the marina.

"Tell Beth and Mason to stay put until backup arrives," I told Brock as I steered the boat through the choppy water.

"Beth, Mason, you copy?" Brock called over the engine and spraying water.

Someone must have answered because he said, "Chris said to stay there until backup gets –" He paused. "You're what?"

I shot Brock a sideways look and saw him watching me warily.

"What?" I asked with a sinking feeling.

"They're headed for the bridge, following the boat."

I swore loudly. "Tell Mason to turn around immediately."

Brock repeated what I'd said and gave me a helpless look. "Uh...Mason's not driving."

"Goddamn it." I motioned for him to give me his radio and to drive the boat while I donned the earpiece.

"Beth," I said in a commanding voice. "Stop whatever you're doing and go back to the marina."

"I'm doing my job," she replied.

"No, you're going back to wait for backup."

"And let them get away?" she bit out. "Not happening."

"We're losing them," Brock shouted.

He was right. The Sea Ray was getting smaller by the minute.

Beth's voice came over the radio again. "You know what will happen to those girls if we lose them. I'm not letting them go."

I cursed myself for giving her the keys to the SUV and for not realizing she'd do something like this. I'd seen how affected she'd been by the news of the missing girls. I should have known better than to bring her into this situation.

"How do you plan to stop them?" I asked her as the boat rocked on the waves and frigid water sprayed my face.

"Beth?" I called when she didn't answer me.

Nothing.

"Beth," I roared.

"She turned off her radio," Mason said hesitantly.

"Mason, where are you now?" I demanded through clenched teeth.

"We're on the bridge." There was talk in the background, and then he came back. "We can see the boat. It's headed right for us. Shit...hold on."

The background noise got louder, and I could hear traffic and Beth's raised voice, followed by the slamming of doors.

"No way, Beth," Mason yelled over the wind. "You're out of your damn mind."

"You have a better idea?" she challenged.

Fear coiled in my stomach. "What's going on?"

"It's too far," Mason shouted, ignoring me.

"It's the only way, and you know it."

Understanding dawned, and my heart leaped into my throat. I gripped the top of the windshield so hard it cracked.

"Beth, don't you dare," I growled. "Do not jump off –"

"Fuck!" Mason bellowed. "She jumped."

11

Beth

I had only seconds to question the sanity of my decision to jump off the Golden Gate Bridge before I plunged feet first into the dark water. The shock of the icy Pacific punched the air from my lungs, and it took me a moment to gather my wits and swim for the surface.

I broke the surface and sucked in air as I looked up at the lights of the bridge looming far above me. *Well, okay then.*

The sound of an engine reminded me why I was currently freezing my ass off in the ocean. I peered through the darkness at the approaching boat that was going to miss me by at least thirty feet if I didn't get a move on.

Thankful for the many hours spent racing Mason in the lake back home, I set out to intercept the boat, slicing through the water with long easy strokes. My Mori was working double-time to strengthen and warm me, and I knew I was going to pay for this little adventure later. Right now, all that mattered was getting to those girls.

I put everything into closing the gap between me and the path of the Sea Ray. It was a fast boat, and I would not be able to chase it down if it passed me. That knowledge sent a fresh burst of adrenaline through me, and I pushed my body harder than I ever had.

The boat came alongside me and sped past. I lunged for the ladder attached to the stern. My fingers grasped a metal rung and I was jerked forward violently, but I held on.

Gasping, I gripped the ladder and let the boat tow me for a minute before I pulled my body to where I could peer over the swimming platform. When I didn't see anyone, I hoisted myself up to lie on my stomach on the platform. From there, I lifted my head until I spotted the male sitting at the cockpit, driving the boat. There was no sign of the girls or anyone else, so I knew they had to be below in the cabin. And the only way to the cabin was past the Incubus, who was not going to let me through without a fight.

I eased the knife from the sheath at my hip, relieved I hadn't lost it when I hit the water. Studying the male at the wheel, I decided the element of surprise was the best thing I had going for me. If he was as strong as the Incubi I saw the others fighting at the marina, he could overpower me, unless I took him down first. What I lacked in strength and speed, I made up for in hand-to-hand combat skills. And the longer I waited, the farther from my team we got.

I inched forward silently to climb over the back seats directly behind the male. Once I cleared the seats, I'd have to move quickly, and there was no room for error.

I nearly screamed when something cold wrapped around my ankle. My hand holding the knife was already descending to ward off God knew what, when I recognized the face of the man sprawled on the edge of the platform.

My legs weakened, and I sank to my knees. "Jesus, Mason," I whispered. "What are you doing here?"

"You didn't think I'd let you have all the fun." His smirk became a grimace. "By the way, Chris is totally losing his shit. I figured it's safer here with you." He crouched and peered over the seat at the Incubus. "Just one?"

"Up here. I don't know if there are more down below."

His eyes met mine. "Guess we'll find out soon enough."

I nodded as new confidence filled me. Mason and I were not as strong as Chris or Brock, but we'd been training partners for years. Together, we could do this.

"Ready?" I asked.

"Whenever you are."

I vaulted over the back seats, landing directly behind the Incubus. My arm went around his head, yanking it back so I could draw my knife across his throat.

The blade had barely touched his skin before he grasped my arm and pulled me over his shoulder into his lap, trapping me between his body and the wheel. His hands were like vices on my shoulders, and I grunted in pain. Wriggling my body, I managed to bring up my hand and plunge my knife between his ribs.

His choked cry of pain ended abruptly, and he went still. I slipped out of his hold and stood to see his head twisted at an unnatural angle. Mason stood on the seat behind him, looking pleased with himself.

"And that's how it's done," he said cockily. "Give me a second to finish the job."

My eyebrows rose. "Look again, pal."

He leaned over the body, and his mouth turned down when he saw the handle of the knife sticking out of the Incubus's chest.

I held back a grin because there'd be time for celebrating later. Reaching past the dead Incubus, I eased back on the throttle and shut the engine off. Then I pulled my knife from his chest and wiped the blade on his shirt. It was my only weapon, and we had no idea what awaited us below.

I expected more Incubi to come charging up from below, but only silence greeted me when I stood at the top of the stairs to the cabin.

Mason touched my arm. "I should go first."

"Why? Because you're the male?"

He pressed his lips together sheepishly, and I shook my head. I already had one overprotective male trying to tell me what to do. I didn't need another one.

"Follow me," I told him before I descended the stairs. There was no need to be quiet. If anyone was down here, they already knew we were on board.

The first thing I saw when I was halfway down the steps was Natalie and Nicole Thomas, lying unconscious on the bed at the far end of the cabin. Relief filled me, but I forced myself to make sure the rest of the cabin was clear before I went to the girls.

"How are they?" Mason asked from behind me.

I checked their eyes and straightened to face him. "I think they're just entranced. Chris will know what to do."

He cocked his head and gave me a worried look. "Speaking of Chris…"

I looked at the door to the cockpit as the sound of another engine reached my ears. Seconds later, my Mori fluttered, and I heard a furious male voice roar my name.

Mason ran for the stairs. "I'll be up here if you need me."

"Coward," I called after him.

"Yep," he shot back as he disappeared from sight.

There was a light bump as the other boat pulled up alongside, followed by the sound of someone jumping onto the deck. I stood beside the bed, trying not to look as nervous as I felt. I'd never heard Chris sound so angry, and I had no idea what to expect when he came down those steps.

I didn't have long to wait. In seconds, he was there, chest heaving, jaw hard, and a storm brewing in his eyes. I gulped and forgot how to speak as he closed the distance between us. Then his arms were around me, hugging me so tightly I could feel his heart pounding and his ragged breaths.

"Goddamn it, Dove, don't ever do that to me again," he said hoarsely against my ear. A shudder went through him, and he buried his face in my wet hair. "I thought I'd lost you."

His desperate words made my chest squeeze, and I forgot for a moment why I should be pushing him away. I allowed myself to relax and pretend he was the Chris I used to love before he'd broken my heart. Closing my eyes, I savored the feel of his strong arms and the warmth of his body through our wet clothes. My Mori was drained after my swim in the bay, but Chris was putting off heat like a furnace despite his own dunk in the water.

"I'm sorry I worried you," I said at last.

"Worried me?" He held me away from him and stared at me with wild eyes. "You scared the hell out of me. I think you took twenty years off my life when you jumped off that bridge."

"I'm not human, Chris. That jump wouldn't hurt me."

"No, but you're not invincible either. What if you'd come on board this boat and you'd been overpowered? They could have killed you or taken you with them."

"Mason was with me," I argued, even though I'd had no idea Mason would follow me into the water. "And I couldn't let them take the girls, not if I could stop them. You'd do the same thing."

"Yes, I would. But I'm a lot stronger and faster than you are." He dragged a hand through his wet hair. "You can fight, but you're not ready for situations like this. It's why I told you and Mason to stay with the car."

I started to object, and he held up a hand. "And this is not about who you are. I'd say the same thing to any new warrior. Nikolas would say it, too, if he was here instead of me."

I pressed my lips together, knowing I had no argument. As much as I hated it, he was right.

He reached out and rubbed his hands up and down my arms. "I understand why you did it, and I think you're amazing for saving these girls. That's the kind of warrior I want fighting at my side."

"Really?" I asked, sure my face must be glowing with pleasure at the praise.

"Really." He pressed a light kiss to my forehead, and I could feel it all the way down in my toes.

Chris released me and leaned over the unconscious girls. He checked their vitals and smiled when he straightened to look at me.

"They should wake up in an hour or so. We'll take them to the hospital, but I doubt they'll have any physical injuries. The Lilin would not tolerate his sons harming any of the girls."

My shoulders sagged in relief. "Can we give them gorum to make them forget what they've been through? This will probably scar them for life."

"Gorum won't work if they've been gone longer than a day," he reminded me. "The Incubi would have kept them in trances for most of it, so the girls won't remember much anyway."

"At least, they're safe, and they'll be home with their parents soon."

It was more than the other missing girls had. I forced myself not to think about what the other girls might be going through at this very moment.

"All good down there?" Brock called from above.

Chris walked to the bottom of the steps and looked up at him. "We're good. Call Charles, and tell him we're coming back with the Thomas sisters. His team will take over when we get there."

"On it."

The engine came to life, and I felt the boat turning. Unsure of what to do now, I sat on the small sofa so I could be near the girls in case they woke up.

As soon as my body hit the comfortable seat, I knew I should have stayed standing. I'd used up most of my and my Mori's strength with that swim through the frigid water, and for the last few minutes I'd been going mostly on adrenaline. Now that the excitement was over, my body decided it was time to crash. A wave of dizziness hit me, and I sagged against the cushions, shivering.

Chris was by me in an instant. "Are you okay?"

I gave him a weak smile. "Yes. Just a little tired. The water was cold, and I might have overtaxed my Mori a bit."

He frowned and pressed a palm to my cheek. The heat of his body felt like a brand against my cold skin. "You're freezing. You're so drained, your Mori can't even regulate your temperature."

He rooted around in the cupboards and pulled out a thick wool blanket. Sitting on the sofa, he lifted me onto his lap and tucked the blanket around me.

I protested and tried to get off him, but I was no match for his strength. The small struggle wore me out, and I laid my head wearily against his chest in defeat. Soon, I didn't want to move as heat came off him in waves, soaking into my chilled body and making it hard to keep my eyes open.

We were always warned about pushing our Mori past their limits, and now I finally understood the warning. It felt as though all the strength had been sucked from my body, and my poor Mori was so tired it was almost asleep. Older warriors could push their Mori for days without tiring. Younger warriors had to rest a lot more often.

Chris drew my feet closer and pulled off my shoes and socks. When his warm hand began to massage my icy toes, I was sure I'd died and gone to heaven.

A part of my brain told me I shouldn't be letting him hold me like this, but I quieted that voice with the promise that it would only be for a few minutes, just until I stopped shivering.

"Better?"

"Mmm," was all I could manage.

"Remember the last time I held you like this?" he asked softly, pulling me from the dreamy state of bliss I was in.

"No." I frowned because I'd remember being in Chris's arms.

He chuckled. "You don't remember the day I brought you to Longstone? You wouldn't go to anyone else, and I held you like this for the whole drive."

"Oh, yeah," I murmured as the memories washed over me. I'd been wet and cold, and Chris had held me in his arms and warmed me. I'd never felt as safe as I had with him that day.

A hand came up beneath my chin to tip my face toward his. His eyes were the color of soft, dark moss, and I couldn't look away from them.

"I have to admit I like holding you a lot more now."

I licked my suddenly dry lips. "I –"

My words ended on a gasp as he tilted his head and fitted his mouth to mine. Shock and pleasure threatened to short-circuit my brain as his firm lips caressed mine with a tender possessiveness that left me breathless.

I murmured a weak protest that became a soft moan when his tongue swept between my parted lips to explore my mouth with exquisite slowness. My hand crept up behind his head to hold him as I surrendered to the kiss.

I'd been kissed before, but those seemed like sweet touches compared to the raw sensuality of Chris's kiss. This wasn't foreplay or a heat of the moment thing. It was a searing, deliberate mark of ownership that sent fire racing through my veins, and God help me, I didn't want it to end.

My breathing was faster when Chris brushed his lips over mine one last time. He wrapped his arms around me again, tucking my head under his chin, and the fast rise and fall of his chest told me I wasn't the only one affected by the kiss.

I felt lightheaded, and I wasn't sure if it was because I was running on empty or if it was from the most mind-blowing kiss I'd ever had. Closing my eyes, I decided I'd figure it out later when my brain was working right again.

"Go out with me," Chris said against my hair.

"What?" I murmured, too loopy to even look up at him.

"On a date. Dinner, dancing, whatever you want."

Don't do it, said the voice of reason at the back of my foggy brain.

"I don't think –"

"Just one date," he cajoled softly.

"Why?"

"Why?" Laughter rumbled in his chest. "You're going to make me work for it. Okay. I want to spend time with you away from all of this. I want us to get to know each other again." He kissed the top of my head. "I miss you, Dove."

My throat tightened, and I felt my resolve slipping. Maybe we should have a date. Then I could say I gave it a shot before I ended this. It wouldn't change anything between us. No matter how good his arms felt or how dizzying his kisses were, none of that could make me forget the past.

"Fine," I said drowsily. "Just dinner."

"Just dinner," he agreed. I didn't need to see his face to know he was smiling.

The sound of a car backfiring woke me as the sky began to lighten the next morning. I shifted slightly and groaned as every muscle in my body ached. It took me a good thirty seconds to remember the events of last night and the reason for my current discomfort. There was a price for pushing your Mori past its limits, and I'd paid it willingly. What was a little stiffness compared to the safe return of two missing girls?

My Mori fluttered happily, a sensation I'd gotten used to, spending so much time near Chris these days. Suddenly, I remembered being in his arms last night and his mouth on mine. Heat rushed through me, and my stomach dipped as I lifted a hand and touched my lips, reliving every second of the kiss.

How could I let him kiss me like that? And then I'd agreed to go on a *date* with him. What the hell was I thinking? I rubbed my aching temple. I hadn't been in my right state of mind. That had to be it. I never would have done any of those things, otherwise. How on earth was I going to face him after last night?

Groaning silently, I moved to get up – and let out a squeak when I found myself pinned to the bed by a male arm around my waist. I held my breath as my eyes followed the arm to its owner and saw Chris asleep on his side next to me.

Oh, my God. What did I do?

My heart sped up, and I tore my gaze from Chris to look down at my body, which was dressed in the tank top and cotton pants I normally wore to bed. I snuck a peek at Chris and saw he wore a T-shirt and a pair of sweatpants. Seeing we were both clothed made me feel a little better, but it didn't explain how the hell I'd ended up in bed with him.

I wracked my brain for memories of last night. I was exhausted when we got back to the marina, and I remembered getting into one of the SUVs and Chris driving us back to the safe house. He had forced me to take some gunna paste, and I'd managed to stay awake long enough to get a shower. After that?

Panic gripped me. Why couldn't I remember what happened after that?

"You're going to hyperventilate if you keep that up," rasped a sleepy voice.

I turned my head and met his green eyes.

His full lips curved into a lazy, contented smile. "Morning."

"Morning," I croaked. "I... How...?"

"Nothing happened," he said, making no move to release me.

I cleared my throat. "Why are you in my bed?"

"I'm not." His eyes lit with amusement and something else that made my stomach flutter. "You're in my bed."

"What?"

I lifted my head and looked at the room – and my bed near the window. The covers were crumpled like I'd slept there. Only I wasn't there. I was across the room in Chris's bed.

A memory surfaced of me getting out of bed and walking over to his. Pulling back his covers...

Heat flooded my face, and I couldn't look at him. My voice was barely a whisper.

"I got into bed with you?"

"Your Mori needed to be close to mine." His arm tightened slightly around my waist. "It's natural and nothing to be embarrassed about."

Easy for him to say. My cheeks burned at the knowledge that I'd actually left my bed and climbed into his. I'd slept in his arms.

I was still in his arms.

I pushed his arm off me and got out of bed. Tugging the bottom of my shirt down, I crossed the room and pulled a change of clothes from my bag. The silence in the room felt heavy and awkward, and I couldn't get away from it quickly enough.

"Beth."

I paused with my hand on the doorknob but didn't turn around.

"Leave some hot water for me."

I glowered at the door, a reluctant smile lurking at the corners of my mouth. "Sure."

"Oh, and Beth?"

I don't know what made me look back at him. I knew it was a mistake the second I saw him lying in the bed with his arms behind his head, making his T-shirt stretch tight across his well-defined chest. His blond hair was ruffled, and he wore an infuriatingly sexy smile as he watched me with heavy-lidded eyes that silently invited me back into his bed.

My breath hitched, and all the heat in my body seemed to pool at my center. "Yes," I said in a husky voice I didn't recognize.

"I like bunking with you a lot more than my old partner."

There was no mistaking his suggestive little smirk. Huffing loudly, I yanked open the door and closed it not too quietly behind me. Arrogant ass. He was so full of himself, and delusional if he thought there'd be a repeat of last night.

I told myself I was only being considerate and saving him some hot water when I set the water temperature in the shower to cool. It had absolutely nothing to do with my flushed skin or the heat in my veins. Nothing at all.

Chris

"Here she is, folks. Supergirl, who leaps off tall bridges."

Brock's loud teasing voice filled the foyer as he entered the house ahead of us, and there were answering cheers and whistles.

Beth heaved a sigh before she followed him inside. She'd been the subject of good-natured ribbing ever since she got up this morning, and she'd taken it all in stride. But her downcast eyes told me she was a little embarrassed by the homecoming reception.

I entered the living room, and my eyes immediately found Nikolas, who was standing near the French doors with Geoffrey, the leader of the team that was staying here for a few days. Geoffrey had been stationed in Las Vegas for the last two years, and Nikolas and I had stayed at his safe house a few times.

"Heard you had quite the night," Geoffrey quipped when I joined them.

I thought about Beth climbing into my bed. "You have no idea."

Nikolas smiled. I'd called him once we got back to the safe house last night and filled him in. He'd laughed so hard when I told him about Beth's dive off the Golden Gate Bridge that I had to growl at him to shut up. Of course, that had only made him laugh even more. I was starting to sense payback here for my amusement over some of Sara's old stunts.

Geoffrey chuckled. "She really jumped off the bridge and caught that boat?"

"Yes and worked her Mori to exhaustion in the process," I grumbled, watching Beth talking to Sara in the kitchen. She looked like she was back to her full strength, but she'd scared the hell out of me for a while there. Not that I was complaining about being able to hold her or her seeking out my bed. But I wished it had been under different circumstances.

"It's easy to forget your body's limitations when the adrenaline's flowing," Geoffrey said, smiling. "I drained my Mori a few times in my first year out of training. One time, I was laid up for two days."

I kept my gaze on Beth. "Great."

Nikolas and Geoffrey laughed, drawing the attention of Beth and Sara. Sara smiled and waved at us. Beth's eyes met mine and quickly looked away. It had been like that since she'd woken up in my bed this morning. Her tell-tale blushes every time I caught her gaze told me she was remembering it, too, and she hadn't found it as unpleasant as she tried to let on.

There was no way, however, that she could pretend she hadn't enjoyed our first kiss as much as I had. My blood heated every time I remembered the feel of her lips beneath mine and how she'd pulled me closer, deepening the kiss. I'd told myself I could go slow and give her all the time she needed to forgive me for the past. But now that I'd had a taste of the passion simmering below the surface, all I could think about was how to get her back into my arms again.

Beth laughed at something Sara said, and my body reacted as if she'd physically touched me. My Mori growled possessively, its need for its mate mingling with mine and making it increasingly hard not to give in to the urge to touch Beth. I'd known that holding and kissing her would strengthen our bond, but I hadn't expected it to affect me this deeply so soon.

I was starting to have a whole new level of respect for Nikolas. I'd known it was difficult for him to hold back his feelings for Sara, and being bonded for as long as they had before they'd mated was unheard of. I wished I could say I had his willpower, but I knew I wouldn't be able to hold back with Beth like he had with Sara. Beth was like a drug in my system, and I was already craving my next taste.

"The one in San Francisco was opened a month ago," Nikolas said, drawing my attention back to the conversation. I realized they were discussing the club we'd found.

"Same owner as the one in Los Angeles?" I asked.

He shook his head. "We don't know yet. David is still following the paper trail. Whoever set it up is good at hiding their tracks. Fortunately for us,

David is better than them. And Kelvan thinks he's found another club in San Diego. One of the teams there is going to check it out."

"The Lilin is not going to be happy to have all his clubs shut down in a matter of days," I said. "And Charles said the Thomas family has already left for an undisclosed location. Losing the clubs and the girls is going to force the Lilin's hand."

"I know," Nikolas said gravely.

"I took pictures of the Lilin's tattoo on the Incubi we caught last night and sent them to David and Kelvan. They're going to see if they can find something in the demon archives. It's a long shot, but you never know."

"Did you get anything out of the Incubi?" Geoffrey asked me.

"We tried but no luck. Charles is going to keep interrogating them, but I doubt they'll give up anything useful. They're fanatics and so devoted to their sire they'll die before they betray him."

Geoffrey frowned. "Why don't we let them go and see if they'll lead us to him?"

"Won't work," Nikolas said. "It's been tried before with other Lilin. The captured Incubi never returned to their sire. They committed suicide to protect him."

"They really are fanatics."

I expelled a long breath. "That's what makes them so dangerous. There's nothing they wouldn't do for their sire."

Nikolas's gaze went to Sara. "I never thought I'd say this, but I wish Eldeorin hadn't chosen now to take a vacation in Faerie."

I felt my eyebrows shoot up. Nikolas couldn't stand Eldeorin, who took every opportunity to annoy the hell out of him. The only reason Nikolas tolerated the arrogant faerie at all was because Sara liked him. She thought of Eldeorin as her cousin and mentor, and under his tutelage, she was learning to master her Fae power.

The fact that Nikolas wished Eldeorin was here spoke volumes about how serious the situation was, and it doubled my worry for Beth's safety.

Two of Geoffrey's guys called to him, and he went to see what they wanted. After he walked away, I looked at Nikolas and found him watching Beth and Sara.

"They've become close," I said.

I was happy Beth and Sara had hit it off. Not only was Sara mated to my best friend, she was one of my favorite people to be around. After Beth, that was. I imagined the four of us traveling together and working as a team, and I liked the idea very much.

"Sara cares a lot for Beth." He gave me a sideways glance. "She's rooting for you to win Beth over."

"Tell her I'm working on it and I appreciate the cheering section."

Nikolas chuckled. "How is it between you two? She seems less tense around you."

"She's fighting it, but she's coming around. She agreed to go to dinner with me."

"Tonight?"

"Yes."

I hadn't told Beth that yet. She was shy about going on a date with me, and I wasn't going to give her time to talk herself out of it.

I knew from overhearing one of her conversations with Sara and Jordan that she liked a particular French restaurant, and I'd called them from the plane to reserve one of their private dining rooms for tonight. It was romantic and intimate, and the perfect setting to woo my beautiful, reluctant mate.

And if all went well, we'd end the night with another one of those incredible kisses. Or two.

12

Chris

"I give up." Brock lifted his head from the mat and waved in surrender. "Mercy."

I walked over and grasped his hand, pulling him to his feet. He staggered slightly before putting a hand against the wall to steady himself.

I went back to the center of the gym. "Come on. We've only been sparring for thirty minutes."

He groaned. "Is that all?"

"You sound like a new trainee," I taunted, bouncing on my feet. "Let's go."

"I'll go a few rounds with you," Nikolas said from the doorway.

"Oh, thank God," Brock muttered, limping past him.

Nikolas stepped into the room, dressed in sweats and a T-shirt, and joined me at the center of the mats with a familiar gleam in his eyes. He was the only one who could best me in hand-to-hand, and we both knew it.

His attack came lightning fast and without warning. I parried the strike with equal speed and countered with a kick to his thigh that would have put Brock on his ass. Nikolas gave me the little smile that caused younger warriors to tremble in fear and landed a numbing blow to my shoulder. I smiled back. This was more like it.

The thing about sparring with your best friend and longtime partner is that you know each other's fighting moves better than anyone else. Nikolas and I had fought together so many times I could predict his reaction before I made a strike. And the same was true for him. We were so evenly matched that all we could do was fight and wait for a sliver of an opportunity to land the winning strike.

We traded blow for blow until I lost track of time and my body was slick with sweat. A group of people had gathered outside the door to watch, but my focus was on my opponent. He'd beaten me in our last full-on sparring session, and I was determined to win this one.

My Mori fluttered excitedly, telling me Beth was nearby. Out of the corner of my eye, I caught a glimpse of long blonde hair, and I shifted my gaze to her for one brief moment.

It was all the opening Nikolas needed. In the next instant, I was on my back staring up at the ceiling with his heavy weight on top of me. Hoots and clapping came from the doorway as I conceded defeat and shoved my friend off me.

He rolled over onto his back and to his feet in one movement. Reaching down, he extended his hand to me. I took it and let him haul me up. We walked over to a set of metal shelves where he grabbed two towels, tossing one to me.

"Thanks," I said, wiping sweat from my face and neck.

"You good now?"

"Yeah."

He slung his towel over his shoulder and gave me a dry look. "You want to tell me what has you in such a pleasant mood?"

"I'm not in a mood," I muttered, causing his brows to lift.

"I thought things were going better between you and Beth. You said she agreed to go to dinner with you."

"They were, and she did agree." I exhaled loudly in frustration. "But dinner didn't happen. *Nothing* has happened since we got back. Except work."

"Ah." Nikolas nodded in understanding.

The day we'd returned from San Francisco, I'd told Beth we were going out that night. She'd looked surprised but shyly agreed. An hour before we were to leave for our date, a call had come into the command center from one of the other teams about a large lamprey demon infestation in the subway. Almost every warrior at the command center had gone down in the subway tunnels, dealing with the problem.

The next day, we'd gotten word from one of Sara's demon contacts about a new gulak slave operation in Baldwin Park. That night, there was a rash of vampire attacks, and we'd spent the whole night answering calls and patrolling.

Yesterday, Nikolas and I had spent the better part of the day following up with informants and in conference calls with the Council about the Lilin situation. By the time I'd gotten free, it was too late for dinner. I was starting to think some higher power was determined to keep me from my date with Beth.

It wasn't like I hadn't seen her in the last three days. She'd worked alongside me on every job, but there was never time for personal talk. At home, there was always someone around, making it impossible to get her alone, even when we had some time to spare.

I didn't know what was worse, the time I spent away from her or being close to her and not able to touch her and talk to her like I wanted to. The need for physical contact with her created a dull ache in my chest, and I caught myself fantasizing about kissing her at the most inconvenient times. If I didn't get some alone time with her soon, I wasn't going to be fit to be on duty.

"It's been a busy few days," Nikolas said as if he'd read my mind. "Things seem to be back to normal, and we can handle it if anything comes up tonight."

"You sure?"

He smiled and thumped my shoulder. "Go spend some time with your mate."

"Thanks."

I tossed my towel in the hamper and left the gym, letting my Mori lead me to Beth. I found her in the kitchen with Mason, who eyed me warily as I strode up to them. Beth gave me a confused look when I stopped in front of her.

"Are you free tonight?" I asked her.

Her eyes widened a little. "Uh...yes."

I smiled as some of the tension left my body. "Will you go to dinner with me?"

I would have been happy to share a pizza with her in the guesthouse living room, but the odds of us having an uninterrupted meal were unlikely. Going out meant we were guaranteed at least three hours alone. More if things went as well as I planned.

She hesitated, and I caught the flash of uncertainty in her eyes. I was sure she would say no, and I let out a breath when she nodded.

"Yes."

"Great. Six o'clock?"

"Sure," she said breathlessly, making it hard for me not to close the distance between us and kiss the hell out of her.

"See you at six," I said, backing out of the kitchen.

I knew I was grinning like a fool, and I didn't care one bit. I turned and headed for the French doors, ignoring Mason and the three people in the living room who had all stopped talking to follow our exchange. I was going on a date with my girl, and I didn't care who knew it.

I was buttoning my shirt when my phone rang at 5:30. I went into the living room to answer it and smiled when I saw Beth's closed bedroom door. She was in there right now, getting ready for tonight, and knowing that made me as excited as a teenager going on his first date.

Distracted by thoughts of Beth, I answered my phone without even knowing who was calling. "Hello?"

"Chris, tell me you haven't left yet," Brock said in a rush.

My attention snapped away from Beth's door. "I'm still here. What's up?"

"We have Adele on the phone. Her club is under attack, and she's asking for our help."

"Under attack from who?" Adele had warlock wards on her place to keep vampires out, and there were few who would mess with the ogres she employed as security.

"Incubi," Brock replied. "She's holed up in her office, but they'll break through her protections eventually."

"Where is Nikolas?"

"Sara got a call about a disturbance at the local wrakk. She and Nikolas left half an hour ago to check it out."

I rubbed my face and stared up at the ceiling. *Is this some cosmic joke on me?*

"Assemble whoever we have available and tell Adele we're on the way," I told him before I hung up.

I walked over to the closed door and knocked. A moment later, it opened and Beth stood before me, barefoot in a teal dress that made me forget what I'd been about to say to her.

She stared at me for a few seconds, waiting for me to speak. When I didn't, she said, "Am I late? I just need a few more minutes."

"You don't need anything else," I answered roughly. "You're perfect."

Pink tinged her cheeks. "I need shoes. I can't go to dinner barefoot."

Her comment brought me back to my senses, and I sighed regretfully. Now that I saw what I'd be missing tonight, I almost wished I hadn't answered my phone.

"We have to postpone our date again. Adele's club is under attack, and she needs our help."

"Oh." Her smile dimmed. Was that disappointment in her eyes?

She blinked, and it was gone. "Give me a minute to change," she said before she shut the door.

Muttering a litany of curses, I yanked off my date clothes and dressed in jeans and a thin sweater. By the time I was pulling on my boots, Beth emerged from the bedroom, similarly attired and pulling her hair back into a ponytail. She walked over to a duffle bag near the table and began arming herself with knives and a long slender sword. I'd thought she looked hot in the dress, but damn, she took my breath away when she was dressed for battle.

Brock and Mason were waiting for us when we got to the control room, and the two of them were armed and ready to go.

"Who do we have?" I asked.

"Raoul and Jordan are meeting us there, along with Geoffrey's team," Brock said.

"Okay."

Geoffrey's team was seasoned and formidable. If I had to choose a team to be at our back, they were one of the best.

We took our bikes because they were faster, and we pulled up outside Blue Nyx ten minutes later. Dismounting, I removed my helmet and studied the building. There were no signs of trouble out here, but that meant nothing. Adele's club was soundproofed so well that a bomb could go off in there and you wouldn't hear a thing on the outside.

Jordan and Raoul arrived a minute behind us.

"Geoffrey's less than ten minutes out," Raoul said, walking over to us. "Should we wait?"

My first instinct was to say yes because I didn't want to take Beth in there without backup. But my gut told me Adele might not have time for us to wait.

"No. But we don't know what we're walking into, so let's stick together until we know more. Beth, Mason and Jordan, don't engage the Incubi unless there are too many for us to handle."

Jordan scoffed, and I held up a hand.

"The Incubus you fought in the tunnel was strong, but the ones we encountered in San Francisco were a lot more powerful. We don't know what we'll find in there. You take your lead from us." I looked at Beth. "And no heroics."

My tone brooked no argument. Jordan huffed softly, and the two of them nodded.

"Okay. Let's do this."

Adele kept the club doors locked at all times, so I pulled out my picks as we crossed the street. When I reached for the door handle, it turned easily in my hand and the door clicked open. Not a good sign.

I looked behind me, and my eyes met Beth's excited ones. My protective instincts were screaming at me to keep her outside, away from danger. But singling her out would embarrass her, and I couldn't stop her from being a warrior. I didn't want to.

"Everyone, stay close," I told them, but my eyes were on her when I said it.

I eased the door open quietly and entered the short hallway, which led to the inner door to the club. I held up a hand to motion for the others to stay still, and then I enhanced my hearing. Faint thumps and shouts came from inside the building, telling me the hostiles were still here.

The inner door was unlocked as well, and I opened it quietly. The interior of the club was dimly lit, and the first floor appeared empty. From upstairs came loud pounding and sounds of fighting that told me the Incubi hadn't been able to force their way into Adele's inner sanctum.

I stepped inside and caught sight of Dolph's massive body lying a few feet to the left of the door. I knelt beside the ogre and took in the deep gash in his stomach and the blood soaking his shirt. The slight rise and fall of his chest told me he was still alive.

I reached for his shirt to check the damage, and a large hand grabbed my wrist in a bruising grip.

"Easy, big guy," I whispered. "The cavalry is here."

His eyes opened, and his mouth twisted in pain. "Mistress," he gritted, trying to sit up.

"Whoa." I pushed him back down. "We got this. How many are there?"

"Ten...maybe."

I waved Mason over. "Stay with him, and keep pressure on the wound. He'll start to heal as soon as we slow the bleeding."

Leaving Mason with Dolph, the rest of us quietly moved farther into the club. Movement on the far side of the dance floor caught my eye, and I swerved in that direction. Fury built in me when I saw the scene before me.

One of Adele's human waitresses lay on a leather couch, crying and feebly pushing at the Incubus leaning over her. Her top was ripped, exposing her bra, and a bruise was already forming on her pale cheek.

Beth let out an enraged gasp, and the Incubus's head jerked up. The hunger in his eyes changed to anger at being interrupted and then to fear

138

when he saw us. Whether he was one of the Lilin's offspring or not, he didn't stand a chance against five Mohiri warriors.

He moved quickly, leaping over the back of the couch and racing into the dark hallway that led to the back entrance. Before I could go after him, metal flashed and a dagger sailed through the air to disappear into the darkness. A choked cry sounded, followed by a crash.

I ran down the hallway with Brock at my heels and found the Incubus sprawled facedown on the floor, gasping his last breaths. Pulling out the knife, I used it to finish him off, then cleaned the blade on his shirt.

We went back to the others where Beth was trying to comfort the girl. Raoul offered up his jacket, and Beth laid it around the girl's shoulders.

"Jordan, you and Beth stay with her," I said.

I didn't want to split us up, but the girl was in no shape to be left alone. And I wasn't leaving either Beth or Jordan here by themselves.

Motioning to Brock and Raoul, I ran to the stairs to the second floor. We passed the bar, where I spotted the bodies of the two human male bartenders and another waitress. Brock went over to check for signs of life and shook his head grimly. The Incubi obviously planned to leave no survivors.

We were halfway up the stairs when the main door opened and Geoffrey entered with the rest of his team. I caught his eye and pointed up. He nodded and told two of his people to stay downstairs while the rest of them followed us to the second floor.

At the top of the stairs, I quickly assessed the scene. Bruce and Lorne, Adele's two other security guys, were embroiled in battle with six Incubi. The ogres had sustained numerous cuts from the Incubi blades, but they fought valiantly to protect their mistress.

Behind them, three more Incubi were viciously kicking the steel door to Adele's office. The door was dented badly, but it held under their assault. Adele's office was warded by warlock magic, most likely by Orias, who was one of the most powerful warlocks in the country. It was going to take more than brute force to break down that door.

The biggest threat was to the ogres, so I jumped in to help them. Bruce was closest to me, so I put myself between him and the three Incubi who were taking turns slashing at him with their knives. I brought my sword up in an arc, and one of the Incubi stumbled backward, clutching at the stump where his hand used to be. On the downward swing, my blade laid open the chest of another Incubi. He staggered, and I went in for the kill, relieving him of his head.

A minute after we joined the fight, it was over. I studied the bodies littering the floor, glad to see that none of ours was among them.

I looked up at Bruce, who towered over me. "You okay?"

"Yeah." He grinned, showing off his fangs. "What took you so long?"

I laughed and walked to Adele's office door, which looked battered but stood firm. Knocking loudly, I called, "Adele, it's Chris. You can come out now."

I had to knock two more times before the door flew open to reveal Adele's pale face. The succubus wore jeans and a shirt instead of her usual slinky dress, and she had on very little makeup. Her hair was uncharacteristically messy, and the sleeve of her shirt was ripped at the shoulder. I'd never seen her look so disheveled or frightened.

I opened my mouth to ask if she was okay, but my question was cut short when she threw herself at me, wrapping her arms around my neck. Her body shook, and a ragged sob escaped as if she couldn't hold it back.

"You came," she choked out. "Thank you."

I'd never seen Adele when she wasn't put together and composed, and her current state took me aback. I wasn't sure how to deal with the scared woman clinging to me. My Mori wasn't too happy either, and it growled, shrinking away from the touch of a female who wasn't my mate.

When my demon suddenly fluttered, I looked up to see Beth standing at the top of the stairs. Her eyes were narrowed on the woman in my arms, and the straight line of her mouth told me she was not happy about what she saw.

Heat shot through me at the possessive glint in her eyes, and I felt a rush of elation. She wanted me even if she refused to admit it.

I gently set Adele away from me. She wavered a little, but Bruce rushed over to steady her.

"Mistress, are you hurt?"

She patted his arm affectionately. "I'm okay, Bruce. You look worse than I do." She looked around in alarm. "Where's Dolph?"

"He's downstairs," I told her. "He's hurt, but he'll make it."

She sagged in relief against Bruce. "He took the blade meant for me. I'd be dead if it wasn't for my men."

"Can you tell us what happened?" I asked her.

Adele's gaze swept over the bodies, and her face began to harden, her anger surfacing to replace the fear. "I was downstairs making sure everything was ready for tonight when they came through the front door. There were so many of them that it was impossible for Dolph and Bruce to stop them all." She drew a shuddering breath. "One of them came at me with a knife, and Dolph threw himself in front of me. Lorne and Bruce held them off long enough for me to get to the office."

I crouched near the closest body and pulled back one of the sleeves, confirming what I already knew. Standing, I looked at Adele again. "Why does the Lilin want you dead? He left you alone until tonight."

Adele rubbed her arms. "He found out I'm in contact with the Mohiri, and he thinks I'm helping you against him. There's no reasoning with a Lilin when his mind is set on something."

I surveyed the carnage. "It might be best for you to leave town for a while."

"I'm leaving tonight." She stood and looked at Bruce. "You're in charge while I'm gone. Can you call someone to clean up the club? And let the staff know we'll be closed until further notice. They'll be compensated as usual."

"I'm afraid most of your staff didn't make it," I said.

She put a hand to her chest. "They're all dead?"

Beth stepped forward. "All except one. We got to her before they could..." She pressed her lips together.

Adele pushed past me and went to Beth. "Where is she? I need to make sure she's okay."

I watched them go then looked at Geoffrey. "We should go through their pockets before Adele has the bodies disposed of. We might find something to lead us to their sire."

"I was thinking the same thing."

We found a few wallets with cash but no credit cards or identification of any kind. Other than the tattoos on their wrists, there was nothing to tie them to the Lilin.

I headed downstairs to where Beth and Jordan stood talking to Raoul while Adele sat with the waitress.

Walking over to join them, I held up the knife I'd pulled from the Incubus's body earlier. "Who owns this?"

"I do."

I couldn't stop the look of surprise that crossed my face when Beth held out her hand. I'd expected Raoul to claim the weapon because the strike had been so fast and clean, something you'd expect from a more experienced warrior.

The corner of Jordan's mouth lifted. "Wicked aim, right?"

"Perfect shot," I praised Beth as I passed her the knife.

She smiled shyly and sheathed the blade. "Thanks."

After we'd escorted Adele to a private hangar at the airport, we headed back to the command center. I pulled my bike up beside Beth's in the garage and removed my helmet.

"I'm sorry we had to cancel our date."

She lifted a shoulder. "It's okay. Duty calls."

Jordan snorted. "What are you guys, senior citizens? It's barely nine. Plenty of night left."

"It's too late for dinner," Beth said as we went into the house.

"But not for dancing." Jordan swiveled her hips. "And that's a lot more fun than dinner anyway."

"I'm up for dancing if you are," I said to Beth. I wasn't willing to give up on our date just yet.

Beth bit her lip and shot me a nervous glance. "I –"

"We'll all go," Jordan announced. "We can wear those hot new dresses we bought last week."

I smiled gratefully at Jordan. "I think that's a great idea."

I wanted Beth all to myself, but if having Jordan there made her more comfortable, I was all for it. Plus, I really wanted to see her in her hot new dress.

Sara was in the kitchen when we came in. "What's a great idea?" she asked around a mouthful of apple.

Jordan stole a slice of apple from her. "We're all going dancing tonight."

Sara didn't look nearly as excited as Jordan. "Didn't you guys just fight a dozen Incubi or something? That wasn't fun enough for you?"

"If you call watching someone else do all the killing fun. Now I have all this pent-up energy I need to burn off." Jordan laid an arm across Beth's shoulders. "What do you say?"

Beth thought it over for a moment. "Okay."

"Don't sound so excited." Jordan laughed as she released Beth and headed for the door. She looked back over her shoulder. "I'm going to my place to get gorgeous. And then we're going to show this town how to party."

13

Chris

"You're staring again."

I gave Nikolas a sideways look before directing my gaze at the dance floor.

"Half the males in this place are staring," I growled. "Could that dress be any smaller?"

Beth's dress – if you could call it that – was a short, strappy, burgundy creation with an open back and a neckline deep enough to reveal the smooth swells of her breasts. The fabric was gathered at one side of her waist, and it looked like a good tug would unwrap her like a present.

"It's no smaller than what any other woman here is wearing," Nikolas pointed out unhelpfully.

"I don't care about other women." I waved a hand at the three girls dancing together. "Sara's not wearing a dress."

Nikolas's eyes practically devoured his mate, who was dressed in skinny pants and a black sequined tank.

"Sara doesn't own a dress," he said with satisfaction.

I'd never been jealous of my best friend until that moment. Sara had her share of admirers, but her outfit left a lot more to the imagination.

It wasn't that I didn't like Beth in the dress. She had a gorgeous body, and I'd nearly forgotten how to speak when she'd walked out of her bedroom earlier wearing that thing. My first thought had been, *She's all mine*, and my chest had nearly burst with pure male satisfaction and pride.

That had lasted until we'd entered the club and I saw the male heads turn and the naked lust in their eyes. I didn't care that none of these males would ever touch her. I knew what they were thinking, and it made me want to take off my shirt and cover her with it. I wanted to stand by her and growl at any male who dared to even look at my mate.

The tempo of the music increased, and Beth and Jordan raised their arms over their heads. Beth's hem rose a few inches, and I choked on my saliva.

Nikolas slapped me hard on the back and forced me to turn around to face the bar we'd been leaning against.

"You're two seconds away from doing something that will embarrass her and won't end well for you." He waved at the bartender. "What you need is a stiff drink."

I wrung my head in my hands. "This is killing me. How did you survive it for so long?"

"A few months of pain was nothing compared to the thought of a lifetime without Sara," he replied quietly. "I'd do it all again for her."

When he said it like that, it put everything into perspective. What I felt for Beth went beyond a physical attraction or the influence of the bond we shared. I'd loved that girl almost since the day I met her. My feelings for her had changed and grown over the years, but the roots of that love went deeper than any I'd ever known. I couldn't imagine a future without her by my side.

If I thought it would help my case with her, I'd declare my love for her right now. But Beth was skittish and afraid of her feelings for me. I'd seen it in her eyes when she realized she'd sought me out in my bed. She was wary of letting me in because of her fear of being hurt again. As much as I wanted to lay my heart open to her, I was afraid of driving her away.

I lifted my head to meet his serious gaze. "Beth is worth it, too."

"I know."

The bartender laid two glasses of Scotch in front of us. Nikolas picked up his and raised it to me. "Drink up. You're going to need it."

We downed the contents of our glasses and called for a refill. After the third one, we slowed and talked about work. Or Nikolas talked and I did my best not to turn around and see what Beth was doing.

"We're delaying our trip to New York until the Lilin threat is over," he said, swirling the amber liquid in his glass. "Tristan agrees that now is not the best time to take resources from here to start a new command center."

"New York has gone this long without one. They can last a little longer."

He nodded and drained his glass. I knew it was bothering him that Sara wouldn't leave Los Angeles, even if she was stronger than the Lilin. It was built into our DNA to be protective of our mates no matter how capable they were of defending themselves. I was going to worry about Beth's safety every second until the Lilin was dead or gone from here.

Sara came up behind Nikolas and slipped her arms around his waist. "Hey, handsome. Want to dance?"

He set his glass on the bar and turned to take her in his arms. I watched unabashedly as they kissed like they were the only two people in the room. Someday, it would be like this for Beth and me. I just needed to be patient and keep whittling down her defenses.

I looked at the dance floor, but there was no sign of Beth or Jordan. I could sense Beth, so I knew she wasn't that far away. Still, I didn't like not being able to see her, and I scanned the crowd for a glimpse of her.

Being taller than the average male and having enhanced vision came in handy at times like this. I caught sight of Jordan first, leaving the restroom on the other side of the club. I let out a breath when I saw Beth exit a few seconds later.

My eyes narrowed when they were intercepted by a tall man with blond hair. His back was to me, but Beth's and Jordan's smiles told me they knew him. Jealousy flared in me as I watched the man move closer to Beth, who didn't seem to mind his nearness. She'd been in Los Angeles for weeks before I got here, and I had no clue whether or not she'd seen anyone during that time. Was this man someone she'd dated?

I had no right to be jealous of anyone she'd been with before me because I'd had my share of lovers in the past. But the thought of another male touching her made my Mori growl and my jaw clench.

The man gestured toward the smaller bar on that side of the room, and Beth smiled and shook her head. They talked for another minute before she pointed in our direction.

He nodded. Then he reached out and took her hand, lifting it to his mouth.

Mine.

Something dark and primal surged in me, and my vision tunneled on the lips brushing against the back of Beth's hand. I heard the sound of breaking glass, but my attention was riveted on Beth.

The man released her hand, and she smiled again before she and Jordan walked away from him.

"Feeling a little *rage* there, my friend?" asked a voice laced with laughter.

I looked over at Nikolas and followed his gaze to the crushed glass in my hand and the Scotch-soaked patch on the front of my shirt.

"Here."

Sara passed me some cocktail napkins, and I wrapped what was left of the glass in them. I used more napkins to press to the cuts on my hand.

She reached for my hand. "Let me see."

I waved her off. "They're shallow. They'll be gone in no time."

I watched Beth weave through the crowd. She walked up to us, and her eyes immediately dropped to my hand.

"What happened?"

The concern in her voice warmed me until I could no longer feel the tiny pricks of pain from my cuts.

"Nothing. Minor accident."

I pulled the napkin away from my hand, pleased to see the small cuts were already closing. Stuffing the napkin in my pants pocket, I took Beth's hand in my uninjured one.

"It's my turn to dance with you."

Heat flared briefly in her eyes, and I wondered if she was remembering our dance at Blue Nyx. I hadn't forgotten a second of it, and I had every intention of getting just as close to her tonight.

The DJ must have read my mind because the music changed to a slower tempo as I led Beth to the dance floor. I tugged her gently to me until our bodies touched, and I heard her soft intake of breath when I ran my hands down her arms and lifted them, placing them around my neck. I put my hands on her hips and locked my gaze with hers as we moved with the music.

"Are...you having fun?" she asked a little breathlessly.

"I am now. I was disappointed we didn't have our dinner, but this more than makes up for it."

She gave me a coy smile, and it took an enormous effort not to kiss her. I cast about for something to say that would keep me from thinking about her soft lips.

"Jordan was right earlier when she said you have wicked aim with a knife. You also have great reflexes. That was a perfect kill shot tonight."

I felt her body relax as she beamed at me.

"Thanks."

"I haven't seen you sparring yet, but Nikolas tells me you're one of the best young warriors he's seen in hand-to-hand."

Her lips parted in surprise, and she flushed with pleasure. "He said that?"

"Yes, and he doesn't throw out compliments often."

She bit her bottom lip as if she was trying to contain her excitement. "I've learned a lot from him since I came here, although I'm not brave enough to spar with him yet."

I laughed. "Few people are."

"You are."

"I'm a sucker for punishment."

"No," she said earnestly. "You're an amazing fighter."

Pleasure rippled through me. I'd been complimented many times on my fighting, but hearing it from her made my chest swell.

"Everything you taught me helped me excel in training. I finished at the top of my class."

I smiled, and she averted her eyes. It was the first time she'd spoken about the past without anger. It felt like we'd moved past an important hurdle and she was one step closer to forgiving me.

"We can start practicing together again if you want to. Mason, too," I added quickly before she balked, thinking it was an excuse to spend time with her. It was, but I also wanted to teach her everything I knew. As a warrior, she was going to face dangers no matter how much I hated it. The best way I knew to keep her safe and my sanity intact was to make sure she was prepared for anything.

Her gaze met mine again. "Okay."

"Good. We'll start tomorrow...if you're up for it."

Her eyes narrowed at my challenge, and I saw the competitive spirit that had put her at the head of her class. I held back a grin. This was going to be fun.

Talk of training had put her at ease, and she relaxed in my arms. When someone nudged her from behind, pushing her closer to me, she didn't stiffen and pull away like she would have a few days ago. I could have stayed there with her like that all night.

The music switched to a faster song and I reluctantly released Beth, but I didn't let her leave the dance floor. Jordan joined us, and Sara even managed to drag Nikolas out onto the floor. Beth spent more time dancing with the other girls than with me, but I didn't mind. She was having fun, and I loved watching her lithe body move with the music. I was already anticipating the next slow song when I could hold her against me again.

Four songs later, Beth declared she needed water and we headed for the bar. As soon as we left the crowded dance floor, I heard someone calling my name. I turned to see an attractive blonde woman, who squealed and launched herself into my arms.

"Chris! It *is* you," she gushed, hugging me tightly. "I can't believe it."

"Hey," I said, acutely aware of Beth, who stood beside me looking on.

The woman stepped back, smiling, and I suddenly remembered where I knew her from. A pit opened in my gut as my past collided head-on with my present.

"What are the odds of running into you here?" she said. "And wow, you haven't changed a bit. How long has it been?"

She snapped her fingers before I could reply. "Four years."

"That long?" I asked lamely, feeling like a deer in headlights.

"Oh, yeah." Her smile turned sultry. "Best July Fourth weekend *ever*."

Beth's gasp was almost inaudible, but there was no mistaking the faint wave of pain that flowed into me through our bond. I reached for her hand, but she jerked it away from me. I caught the wounded look in her eyes before she spun and disappeared into the crowd.

"Excuse me," I said to the woman as I turned to go after Beth.

I caught up to her outside the restrooms. "Beth, wait."

"Don't touch me." She shrugged off the hand I laid on her shoulder as if it repulsed her and went into the ladies room.

"Fuck."

I paced outside the restroom, trying to figure out how to fix this mess. God, the timing for that little reunion could not have been worse. Things had been going so well, better than I'd hoped, and this was going to undo all the progress we'd made tonight. Worse than that, Beth was hurting and it was my fault.

Beth

Stupid! I'm so stupid.

I swiped angrily at the tear that trailed down my cheek, ignoring the curious glances from the three other women in the restroom. What were they staring at anyway? I wasn't the first girl to cry over a man who didn't deserve her tears, and I wouldn't be the last.

My chest tightened painfully as my mind replayed the beautiful blonde woman in Chris's arms, the recognition in his eyes, the way she'd smiled and looked at him with the familiarity of a former lover.

Best July Fourth weekend ever.

A fresh wave of tears threatened as old heartaches pushed their way to the surface. In the mirror, I saw the sixteen-year-old me who had been crushed by the same man I'd unwittingly let back into my heart.

One of the women grabbed several tissues from a box on the vanity and carried them over to me. She was my height with inky black hair, dark skin, and the face and body of a runway model.

"He's not worth it."

I sniffled and blotted away the wetness on my face. "How do you know?"

Her smile was understanding as she met my eyes in the mirror. "Honey, any man who would make you cry when you look that gorgeous is not good enough for you."

"Amen," said a petite redhead as she retouched her lipstick. "Too many great guys out there to waste your time crying over one."

The door opened, and Sara entered the restroom, her eyes immediately finding me. Her brow furrowed in concern as she walked over to me.

"What happened? Chris looks miserable, and you're in here crying. I thought you two were having a great time together."

"We were."

"So, what went wrong? Did he say something to upset you?"

No, he said all the right things. And I fell for them.

I wiped away a few smears of mascara below my eyes and straightened to face her. This wasn't a conversation I wanted to have here in front of an audience.

"Can we talk about it later? I just want to get out of here."

"Sure." She glanced at the closed door. "He's outside, waiting for you."

I knew exactly where Chris was, thanks to the bond between us, the bond I should have broken days ago if I hadn't been so weak. God, I was such a fool.

Steeling myself, I went to the door and opened it. The first person I saw was Chris, standing a few feet away, his expression one of worry. And guilt.

"Beth," he said as I walked up to him.

"I can't do this," I managed to say as my throat tightened, almost cutting off my air. I moved to go around him, and he took my wrist in a loose grip.

"Let's talk about this," he pleaded softly. "We'll go home and –"

I pulled out of his grasp. "There's nothing to talk about. Please, just leave me alone."

Sara spoke to Chris as I walked away, but I was too focused on putting distance between us to hear what she said. I thought about looking for Jordan to tell her I was leaving and abandoned the idea when my gaze landed on the woman from Chris's past. Pain flared in my chest again, and something ugly burned in my stomach at the knowledge of exactly what she had been to him.

I wasn't stupid or naïve. I knew a man like Chris didn't live like a monk and that he'd probably had a lot of lovers. It wasn't something I liked to think about, so I tried to never let my mind go there. But coming face-to-face with an ex-lover of his had almost gutted me.

"Beth, are you okay?"

I stopped outside the main exit and turned to look at Adam, who approached me with concern etched on his face. Jordan and I had run into him in the club earlier, but I hadn't seen him since. Or maybe I'd been too caught up in Chris's spell to notice anyone else.

I forced a smile. "Yes. I'm just a little tired."

"Wes went to get the car. Can we give you a ride home?"

"I'm good, thank you."

I appreciated his chivalry, but I also knew he was interested in more than friendship. I didn't want to send him any false messages. Not to mention what could happen if I arrived at the house in the company of another male. For the moment, I was still bonded to Chris, and bonded males were possessive and volatile. I would not drag Adam into that.

Adam frowned. "At least, let me get you a taxi."

I nodded gratefully, and he hailed one of the many cabs cruising the street for fares. He opened the back door for me, and I thanked him as I got in. At the light I looked back, but Adam had already gone. In his place stood Chris. I couldn't see his face, but I could feel the weight of his stare even after we rounded the corner and he disappeared from sight.

When I could no longer sense him, I sank back against the seat with a ragged sigh. It was a brief reprieve because he wouldn't be far behind me. I thought about telling the driver to take me to a hotel instead of the house because I felt too fragile inside to deal with anything else tonight. But if Chris went home and I wasn't there, he'd freak and everyone would worry.

I beat everyone else home, and I was dressed in jeans and a comfortable sweater by the time I felt Chris arrive. I stood in the living room and waited, knowing he'd come directly to me. The door opened, and he entered, closing it behind him before he faced me. In his eyes, I saw pain and regret, but also determination.

He entered the living room, but something in my expression must have warned him against coming too close. Stopping a few feet away, he held up his hands.

"Let me explain, please. That woman –"

"I know all I need to know about her. I know you had a life before this and that you didn't spend it alone." My voice cracked, making me sound younger, which fueled my anger. "I don't care about your love life or who you share your bed with."

His eyes narrowed. "The only woman I'll share my bed with is you."

The possessive gleam in his eyes sent a rush of heat through me. But it was only my body reacting to the bond, nothing more. I needed to remember that if I was going to come out of this with my heart intact.

Fated

I crossed my arms and stood my ground, determined to say my piece and get this over with.

"Do you know where I was four years ago, on July Fourth?" I asked with as much coldness as I could muster. "I was sitting in my bedroom, waiting for you because you never missed a holiday. I figured it had been a month since my birthday, so that whole thing would be forgotten and you'd show up like nothing had happened."

"Beth –"

"But you never came, not then, not ever. I cried myself to sleep that night, hating myself for telling you how I felt and for driving you away. And all that time, you were with some woman whose name you probably can't even remember. But she was obviously more important to you than I was." My voice broke on the last few words, but I got them out.

Chris's eyes filled with anguish. "I'm so sorry, Dove. I never meant to hurt you. I thought I was doing the right thing not going back."

"You were wrong," I said hoarsely.

"I know." He took a step toward me. "I swear I'll make it up to you. I'll do whatever it takes."

My heart felt like it was breaking for the second time.

"In a way, I'm glad we ran into that woman. It reminded me how much you can hurt me. I can't go through that again. I won't."

He went still. "What are you saying?"

My Mori howled and pressed forward, trying to take control and stop me from doing what it read in my thoughts. I never should have let it go on this long, never should have let my Mori get close to his. I never should have allowed myself to fall for him again.

"I..."

I choked. I knew the words I needed to say, but I couldn't form them. It was like hands were squeezing my lungs and making it impossible to draw a breath.

A sob welled in my chest, working its way up my throat, and I put a hand over my mouth to keep it in. I spun away from Chris, trying to pull myself together. I would do this. I had to.

Hands gripped my shoulders, turning me and crushing me against his hard chest. I tried to pull away, but he refused to release me as he buried his face in my hair.

"Don't," he said harshly. "Don't say it."

The desperation in his voice was my undoing, and the last of my composure crumpled. Years of hurt and abandonment spilled forth in a torrent of tears that soaked his shirt and left me feeling achy and hollow.

151

Chris held me the whole time, his strong arms wrapped around me like they would shelter me from the world. For a few minutes, I pretended that was true. I closed my eyes and let his warmth and strength envelop me. I felt like I was exactly where I was meant to be.

When I could stand on my own again, I pushed away from Chris. His arms fell slowly to his sides, and he stood there quietly, waiting for me to say something. I avoided his gaze as I summoned the energy to speak.

"I need to be alone."

"You're upset. Let's just talk," he said gently.

"I need space." I took a breath and met his eyes. "From you."

Pain flickered in his eyes. It wasn't my intent to hurt him, but I didn't know what else to say. I hadn't been able to break the bond, and I needed to figure out what that meant. One thing I knew was I couldn't think straight with him around.

"Please." I hugged my waist trying to hold back the emotions that threatened to burst from me again. "Please, go."

He raised a hand and let it fall. Then he turned away and did what I'd asked.

14

Beth

When the tall iron gates of Longstone came into view, I felt the tears I'd warded off all day burn the back of my throat. I lifted my visor to greet the warriors manning the gate, but I didn't stop to talk. I'd ridden all day to get here, and there was only one person I wanted to see.

I'd left Los Angeles long before dawn, stopping once for gas and food and to finally return Mason's frantic voice mails and texts. He'd had a minor freak out when he read the note I'd left for him on our fridge, and he'd wanted to know why I'd left without him. He would have gladly come with me.

I'd explained to him that I needed to do this alone and promised I'd text him as soon as I got home. Immediately after I parked my bike near the main garages, I sent off a text to tell him I'd arrived safely. His response came less than a minute later.

About time. I'll let everyone know.

By *everyone*, I knew he meant Chris, who had called and left texts for me, too. I'd asked Mason to let him know I was going home and to tell him to please not come after me.

I'd gotten about five hours from Los Angeles when I'd surfaced from my misery long enough to realize what my leaving would do to Chris. Last night, I'd tried to break the bond, and today I'd taken off without a word. He had to think I was running with no intention of going back.

Am I?

I'd been asking myself that question ever since I rode away from the command center, and I was no closer to the answer now than I was then. Mostly because it hurt too much to think about what would happen if I walked away from Chris forever.

Tell him, I started to type. I deleted it and sent a simple **Thanks.**

Grabbing my small duffle, I walked across the compound to the residential area. Unlike military strongholds, Longstone was laid out more like a small town with actual houses, a school, and even a park. There were a lot more families here, too, which meant more children of all ages. I recognized many of them as I passed by, and they all called greetings to me. I waved and smiled, but continued on without stopping.

In no time, I stood outside the pretty little house I'd grown up in. It felt like I hadn't seen this place in years, although in reality, it had only been a month. Maybe it just seemed that way because so much had happened since Mason and I had set out from here to see the world.

I opened the door and went inside, setting my bag down in the living room. I hadn't told Rachel I was coming home, but when I'd talked to her a few days ago, she'd said she was just back from a job in Portland and would be here for the next two weeks.

"Rachel," I called in a voice that cracked from pent-up emotion.

She hurried out of her bedroom, her eyes wide. "Beth? You didn't tell me you were –"

Taking one look at my face, she ran to me. "What's wrong?"

"Everything," I whispered before the dam broke and I began to cry.

She gathered me in her arms, and I buried my face against her shoulder like I used to do when I was younger. The last time I'd cried like this in her arms was the day Chris left Longstone without saying goodbye. I'd thought my heart was going to break in two that day, but that pain had nothing on what I felt this time.

Rachel held me while I cried, rubbing my back soothingly like moms do. When I started hiccupping, she led me over to sit on the couch and waited until I found my voice again.

"Do you want to tell me what happened?" she asked softly.

"I don't know where to start."

A few days after Chris had shown up in Los Angeles, I'd called Rachel and told her. I'd assured her I was okay with it and that he wouldn't be there long anyway. She'd been satisfied with that, and she hadn't pressed for more information about him. How did I tell her now that Chris and I had been bonded for almost two weeks and this was the first she would hear of it?

She tenderly brushed my hair back over my shoulder. "Is it Chris?"

"Why do you ask that?"

"In all the years I've known you, you've only cried like this for one person."

I wrapped my arms around my waist as a fresh wave of pain hit me.

"It hurts so much. I can't make it stop."

"Oh, sweetie. What happened?"

It was several minutes before I could answer her. I took a breath and met her worried eyes.

"We bonded."

"What?"

The word came out almost as a shout as Rachel gaped at me with wide disbelieving eyes. I was pretty sure that was the last thing she'd expected me to say.

Her mouth worked for a few seconds before she managed to speak again.

"Last night? Is that why you left Los Angeles?"

I bent my head so I didn't have to see her face. "Two weeks ago."

"I...don't understand," she stammered. "You never said anything."

"I didn't know what to say. I think I was in shock at first, and then..." I swallowed hard. "I was going to break it, but Chris said he didn't want to. I was so confused, and before I knew it, I fell for him again."

My throat closed up, and I took a few breaths to compose myself. Rachel didn't speak as she waited for me to continue.

"I was starting to think I could get past what happened before, but last night...we had a big fight, and I knew it was over." I told her what had happened at the club and after. By the time I got it all out, my words were coming between broken sobs. "But when I tried to break the bond, I couldn't. And I don't know what to do."

Rachel's arms came around me, and I curled into her as she stroked my hair.

"Is that why you left Los Angeles – to break the bond?"

"No. I was so upset, and all I could think of was coming home to you." I let out a shuddering breath. "I'm sorry I didn't tell you."

"I wish you had, but I understand how overwhelming this must be for you. Bonding is emotional enough without him being someone you were once so close to."

"Why did it have to be him?" I wailed against her chest.

She heaved a sigh. "It was always going to be him."

I went still. "What do you mean?"

"Maybe if I'd ever bonded, I would have seen the signs. Looking back now, it's so obvious. There was a special connection between you and Chris from the moment he brought you home. You were already attached to him, and he went out of his way to help you settle in here."

"He saved my life, and I was traumatized," I said, sniffling.

"It was more than that, and I can't believe I didn't see it. Chris has always been overly protective of you, and he couldn't stand to see you upset. Any time he thought he might be late coming home, he called me to give me a heads-up just in case. Beatrice used to joke about how Chris could never remember birthdays, but not once did he forget yours.

"You were happiest when he was around, and I wasn't surprised when you developed a crush on him. I thought it would pass, and it wasn't until after he left that I saw you were in love with him. No one is that devastated from a crush. I think your Mori was mourning, too, because it already knew Chris was your mate."

I lifted my head to give her a disbelieving look. "You think Chris knew all along?"

"No, but I think his Mori might have."

"Then why did he leave?" I asked angrily. "Why did he hurt me like that if he cared so much for me?"

"He wasn't trying to hurt you. He was doing what he always did – protecting you."

I let out a harsh laugh. "Protecting me from what?"

"Look at it through his eyes. You were sixteen and still a child compared to him. He couldn't return your feelings, and he felt his presence would cause you more pain than his absence."

"He told you that?"

"No, but I talked to him before he left, and he was beating himself up for making you cry. He called me every week for the first few months to see how you were."

Shock rippled through me. "He called?"

"Yes. He was waiting for you to get over your crush before he came home again."

I wasn't sure what to make of the things Rachel was telling me. I knew she'd gone to see Chris that day, but not once had she mentioned being in contact with him afterward. All this time, I'd thought he'd left and forgotten me.

"But he didn't come back," I argued. "He never even called me."

"I don't know why he stayed away and didn't call you. Those are questions only he can answer. But I do know he cared about you very much."

I wiped the wetness from my cheeks. "It doesn't matter anymore."

"Doesn't it? You love him."

I didn't deny it. In San Francisco, I'd felt something shift inside me when he'd kissed me on the boat and again when I'd woken up in his arms the next day. I'd started to wonder if there really could be something between us. It was why I'd agreed to go to dinner with him, and why I'd felt so comfortable dancing with him at the club.

When I couldn't break the bond, I'd thought it was because I was weak. But as the hours passed during my ride here, the growing ache in my heart told me the real reason we were still bonded. I was in love with him.

"Sometimes, love isn't enough," I said hoarsely.

Rachel squeezed my hand. "And sometimes, all you need is a little time and space to put things into better perspective. And your mother."

I rested my head against her shoulder. "I'll always need you."

We sat like that for a while before Rachel stood and smiled down at me.

"I'm going to make dinner, and then we'll have a nice quiet evening, just the two of us."

"I'd like that."

I carried my bag into my old bedroom to shower and change after the long day on the road. Standing in the door to my bathroom, toweling my hair dry, I couldn't help but think about all the laughter and tears this room had seen. The best years of my life had been spent here, and every picture and object held a memory for me.

I tossed the towel in the hamper and opened the closet door. At the back of my closet were three large plastic storage containers that held almost every gift Chris had given me over the years. I hadn't opened these containers in years, except to add the things he'd sent me after he left. I didn't know if seeing what was in the containers would help or hinder me, but I felt a sudden urge to look in them now.

Grabbing the top container, I carried it over and set it on the floor by the bed. I sat on the rug, pried off the lid, and immediately lost myself in the past.

This box was from my younger years, so it was full of mostly toys and plush animals. Among the contents, I found a delicate china doll, a ragged stuffed bear I'd slept with for years, a tiny bow and a quiver of arrows, and a wooden sword with a real leather sheath.

A small smile curved my mouth as I remembered how excited I'd been to get the sword on my ninth birthday and how Chris had spent hours engaging in mock duels with me. I'd practiced every day for a month so I could show him how good I was on his next visit. Rachel had finally ordered me to take the sword outside and to stop hitting the furniture. It was a good thing the blade was dull, or I would have sliced up everything in sight.

At the bottom of the box, I found a thick photo album, and I hesitated before I lifted it out. I knew it was full of pictures of Chris and me. Otherwise, it wouldn't have ended up in this container.

I opened the album to the first page, and I was filled with memories of my first Christmas at Longstone, six months after Chris had found me. The first few photos were of me opening gifts, my face flushed with excitement. Turning the page, I saw a picture of Chris and me in front of the tree. My head barely reached his waist, and I had my little arms wrapped around his leg as I grinned up at him. He was smiling back, and it was easy to see the affection we'd had for each other.

Could Rachel be right? Had Chris and I been drawn to each other because our Mori somehow knew we were mates? Was it even possible for a young Mori to sense a potential mate?

With those questions at the front of my mind, I flipped through the whole album, reliving the memories associated with each photo. One thing I couldn't dispute was that whatever his reason for leaving, Chris had loved me once. The proof was in every picture of the two of us together. But was that enough to forgive him and let go of all the hurt I'd carried with me for years?

I lay back on the floor, hugging the photo album to my chest. My heart still felt like it was in a vise, but I had no tears left to cry, at least for today.

I was still there when Rachel appeared in the doorway thirty minutes later. She took in the photo album in my hands and the things spread out around me and gave me a small smile.

"I made chicken fajitas. Do you want me to bring you some?"

"No. I want us to eat together."

I sat up and laid the photo album on the bed. I hadn't come all this way to hide in my room.

She held out a hand to me. I took it, and she pulled me to my feet.

"Come on." Still holding my hand, she led me from the room. "You know my fajitas always make you feel better."

"I think it's going to take more than that this time."

"What if I told you I have your favorite dessert in the fridge?"

"Cheesecake?" I asked hopefully.

"Call it mother's intuition, but I had the sudden urge to make New York-style cheesecake this morning."

I pulled my hand from hers so I could give her a hug. "I missed you."

"I missed you, too. Now let's go eat a cheesecake."

I laughed for the first time in what felt like days and followed her to the kitchen.

Fated

Chris

The vampire grinned, showing off his snakelike fangs, as we circled each other in the lobby of the abandoned apartment building. Off to one side, two more of his brethren cheered him on like boys at a street fight. Fools had no clue they were taking their last breaths.

I struck, and the vampire darted away, alive but sporting a nasty gash across his chest. He shrieked and spun back to me, his smile gone.

"When I'm through with –"

His threat ended abruptly as my sword sliced through his neck. Before his head hit the floor, I was on the next one, thrusting my blade through his heart. The third one ran, but I took him down with a knife to the back. He was writhing on the dirty carpet when I strode over to finish him off.

I surveyed the room as I wiped my blades clean on their clothes. Usually, killing three vampires in less than two minutes would fill me with satisfaction, but it would take a lot more than that to lighten my mood.

It had been three days since Beth left, and with each hour that passed, it was getting harder to not get on my bike and go after her. I knew she was at Longstone and that the worst move I could make was to follow her, but being away from her like this was tearing me apart inside.

All I could see when I closed my eyes was the pain on her face when she'd asked me to leave the other night. I didn't know what had stopped her from breaking the bond, and I was afraid she would be able to do it after she spent time away from me. Every time I thought of that possibility, it felt like a knife was twisting in my chest. I'd spent most of the last three days working and doing anything I could to keep me from thinking about it.

"Took out two. All clear up here."

Nikolas's voice came through my comm, pulling me from my thoughts and reminding me I was supposed to be sweeping the bottom floor. I was the one who had suggested he and I be the ones to clean out the abandoned apartment building after we'd gotten word some vampires were squatting here. Normally, we'd send a team for a job like this, but I'd needed the distraction.

The barest whisper of a shoe against carpet alerted me to the fact I was not alone. I spun to the left and felt the sharp sting of claws across the back of my neck.

The vampire flew past and whirled to face me, her face contorted with rage as she looked down at the bodies around us. She was faster than the three I'd killed, and she'd almost gotten the drop on me. I couldn't remember

159

the last time a vampire had been able to sneak up on me like that. This thing with Beth wasn't just driving me insane. It was making me sloppy.

"Friends of yours?" I taunted.

Two things I'd learned about vampires was that they had short tempers and tended to act rashly when they were angry.

"Bastard," she screeched and lunged at me.

I was in no mood to play around. I hit fast, slicing deep across her thigh. My second strike went straight through her chest. She let out a strangled gasp as her body sank to the floor.

"Chris?" Nikolas said through the comm.

"Four down. Continuing my sweep."

By the time I finished checking the four apartments on this floor, Nikolas was in the lobby, calling for a cleanup team.

"Not a bad night's work," he said as I walked up to him.

"No. Though part of me wishes these were Incubi instead of vampires."

There had been no sign of the Lilin or his sons since the attack on Adele's nightclub, and the lack of activity worried me. A Lilin didn't give up on his quest to procreate.

If one good thing had come from Beth leaving, it was that she was at Longstone and far from the Lilin. I'd suffer her absence if it meant she stayed safe while we hunted the demon.

Nikolas and I walked outside to wait for the cleanup team. His phone buzzed with a text, and his smile told me it was from Sara. She hadn't been happy we'd left her behind tonight. She understood it had nothing to do with her abilities, but she still didn't like it.

"She still angry texting?"

He chuckled. "She said she's going to zap us both if either of us gets hurt."

I laughed, but my good humor was fleeting. My thoughts went to Beth for the hundredth time today, and I wondered if she and I would ever have what Nikolas and Sara had. Or had I hurt her too much to move past all of this?

"How are you holding up?" Nikolas asked.

"I don't know what's harder – being away from her or not knowing what she's going to do."

"Still no word from her?"

"No." I leaned wearily against the side of the building. "She's been in touch with Mason, but no word on when she's coming back."

He nodded sympathetically. If anyone knew what it was like to be separated from their mate, it was him.

"I know this is not what you want to hear, but give her time."

"You're right. I don't want to hear it."

I'd give Beth all the time in the world. I just couldn't bear this silence and not being able to feel her nearby.

A white van and an SUV pulled up outside the building. We gave them a rundown on what they'd find inside before we walked to our bikes, which we'd parked down the street.

"You heading back to the house?" I asked Nikolas as he picked up his helmet.

"You're not?"

I straddled my bike. "It's still early. I think I'll patrol for a few hours."

Nikolas didn't hesitate as he pulled out his phone and sent off a text. I gave him a questioning look, and he smiled.

"I told Sara we were patrolling together so she doesn't wait up."

"Okay then. Let's ride."

15

Beth

My body buzzed with equal parts anxiety and anticipation as I turned into the driveway of the command center. It had been four days since I'd taken off for Oregon, and I wasn't sure what kind of reception I'd get upon my return.

I was worried about what my friends thought of me for running out on Chris, but more than that, I wasn't proud of myself for what I'd put him through. Yes, he'd hurt me, but what I'd done was almost as bad. I'd left him just hours after trying to break our bond, and I hadn't spoken to him once since then. Separation was hard on bonded couples, but doubly so for the male. I'd known that, and I'd done it anyway. I hadn't meant to be cruel to him, and this wasn't some form of payback. I'd been so wrapped up in my own pain I'd selfishly ignored his.

The first thing that struck me when I neared the house was that I couldn't sense Chris inside. The longer I'd stayed in my self-imposed exile, the more I'd missed feeling him nearby, until I was as jittery as a drug addict in withdrawal. My stomach clenched in disappointment, even as I felt a small measure of relief that I didn't have to face him yet.

I parked my Harley in my usual spot and groaned as I stretched my aching muscles. I loved riding, but I'd been on the road since early this morning, after a short rest at the safe house in Sacramento. My butt was sore from sitting for so long.

I dropped my bag off at the empty guesthouse and went to the main house to see who was around. I found Raoul, Will, and Sara in the control room.

"You're back." Sara hugged me tightly, and her smile was wide when she let me go. "Did you just get here?"

"A few minutes ago. Where is everyone?"

"Nikolas and Chris are out checking on some properties David found. Mason and Brock went with them. I don't know where everyone else is."

Guilt pricked me again. While I'd been hiding out at home, everyone else had been dealing with the situation here and trying to find the missing girls.

"Is there anything I can do to help?"

"Not much anyone can do until we get a solid lead," Raoul said. "But it's good to have you back."

I rubbed the stiff muscles of my neck. "Good to be back."

"You okay?" Sara asked.

"Too long on the bike. I'll be fine after I move around a bit."

"Let's go for a hike. We haven't done that in a week, and it'll help you work out the kinks. I could use some nature time, too."

A vigorous hike sounded pretty good, and it would keep me occupied. Otherwise, I'd spend the day moping around here, waiting for Chris to come back. I had no idea what I was going to say to him, but he and I needed to talk. If I sat around thinking about it, I'd be a mess by the time I saw him.

"That sounds great."

"Is this a hike or an expedition?"

I grinned at Sara, who was several yards behind me on the narrow ridge. "We're almost there. Come on. The view is worth the trek."

We continued along the ridge for a few more minutes, and I let out a deep breath when we reached the summit of Mount Baden-Powell. I loved coming up here, where all you could see were mountains and desert and sky.

Sara came to stand beside me. "Wow. Is that the Mojave Desert over there?"

"Yes. You like it?"

"I love it." She took a long pull from her water bottle as she scanned the area. "I bet there are trolls in those hills."

I jerked my head in her direction. "Trolls?"

She nodded. "Yeah. They love mountains and cliffs. Not that we'd ever find one of their caves. We could be standing on top of a troll clan right now and never know it."

A laugh burst from me, and my whole body suddenly felt lighter. "I bet you're the first person to stand up here and wonder where the trolls are."

Sara chuckled. "Probably so."

We sat on the rock, neither of us saying anything for several minutes as we enjoyed the view. One of the things I loved about Sara was that she never needed to fill the silence with conversation. If I'd brought Mason up here, he would have talked my ear off by the time we hit the summit.

"How is he?" I asked before I could stop myself.

Sara let out a breath. "Honestly? I've never seen him like this. Chris is usually the easygoing one, the one who makes others smile. I don't think he's smiled in days."

I drew up my legs and rested my forehead on my knees. "You must think I'm a terrible person for leaving the way I did."

"Of course not." Sara's hand rubbed my back. "I know how difficult bonding can be, especially in the beginning, and I'm pretty sure I put Nikolas through a lot worse."

"You thought Nikolas didn't want the bond when you tried to break it. I know Chris wants ours, and I still tried to end it."

Her hand stilled. I felt her staring at me, but I kept my gaze on the wide stretch of desert below.

"You tried to break the bond?"

"Yes." Pain pricked me as it did every time I remembered the look on Chris's face the last time I saw him.

"Because of the woman at the club?" she asked softly, without judgement.

"You know about her?"

I hadn't told anyone except Rachel and Mason about running into Chris's former lover that night, and they would never break my confidence.

"Chris told me about her." She was quiet for a moment. "You were getting along so well that night. I find it hard to believe that seeing a woman he went out with years ago would make you want to break the bond."

"It wasn't that he'd been with her. I admit that bothered me, but it's not the reason I got upset."

I told her about the encounter with the woman, and me realizing he'd been with her a month after he'd left Longstone for the last time.

Sara exhaled slowly. "I can see why that upset you. I'd feel the same way."

"When I was younger, the last person I thought could ever hurt me was Chris. But he did, and it took me a long time to get over him. What happens if I bind myself to him and he hurts me like that again? It would destroy me."

"Loving someone means putting your heart in their hands and trusting them to keep it safe."

My throat tightened. "What if I can't trust him to do that?"

She was quiet for a moment. "You need to ask yourself if you can learn to trust him, and you need to figure that out before either of you get in any deeper. Chris is crazy about you. It'll kill him if you let the bond grow and then decide you don't want it."

"I don't want to hurt him," I whispered hoarsely.

"Do you love him?"

"Yes," I breathed.

"Can you imagine a life without him?"

Tears suddenly clogged my throat, making it impossible to speak. I shook my head.

"Then you have your answer."

Sara and I stayed up on the mountain for hours, talking about everything from relationships to books and music to places we'd like to see. When we finally returned to the car, it felt like a weight had been lifted from me. I wasn't ready to jump into Chris's arms, and the thought of trusting him with my heart still scared me, but I didn't want to walk away, either.

Admitting that last one filled me with a nervous energy that had my fingers tapping the steering wheel. What would I say to Chris when I saw him? What would he say to me? Was he angry at me for not hearing him out that night and then leaving without a word? I wouldn't blame him if he was.

Sara laughed and reached over to lay a hand over one of mine on the wheel.

"You look like you just drank a gallon of espresso."

"Sorry."

"Don't be. You seem to be happier than when we left the house this morning."

I smiled at her. "I am. Thanks for coming with me today and for the things you said up there. It helped a lot."

Her stomach growled loudly in response, and the two of us laughed.

"Late lunch?" she asked, already looking around to see what was available.

"God, yes. I ate breakfast at 4:00 a.m., and my stomach is about to eat itself."

We found a little Mexican place where we shocked the waitress by demolishing four baskets of tortilla chips and salsa *before* our meal came. I was sure I caught her peeking at us once to see if we were dumping chips in our bags. When we ordered the fried ice cream for dessert, she just shook her head and smiled.

It was a late afternoon by the time we got back to the house, and I was full of nervous anticipation over seeing Chris. As soon as I pulled up to the garage, I knew he wasn't there, and I swallowed my disappointment as I got out of the SUV. I'd made him wait four days, so it was only fair that I be the one to wait for him now.

"Lass," boomed a loud voice when we walked through the garage door into the kitchen. I watched as Sara was lifted off the floor by a big red-haired warrior I didn't know.

Sara let out a strangled laugh. "You're crushing me, you big oaf."

"My turn, bro," said a second male with the same Irish brogue.

I thought I was seeing double as Sara was passed off to another warrior, identical to the first one. Twins?

"Don't make me zap you again," Sara threatened in a muffled voice.

Laughing, the warrior set her on her feet. "We missed you, lass."

"Right." She scoffed, but her smile said she was happy to see them. She turned to me.

"Beth, this is Seamus and Niall."

"Nice to meet you," I said as the one named Seamus took my hand in a firm grip.

He grinned boyishly. "Pleasure's all mine."

Niall shoved his brother aside to claim my hand. "If I'd known the lasses were this pretty here, I would have come a lot sooner."

Sara scoffed and gave him a friendly shove. "What does bring you guys to California?"

"Tristan thought with all the people we have in LA, you could use a healer," Niall said. "We volunteered to escort Margot and to see if you could use a few more pairs of hands. It's too quiet at home these days with all the extra security Dax has on the stronghold."

Seamus nodded. "And with Sara's two beasties running loose about the place, no one would be daft enough to attack."

Sara's *beasties* were two hellhounds she'd adopted and named Hugo and Woolf. I'd heard all about them from Sara and Jordan. Sara missed them terribly, but she couldn't travel with a pair of hellhounds. She said they were happy at Westhorne, and she went home between jobs to see them.

"Will you be staying here at the command center?" I asked, noticing the two large duffle bags on the living room floor.

While I was gone, Geoffrey and his team had moved into the new safe house we'd set up in the city. This place seemed almost empty without all the extra bodies.

"For now," Niall said. "We're about to head out to meet up with Nikolas and Chris for a pint."

"We won't keep you then," Sara told them. "I'm sure we'll have plenty of time to catch up."

Seamus smiled. "That we will."

The brothers left, and Sara and I went to clean up from our hike in the mountains. Nikolas called Sara around 6:00 to let her know he wouldn't be home for dinner, so the two of us ordered Chinese and hung out with Will and Raoul in the control room. It was a quiet night, and the only call that came in was from one of the teams reporting they'd killed two vampires outside a bowling alley.

At 11:00, I decided to call it a night. Mason was out on patrol with Brock, so the guesthouse was quiet as I undressed. Lying in bed, I found it impossible to settle down. Every night that I'd slept in this bed since Chris and I had bonded, I could feel him nearby, even when I hadn't wanted him there. My Mori was agitated now, not being able to sense him, and I had a feeling it was going to be a long night.

I was finally dozing off when a commotion outside woke me. I heard shouting, which was cut off abruptly by a loud splash. That was followed by male laughter and more shouts.

Lifting my head, I glanced at the clock on my nightstand. 2:00 a.m. What the hell was going on out there at this hour?

I got up to see what was happening, and I was halfway across my room when I realized I could feel Chris's presence. Before I could think about that, a knock came on the front door.

I hurried to answer the door and found Nikolas on the doorstep wearing an apologetic smile.

"I'm sorry to wake you, but we have a small situation."

"Dove," called a drunken male voice I'd know anywhere. "I need to see Dove."

I leaned to one side to peer around Nikolas, and my mouth fell open at the sight behind him. Chris stood supported between Seamus and Niall, and he looked wasted. He was also drenched from head to toe.

"What happened to him?" I asked Nikolas.

"He fell in the pool, and we had to fish him out."

"I can see that, but he's drunk. How much alcohol did he have tonight?"

We had a high tolerance for human alcohol, and a warrior would have to consume a vast amount to get this intoxicated.

Nikolas shook his head. "It wasn't normal alcohol. He drank murren."

"What's that?"

"Demon liquor."

I put my hands on my hips. "Where the heck did he get demon liquor?"

"Demon bar," called either Seamus or Niall. How could anyone tell them apart?

"Don't yell at her," Chris growled.

Someone let out a loud "oomph." Nikolas and I looked behind him to see one of the twins rubbing his side.

Chris spotted me and stared as if he wasn't sure I was real. "You came back," he said in a hushed voice.

"Yes."

He gave me the saddest smile I'd ever seen. "I'm sorry, Dove."

Nikolas turned to me again. "I'd leave him to sleep it off in the grass, but he'd wake up the whole neighborhood. He insisted on coming over here."

I sighed heavily. "Bring him in."

"Where do you want him?" one of the twins asked after they'd helped Chris into the house. "Bedroom?"

I huffed. "Absolutely not. Let me get some towels, and you can put him on the couch."

I grabbed a stack of large towels from the linen closet and spread them over the cushions. Seamus and Niall sat Chris on the couch where he immediately toppled over onto his side.

"I think he's finally passed out," Nikolas said.

"Will he be okay?" I asked no one in particular. I had no idea what the effects of demon liquor were.

"He'll have a bad hangover. That's it."

"I'm not going to ask why you all were at a demon bar," I said crossly. "But if he pukes in here, you three are cleaning it up."

"Yes, ma'am," one of the twins said, and they all chuckled.

They left, and for the first time in four days, I was alone with Chris. He was asleep, but his presence filled the room, surrounding me and soothing my Mori. I hadn't known just how much I'd missed him until that moment.

I walked over and stood behind the couch, looking down at him. How was it possible for someone to be passed out drunk and still look this handsome?

He'll probably look good tomorrow, even with a hangover.

I turned off the lights and went back to bed. Barely five minutes passed before I heard thumps and swearing coming from the living room.

Fated

I found Chris half sitting and trying to pull off his boots. Shaking my head, I went to him and helped him out of the wet boots. He rewarded me with a lopsided smile that made my heart flutter.

"Thanks," he murmured as he reached for the top button of his shirt.

My pulse jumped. "What are you doing?"

"Wet."

I watched him try unsuccessfully to unbutton his shirt for several minutes before I gave in and did it for him.

"I should let you sleep in your wet clothes," I grumbled as I released his arms from the sleeves. I kept my eyes on his face so I didn't stare at his sculpted chest and rock-hard abs. Nope, wasn't going there.

As soon as his hands were freed, they went to the button on his jeans. He got the button undone, but the wet denim was plastered to his body. There was no way he was getting out of those without help.

"Lie down."

I pushed him back on the couch, and he complied without argument. Grabbing the waist of his jeans, I worked them over his hips and down his long legs. I had one heart-stopping moment when his boxer briefs started to slide down with the jeans, and I had to stop to tug them up. By the time I dropped the wet jeans on the floor, I felt overheated and my stomach was a quivering mess.

Needing to compose myself, I took my time getting him a blanket, which was more for my benefit than his. I laid it over him, and he opened his eyes and gave me another one of those devastating smiles.

"You're so beautiful."

I smiled in spite of myself. "And you're drunk."

His eyes grew sad. "I was trying to forget."

"Forget what?"

"That you hate me. Can't bear you hating me."

My chest started to ache. "I don't hate you. I don't like you sometimes, but I could never hate you."

He closed his eyes and let out a breath. When he opened them again, a smile played around the corners of his mouth.

"Do you like me now?" he asked playfully.

"I'm on the fence."

He lifted his hand, and I foolishly let him take hold of one of mine. The next thing I knew, I was sprawled on top of him with his arms wrapped securely around me.

I wriggled to free myself and froze when I felt the hard length of him against my thigh. Drunk Chris I could handle. Drunk, aroused Chris was a whole different story.

He seemed to sense my anxiety, even in his drunken state, because he lifted me until my face hovered just above his. I used my arms to prop myself up on his chest, but he wouldn't allow me to go any farther.

"Let me up."

"Tell me you like me."

I scrunched my nose at the alcohol fumes on his breath. "Oh, my God. What do they put in that demon liquor?"

He grinned crookedly. "You don't want to know."

Something told me he was right about that.

"You're looking awfully happy for a guy who's going to have a hangover from hell tomorrow." Literally.

"I'm happy because you like me."

I arched an eyebrow. "I didn't say that."

His mouth turned down into what was most definitely a pout. My chest fluttered. God, I was hopeless.

"Fine, I like you. Now, can I get up?"

I expected him to smile and make a funny comeback. I wasn't prepared when his eyes filled with longing.

"I miss you."

"I miss you, too," I admitted softly.

His face lit up. "Yeah?"

I scoffed. "Don't let it go to your head. I'm still working things out."

"Does that mean we can be partners again?"

"Maybe," I conceded.

Chris's gaze burned into mine for a long moment, and I thought he was going to try to kiss me. My one kiss with him had rocked my world, but no way was he putting that mouth on mine without using a bottle of mouthwash first. If murren smelled this bad, I didn't want to know what it tasted like.

And why am I thinking about kissing him anyway?

I'd just told him I was still working it out. The last thing I need to be doing now was making this more complicated when I wasn't ready to go there yet.

I think he knew that, too. He moved me again, but this time, it was to tuck my head under his chin like he was settling down for the night.

I tried to push myself up, but he wasn't ready to let me go.

"Not yet," he implored sleepily.

There was a vulnerability in his voice I'd never heard before, and it tugged at my heart. What could it hurt to stay here a few more minutes?

My arms were uncomfortable, tucked under me in this position, so I let them fall to either side of him. He sighed contentedly, and I felt his breathing slow as he finally began to succumb to sleep.

"Dove," he murmured so softly that I couldn't tell if he was awake or dreaming.

"Yes," I replied, starting to feel drowsy, too.

His next words were barely discernible, but they were still able to knock every bit of air from my lungs.

"I love you."

16

Chris

S omeone was going to town on the top of my head with a steel bar. That was the only explanation for the excruciating pain in my skull and the feeling that my eyes were about to explode from their sockets. I moaned, wishing they'd just get on with it and kill me already.

A sound penetrated the haze of pain, a soft feminine sigh that momentarily made me forget my suffering. Suddenly, I was focused solely on the soft, warm body I was spooning. Silky hair tickled my nose, and a delicate floral scent invaded my senses.

I opened my eyes and saw that I was on the couch in the guesthouse... with Beth. God, she felt amazing in my arms. I had to be dreaming this.

It took me a minute to realize the crushing weight that had sat in my chest for days was gone. The next thing I noticed was the blissful state of my Mori. The demon was so happy it was practically purring.

Beth stirred, and so did my body. Apparently, my Mori wasn't the only one excited to be this close to our mate. I willed my body to relax. The fact that I could feel desire with my head threatening to split open was a testament to how much I wanted this woman. But I needed to hold her now more than my next breath, and I didn't want to do anything to drive her from my arms.

I would have killed for some gunna paste, and there was a can of it in my bag a few feet away, but nothing could make me move from this couch.

Something told me Beth wouldn't let our sleeping arrangement continue when she woke, and I wanted to enjoy it as long as possible.

Doing my best to ignore the relentless pounding in my head, I ran through the events of the previous night, reliving every minute from the moment I saw Beth. Some of my memories were a little foggy from the alcohol, but there was no way I could forget her hands on me as she undressed me or the feel of her body when I'd pulled her down on top of me. Just the thought of it sent a fresh wave of heat through me, and I had to fight the urge to press closer to her.

I focused on remembering her demeanor as she'd tended to me and the things she had said. She'd told me she could never hate me and she'd missed me. She'd even smiled a few times. Did that mean she'd forgiven me? Was she willing to give us a chance? She'd come back. That had to mean something.

I'd left here the night she'd almost broken the bond, feeling like my heart was being ripped from my chest. Hearing her talk about waiting for me to come home and how she'd blamed herself for me leaving filled me with so much regret. I hadn't realized until that moment just how much I'd hurt her, and I hated myself for it. The pain I'd felt the last four days was nothing compared to what I'd put her through.

"Mmmm," Beth murmured softly.

She shifted and let out a small gasp before she lay still. Not wanting to startle her, I didn't move as I waited to see what she would do.

Minutes passed before she started to ease away from me. Instinctively, my arm tightened around her waist, not wanting to let her go yet. She lay back down with a resigned sigh.

"I did not crawl into your bed this time," she grumbled.

Lightness spread through my chest. Despite her words, she didn't sound unhappy to be with me. I hadn't imagined it or dreamed it. Something had changed between us.

I smiled against her hair. "I don't think this qualifies as a bed."

She huffed softly and moved again to get up. This time I didn't try to stop her, but when her elbow accidently knocked the side of my head, I couldn't hold back my groan of pain.

Beth sat up and looked down at me, her brow furrowed with concern. "Are you okay?"

I winced and put a hand over my eyes. "I'll let you know as soon as my head stops threatening to explode."

Her laugh was unexpected and the most beautiful sound I'd ever heard. Less than a day ago, I'd been afraid I would never hear it again.

"That's what you get for drinking yourself into a stupor," she scolded. "Whatever possessed you to drink demon liquor?"

"It was Niall's fault," I moaned into my hands.

The details about how we'd ended up at Sal's were cloudy, but I remembered Niall challenging me to a round of *nobs*, a demon drinking game. I hadn't been thinking clearly, or I never would have accepted a challenge from an Irishman whose favorite pastime was drinking.

"Yes, I'm sure he forced it down your throat," she said without an ounce of sympathy before she got up and strode into her bedroom.

I eyed the duffle bag on the other side of the coffee table, wondering how much it was going to hurt to stand up and walk over to it. With tremendous effort, I managed to sit up, only to sag back against the cushions as the room spun wildly. Sweat broke out on my brow, and I swallowed as my stomach began to revolt.

"Kill me now."

I let my body fall back to a horizontal position, taking slow deep breaths to calm my churning stomach. I'd overindulged in murren once before, and I should have remembered that moving only makes the hangover worse.

"Here."

I opened my eyes to see Beth standing over me, holding out a can of gunna paste. I took the can from her, but my hand was shaking so much I couldn't open it.

Beth made a sound of exasperation and perched on the edge of the couch. She opened the can and scooped out a large amount of the green paste with two fingers.

"Open," she ordered briskly. I did, and she placed the gunna paste on my tongue.

Before she could withdraw her fingers, I closed my mouth and sucked the last of the paste from them. The stuff tasted awful, but seeing her lips part and the flush in her cheeks was worth every bit.

She pulled her hand away, and I swallowed the paste like a good patient. "Thanks," I rasped.

"You look green. Are you going to throw up?"

I closed my eyes. "No. Just need to lie still until the gunna paste kicks in." "Okay."

She stood, and I heard her set the can of paste on the coffee table before she went into the kitchen. Soon, the sounds and aroma of brewing coffee filled the room. In a few minutes, she was back, setting a mug on the coffee table near me.

"Drink that when you no longer feel like vomiting."

"You're an angel," I said without opening my eyes.

There was no mistaking the amusement in her voice. "Just try not to puke. Murren smells bad enough on your breath. I do not want to know what it smells like coming back up."

"I'll do my best."

I heard her sit in one of the arm chairs and take a sip from her own cup. She seemed content not to speak, so I didn't either. It was enough to know she was in the same room with me. I was happy to lie there with her close by and let the gunna paste work its magic.

After about twenty minutes, the pounding in my head lessened and my stomach stopped threatening to erupt. Five minutes after that, I was able to lift my head off the couch without going into a tailspin. I eased myself into a reclined position and picked up my mug with a hand that still trembled slightly.

The coffee was cold, but I didn't care because it felt so good to my parched throat. I drained the mug and wiped my mouth with the back of my hand.

"I needed that," I said to Beth, who still sat in her chair. "Thanks."

She came over and took the mug from me. "Feeling better?"

"Much."

"Good."

She turned away, but not before I saw her face take on a tender expression. She cared more than she wanted to let on. I didn't know what had softened her toward me, but I'd take it.

She carried our mugs to the kitchen and rinsed them, returning with a bottle of water for me. When she started to move away, I took hold of her wrist in a loose grip.

"Sit with me."

She arched an eyebrow but didn't pull away. "You're milking this sick patient thing."

I started to make a joke and went with honesty instead. "My Mori needs to be close to you." I caressed the back of her hand with my thumb. "I need to be close to you."

She hesitated, and I watched the play of doubt and worry across her face. But those emotions were not as strong as the answering need I saw in her eyes.

I let out the breath I was holding when she sat on the edge of the couch and turned toward me. I released her wrist and took her hand, pleased when she didn't object or pull away. The feel of her skin against mine did more to relieve my pain than anything else could.

"How have you been since...?" I trailed off, unsure of how to finish the question.

She looked down at our joined hands and whispered, "Fine," which I knew meant she'd been anything but that.

"How about now?" I pressed softly.

Her teeth worried her lower lip. "A little better."

I smiled at her quiet admission. I understood her reluctance to open up to me, and I knew I had to be patient and gentle with her, now more than ever.

"I'm feeling better, too, and not just because of the gunna paste."

That got a little smile from her, and she lifted her gaze to mine. "You did look a dangerous shade of green."

I nodded. "It was touch and go for a few minutes. Thanks for taking care of me today...and last night."

She made a face. "I almost told Nikolas to leave you on the lawn."

I laughed and then winced at the lingering pain in my head. I was never touching murren again.

"I'm sure I deserved it."

"Probably, but I was afraid you'd end up drowning yourself in the pool."

"So, you *do* like me," I teased, earning an eye roll from her.

"You're not going to let that go, are you?"

"Not until you admit it."

She looked down again, going quiet for a long moment. I watched her bent head and hoped I hadn't pushed her too soon to talk about her feelings. This was all new territory for me, and I didn't want to mess it up. I'd never been one to go slow when it came to women, but then, I'd also never been in love with anyone until Beth.

"Today, I like you," she said at last. "Tomorrow remains to be seen."

I gave her hand a little squeeze. "Then I'll have to do what I can to make sure you still like me tomorrow."

She fell silent again. After a minute, I tugged on her hand to get her attention. "What's wrong?"

Her eyes were troubled when she looked at me again. "I'm sorry I ran away. I wasn't trying to hurt you."

"I know that."

I let go of her hand and reached for her to pull her into my arms, but she resisted, shifting so she was facing away from me.

"I'm not ready to..."

"I understand."

I was disappointed that she didn't want me to hold her, but I wasn't surprised after what had happened a few nights ago. It was enough for now that she was sitting here beside me.

"None of this is your fault. I'm the one who screwed up, and I should be begging you for forgiveness. Just tell me it's not too late to make it right."

"No... I mean it's not too late," she said in a rush.

My heart began to race, but I forced my voice to sound calm. "So, going home was good for you."

"Talking to Rachel helped a lot. But then Sara asked me something yesterday."

I could barely speak around the breath that was bottled up in my chest. "What did Sara say to you?"

Beth stared at the far wall, but I could see her throat working before she spoke.

"She asked if I could imagine my life without you."

I didn't speak as I waited for her to continue.

"I can't," she said hoarsely.

I closed my eyes briefly as relief coursed through me.

She turned slightly to look at me, and my heart constricted at the hurt in her beautiful eyes. The need to hold her was fierce, but I was afraid to make any advances that might undo the progress we'd made.

"I want you in my life, but I'm scared. This is all happening too fast, and I..."

"It's okay."

I held out my hand to her, and slowly, she slipped hers into mine. I laced my fingers with hers and let our joined hands lie on the couch between us.

"Bonding is difficult in the beginning, no matter how easy Sara and Nikolas make it look."

I raised my eyebrows meaningfully, and she rewarded me with a small smile. Taking that as a good sign, I continued. "It's normal to have doubts, especially considering our history. I hurt you, and you're afraid I'll do it again. Give me a chance to earn back your trust and love."

She pressed her lips together, but her eyes betrayed her inner struggle. She wanted to say yes, but fear made her question everything.

"If I say yes, what happens next?" she asked in a voice laced with uncertainty.

"Well, right now, I'm going to lie here until I'm able to stand again."

Her eyes widened, and a startled laugh bubbled from her.

I smiled back. "After that, we'll take it one day at a time."

She nodded slowly. "I think I can do that."

Beth

The door opened as I was tying the laces on my gym shoes, and I looked up to see Mason hesitantly enter the house. He glanced around before he came all the way in and shut the door.

"What are you doing?" I asked him.

"Checking to see if the coast is clear." He walked over and pulled me up into a tight hug. "So glad you're back."

"Me, too."

He let me go and sat on the end of the coffee table nearest me. "I take it Chris left."

I flushed even though there was nothing to be embarrassed about. "How did you know he was here?"

Mason gave me a crooked smile. "I walked in here at 6:30 after my patrol and found the two of you asleep on the couch. I figured it was best if I made myself scarce, so I crashed on the couch in the control room for a few hours."

"You didn't have to –"

"I wanted to." He studied my face. "Does this mean things are okay between you and him?"

"Yes. We agreed to take things slow."

His serious expression dissolved into a relieved smile. "Good, because I hated seeing you so miserable."

"I wasn't that bad."

He gave me an incredulous look. "Beth, you cried all night and left without a word. Then it took me two days to get you to tell me what happened. You had me pretty worried there for a while."

"I'm sorry."

He leaned in and took my hands in his. "You have nothing to apologize for. You were hurting, and you needed to cope with it in your own way. I'm just glad you worked it out."

"Yeah, me too."

I let out a long breath. Things were a lot better between Chris and me, but I was confused about his feelings for me. He'd called me Dove when he'd said he loved me last night. Had he been dreaming about the young girl he used to know when he'd said that? Or had he meant he was *in love* with the adult me? He hadn't repeated the declaration this morning, so I was left wondering if he'd even meant to say it. It was enough to drive me crazy.

"Are you up for some training?" I asked Mason. "I'm headed to the gym, and I could use some company."

He smirked. "Need to work off some energy?"

"Something like that."

"Sure. Give me a minute to change."

Five minutes later, the two of us entered the gym to find Chris and Seamus exchanging blows that would have knocked me into next week. I stood by the door, watching them move with speed and grace I hoped to have someday. Their bodies were slick with sweat, and it was impossible not to admire the play of muscles under Chris's T-shirt or his strong arms. It amazed me that someone so powerful could also be as gentle as he was with me.

Of course, he chose that moment to look at me, and his cocky little smile told me he'd caught me checking him out. Great.

Heat spread across the back of my neck as he ended his fight with Seamus and walked over to me. It had only been an hour since he'd left the guesthouse, but he looked at me like he hadn't seen me in days.

"Your turn," he said to me.

"Me?" I let out a short laugh. "I'm no match for you."

His smile turned sensual as he stepped into my space. "You're the perfect match for me."

I put a hand against his hard chest and shoved him. It was about as effective as pushing a brick wall.

"You know what I mean. I'm not fast enough to fight you."

"That's why you should fight me. You and Mason are at the same level, and you know each other's every move. Sparring with a better partner will challenge you more."

He was right. I hadn't felt challenged in training for months. I needed to bump up the intensity to push myself to the next level.

"Okay, but don't blame me if you get bored."

"You could never bore me," he said with a meaningful look before he turned and walked back to the center of the room.

"Good luck," Mason called in a stage whisper as I followed Chris. I could hear the laughter in his voice, but I resisted the urge to glare at him over my shoulder.

I faced Chris on the mats, feeling uncertain and self-conscious. He was so good. How could I hope to land a strike against him? I knew he wouldn't hurt me, but that wasn't enough. I hated losing.

"I'm going to fight without my Mori's help to make it even," he said.

"But it won't be even if I use mine," I protested.

Chris chuckled. "I think I can hold my own. Ready?"

I assumed my fighting stance and nodded.

Chris's expression didn't change as his left hand shot out. I brought mine up and blocked his strike before it could connect. The force of his blow shocked me, not because it would have hurt me, but because he was a lot faster than I'd expected. Even without his Mori speed, Chris was fast and most likely stronger than I was.

Recovering from my surprise, I struck back with a right hook, followed by a kick. Chris blocked me easily on both strikes, and then he shot me a taunting little smile that said, "Is that all you've got?"

Game on.

I went at him with everything I had, using every trick and technique I'd learned in training. I even managed to land some hits, but those victories were few and far between. Chris was a masterful fighter, his skills honed by many years in the field, and he maintained an infuriatingly neutral expression that gave nothing away.

After twenty minutes, I retreated and bent down with both hands on my knees, panting. I was sweating and breathless like a first-year trainee. And I'd never felt so exhilarated by a fight. I loved sparring, but I'd been missing out. Nothing compared to going up against the best, even when he was holding back.

"You done?" Chris asked with amusement lacing his tone.

I lifted my head and scowled at him. "Hardly."

Mason snickered. "Oh, boy. I know that look. You're in for it now."

I straightened and studied Chris as my old trainer's voice filled my head.

"You're going to face fighters who are stronger and faster than you. But most fights are won with the mind, not the body. If you can win the mental battle, you can defeat any opponent. It's up to you to find out how to get into their head and find their weakness."

Her advice was all well and good, but Chris was a fighting machine. From where I stood, he didn't have any weaknesses.

Except one.

I struck first this time, and he blocked it as expected. We fell back into the same pattern of trading blows. A few minutes lapsed before I deliberately moved too slowly, allowing his fist to graze my shoulder. I staggered backward and let out a small sound of pain.

Chris rushed forward to catch me. As soon as his hands landed on my shoulders, I swept my leg around, hooking his knees and sending him to the floor. I followed him down, twisting us so his bigger body was facedown with me on top of him, my signature move that had bested everyone in my training class. I had his arms pinned behind his back and my legs twisted around his before he could utter a sound.

I lowered my head until my mouth almost touched the rim of his ear. "You done?"

A hoot of laughter came from Seamus, and I heard the unmistakable sound of hands slapping in a high five. I was no fool. I knew the only reason I'd been able to take Chris down was by using his concern for me against him. But I was still going to enjoy the moment while it lasted.

It lasted all of ten seconds.

Chris moved so fast I was on my back before I could blink, his big body pressing me into the mat. He rose up on his elbows and gave me a wicked smile that made me breathless and tingly all over.

"You cheated," he admonished huskily.

"Did not. My opponent had a weakness, and I used it against him."

"Smart girl."

He brushed away some of my hair that was plastered to my cheek. I was a sweaty mess, but the warmth in his eyes told me he cared about that less than I did. I didn't move, willing my heart to slow down and my lungs to function normally.

"You're not bad for a newbie."

I quirked an eyebrow. "Not bad?"

He rewarded me with another slow smile. "Above average."

"Whatever."

I huffed and tried to buck him off, which proved to be a big mistake. His eyes darkened perceptibly when our lower bodies pressed intimately against each other, and heat suffused me. My lips parted slightly, and his gaze fell to them.

"You guys want us to give you some privacy?" Mason called with a snort of laughter.

My face flamed. Chris grinned.

He rolled off me and to his feet. Before I could move, he reached down and took my hands, pulling me up. I hoped the others would attribute my red face to exertion from the fight and not from my embarrassment at nearly making out with Chris on the gym floor.

Seamus smirked at me as I walked over to grab a towel.

"You've got some moves, lass."

"Thanks."

"I taught her everything she knows," Mason joked.

Chris laughed. "Good, because you're up next."

Mason's smile fell. "What?"

Chris picked up my water bottle and carried it over to me. He gave me a conspiratorial wink before he turned to Mason.

"You need to up your game, too, if you don't want Beth kicking your ass. So, who do you want to take on? Me or my Irish friend here?"

Mason swallowed. "That depends. Who likes me more?"

Seamus let out a guffaw. "Come on, lad. I'll take it easy on you. Chris is still sporting a hangover from last night, so he's a bit testy this morning."

I looked at Chris, who was showing no signs of the terrible hangover he'd had when he woke up. He'd been in such a sorry state that it had been impossible not to feel bad for him, even if he had brought it on himself.

"I thought you were feeling better," I said when Mason and Seamus walked away.

"The gunna paste and your nursing skills took care of the worst of it, but it takes a few hours to work the effect of murren out of your system."

"Oh."

"But I definitely wouldn't say no to more nursing."

I scoffed. "Nice try."

We watched Mason and Seamus exchange blows for a minute before I broke the comfortable silence between us.

"Did I look that slow when I fought you?"

Chris leaned in, lowering his voice. "Seamus is tapping his Mori's speed to play with Mason. You both fight well."

Pleasure washed over me. "Thanks."

"We can do this again tomorrow if you want to. I did promise to practice with you."

"Yes," I said quickly.

He chuckled, and I grinned at my own eagerness.

"I should warn you I know your tricks now and I won't fall for them next time."

I lifted a shoulder, feigning nonchalance. "Guess I'll have to come up with some new ones."

17

Chris

If I'd known getting drunk on demon liquor was the way to get Beth back, I would have downed a gallon of murren weeks ago. The hangover was brutal, but it was more than a fair price to see her smile again.

I watched her laugh at something Sara said as they carried plates and a large bowl of salad outside and set them on the patio table. As if Beth sensed my gaze on her, she looked my way and quickly averted her eyes. But not before I saw the telltale pink in her cheeks.

It had been like that between us ever since our practice session in the gym this morning. Every time she did it, I wanted her a little more, but I'd promised her we'd go slow, and I meant to keep that promise, even if it killed me.

"You better turn those steaks unless you want them well-done," Nikolas said as he walked past me.

I pulled my attention away from Beth and finished grilling the steaks for dinner. Piling them on a plate, I brought them to the table where Beth, Sara, and Nikolas were already seated. I took the open chair next to Beth, and she gave me a little smile when I sat closer than was necessary.

When we'd talked about grilling steaks for dinner, I'd figured there would be more of us, considering how many people we had staying at the house. I had a suspicion the rest of them had deliberately made themselves scarce to allow the four of us to have a quiet evening together.

The conversation was light as we talked about Westhorne, and Sara lamented over missing her pets and the imps. I'd long since stopped shaking my head whenever she talked about the three imps that lived in their apartment at home. Only Sara could convince Nikolas to share his home with those pesky little fiends.

Talk turned to motorcycles, and Beth's face lit up when we started discussing what bikes would be right for Sara's smaller frame. Beth knew her motorcycles, and she soon engaged in a lively debate with Nikolas on the pros and cons of the models he was considering. Few people, other than Sara, could hold their own against Nikolas in an argument, even a friendly one, but Beth didn't back down.

Eventually, the conversation came around to the topic that was foremost in everyone's minds these days. Where was the Lilin, and why had he been so quiet lately?

"Maybe he left Los Angeles because we were getting too close," Beth suggested.

I almost wished she was right because it would mean he was far away from her, but I knew better.

"Based on how long he's been active here, he's close to the peak of his breeding cycle. It would take too long for him to set up in another city, and it's too risky to move the girls he's taken."

The mood around the table grew more somber at the reminder that those girls were running out of time.

Sara tapped her water glass thoughtfully. "Could it be that he has all the girls he wants, and that's why he's being so quiet?"

Nikolas nodded grimly. He and I had discussed this exact possibility today. We hadn't heard of any girls disappearing since the two we'd rescued in San Francisco, but the Lilin could have taken girls from outside the state and had them brought here if he was growing desperate.

Beth's brow creased with worry. "I can't bear to think of what those girls are going through. They must be so scared."

"Lilin treat their female captives well," I told her. "He will pamper them and keep them in luxury."

"But they're still prisoners."

"Yes. But they probably don't know that. He'll keep them under the influence of his power to make sure they are calm and happy and in the best physical health."

Beth paled. "God, it sounds like a breeding stable for horses."

I had no response to that because she was right. A Lilin was methodical in his selection, and he collected what he considered to be the best breeding stock. His one goal was to ensure he got strong, healthy offspring.

Beth grew quiet, and I worried for the hundredth time that this job was too much for her. Most new warriors worked at strongholds for the first few years, and they were gradually exposed to the worst this world had to offer. No one fresh out of training should have to deal with something this serious.

Sara leaned back in her chair and took a deep breath of cool evening air.

"This California weather is spoiling me. I guess I'll have to get used to the cold again when we go to New York."

"We can stay here if that's what you want," Nikolas told her.

Her eyes gleamed with excitement. "Oh, no. California's great, but I can't wait to see New York."

Beth leaned forward in interest. "When do you leave?"

"We'll stay here until the current threat is over," Nikolas said. "The Council purchased a property there, and it's being renovated now."

"There's a huge demon community there, almost as big as the one here," Sara added. "I'm going to get to know them while Nikolas does his thing."

I met Nikolas's gaze across the table and fought back a laugh. I already knew his thoughts on Sara's plans to build relations with the demons. He wasn't against it. He just wasn't sure he and New York were ready for it.

Beth smiled. "That should be fun."

"You guys have to come visit us," Sara told her. "There's so much to do there."

I watched Beth's reaction to Sara's assumption the two of us would be together then, and I felt a surge of relief when she smiled.

Beth looked at me. "I thought you were going to New York with them."

I realized then that I hadn't told her I planned to assume leadership of this command center after Nikolas left. Although, I'd made that decision before she and I had bonded, and having a mate changed things. Did she even want to stay in Los Angeles?

"I'll stay here for now. I'm not sure about long-term. What about you? Do you want to see New York?"

Her smile grew. "Yes. It's on my list of places to visit."

"I want to travel, too," Sara said eagerly. "Nikolas and I are going to Africa next year." She grinned at him. "He promised to show me the best sunsets in the world."

Nikolas gave her an indulgent smile. "And I always keep my promises."

Sara turned to Beth again. "Maybe we can all go together."

One of the French doors opened before Beth could reply, and Raoul strode out, his serious expression telling me he wasn't coming to hang out.

KAREN LYNCH

"We got a call from someone at the mayor's office. There's a problem on a container ship down at the port."

"What kind of problem?" I asked, pushing back my chair. City officials only contacted us when it was something big.

"The bazerat kind," Raoul answered wryly. "Some genius tried to ship a whole container of them, and it broke open when they loaded it on the ship. The ship is overrun. Luckily, most of the crew weren't on board yet. The ones who were are holed up on the bridge."

Nikolas and I stood at the same time. Bazerats were rat-like demons about the size of a small dog that were normally found in the Amazon. A single bazerat was harmless, but a whole pack was deadly, especially once they picked up the scent of blood. We had to contain them before some of them managed to get off the ship, if they hadn't already. The last thing we needed was those things breeding in the sewers.

"Call in everyone you can find," Nikolas told Raoul.

"Will's already on it."

I looked at Beth. "Ever work with bazerats in training?"

"No."

Sara laughed. "Then you're in for a real treat." She tossed her napkin on the table. "What are we waiting for? We have a pack of demon rodents to round up."

I looked up from my tablet when I sensed Beth approaching, and I watched her enter the house through the French doors. She was dressed comfortably in leggings and a T-shirt with her hair piled on top of her head in a loose knot. In one hand, she carried a large mug. The other hand was wrapped in a bandage.

"How's your hand?" I asked when she sank down on the other end of the couch.

"I should be able to take this off in an hour or so."

I laid the tablet on the couch and slid over to her. "Let me check it."

"It's fine," she protested, but she couldn't hide the slight wince when I started unwrapping the bandage.

I gave her a stern look. "I'll be the judge of that."

I gently removed the wrapping and examined the two puncture wounds that went from the back of her hand to her palm. The holes were puckered, but there was no sign of infection. Bazerats, like many demons, had bacteria in their saliva that could cause infection if not treated carefully.

"I told you it was okay," Beth grumbled.

I took my time wrapping her hand again. When I finished, I couldn't resist lifting her hand and pressing a light kiss to her fingers.

"Do you do that for all your patients?" she joked a little breathlessly.

"Only the beautiful ones who jump into the hold of a ship to save me from a pack of hungry demons."

She smiled and rolled her eyes. "A simple thank you will do."

"Thank you," I said with a smile that hid my true emotions. I couldn't let her know I was still worked up from watching her go down under a pile of bazerats. She'd come out of it with one bite and some scratches, but that was something I never wanted to see again.

It had been utter pandemonium when we'd arrived at the container ship last night, and it had taken the better part of the night for us to capture or kill every last bazerat and to deal with the injured. Not to mention the frightened crew who now believed they'd been overrun by a shipment of exotic rats from New Guinea.

When I'd followed the screams of a terrified dock worker into the hold, I found him trying to climb the side of a container with several bazerats hanging off him. The blood from his injuries had soon attracted dozens of the creatures. I'd tossed the man up on top of the container and set about dealing with the immediate threat.

What I hadn't expected was for Beth to come running to my rescue, or for the bazerats to turn on her instead. I was pretty sure I'd lost decades off my life when they attacked her, and hours later I was still trying to calm my agitated Mori.

"You want breakfast?" I asked her, needing something to keep me busy.

"Sure."

Sara walked into the living room. "I'll have some."

I cooked up eggs and sausage for the three of us, and we ate it at the breakfast bar. Sara and Beth kept the conversation light, and I felt a lot calmer inside by the time we finished eating.

Nikolas came in as Sara and Beth were cleaning the kitchen, and his grave expression immediately put me on edge again. Sara must have sensed something was off, because she dropped the dish towel and hurried to Nikolas.

"What's wrong?" she asked.

"We just got word that five more girls went missing last night."

Sara gasped. "The Lilin?"

"They were all in the right age range." His eyes met mine briefly. "One of them was Mei Lin."

Beth put a hand to her mouth. "No."

Mei was the girl we'd saved the night of the rave. Her parents had taken her away right after it happened, and I'd had no idea they had come back to town. Otherwise, we would have had someone watching her.

"The bazerats were a decoy," I said almost to myself.

We'd been wondering why the Lilin was so quiet and now we knew why. He'd been arranging a distraction to keep us busy while he moved in and snatched those girls.

Nikolas's face hardened. "Yes."

Beth looked from Nikolas to me. "What do we do now?"

"We work harder to find the Lilin," I told her, wishing I had a better answer. Without a solid lead or a stroke of good luck, it would be almost impossible to track him down. And in a city this big, there was no way we could know where he'd strike next or who his intended victims were.

"You and I have a call with Tristan in thirty minutes," Nikolas told me. "He's speaking with the governor now."

I picked up the tablet I'd left on the couch. "Better him than me."

"Is there anything we can do to help?" Sara asked Nikolas.

"We'll work out a plan of action after we talk to Tristan," he said. His expression told me he still had no idea what that would be.

The call with Tristan went pretty much as I'd expected.

"The latest kidnappings have everyone on edge from the mayor of Los Angeles to the governor," Tristan said with the weariness of a man with far too much responsibility on his shoulders. "They're thinking of warning the public that we have a possible serial killer targeting young women in California."

"They must know that would only cause a panic," I said.

Tristan sighed. "I pointed that out, along with the fact that it would make our job a lot more difficult. It took some convincing, but I think I managed to put them off that idea for now."

Nikolas leaned back in his chair with his arms across his chest. "Do they know that the Lilin will soon have all the girls he needs, if he doesn't already?"

"Yes, but that did little to appease them, especially when I told them none of the missing girls would be recovered if we don't find the Lilin before it's too late. A rash of unsolved missing persons cases doesn't look good on a mayor's record when re-election time comes around."

I shook my head. I'd never understand how humans could put politics above lives. There was some politics around the Council, but in the end, our governing body always worked together to serve one purpose – protect our people and humanity.

Tristan's chair creaked, and I knew he'd gotten up to walk around his office, something he did when he was agitated.

"I assured the governor that we have our best people on this, and we are sending every available warrior to California. Although, at this point, I'm not sure how much can be done."

Nikolas and I shared a look because Tristan was right. The Lilin must be getting close to breeding, which meant we were running out of time and so were the girls he'd taken. Once he started breeding, he wouldn't emerge from his lair until after his offspring were born. Our window to find him was growing smaller with each day that passed.

Someone rapped sharply on the office door before it flew open and Beth rushed in, her face flushed. I was on my feet in an instant.

"He didn't get them all," she cried, waving a piece of paper.

"Get what?" I asked.

Beth could barely contain her excitement. "The girls. Last night, he took five girls, but he went after six. One got away."

Nikolas stood. "How do you know that?"

She held up the paper. "A student at UCLA was attacked walking to her sorority house last night. She tasered the guy and managed to get away."

Beth's smile grew. "She told campus police her attacker had a flame tattoo on his wrist."

I looked at Nikolas. "If the Lilin wants her, he'll come back for her like he did for Mei Lin."

"Yes."

Tristan cleared his throat. "I'll let you get to it then."

Beth's startled eyes darted to the phone on the desk and then back to me. "I'm so sorry. I barged in here without thinking."

"You had a good reason," Tristan said. I could hear the smile in his voice.

"Beth, I don't believe you've met Tristan."

Her eyes widened, and she shook her head mutely. Then, as if realizing he couldn't see her, she blurted, "No."

She was adorably flustered. I didn't think it was in my best interest to laugh, so I hid my smile.

"It's nice to meet you, Beth," Tristan said warmly. "Hopefully, next time we'll meet in person."

"I'd like that," she managed to say.

Tristan said goodbye, and Beth relaxed when it was just the three of us. She didn't say much as Nikolas and I discussed the best way to handle the UCLA attack.

"We'll need to put someone on her in case he goes after her again," I said.

Nikolas nodded. "I'll set up twenty-four hour protection. And one of us should talk to her."

"Beth and I will go see her."

Beth's head swiveled in my direction. "We will?"

"It's your lead. I figured you'd want to be involved."

Her smile lit up the room. "I do."

I waved a hand at the door. "Alright. Let's go."

Beth

"I was at the library with my study group until nine, and I went straight home from there. I walk that route all the time, and nothing's ever happened before. I still can't believe it."

I studied the slender brunette girl sitting next to me in the living room of her sorority house. Paige Collins was remarkably composed for someone who had been attacked less than a day ago. Except for the bruise on her cheek, you'd never know she'd just been through a horrible ordeal.

"Tell us about the attack," Chris urged lightly, ignoring the group of girls whispering and ogling him from the kitchen. It had been like that since we'd arrived ten minutes ago, passing ourselves off as the police.

I brushed off my flash of annoyance at the girls and returned my attention to Paige.

"I was only a few hundred yards from the house when he grabbed me from behind. He was so quiet for a big guy, and I didn't even hear him coming. He wrapped an arm around my throat before I could scream."

Paige shuddered and went on.

"My father made me promise to always carry my Taser when I walk alone. Thank God I had it in my hand. That guy was so strong I had to shock him three times before he let go of me. I think he must have been on drugs or steroids.

"As soon as I got away, I screamed and ran to the house. The guys in the house across the street came out to see what was going on, and the man ran away. They called the campus police for me, but the man was long gone."

"Did you see his face?" I asked her.

"No. All I saw was his arm. As soon as I broke free, I ran."

Chris leaned forward, resting his forearms on his knees. "You told the campus police you saw a tattoo on the man's wrist. Can you describe it for us?"

"It looked like flames. I think there were words too, but everything happened so fast I didn't read them. I'm sorry."

I smiled to reassure her. "You got away, and that's all that matters."

"Have you noticed anyone hanging around campus lately who seemed out of place?" Chris asked.

Paige blanched. "You think he's been following me around campus?"

"For all we know, this was a random attack, but we have to cover all our bases. It's just procedure."

"Oh." She visibly relaxed and thought for a moment. "I did see a man in the dining hall yesterday who looked wrong, if that makes sense."

Chris met my gaze before he asked, "Wrong, how?"

"He was sitting at a table alone, not eating or reading. Just sitting there. I was eating lunch with my friend Jenny, and she noticed him, too. It was just kind of odd, you know?"

Chris nodded. "Can you describe him?"

"He was good-looking with short, dark hair, and I could tell he was tall, even though he was sitting. He looked to be around twenty. If it wasn't for the strange way he just sat there, I'd say he was like every other student."

Paige looked from Chris to me. "Does that help?"

I smiled. "Yes."

"Good." She let out a breath. "I wish I could tell you more. It all happened so fast."

"You're doing great."

Chris gave her an encouraging smile, and I heard a chorus of sighs from his new fan club. Good grief. He should come with a warning label.

Looking directly at the smile may cause swooning and temporary loss of intelligence.

"Thanks," Paige replied, looking at ease for the first time since we'd started questioning her. "You're a lot easier to talk to than the other officers who were here earlier."

"We have a little more experience in this area," I said.

Her eyes widened at my words.

"You must have joined the police force fresh out of school because you don't look any older than me."

And that was our cue to wrap this up.

"We get that a lot." I shot Chris a meaningful look.

He stood, prompting a flurry of murmurs in the kitchen. I resisted the urge to roll my eyes, and followed him and Paige out of the living room.

"We'll keep an eye on things here for the next few days," Chris told Paige as she walked us to the door.

We didn't tell her she'd have around-the-clock protection until the Lilin threat had passed. That would only raise more questions and stir up her fear. She'd been through enough, and aside from leaving Los Angeles, there was nothing she could do to stop the Lilin from coming after her again.

"Thank you," she said. "I feel better knowing you guys are here."

Chris opened the door, and one of the girls called, "Come back anytime."

I must have made a face because his lips twitched as he held the door for me. His expression told me he was used to this reception from females, and he was enjoying my reaction to it.

We said our goodbyes to Paige and left. Chris followed me down the walkway to the SUV, waiting until we were inside before he chuckled softly.

I looked at him as I buckled my seat belt. "What?"

"I saw the looks you were shooting those girls," he said with a smirk.

"What looks?"

"You glared at them every time they moved."

"They were annoying. Don't they have anything better to do than to stand around and gawk at people?"

Chris cocked his head smugly. "Jealous?"

I scoffed. "You are so full of yourself."

"I have good reason to be. The most beautiful girl in the world doesn't like other women looking at me."

A laugh burst from me, and I looked out the passenger window so he couldn't see the effect his words had on me.

"Admit it. You think I'm hot."

I slanted a look at him. "Every woman thinks you're hot. That's nothing new."

"I don't care about every woman," he said in a low voice that sent a delicious shiver through me. "I only care what *you* think."

"I think you should drive."

"Not until you admit you were a wee bit jealous in there."

He was right, but no way was I telling him that. He was already too cocky for his own good.

"No."

"Okay. I can wait," he said, laying his head against the headrest.

Silence filled the SUV, and after several minutes passed, I knew he wasn't going to move until I gave him what he wanted. Stubborn ass.

I crossed my arms and scowled at him. "Fine. I think you're hot."

"And you were jealous."

"Don't push it."

Chris grinned and started the vehicle. "Was that so hard?"

"Yes," I muttered.

He pulled away from the curb.

"Then we'll have to work on that."

18

Beth

"What do you have for us, David?" Chris said to the phone sitting in the middle of the small conference table where he and I sat with Nikolas, Sara, Seamus, and Niall.

David's voice spilled from the phone's speaker. "Kelvan and I have been searching the demon archives since you sent us that picture of the Lilin's mark. The archive is endless, and it's like a needle in a haystack, but we think we might have gotten a hit on it."

The air in the control room seemed to crackle with excitement as everyone leaned forward in their chairs.

"You found him?" Nikolas asked.

"Not exactly. We came up with a name, but no photo to go with it. Problem is, it's from sixty years ago."

I looked at Nikolas, who sat directly across from me. "Why is that a problem?"

"Demons who live a long time change their identity every generation or two to avoid suspicion," he explained. "The Lilin might have changed his several times in the last sixty years."

"Is there any way to know what he changed his name to?" I asked, looking from Nikolas to Chris, who sat next to me.

Chris answered. "Possibly, but he won't leave an easy trail to follow. Lilin are extremely private."

He looked at the phone again. "How reliable is this information, David?"

"Kelvan said it came from the Incubi lineage records. Think of it as the who's who of Incubi. They like to keep track of their family tree, and the Lilin are their royalty. Every Incubus wants to be related to one."

I was starting to think demons were great allies to have. I'd been dubious when I heard that Sara had demon friends, including Kelvan who worked with us now. But there was no way we'd have access to demon archives without inside help. I hadn't even known there were demon archives until recently.

"What do the records say about the Lilin with that mark?" Nikolas asked.

"His name was Charles Prescott, and his last known whereabouts was London. We cross-referenced that with some old Scotland Yard records and discovered there were a bunch of unsolved missing person cases around the same time. Young women."

Chris tapped his fingers thoughtfully on the glossy tabletop. "The time-line matches up with our Lilin. They breed every thirty years, so sixty years ago he would have been in his fertile cycle."

My stomach roiled with revulsion like it did every time someone mentioned the Lilin's breeding habits. How many girls and young women had this one demon killed in his long life to build his family? How many more innocent lives would he take if we didn't stop him?

Chris's warm hand covered mine on the arm of my chair. He gave my hand a light squeeze as if he sensed my discomfort.

Since we'd gone to the sorority house two days ago, our relationship had changed, in a good way. It felt like one of the barriers between us had fallen, and we were building new bridges. Chris didn't try to talk about us, but he was always touching me in a nonsexual way. I think it was his way of giving us the physical contact we both craved from each other. I didn't push him away because I needed it as much as he did.

"Does Kelvan think he can find out the next identity of Charles Prescott?" Chris asked, still holding my hand.

David chuckled. "He's already working on it, and he said to tell you he's a genius, not a miracle worker."

"Tell him I have complete faith in him," Sara said. "Never mind. I'll call him and tell him myself."

"I'd better get back to work," David said, and I could hear him already tapping on his keyboard. "I'm still looking at real estate in the Los Angeles area while Kelvan does his thing."

"Good work," Chris told him. "We appreciate all you've done."

"Are you kidding? I get to work with the Mohiri's top nerds, and I get paid for it. I'm having so much fun I almost feel guilty. Almost."

"Okay. We'll check in with you tomorrow," Nikolas said.

The call ended, and Niall was the first to speak. "Do you think they can track him down?"

Sara nodded confidently. "If anyone can, it's Kelvan and David. They found Madeline when she was hiding behind Orias's glamours."

"Can they find him before we run out of time?" I asked her.

Her face grew serious. "I don't know."

Chris looked around the table. "He hasn't come after Paige Collins again, which means he still doesn't have all the girls he wants."

"Unless he's given up on her and decided to go with what he's got," Seamus said.

"A Lilin doesn't give up," Nikolas replied, with a conviction that sent a shiver through me.

Chris stood. "Then we'd better make sure he doesn't get what he wants. Who's watching Paige now?"

"Mason and Brock," I told him. "Mason texted a little while ago. He said it looks like they're throwing a party at the sorority house tonight."

"If the Lilin is watching her, he might go after her tonight," Nikolas said, and Chris nodded unhappily.

I didn't have to ask what Chris was thinking. He and I were on protective detail tonight for the first time, and he didn't want me there if the Lilin was planning another attack. I waited for him to say someone else would go with him.

Chris looked at the twins. "Beth and I are going to need backup tonight. You guys feel like going to a party?"

Seamus snickered. "Sorority girls and beer. Do you even need to ask?"

"Does this mean I can partner with Beth?" asked Niall, who sat on my other side.

Chris's scowl was almost comical. "No."

Niall shrugged. "You can't blame a lad for trying."

Seamus leaned back with his hands behind his head. "How are we doing this? We all going into the house, or do you want us outside?"

"Paige and her sorority sisters think Beth and I are police officers, so we'll have to stay outside," Chris said. "We'll watch the front of the house, and you two can watch the back."

"Sounds good." Niall leaned sideways toward me. "If you get bored with his company, you know where to find me."

I smiled and shifted uncomfortably in my chair. There was nothing inappropriate in Niall's behavior, but lately I felt uneasy when other males got too close to me.

Chris made a sound that was suspiciously like a growl, and Niall leaned away from me. I was seeing these little displays of aggression from him more often in the last few days. I didn't show it outwardly, but part of me liked the possessive gleam in his eyes, because I'd started to feel the same way toward him. I was just better at hiding it.

I stood, drawing Chris's attention to me.

"If I'm going to be sitting in a car all night, I need to get a good workout in first. Do you have time to spar with me?"

His whole demeanor changed, and a smile curved his lips. "I always have time for you."

"Great. Give me five minutes to change."

I headed for the door, calling over my shoulder. "Today, you're going down."

Chris laughed. "I'm counting on it."

"Where are we going?" I asked Chris as he turned onto a street in the opposite direction of the university campus.

"Getting some food. Neither of us had dinner, and you can't do a stakeout on an empty stomach."

We pulled up to a fifties-style diner, and Chris shut off the engine. When I started to open my door he said, "I'll get it."

"Thanks."

I watched him go inside and stand at the counter. It took me several minutes to realize I was staring at him, a new habit of mine. Not that anyone could blame me. Chris was hot with a hard, powerful body and eyes I could happily drown in.

And he was mine.

I don't know when I'd stopped denying it, but I knew with every fiber of my being that Chris and I belonged together. Did we have stuff to work out? Yes. Was a part of me still afraid of getting hurt? Yes.

Did I love him?

More than my own life.

It was a little terrifying to know that one person owned my heart so completely, especially the man who had hurt me deeply in the past. Maybe that was why I wasn't ready to say those three words to him. But we were getting closer to that moment with every minute I was with him.

The driver's door opened, shaking me from my thoughts. Chris handed me a large takeout bag and bottles of water before he got in.

I hefted the heavy bag and laughed.

"Are we feeding Seamus and Niall, too?"

"I have to keep my partner fed. And those two can fend for themselves."

"You've been friends with them a long time, haven't you?"

Chris smiled fondly. "A little over seventy years. When they were twenty-five, they came to Westhorne for a visit and stayed. They're good guys. Some of my worst hangovers are thanks to them."

Somehow, that didn't surprise me.

"Worse than the last one?"

He grimaced. "No, a murren hangover pretty much tops the list. Well, except for Glaen, although I've never been drunk enough to try that one."

"Glaen?"

"Fae drink," he said as he turned a corner.

I couldn't hold back my gasp. "But I thought Fae food was poison to us. Why would you drink that?"

"I wouldn't. Niall told me he tried it once on a dare, and he couldn't walk for two days." Chris grinned. "Did Sara ever tell you about the time she beat a gulak in a Glaen drinking contest?"

I gaped at him. Gulaks were huge, scaly demons like reptiles on two legs, and they were mean brutes. Not even Sara would befriend one of those.

"You're messing with me."

"You should know by now that most stories about Sara tend to be true, especially the most outlandish ones. Ask her about it tomorrow."

"Did the gulak die?"

"Yes, but not from the Glaen. He made the mistake of pissing off Nikolas."

"Oh."

Having seen Nikolas in action a few times, I didn't want to imagine what a pissed-off Nikolas was like.

We reached the campus, and Chris drove us to Paige's sorority where we parked two houses down on the other side of the street. It gave us an unobstructed view of the house but put us far enough away to not draw attention.

Mason and Brock came over to give us a brief update of the comings and goings in the house before they took off for the night. Then Chris and I settled in for our long shift.

I pulled the food from the bag, not surprised to see burgers and fries. If you send a male for food, chances are you're getting burgers or pizza.

"Are these the same?" I asked, holding up two of the four large burgers.

Chris peered at them and pointed to the one in my right hand.

"That one's yours. No onion or tomato."

"Thanks. I hate picking those off."

"I know," he said as he took his burger from me.

I felt a silly burst of pleasure over the fact that he'd noticed and remembered how I liked my burgers. It was such a simple thing, but it made me smile.

"What's that smile for?"

I lifted a large container of fries from the bag and laid it on the console between us.

"This smells amazing, and I just realized how hungry I am."

It wasn't a total lie. I was hungry, and the food was making my mouth water.

He unwrapped his burger. "Dig in."

Chris and I didn't speak much as we ate our dinner, but it wasn't an uncomfortable silence like it would have been two weeks ago. It was nice just being around him, and my Mori was somewhat content as long as it could sense him. It would never be fully content until I gave it what it wanted and completed the bond with Chris. My heart and mind were getting there, but not fast enough for my impatient Mori.

Activity at the sorority house picked up as people began to arrive for the party. I watched two young men hoist a large beer keg from the back of a truck and lug it up the front steps, and I wondered why humans drank so much. I hadn't been among them much before I came to Los Angeles, and I was fascinated by their behavior, especially their social habits.

Music was filtering from the house by the time I finished my meal. I picked up the bag to throw away my wrappers and realized there was another container at the bottom.

"What's this?" I asked as I pulled the foil container from the bag.

Chris wiped his mouth with a paper napkin. "Dessert."

"Ooh."

I lifted the top off the container and revealed a massive slice of cheese-cake inside.

"New York-style," he said. "I hope you like it."

I stared at him. "You remembered."

A tiny lump formed in my throat. It wasn't the cake that made me emotional, but that he hadn't forgotten it was my favorite.

Chris's answering smile was so tender it made my heart ache.

"I remember everything about you."

The lump in my throat doubled in size. I was incapable of speech as those five simple words broke through another one of the walls I'd erected to protect my heart.

"Hey," he said softly.

He reached across the seat and gently brushed away a tear I hadn't realized was rolling down my face. His fingers lingered against my cheek as his eyes held mine.

"What's wrong?"

How did I tell him I was crying over a piece of cake because I'd spent the last four years thinking the most important person in my world had forgotten about me? That this small gesture meant more to me than I could put into words?

"Why?" I asked in a small voice. "Why did you never come back?"

I hadn't meant to ask that question, but as soon as it came out, I knew it was the one I desperately needed him to answer. All he'd told me was that he'd left because it was for the best. What did that mean? And why had he stayed away?

Sadness and regret darkened his eyes, and his hand left my cheek to hold one of mine. He entwined our fingers as if he was afraid I'd run away.

"That day you came to see me at my apartment, I almost didn't recognize you when I opened the door. I'd gone home expecting to see my sweet little Dove, and I found a beautiful, desirable young woman instead."

My breathing faltered.

"I thought there was something wrong with me," he said roughly. "You were sixteen, at that place between a girl and a woman, and nowhere near ready for what I was feeling for you. Just having those thoughts about you made me ashamed.

"I left because I couldn't face you, feeling like I did. I planned to clear my head, get it out of my system, and then go back."

He looked out the windshield and back at me as if he was trying to find the right words.

"But I never got you out of my system. I never stopped wanting you."

I inhaled sharply.

"I kept in touch with Rachel, and she let me know how you were doing. You seemed happy and I didn't want to confuse or upset you, so I stayed away." He let out a ragged breath. "I missed you, but I told myself I was doing what was best for you."

I found my voice. "You wanted me?"

His green eyes blazed with need so raw it stole my breath.

"Since that day, I've never wanted anyone but you."

My throat worked. "But those other women –"

"Meant nothing to me," he declared. "I enjoyed their company as they enjoyed mine, but I used them to try to forget the one I really wanted."

My head spun from his confession. He'd left to protect me from him. He had to have known I'd never say no if he'd given in to his desire, not after I'd professed my love for him.

"Why didn't you call me? I thought you forgot me." I tried to keep the quiver out of my voice and failed.

"God, Beth. I could never forget you. I thought if I heard your voice, I'd give in and go home to see you. I was weak when it came to you, and you were so young."

"But I became an adult, and you still didn't come," I said accusingly as the old doubts and hurts resurfaced.

"I wanted to. I planned to go so many times." He let out a harsh laugh full of self-recrimination. "Something always came up to stop me. I think a part of me was afraid you wouldn't want to see me after all that time."

I stared at the street and tried to process everything he'd told me. All this time I'd believed he'd left because he didn't want me in his life anymore. Yes, he'd sent me presents for my birthday and Christmas, but I'd thought he did that out of obligation, nothing more.

"Do you think our Mori always knew we were mates?" I asked without looking at him.

His fingers flexed around mine. "Yes."

"Did you know?"

"No."

I closed my eyes. "If you'd known, would you have come back?"

"Beth." He tugged on my hand until I turned to look at him again. "If I'd known that what I felt for you was a natural reaction to my mate, nothing would have kept me from you."

Emotion welled beneath my breastbone, and I released it in a long, shuddering breath. In its wake, I felt lighter as I let go of most of the pain I'd been carrying all these years.

Chris released my hand and leaned over to pull me into his embrace. I pressed my face into the crook of his neck, wishing the console wasn't in the way. All I wanted to do was climb into his lap and start making up for all the lost days.

Chris let me go and said, "Slide your seat back."

I did as he'd said, and I was rewarded when he hoisted his body over the console. Before I could protest that we wouldn't fit, he lifted me and slid into my seat, lowering me sideways onto his lap. It was still a tight fit, but neither of us was complaining.

KAREN LYNCH

He wrapped one arm around my waist and used his other hand to turn my face toward his.

"Do you know how long I've wanted to hold you like this?" he asked huskily, sending a shiver of pleasure through me.

He trailed a finger down my throat to my collarbone.

"To touch you like this."

His mouth was so close I could feel his warm breath.

"To kiss you like this."

"Oh," I breathed.

He brushed his lips chastely against mine, once, twice, before he captured my mouth in a hungry kiss. My lips parted for his demanding tongue, and I clutched his shoulders as he explored my mouth until my entire body buzzed from the sensual assault.

He broke the kiss so his lips could blaze a trail along my jaw. Needing more, I tilted my face up, exposing the column of my throat to him. He let out a low groan that made my toes curl, and he kissed his way down my throat to the collar of my button-up shirt.

My heart began to pound when he tugged the material down and pressed his lips to the swell of my breast. I burned with a need I'd never felt before, but things were moving so fast. The few boys I'd dated at home hadn't gone beyond kissing. But Chris was a man, and he wouldn't want to stop there.

He lifted his head and kissed me again with a reverence that made tears prick my eyes. When he finally ended the kiss, I curled against him with my head on his shoulder and his arms around me. I didn't know why I felt so emotional and needy, but all I wanted was for him to hold me like he'd never let me go.

He sighed as he toyed with the end of my ponytail. I could feel reality about to burst our happy little bubble.

"You make it very hard to think about work."

"But we have a job to do," I murmured.

I reached over and opened the passenger door. As I moved to get out, Chris's arms tightened around me.

"Where do you think you're going?" he demanded playfully.

I swatted at his arm. "You need to get back into your seat, and this is a lot easier than climbing over the console. Not to mention we have garbage everywhere after your little maneuver."

He laughed and let me go. I got out of the SUV, and he followed me. Looking at the mess we'd created, I made a face when I spotted a flattened foil container on the floor.

"I don't think the cheesecake made it."

202

Chris nuzzled the back of my neck. "I'll buy you a whole cake tomorrow."

"Okay," I squeaked.

I heard his chuckle as he walked around to the driver's door. Shaking my head, I picked up our garbage and stuffed it all in the takeout bag. He'd bought dinner, so it was only fair that I cleaned up.

"Beth," Chris said in a low voice that no longer held a trace of amusement.

I looked up from reaching for the cheesecake container to see him staring intently out the windshield. I peered over the dash, but saw nothing out of place.

"What?" I whispered.

"We have company. Four houses down on the other side of the street."

I followed his gaze to a dark sedan parked on the street. Sharpening my vision, I made out the shapes of two people in the front seat.

"How do you know it's them?" I asked, feeling my pulse speed up.

Chris reached for his phone. "They pulled up a few minutes ago, and they haven't moved since."

"Maybe they're waiting for someone at the party."

"I'm sure they are," he said, shooting off a text.

He got a reply less than thirty seconds later. After he read it, he turned to me.

"I need you to promise to stay here when this goes down. Seamus, Niall, and I will handle it."

I started to protest, and he cut me off.

"Some of these guys are a lot stronger than normal Incubi. You're an amazing fighter, but you don't have the strength to fight the stronger ones. It's safer for you to stay here until we know what we're up against."

He was right. The only reason Mason and I had been able to kill the Incubus on the boat was because we'd had the element of surprise on our side. If I'd faced off against him alone, it would have been a different story.

"Okay. I promise."

"Thank you."

I looked at the sedan again. "What will you do?"

"Niall and Seamus are out back. Seamus is going inside to find Paige. Once he does, Niall and I will check out the car."

He reached across me and opened the glove compartment to retrieve a small leather bundle, which he handed to me.

"Here."

"What's this?"

"It's a Taser. I picked it up today."

I removed the Taser from its case and stared at it, not quite sure how to react to the fact he wanted me to use a human weapon. "You want me to use a Taser? I already have weapons."

He gave me a half smile. "I know, but I don't want to take any chances. If a human girl can get away from an Incubus with a Taser, then I want you to have one, too. At least for this job."

When I didn't respond, he said the one thing guaranteed to get me to agree to his request.

"It'll give me some peace of mind knowing you have it."

I huffed. "Fine."

Chris's phone buzzed. He read the text and swore.

"What is it?"

"Seamus can't find Paige. He's checking upstairs now."

"She has to be in there. One of us would have seen her –"

I stared at Chris. We could have had an earthquake, and I wouldn't have noticed it during that kiss. What if Paige had left the house – or worse, been taken – while Chris and I were too caught up in each other to see it?

The front door of the sorority house opened, and I watched anxiously as two couples came out. Their staggering steps said they'd all had too much to drink. At the bottom of the steps, they waved goodbye, and one couple headed toward the house across the street. Without them blocking my view, I was able to see the faces of the other couple.

"Paige," I said in relief.

Chris was out of the SUV in a heartbeat and reaching under his seat for a pair of long knives. With a last glance at me, he ran toward the couple that was almost abreast of the sedan.

The car doors opened, and two people jumped out. If I had any doubt about who they were, it disappeared the second they went straight for Chris at inhuman speed.

The two Incubi came at Chris at the same time, and I saw the glint of metal in their hands. It was two on one, and they were armed.

Chris met them, the three moving so fast I couldn't see who struck first. It was several heart-pounding seconds before they separated, and I saw one of the Incubi stagger a little. Chris looked unhurt, but it was impossible to say for sure.

The uninjured Incubus lunged at Chris, and they circled each other. Behind them, another Incubus was putting Paige in the back of the car.

My hands gripped the Taser so hard it creaked as I frantically searched for Niall. Where was he?

I looked at Chris, who was once again locked in combat with the two

Incubi. God, they were so fast. I couldn't see what was happening, and it terrified me.

Chris stumbled. The Incubi closed in.

"Chris," I cried and reached for the door handle.

Movement by the sorority house caught my eye, and I watched as someone sped toward the fight. My breath caught when I recognized Niall's red hair. He didn't move as quickly as Chris, but he was still a match for the Incubi.

Metal flashed. One of the Incubi went down and didn't get up.

The car lights came on, illuminating Chris and Niall fighting the second Incubus. Chris shouted something, and Niall ran to the car, which had started to back up.

My heart leaped into my throat. *Paige.*

A small scream erupted from me when the door beside me flew open. I caught the glint of silver in the dark eyes as the Incubus grabbed my wrist in a vise-like grip and hauled me from the SUV.

He dragged me toward the back of the SUV, away from the others. I knew immediately why Chris had made me promise to stay in the vehicle. My strength was puny compared to the demon that wrapped one arm around my middle as the other hand clamped over my mouth to silence me.

I experienced a moment of terrifying helplessness, and I knew this must be how Paige had felt when she was attacked. But she'd escaped, and she wasn't nearly as strong as I was.

It took me several precious seconds to twist enough to hit him in the ribs with the Taser. He grunted, but his hold didn't loosen.

I hit him again.

His steps faltered, and the hand covering my mouth slipped.

I sucked in my breath and let out a yell as I struck a third time.

His hand came down and slammed into my wrist. Pain shot up my arm as the Taser flew from my numb fingers.

The Incubus released me. I was free. I spun to face him.

His fist was the last thing I saw before stars exploded in front of my eyes.

Then there was blackness.

19

Chris

I heard Beth shout as my blade sank into the Incubus's chest. I spun toward the SUV, and fear gripped me when I saw the cab light on and the open passenger door. And no sign of Beth.

Blood roared in my ears when I reached the SUV and saw the Incubus's fist slam into Beth's face. Blinding rage consumed me, and I was barely aware I was moving as I caught her before she hit the pavement. I didn't remember the next minute, but when I came to my senses, I was sitting on the ground, holding Beth on my lap, and the Incubus was a bloody lump a few feet away.

Someone spoke to me in a deep, calm voice, and it took a moment for the Irish brogue to penetrate my mind. I looked up at Seamus, who stood at a safe distance with his hands up.

"I know you're still a bit out of it, but we have to see to the lass," he said without coming closer. "Is she okay?"

I lowered my gaze to Beth, who lay silently in my arms. Her eyes were closed, and her face looked pale in the streetlight. A trickle of blood ran down from a cut on her temple.

Her chest rose and fell steadily under my hand, and I closed my eyes as relief made my world spin. A hard blow to the head might have temporarily stunned me, but Beth was a young warrior, and I'd seen how strong these Incubi were.

"Beth," I called to her.

I tried to force myself to sound calm, but my Mori was nowhere near that state. My voice came out harsher than I'd intended.

I tapped her cheek gently. "Dove, you need to wake up for me."

Her eyelids didn't flicker once, telling me she was fully unconscious. I needed to get her to the healer.

I stood with her in my arms and turned to Seamus. He spoke before I could tell him what I needed.

"I'm going to get these bodies out of sight, and then I'll drive you back to the house. Niall will see to the other lass."

"Thank you."

I settled myself in the passenger seat of the SUV with Beth cradled on my lap. A few minutes later, Seamus got behind the wheel.

"Another team is coming to help Niall handle things here," he said as he started the vehicle. "And I called Nikolas. Margot is waiting for us."

It seemed to take forever to reach the house, and Beth didn't stir once during the drive. When we drove around to the garage, we found Nikolas, Sara, and Margot waiting for us in the backyard.

Nikolas opened the door for me, and I got out, holding Beth. Sara gave Beth a worried look before she hurried ahead of us to the guesthouse and opened the door.

I carried Beth to her room and laid her on the bed. It took most of my willpower to step back so Margot could examine her.

When Margot took a syringe from her medical bag, I put a hand on her arm.

"What's that for?"

"It's a healing accelerant, with a sedative mixed in."

"She has a head injury, and you're giving her a sedative?" I asked incredulously.

Margot smiled. "It sounds like an odd combination, but it'll keep her body in a relaxed state so her Mori can heal her. She'll be as good as new in the morning."

I released the healer's arm so she could administer the drug. When she finished, she straightened and began packing up her bag.

"Can I hold her?" I asked. There was no way I could leave Beth tonight. I'd sit by her bed and hold her hand if that was all Margot allowed.

Margot turned to me with bag in hand, and her calmness eased some of my worry.

"I'd recommend it, actually. Her Mori is distressed, and physical contact with you would calm it."

I followed the healer to the living room where Nikolas and Sara waited to hear about Beth. Before either of us could speak, the front door burst open and Mason ran in.

"Is Beth okay?" he asked fearfully.

Sara motioned for him to lower his voice. Understanding crossed his face, and he shut the door quietly.

"Beth has a concussion, but she'll be fine," Margot assured everyone. "I gave her something to help her heal, and all she needs now is a good night's sleep."

The tension in the room dissipated, and everyone seemed to sag with relief.

"Thank God," Sara murmured.

Nikolas put an arm around her, pulling her close. His eyes met mine, and his expression told me he knew exactly how I was feeling. He'd been there a few times.

"We'll get out of here and let her rest," he said, already turning Sara toward the door.

Mason followed them out. Margot stopped at the door and looked back at me.

"I'll be at the house, but I doubt you'll need me anymore tonight. All she needs is rest and you."

"Thanks for everything. I'm glad you were here."

I closed the door behind her and returned to the bedroom. Turning off the light, I kicked off my boots and eased my body down next to Beth without jostling her. She lay on her back, so I turned on my side and laid an arm over her with my head on the pillow beside hers.

I hadn't realized how worked up my Mori still was until I had Beth in my arms again. It strained against me, trying to get closer to her Mori.

"I'm here, Dove," I whispered against her ear, wishing I could do more for her. If she and I had been mated, I would have been able to share my strength with her, and I wouldn't feel so helpless. All I could do was offer her the comfort of my touch.

Gradually, her nearness calmed my agitated demon, and I was able to focus on something other than her attack. I replayed our conversation in the SUV, my chest tightening when I remembered the pain in Beth's eyes when she'd asked me why I hadn't gone back to Longstone. I'd been waiting for the right time to tell her the truth, but it was the last thing I'd expected to talk about tonight. She'd looked happier after our talk, and I had felt the rift between us finally heal. All that was left was for me to make her mine in the only way that remained.

My body burned with need when I thought about our smoldering kiss.

God, she had no idea what she did to me. She was sweet innocence and seduction at once, so responsive yet demure. She'd made me forget where we were and why we were there, and I'd stopped only because I had sensed her hesitation when I'd started to take it beyond a kiss.

I was still awake hours later when Beth stirred. She murmured incoherently then turned and snuggled against me as if she couldn't get close enough to me.

"I didn't break my promise," she slurred.

I smiled and kissed the top of her head. "I know."

She sighed happily and went back to sleep. I followed soon after.

It was daylight when I awoke to the sound of the front door opening. A minute later, a smiling Margot appeared in the bedroom doorway.

"Came to check on our patient," she whispered. "How did she sleep?"

"Good. She only moved once."

The healer entered the bedroom. "Why don't you go get cleaned up? I'll stay with her until you return."

I looked down at my clothes splattered with dried demon blood from last night's kills. The last thing I'd been able to think about when we got back here was changing my clothes, but I should do that now. I didn't want Beth to see me like this when she woke up.

Thanking Margot, I went to the main house to shower. I'd been staying in my old room since Gregory and his team had moved into the new safe house.

Freshly showered and changed, I headed to the kitchen where Nikolas was making breakfast for him and Sara.

"How's Beth?" he asked.

"Much better, I think. Margot is with her now."

He put four slices of bread into the toaster and checked on his bacon.

"Seamus filled me in on what happened. We're doubling the protective detail on Paige Collins until this is over."

I leaned against the breakfast bar. "Does she know she was almost kidnapped again?"

"No. As far as she knows, she drank too much and fell asleep on the back porch."

"If he's set on her, he'll try again," I said.

Nikolas nodded. "Possibly. But he knows we're protecting her now, so he might think she's too much of a risk."

"That's true."

I hoped so for Paige's sake. One thing I knew for sure was Beth was not going on another job that might put her in contact with the Lilin or his sons. She wasn't going to like it, but I was putting my foot down, something I should have done weeks ago. She was too young and inexperienced to be involved in a dangerous situation like this one. And my heart couldn't take another scare like last night's.

"No more jobs like this for Beth," I stated with finality. "Jordan and Mason should be pulled from them as well."

Nikolas nodded gravely. "I agree. I'll call for a meeting this afternoon to let everyone know."

The doorbell rang, and Nikolas and I looked in that direction as Sara walked past us.

"I'll get it," she called over her shoulder.

I heard the door open and the murmur of female voices. Sara reappeared, wearing something that closely resembled a scowl.

The reason for Sara's unhappy expression sauntered in behind her. The newcomer pushed her sunglasses atop her head and tucked her long black hair behind an ear as her lips curved into a genuine smile.

"Nikolas, Chris, how lovely to see you again."

Beth

The pounding in my head woke me, and I opened my blurry eyes to stare up at the ceiling of my bedroom. I was groggy and disoriented, and I lay there for a few minutes until my mind could piece together my distorted memories. Chris...Paige...Incubi...

"Chris!"

I shot up in bed and flopped back down as the room spun.

"Easy there," said a soothing female voice.

I turned my head to see Margot entering my bedroom.

"Where's Chris?" I demanded, my panic rising. If I needed a healer, he'd be here. Unless he couldn't be.

The healer smiled as she walked over to the bed.

"Chris left a few minutes ago to clean up. He was still wearing his clothes from last night, and he wanted to shower before you woke up."

Relief hit me so hard I could barely speak. "He's okay?"

"Yes. How are you feeling?"

I took stock of my aches and pains before I answered her. "I've never had a hangover, but I imagine this is what a bad one feels like."

Margo chuckled. "That's an apt description. You took a hard blow to the head, and I gave you something to help you heal faster. It has unpleasant side effects." She held up a can of gunna paste. "And this will remedy those."

I made a face and dutifully ate some of the horrid paste. No matter how many times you took the stuff, you never got used to the taste.

"Why can't they make that taste like chocolate?" I complained after I'd drunk the glass of water she'd held to my mouth.

She laughed. "Maybe to discourage warriors from getting hurt."

I let my head fall back to the pillow, grateful the room had stopped spinning at least. I was going to need a gallon of coffee once I could get out of this bed.

It took a good fifteen minutes before I felt well enough to shower. I stood under the hot spray of water, all discomfort forgotten as I remembered talking to Chris in the SUV and sitting on his lap, kissing him. God, that man could kiss. Heat spread through me, and it had nothing to do with the water temperature.

I dried and hurriedly dressed in jeans and a soft sweater. My headache was almost gone, but I felt irritable and jittery. Margot had left, so I couldn't ask her if this was another side effect of the medicine. Maybe I just needed to see Chris.

Trying not to analyze this new dependence on him, I left the guesthouse in search of him. I could sense him in the main house, so I let my Mori guide me.

I entered by the French doors and came to an abrupt stop at the sight of Chris on the far side of the room, wrapped up in the arms of another female. Pain lanced through me, but it was immediately burned away by a wave of white hot anger.

Mine, my Mori growled.

I was dimly aware of Sara calling to me as I sped across the room. Grasping the woman's shoulders, I ripped her away from Chris.

"Hands off," I snarled, placing myself between her and Chris.

Her green eyes flashed angrily as she spun back to face me. "How dare you?" she fumed. "Who do you think you are?"

She took a menacing step toward me, and I reacted on instinct. My fist slammed into her jaw, and her eyes widened in shock as she stumbled backward. Not waiting for her to recover, I went after her, only to be stopped by two strong arms that came around me from behind.

"Easy there," Chris crooned in my ear as he turned us so we were facing away from the other woman.

I started to calm until I replayed the image of him holding her. Incensed, I elbowed him in the gut, taking satisfaction from his low grunt.

"Let me go," I bit out. I struggled in vain to break free of his hold. When that didn't work, I elbowed him again.

I let out a strangled cry when Chris swung me up over his shoulder and strode toward the French doors.

"Excuse us, folks. I think my mate and I need some alone time."

"Put me down, you jerk," I railed as he crossed the yard.

He ignored my demands until we were inside the guesthouse. He turned and let me slide down until my feet touched the tile and my back was against the door.

I looked up at his grinning face, and my anger surged again. "You think this is funny?" I yelled, shoving at his immovable chest.

He captured my hands with his and entwined our fingers before he raised my arms above my head. I was helplessly trapped between his hard body and the door, a predicament that made me excited and angry at the same time.

"You're hot when you're jealous," he said huskily, his heated gaze making me squirm with something that was definitely not anger.

"I'm not –"

His mouth covered mine, smothering my denial with a dizzying kiss. His tongue teased the seam of my lips until I opened to him, and then I was swept away. I pressed against him, frustrated because I couldn't get close enough, and kissed him back with delicious wantonness.

Chris made a sound deep in his chest, and I let out an answering moan when I felt his hard arousal against my belly. I didn't know if I was ready to go where this was heading, but in my haze of desire, I didn't care about anything but his touch.

Without warning, Chris broke the kiss. He released my hands and pressed his palms against the door as he rested his forehead against mine. His breaths came in short pants, matching mine.

"No," I whined.

"Give me a minute," he said in a strained voice.

"Why did you stop?" I demanded, squirming against him.

He let out a laugh. "Jesus, Beth. You'll be the death of me."

His lips brushed my temple where the Incubus had hit me, and I could feel his deep shuddering breath.

"If I don't stop now, I'll take you to that bedroom and make love to you."

A fresh bolt of desire shot through me, and my Mori pressed forward, eager to complete the bond we'd forged weeks – or maybe years – ago.

"But –"

"You're barely recovered from a head injury," he reminded me tenderly. "What kind of man would I be if I took advantage of you in a moment of weakness?"

"I want this, too."

He swore softly and captured my mouth in the sweetest of kisses. Then he stepped back with his hands on my shoulders. I felt the sharp sting of rejection until his eyes met mine again.

"I need you more than I need to breathe, and it kills me to wait. But I love you too much to take any chances with your recovery. I promise it'll happen soon."

I stared at him for a long moment, replaying his words to make sure I'd heard them right.

"I... You love me?"

"Beth." His thumb caressed my jaw. "I've always loved you. Don't you know that?"

My lips parted, but no words came out. I think I already knew he loved me, despite all my doubts, but hearing him say it made my heart feel twice its size.

Chris smiled. "You stole my heart the first time I held you in my arms, and it's been yours ever since. It's okay if you're not ready to say the words. I know you love me, too."

"I do love you," I blurted. "I never stopped loving you."

"I know," he murmured as he kissed me again.

And again, and again, and again.

Until my stomach rumbled and we broke apart, laughing.

I rubbed my stomach. "I guess I need some fuel after all that healing."

"Then we need to feed you so you'll be good and strong." His mouth curved into a rakish smile that made butterflies take flight in my belly. "You're going to need it."

I blushed to the roots of my hair, despite the fact we'd just spent the last ten minutes making out. But before I could spend too long being embarrassed, someone pounded on the door.

We stepped back, and Chris opened the door to a grinning Jordan.

"Is it true?" she demanded gleefully. "Did you really punch Celine in the face?"

I scowled, some of my happy glow fading. "If you mean the woman I caught wrapped around my mate, then yes."

Chris laughed and defensively held up his hands. "It was a friendly hug."

"Uh-huh." I had trouble maintaining my stern face when he was so damn cute. "Well, your friend can find someone else to hug. You're taken."

"Yes, ma'am." He leaned closer. "I kind of like this bossy side of you."

Jordan rolled her eyes. "She can boss you around later. Right now, she needs to tell her BFF about the Celine smackdown." She looked at me. "And don't leave anything out."

Chris

My phone vibrated on the desk, and I smiled when I saw Beth's name on the text message.

All done. See you soon.

She'd been checking in with me every half hour since she went out shopping with Mason a few hours ago. I'd been worried about her going out two days after the attack, but she was fully healed and there was no good reason to ask her to stay in.

She must have sensed my reservations because she'd volunteered to take a tracker *and* a Taser. The regular check-ins were a bonus.

Good, I wrote back. **I made dinner plans for us.**

Where?

I smiled. **It's a secret. Now get your pretty behind back here.**

She sent a smiley face. **Now who's being bossy? Love you.**

Love you.

I laid my phone back on the desk and caught Nikolas's knowing smile. I'd been distracted since we sat down to work. I'd tried to focus on the job, but my mind kept going back to my plans for tonight.

If I could, I would have whisked Beth off to some romantic location where I'd spend days doing nothing but making love to her. She deserved that and so much more after all she'd been through. But I couldn't take off in the middle of a crisis and leave Nikolas to deal with it. It was either wait until the Lilin threat was over, or create a special night for her here.

This morning, I'd informed Mason he needed to find somewhere else to sleep tonight. He hadn't needed an explanation. He'd just laughed and said no problem. What I hadn't told him was that I planned to move back into the guesthouse and he was moving to my room in the main house. I figured it was as close as Beth and I could get to privacy for the foreseeable future.

I had also called the French restaurant I knew Beth liked and ordered a three-course meal to be delivered this evening. I'd enlisted Sara's help, and she had run out to buy a cheesecake from a bakery she and Beth loved. Beth hadn't gotten to eat the piece of cake I'd bought her the other night, and I wanted to make it up to her.

The desk phone rang, pulling me from my thoughts. Nikolas answered it then put it on speaker.

"Go ahead, David," Nikolas said.

"We think we found him," David said in a rush. "Or at least his current identity."

Nikolas and I sat up straight, sharing a look that was part disbelief and part hope.

David continued. "Charles Prescott turned up in New York City in the eighties under the new name Jonathan Wells. We just found this an hour ago, and Kelvan is still digging, but we have photos."

"Photos?" I asked.

This was the biggest lead we'd had since we'd discovered there was a Lilin at work here. With a name and a photo, we could probably track him down in a few days or less, depending on how well he'd covered his tracks here.

"Actually, it's photos from a big society gala Jonathan Wells attended," David explained. "Kelvan's not positive, but he thinks the Lilin is in them. One second. I'm sending them now."

Nikolas opened his laptop and turned it so the two of us could see the screen. It took a minute for David's email to arrive, and I held my breath as Nikolas clicked on the attachments.

The first photo showed a group of men and women in black and white evening wear. They were talking and seemed unaware that someone was taking their picture.

I scanned the male faces, even though I didn't expect to recognize the Lilin. He'd be careful to keep his distance from us when he knew we were hunting him. But we could have Dax run facial recognition on every male in the photos and see what came up.

"See that man standing by the fountain in the second photo?" David said.

I studied the two men closest to the fountain. They were tall and handsome like all Incubi, but there was nothing to distinguish them from every other male in the photos.

"The blond man?" I asked.

"The dark-haired one. We think he's your Lilin."

"Great work," Nikolas said as he forwarded the email to the head of security at Westhorne. "Can you find out if Jonathan Wells has property in Los Angeles?"

"Already on it. I'll let you know as soon as I find something."

David hung up with a promise to call with an update in a few hours. I continued to stare at the man David had singled out as if I'd suddenly see something new to identify him.

"I'm going to send these to Celine," Nikolas said, opening a new email. "I think she's going to that charity event tonight."

"Good idea."

Celine, after she'd calmed down from her run-in with Beth, had informed us she'd come at the request of the Council. Unlike most of us who avoided human social events, Celine loved them, and she rubbed elbows with the social elite all over the world. It had taken her less than half a day to insert herself into the Los Angeles social sphere and get invites to all the big parties.

Lilin were wealthy, and the likeliest place to see one in public was at a party or event thrown by someone equally rich. That's where Celine came in. Lilin had no distinctive physical characteristics, but she could look for suspicious behavior or try to match a face to a photo.

Much to Nikolas's and my relief, Celine had informed us she was staying in a suite at the Beverly Wilshire. I would have gladly given up my room to her, but sleeping arrangements were the least of our worries. Sara disliked Celine from their past encounters at Westhorne, and Beth hadn't exactly made a new friend by punching Celine before they'd even been introduced.

Although, I had to admit seeing Beth's little jealous rage had been a major turn-on. And kissing her after had left me wanting more. If just making out with her could affect me that way –

"Chris?"

I looked at Nikolas, who wasn't trying to hide his grin.

"Sorry. What were you saying?"

"I said we have a call with Tristan in ten minutes. Are you going to be up for that?"

I smiled sheepishly. "Yes."

He rested his elbows on the desk. "It gets easier. Your Mori will settle down once you complete the bond, and you won't be quite so..."

"Distracted?"

He chuckled. "I was going to say obsessed."

"God, I am." I scrubbed my face with my hands. "Okay, I promise to focus on work and not think about Beth for the next hour."

He smirked. "Good luck with that."

Beth

"You're texting him *again*?"

I stuck my phone in my pocket and met Mason's amused gaze.

"Just letting him know we're done shopping. We are, right?"

He held up the shopping bag that held the birthday present he'd picked out for his mother. She loved glass blown art, and we'd spent the last hour looking through the glass displays in the cute little shop he'd found in Long Beach.

"Got a hot date or something?" he teased as we left the shop and headed for the rear parking lot where we'd left our bikes.

"Maybe."

My body grew warm as it did every time I thought about being alone with Chris. Since our make out session yesterday, all I could think about was his promise that we would make love soon. He hadn't said exactly when that would be, but something told me it was tonight. My insides quivered every time I tried to imagine what it would be like. Soon, I wouldn't have to imagine it anymore.

We reached our bikes, and I couldn't resist checking my phone one more time before I donned my helmet. Mason snickered, and I turned to glare at him.

"Mason," I cried when I saw the four Incubi sneaking up on him.

Mason spun as the nearest Incubus swung his fist, and Mason's head snapped back under the force of the blow. He went down, and a second Incubus kicked him hard in the ribs.

"Stop," I screamed.

I fumbled in my coat pocket for the Taser Chris had given me. I had it in my hand when one of the Incubi came for me. Before he could grab me, I struck, shocking him twice.

A fist glanced off my cheek, and I staggered backward into someone. Terror gripped me when an arm came around my neck and tightened, cutting off my air. Blood roared in my ears and blackness crowded the edges of my vision as I fought to stay conscious.

My body started to go limp from lack of oxygen. The Taser slipped from my fingers and clattered against the pavement. And then I felt nothing.

20

Beth

My body felt like someone had used it for a punching bag. There were so many aches I was afraid to open my eyes and see what I looked like. Chris was never going to let me go on another job with him after this one. How had I not seen that Incubus sneaking up on the SUV?

I forced my heavy eyes open and stared at a pale gray ceiling. Wait, that didn't look right.

"Chris," I croaked and winced as pain shot through my face. But it was only half as bad as the raw burning in my throat.

I swallowed, and a coughing fit hit me. Rolling to my side, I tried to catch my breath.

I stared in confusion at the white dresser against the far wall, which was covered in gray and white striped wallpaper and looked nothing like the wall in my bedroom.

My eyes moved from the dresser to a silk upholstered chair I'd never seen before. Was I in a bedroom in the main house? Why would they put me here?

"Chris?" I called hoarsely again. "Mason?"

A chill went through me when I said Mason's name. Something was very wrong, but I was too disoriented to figure it out.

I sat up, closing my eyes against a wave of nausea. It passed, and I was able to open my eyes and survey my surroundings.

I was on a bed in a bedroom I'd never seen before. The room was tastefully decorated with white furniture and soft lighting. It looked like any other bedroom except for one thing: there were no windows.

It all came back to me then in one huge rush of memories. I'd been shopping with Mason and the Incubi had ambushed us. I'd seen Mason fall.

"Oh, God. Mason."

I threw back the thick down comforter that covered me. Shock rippled through me when I saw I was wearing only my bra and panties.

I jumped off the bed like it was on fire. My feet hit the rug, and I took a step, only to trip over something. It made a loud clinking sound as I fell to my hands and knees. I looked down at my feet and gasped at the thick chain attached to a padded shackle around my left ankle. The other end of the chain was connected to a bolt in the concrete floor.

Sitting on the rug, I grasped the chain in both hands. It looked like an ordinary chain, and I should have been able to break it. I pulled on it as hard as I could, and the effort left me panting like I'd run ten miles. I dropped the chain and lay back weakly on the rug.

I heard the door open, but I was too exhausted to move. I watched warily as a man came into view, and I had to stare at him for several seconds before recognition set in.

"You," I rasped in disbelief.

Adam Woodward's smile faded into a hard line as he took in my appearance. He turned on his heel and went to the door. A second later, there was a scuffle and he was back, dragging the Incubus I'd shocked with the Taser.

He gripped the Incubus by the throat and pointed at me with his other hand.

"Why is she bruised? I specifically told you she was not to be harmed in any way."

The Incubus swallowed nervously. "It was an accident. She had a weapon, and we had to subdue her before she hurt herself."

"Four of you couldn't do that without bruising her?" Adam shouted.

"We had to deal with the male she was with."

Mason. Fear for my best friend overrode everything else.

"What did you do to Mason?" I screamed. "Where is he?"

The Incubus darted a look at me before addressing Adam. "He lives."

Adam pushed the cowering Incubus toward the door. "I'll deal with you later. Leave us."

"Yes, Father."

Father? Coldness spread through me as Adam turned his attention to me again. Adam was the Lilin? It couldn't be. I would have known, wouldn't I?

"Let's get you off this floor."

He leaned down and picked me up as if I weighed nothing.

"Don't touch me," I cried.

My Mori shrank away from the touch of a male who wasn't my mate. Revulsion made my skin crawl, and I struggled to get away from Adam.

"Shhh," he crooned as he laid me gently on the bed.

I scrambled away as far as the chain would allow, which was only to the middle of the bed.

"What did you do to me?" I demanded, hating how feeble I sounded. "You drugged me."

He pulled the comforter up over me and tucked me in. Then he sat on the edge of the bed.

"Incubi power doesn't work on your people. My sons had to give you a sedative so you didn't wake up before they got you here. It has no lasting effects, I assure you."

I hugged the comforter to my chest. "Where are my clothes?"

I was chained in a room, almost naked, with a sex demon who was ten times stronger than I was. Panic rose up in me, and I tried to swallow it down.

He smiled apologetically. "Unfortunately, my sons had to remove your clothing before they brought you here, in case you were wearing a tracking device. I know how much the Mohiri love their technology."

"They undressed me?"

Bile rose in my throat at the thought of four Incubi taking off my clothes and touching me while I was unconscious and helpless.

Adam held up his hands. "Beth, you have no reason to fear me. I'd never hurt you or allow my sons to hurt you."

"Tell that to your son who nearly choked me to death," I spat.

His expression darkened. "I apologize for that. It will never happen again. You're my honored guest."

"Do you always chain your guests?" I laughed bitterly, and it turned into a dry cough.

Adam stood and went to a table that held a carafe and two glasses. He filled one of the glasses and brought it to me.

I stared at it suspiciously. I was so thirsty, but for all I knew he could be trying to drug me again.

"It's just water."

He took a sip and held the glass out to me again.

Giving in to my thirst, I accepted the glass and gulped the cool water greedily. When I finished, Adam took the glass and went to refill it. I drank half of the second one before I'd had enough.

Adam sat on the bed watching me, looking like the nice college boy I'd met, and nothing like the powerful, ruthless demon I'd learned about. I stared at his blue eyes, looking for some sign he wasn't human. There was nothing.

"I don't have the eyes of an Incubus, if that is what you're looking for," he said, sounding amused. "I did once, but my eyes changed when I became what I am now."

"A Lilin."

"Yes."

His simple confirmation sent a shiver through me, and my hand holding the glass trembled. Adam reached out and took the glass from me.

"Why don't you try to sleep some more? You'll feel better when you wake."

He was talking as if I really was a guest and not his prisoner. I couldn't hold off any longer. I had to know why I was here.

"What are you going to do with me? Are you using me to get the Mohiri to back off?"

I didn't know how the Council handled hostage situations, or if there even was a policy in place for something that happened so rarely. But Chris would do anything to get me back.

Adam shook his head. "You are not a bargaining piece. I'd never devalue you that way."

I rubbed my temple, which still throbbed slightly. "I don't understand. Why am I here then?"

He smiled without a hint of menace. I'd almost call it tender. For some reason, that unsettled me more than his anger.

"I brought you here for me."

My stomach dropped. "What?"

"I never planned to take a Mohiri female, until I met you that night at Luna. You were so beautiful and charming. I was completely enamored of you. I wanted to take you that night, but Weston pointed out how reckless and dangerous it would be. I was forced to wait and watch you from afar until all my chosen females were gathered."

I felt the blood drain from my face. Silently I cried, *NO, NO, NO.*

Adam continued as if he hadn't just dropped a bombshell on me.

"I've been alone for too many years. Even surrounded by my sons, my life is a lonely one. I've wanted to take a mate for a long time, but I never found someone I wanted to share my life with. You're immortal, so I'd never have to worry about losing you. And you're strong and beautiful. We will make magnificent sons together."

"No," I uttered, swallowing back the nausea that threatened. "I'm Mohiri. We can't..."

"You forget my power is much stronger than that of an Incubus. I've bred with other demons to see what our offspring would look like. As long as I feed the mother my energy every day, the baby is born strong and healthy, and a pure Incubus. Ours will be even stronger, and we'll raise them together."

"I won't," I cried shrilly. "I'll kill you if you touch me."

I expected my declaration to anger him, but he merely smiled.

"You're upset right now, and that's understandable. But you'll feel differently with time, and you'll come to love me."

I recoiled at the thought of being with anyone but Chris. I could never love anyone but him, and I'd die before I let another male have me.

Adam seemed to care for me in his own twisted way, so I appealed to that side of him.

"Please, don't do this. I have a mate, and I love him." My voice broke. "If you care about me at all, let me go back to him."

Annoyance flashed in his eyes for the first time. "You may love him, but you haven't mated him. I can tell you are still pure just by being near you. It's the other reason I chose you."

I fought back a sob. If I hadn't pushed Chris away for so long, we would have completed the bond, and I wouldn't be here wondering if I'd ever see him again.

Adam's face softened. He reached for me, but I flinched away, which made him sigh. "You don't have to fear me. I'd never hurt you."

"You *are* hurting me."

"Once you've fed on my power, you'll change your mind. And then you'll see how happy we'll be together."

I clutched the comforter tightly. "Incubus power doesn't work on me. You said so yourself."

He smiled indulgently. "You keep forgetting I'm not a normal Incubus. It will take several feedings to weaken your resistance, but you'll come to want me as much as I want you."

I stared at him in horror as the weight of his words hit me. "If you take away my resistance, it's the same as drugging me and forcing yourself on me."

Adam looked as if I'd slapped him. "I would never take a female by force or use violence against one. Females are to be cherished, and I've never been with one against her will."

"Don't you see that using your power on them is taking away their free will?" I pleaded, though I already knew there was no getting through to him. How could he not see that what he was doing was the ultimate violation?

I put my hand to my face as a wave of dizziness washed over me. My eyes suddenly felt heavy and unfocused as I stared at the glass in Adam's hand. "You drugged me again," I accused.

He stood and set the glass on the night table then leaned over me. "It was a mild dose, just enough to make you compliant."

I shrank away from him as fear mingled with the lethargy stealing over me. "Compliant for what?"

His hand caressed my face lovingly. I loathed his touch, but I couldn't raise an arm to push him away. All I could do was stare at him helplessly as he leaned over me.

"Shhh. Don't be afraid," he said softly. "I have no desire to make love to a drugged female. All I would take now is a kiss."

"No," I protested drunkenly as the room dimmed.

"Yes," he murmured.

The last thing I felt as sleep took me was his mouth on mine.

Chris

I glanced at my phone for what seemed like the hundredth time. I'd gotten used to Beth texting me often, but I hadn't heard from her since she'd let me know she and Mason were done shopping. That was almost two hours ago. Los Angeles traffic was bad this late in the afternoon, but she should have been home by now.

Forcing my attention back to the report on the computer screen, I managed to get through two pages before I looked at my phone again.

"She's probably held up," Nikolas said.

I rubbed the back of my neck. "I know, but I can't stop feeling like something's wrong."

"Call her. No sense worrying for nothing."

"You're right."

I picked up my phone and dialed Beth's number. It went immediately to voice mail.

A cold lump formed in my gut, and I tried her number again to no avail. This time, I left a short message for her to call me.

I hung up and called Mason next. His phone rang four times before it went to voice mail. I left a message for him, too, and met Nikolas's questioning look.

"Neither of them is picking up. I don't like this."

His brows drew together thoughtfully. "Beth's wearing a tracker?"

"Yes."

I was out of my chair before he finished the question. Out in the control room, I went to Will, who was monitoring all the team locations.

"Can you bring up Beth's location?" I asked him.

"Sure."

He typed her name into the search bar on one of his screens, and the map zoomed in on a blinking blue dot in Long Beach.

Will pointed at the screen. "I know that area. It's a bunch of little craft shops. There's a seafood place I go to close by."

The coldness in my stomach grew. It had been almost two and a half hours since Beth had said they were heading home.

"Something's wrong," I said to Nikolas, who had followed me. "If they'd decided to shop some more, Beth would have let me know. And neither of them is answering their phone."

Grabbing a mobile receiver, I entered the device number for Beth's tracker.

"See if anyone is close to Long Beach, and have them meet me there," I told Will. "Tell them to call me if they find Beth and Mason."

"On it."

I headed for the garage, and I didn't need to look to know Nikolas was behind me. Neither of us spoke as we straddled our bikes and donned our helmets. My mind was too full of worry to make conversation, and if anyone understood, it was Nikolas.

I alternated between calling Beth and praying she was okay during the ride to Long Beach. Traffic was terrible as always, but Nikolas and I knew how to maneuver through it and get there in half the time it would take a normal commuter.

Dusk had fallen when we reached the little row of shops. I looked at the receiver mounted on my dash. The map showed that Beth was in a parking lot behind one of the shops.

I followed a parking sign to a wide alley between two buildings. The alley opened into a small parking lot with a handful of cars and a large black SUV.

It wasn't until I pulled up to the SUV that I saw what was beside it. Fear knifed through me when I took in the sight of Raoul and Jordan kneeling beside Mason, who lay on the ground. His Ducati stood nearby beside Beth's Harley. Beth was nowhere to be seen.

Raoul stood when I shut off my bike, and his grim expression made it impossible to breathe for a moment. My hands shook when I removed my helmet and met his gaze.

"What happened?" I heard Nikolas ask.

Raoul's eyes shifted to him. "Incubi. Mason said there were at least four of them. Maybe more. They jumped him and Beth as they were walking to their bikes."

"Beth?" was all I could say.

"Took her," Mason said weakly.

I fought to control the rage building inside me. Losing control now would not help Beth, and finding her was all I cared about. Forcing myself to stay calm, I went to Mason.

One side of Mason's face was a massive bruise, and one of his eyes was swollen shut. Jordan had his shirt pulled up to expose the dark bruising along his ribs.

"Bastards were...waiting for us," he said between gritted teeth. Remorse filled his eyes. "I'm sorry. I couldn't help her."

"It's not your fault," I told him, sounding a lot calmer than I felt. "Did they say anything? Give you any clue to where they were taking her?"

Mason tried to sit up and fell back to the pavement.

"No."

I looked at Beth's bike as if it could tell me something. A glint of silver near the back wheel caught my eye, and I crouched to see what it was. My gut clenched when I saw the silver chain with the tiny dove pendant. I picked it up and tucked it into the inside pocket of my jacket.

Going to my bike, I grabbed the receiver, which showed a blinking blue dot close by. I scanned the parking lot, and my gaze landed on a blue dumpster.

My mind filled with images of Beth lying on a pile of trash. I couldn't feel her. What if she was –?

No. I'd feel it if she were gone. The bond was still there, so she was alive.

Raoul ran to the dumpster and peered inside. Then he leaned in and grabbed something. When his hand reappeared, it was holding Beth's brown leather jacket. I'd know it anywhere because it was her favorite, and she wore it whenever she rode her Harley.

I walked over and took the jacket from him. Reaching into the inside pocket, I found the tiny round tracking device, exactly where I'd placed it before Beth left the house. A search of the other pockets turned up the key to her bike.

"Do you see her phone in there or her Taser?" I asked Raoul.

He looked down into the dumpster and pressed his mouth together like he was reluctant to speak or like he didn't know how to tell me what he saw.

My heart thudded painfully against my ribs. *Please, God, no.*

"Tell me," I said in a voice I barely recognized.

"She's not here," Raoul rushed to say. "But..."

He reached into the dumpster a second time and lifted out a pair of women's jeans, a white shirt, and a pair of women's biker boots. I didn't need to smell them to know they carried Beth's scent, because I'd seen her in that outfit a few hours ago.

The world tilted. I couldn't think about why the Incubi would undress Beth before they took her away. If I did, I'd completely lose it.

"If they found her tracker, it's likely they removed her clothes in case she was wearing another device in them," Nikolas said.

"But why would they take her?" I asked, hearing the desperation in my voice. "What use is she to them?"

"Maybe they plan to use her as a hostage to force us to back off," Jordan suggested.

Raoul frowned. "Then why not take Mason as well? Wouldn't two warriors be better to bargain with?"

Jordan looked up from helping Mason. "It seems to me that Incubi place a higher value on females than males. They probably think we do the same and would be more likely to give them what they want for Beth."

I felt a flicker of hope, but it did nothing to ease the fear clawing at me. Beth was at the mercy of a monster, and I had no idea what she was going through right now. She could be hurt or afraid, and all because I hadn't kept her safe. I should have listened to my instincts and taken her away from here. She would have been furious with me at first, but at least she'd be safe.

I turned to Nikolas. "I can't stand here waiting for them to call us. I'm going to ride around and see if I can find anything."

"I'll go with you."

I shook my head. "I'd feel better if you were running things at the house."

He started to speak but let out a heavy breath instead. "Check in regularly. I'll let you know if we hear anything."

"Thanks."

I turned to my bike, and Nikolas called after me.

"We'll get her back."

I couldn't answer because I was struggling to hold myself together. The most fear I'd ever felt was when Nikolas and Sara were taken by a Master last year. The odds of finding them alive had been so small I'd thought I would never see them again. I'd comforted myself with the knowledge they were together at least.

That fear didn't come close to the terror gripping me now. Beth was alone with a demon almost as powerful and dangerous as a Master, and she didn't have Sara's power to protect herself.

I didn't have a destination in mind when I got on my bike. Without a clue to the Lilin's whereabouts, all I could do was ride around and cover as much ground as possible, trying to sense Beth. She was still in the Los Angeles area. It wasn't just wishful thinking. The Lilin's activity was heaviest here, which meant he had a lair close by. And if he took Beth to force our hand, he'd keep her here.

All night, I rode through countless streets, stopping only once for gas. Nikolas called every few hours, but there was never any word about Beth. I knew he was worried about me, but I couldn't go back to that house, not yet. Beth was out here somewhere, and until we got a new lead, this was my best chance of finding her.

I tortured myself, thinking about the years I'd spent trying to get Beth out of my system, believing there was something wrong with me for wanting her. So many wasted years. My heart gave up the fight the first moment I saw her get off that Harley. She'd been back in my life for less than a month, and I knew I couldn't live without her.

It wasn't until the following afternoon that Nikolas tracked me down at a food truck in Santa Monica. I hadn't eaten since lunch the day before, and I was forced to eat to keep up my strength. I was leaning against my bike, making short work of a hot dog when he pulled up beside me.

"How did you find me?"

"We've been tracking your phone all night."

"How's Mason?" I asked.

"Better. Margot fixed him up."

He gave me an assessing look, and I knew what he was going to say before he spoke.

"You need to sleep."

I clenched my free hand into a fist. "I'll sleep when I find her."

"You pass out on your bike and you'll be no good to anyone, especially Beth," he replied in his no-nonsense way.

"I can't sleep, not when she needs me."

He crossed his arms and sighed. "When I was looking for Sara, I would have driven myself into the ground if you hadn't been there. You said I was thinking with my heart and not my head. I'm telling you the same thing now. You need to rest."

I wanted to argue that Sara had taken off of her own free will, and Beth was a captive. But it wouldn't change the fact that he was right. I was exhausted, and my body needed more than food to keep going.

"I'm supposed to protect her, and I failed her. It's killing me, thinking about what she might be going through."

"We'll find her," he stated with conviction. "A dozen warriors arrived from Longstone this morning, and we have more coming from other strongholds today. David and Kelvan are closing in on him, and they're sure they'll have something soon."

His last comment gave me the first hope I'd had all night. David and Kelvan had tracked down a Master from nothing more than a drawing of a house Sara had taken from a vampire's memory. If anyone could do this, it was them.

The driveway at the command center was so full of vehicles I had to park my bike on the patio. I told Nikolas I'd see him in a few hours and let myself into the guesthouse. The silence of the empty house pressed down on me as I entered Beth's bedroom and lay down on her bed. Her unique floral scent surrounded me, comforting and tormenting me at the same time.

Solmi, my Mori wailed, its anguish mixing with my own until I could barely breathe from the pain in my chest.

We'll find her, I swore to us both.

The Lilin had made a fatal mistake when he stole my mate from me. I wouldn't stop hunting him until I found her or avenged her. Either way, he'd signed his own death warrant.

It was almost dark when I woke, but a glance at the clock by the bed told me I'd slept for less than four hours. I was surprised I'd managed that many.

There was no way I'd go back to sleep, so I got up and went over to the main house to shower and change before I headed out again.

The house was less crowded than I expected, considering all the vehicles I'd seen when I arrived. Wondering where everyone was, I went to the control room. I already knew there was no news, because Nikolas would have woken me the moment he heard something.

I found Sara, Jordan, Raoul, and Nikolas sitting at the conference table talking. Mason, who looked paler than usual, was sitting on the couch with a red-haired warrior I hadn't seen in four years.

Rachel's tired eyes widened slightly when she saw me, and she stood as I headed for her. I took in her drawn complexion and the dark shadows under her eyes as I wrapped her in a warm hug.

"I'm so sorry, Rachel. I should have taken her away from here as soon as we knew what we were dealing with."

She hugged me back then held me at arm's length. "None of this is your fault. Just focus on getting her back."

Someone entered the room, and I turned to see who it was. I sucked in a breath when I saw the blond couple who watched me with worried eyes.

"Mom? Dad? When did you get here?" I asked as they crossed the room to me.

"Landed an hour ago," my sire said as my mother hugged me tightly. "Tristan called last night, and we left as soon as we could."

My mother let me go and stood back, wiping her eyes. "No word?"

"No," I said roughly.

"What can we do to help?" she asked, businesslike again.

My mother was one of the most coolheaded people I'd ever known. In a crisis, she was the person you wanted overseeing the situation. It was a trait she shared with Tristan.

"Beatrice, James, great to see you," Nikolas said, coming over to us. "It's been a while."

"Too long," my mother replied. "I wish it was under better circumstances."

Nikolas's smile was grave. "So do I."

He waved for the others to come over and introduced them to my parents. My mother surprised Sara by pulling her into a tight hug.

"Tristan talks about you so much I feel like I already know you. And Chris has told us so many stories about your adventures together."

Sara gave me a sidelong look. "I bet he has."

"Where are you two staying?" I asked my parents.

My sire looked from my mother to me. "We haven't even thought about that yet."

"Stay here," I told them. "You can take my room."

My mother frowned. "Where will you sleep?"

"I'll stay in Beth's room." Not that I expected to sleep much.

I turned to Rachel, who had joined us. "Unless you need a room."

Mason spoke up. "I already gave her mine."

"It's settled then." My mother smiled. "Now, put us to work. That's what we're here for."

Nikolas motioned for us to sit. I stood while the rest took seats at the conference table. I didn't plan to be here much longer because I still had a lot of ground to cover.

"We've been contacting everyone we know in the local demon community," Nikolas said. "Many of them are too afraid of the Lilin to even talk to us. Sara's managed to reach out to a few of them, but all we've gotten so far is suggestions for places to look. Most of our people are out there checking out these places. So far, we've found nothing."

"Is there nothing else we can do?" my sire asked.

Sara answered him. "We also have some guys trying to track down any property the Lilin might have here. We're expecting an update from David any minute."

As soon as the words left her mouth, the phone rang. I leaned over and hit the speaker button before anyone could move.

"David?"

"Yeah. Is the gang there?"

"We're here," Nikolas said. "Any luck?"

"Yes."

My heart leaped. "What?"

David cleared his throat. "Kelvan found two names linked to Jonathan Wells from his time in New York. Henry Durham and George Ramsey. I decided to add them to my property search, and I got a hit for one of them. Henry Durham has a house in Bel Air that he's owned since the seventies. And he's an Incubus."

Hope flared in me. This was it; it had to be. It was too much of a coincidence.

"What's the address?" I asked, already calculating how long it would take me to get there.

"Hold on, Chris," Nikolas said as everyone stood. "We don't know what we might be walking into. Let's make sure we have plenty of backup before we go."

"Beth might not have time for us to wait for backup," I snapped. "I'm going."

"I am, too," Mason and Rachel said at the same time.

Jordan held up a hand. "We have all of us and Sara. I think we're covered."

Nikolas looked unhappy, and Sara scowled at him.

"Oh, no. You are not pulling that protective mate thing on me. I'm going."

"David, the address," I called over the clamor of voices.

He read off an address, and I plugged it into the GPS on my phone as I was hurrying out the door. I heard footsteps behind me, but I didn't look back to see who followed. All I cared about was Beth. Every minute we waited was another minute she was in danger.

I would tear that place apart to find her if that was what it took. And I would kill anything that got in my way.

21

Beth

I sat on the floor, panting and covered in a fine sheet of sweat from my latest attempt to break the chain on my leg. I couldn't even bend the links a little, and I was starting to think they were infused with some kind of magic.

"Argh!"

I slapped the floor as tears of desperation burned my eyes. I had to get out of here before he came back.

I couldn't even think about what Adam wanted to do with me. The idea of someone other than Chris touching me made me physically ill. And the thought of spending my life as a prisoner, of never seeing Chris again, was almost more than I could bear.

I rested my forehead on my knees, trying not to give in to despair. I wasn't sure exactly how long I'd been here, but it didn't feel like more than a day. Chris would find me, or I would find a way to escape on my own. There was no other acceptable option.

Adam hadn't come to see me since last night. I didn't want to see him, but his absence made me worry more about what he was doing. I wouldn't delude myself into thinking he'd lost interest in me, not after seeing the intent in his eyes. Chris had said a Lilin didn't stray from his course once he was set on something.

My stomach growled, but I pushed the hunger aside. Twice today, a gray-skinned mox demon, accompanied by an Incubus, had come with food and to take me to the adjoining bathroom to relieve myself. During her first visit, the mox demon had smiled meekly at me as she set the tray on the night table. A few hours later when she returned with a second tray, she'd frowned and cast a worried glance at me when she saw the untouched food from earlier.

The Incubus had scowled and ordered me to eat. I'd informed him I would starve and die of thirst before I'd eat or drink anything else here. My declaration had angered him, but he'd left without another word. I didn't care what anyone here said. After Adam's deception last night, I didn't trust them to not drug me again. Whatever happened to me, I was going to face it with a mind free from drugs.

Someone knocked softly on the closed door, and I looked up in surprise. Since I'd been here, no one had knocked before entering the room.

The door creaked open, and the mox demon entered timidly, closing the door behind her. She was alone this time, and she carried a garment bag over one arm and what looked like a toiletry bag in her other hand. She laid the bags on the foot of the bed and bowed her head subserviently.

"Master sent me to help you dress for dinner," she said quietly, her long white hair hiding her face.

I stood and sat on the bed, pulling the comforter over me. I still wore nothing but my underwear, and I felt vulnerable without clothes, even with this shy female.

"Tell your *master* I'm not hungry and I'll stay in my prison cell."

Her head came up, and her eyes widened. "You must go. Master is expecting you."

"He'll get over it," I said coldly. "He has plenty of girls here if he needs a dinner companion."

"But you are his special guest. He has been waiting for you to join him here to have this dinner."

I let out a harsh laugh. "I didn't join him; I'm his prisoner. So, I think I'll pass."

She wrung her hands. "Master will be very displeased with me if you don't go."

"Why would he be mad at you? I'm the one who doesn't want to be there."

"He gave me the responsibility of seeing to you. If I fail him, he'll punish me."

A feeling of helplessness washed over me. My stomach twisted at the thought of going to Adam's dinner, but I couldn't let his servant be punished because of me. Mox demons were passive, which meant they were easily enslaved and abused by more aggressive demons. She was just as much a prisoner here as I was.

"What's your name?"

"Ree, my lady," she stammered.

I sighed. "Okay, Ree. The first thing you can do is stop calling me my lady. My name is Beth."

Her title for me implied a relationship I would never have with Adam, no matter what he thought was going to happen. It unnerved me just hearing her call me that.

"But Master said –"

I held up a hand to cut her off. "It's Beth, or I'm staying right here."

She nodded meekly. "Yes...Beth."

"Now, can you please take this thing off me?" I uncovered my shackled leg. "Or am I wearing a ball and chain to this dinner?"

A smile curved her lips, and she pulled a small key from the pocket of her simple black dress. She hurried over and unlocked the shackle, letting it fall to the floor with a clank.

I rubbed my freed ankle. The shackle hadn't hurt me, but wearing it was degrading, and it put me completely at the mercy of anyone who entered the room. I was still a prisoner without it, but I didn't feel quite as vulnerable.

Ree picked up the toiletry bag. "Shall I draw you a bath?"

"No. I can bathe myself."

I got off the bed and took the bag from her before I shut myself in the bathroom. It was luxuriously done in pink and gray marble with a deep claw-foot tub. I pulled off my bra and panties, hoping Ree had fresh ones in that garment bag. There was no way I was going commando, especially considering whose company I'd be in tonight. I shuddered at the thought.

I showered quickly and made use of the hair dryer and brush I found in a drawer of the vanity. The bag Ree had given me contained a cosmetic bag, but I decided to forego makeup. This wasn't a social event. My captor had requested I dine with him. I didn't need mascara for that.

Ree was waiting for me when I left the bathroom. She'd laid out the contents of the garment bag, and I was relieved to see a matching bra and panty set on the bed next to the red dress. I donned the underwear then picked up the dress, frowning at its sheer material. It wasn't see-through, but it was too thin for my comfort.

I pulled it on and looked at myself in the floor-length mirror. The dress was sleeveless with a V-neckline and a fitted skirt that fell to mid-thigh. It wasn't unlike some of the dresses I'd worn to clubs with Jordan, but it was definitely not dinner wear.

I set my shoulders and leaned down to slip on the red heels Ree had brought with the dress. Something told me a request for a change of wardrobe would be denied, so I'd have to go with this one.

Straightening, I saw Ree holding a black leather jewelry case. I put up my hands and shook my head. "No."

She opened the case to reveal an exquisite diamond necklace that had to be worth at least a hundred thousand dollars. It was breathtaking but not something I'd wear. I might have to wear the dress, but I refused to adorn myself in jewels for him.

"Master bought it especially for you. It would please him to see you wear it."

"It would please me not to wear it," I said firmly.

Ree unhappily closed the case and tucked it into the pocket of her skirt. She looked me up and down and smiled.

"You look beautiful, my lady...Beth. Shall we go?"

I pretended to adjust my dress to cover my sudden dread over what was waiting for me on the other side of that door. But if I was going to get out of this place, I had to leave this room and see what I was up against.

You can do this.

"Lead the way."

Ree opened the door for me, and I stepped into a hallway where two Incubi waited for us. I immediately recognized Adam's dark-haired friend Wes. His eyes now had a silver ring around the irises, telling me he must have worn contacts the other times I'd seen him.

"Welcome to the family, Beth," he said with a salacious smile.

I glared at him in contempt but didn't say anything. I had no intention of making nice with anyone here. Ree was a slave, so I'd tolerate her, but I wouldn't trust her or forget where her loyalties lay.

The mox demon was even more timid in the presence of the Incubi. She kept her eyes downcast, and her voice was little more than a whisper.

"This way, if you please."

I followed her down the hallway, which was lined with doors, and it took me a moment to realize this must be where they were keeping the other girls. I'd been so caught up in my own predicament that I'd forgotten I wasn't the only prisoner here. The weight of our situation pressed down on me. How was I going to get us all out of here?

I studied my surroundings, looking for escape routes, as I was escorted through the building. It didn't take me long to see there were no windows, which meant we were most likely underground. I felt a moment of panic over that discovery. An underground structure would probably have only one way in and out, and that would be heavily guarded. The girls were too important to the Lilin, and he wouldn't take any chances of them escaping.

Up ahead, I heard the murmur of voices, and my steps faltered when we entered a large opulent drawing room where at least two dozen girls milled about, sitting on couches or standing in little groups. The girls wore pretty pastel dresses with their hair down, and a hint of makeup. They looked innocent and virginal, exactly what the Lilin preferred.

I looked down at the revealing red dress I wore, and my stomach lurched again at the reminder that he'd singled me out to be his mate. These girls would serve their purpose, and they'd die giving birth to his offspring. He intended to keep me forever.

"Beth."

A petite Chinese girl ran up to me, her face glowing with happiness. She wore a white dress, and a white orchid adorned her glossy black hair.

"Mei," I said, not sure how to greet someone under these circumstances.

"Isn't this place amazing?" she gushed. "I wish Alicia was here to see it, but Adam said only his chosen can come here."

A dreamy expression came over her face when she said Adam's name, leaving no doubt she was under his power. The Mei I'd met at Luna had been shy and quiet, nothing like the bubbly girl before me now. Chris was right when he said the girls would be happy and they wouldn't even realize they were prisoners.

Thinking about him made a lump form in my throat. He had to be going out of his mind looking for me. My heart constricted when I imagined the pain he must be feeling, not knowing if I was safe or hurt or whether he'd see me again.

I thought about the last time I'd seen him, before I'd left to go shopping with Mason. He'd taken hold of the open front of my leather jacket and tugged me to him for a slow, deep kiss that had left me unsteady on my feet. Then he'd given me a smile that said he knew exactly what effect he had on me and that there was more of that waiting for me when I got home.

"Adam's estate in France is way bigger than this place," Mei said with awe in her voice. "He said there are gardens and a lake, and we can go outside. And we'll have more dresses than we can count. But best of all, he won't have to leave us for business anymore, and we'll see him all the time."

She sighed happily, lost in the dream he'd fed her of the perfect life waiting for her. Anger boiled in my chest. Mei and all the other girls here thought Adam cared for them. They had no idea of the real fate awaiting them.

A girl squealed. "He's here."

All eyes turned to the doorway. I followed their gazes to Adam, who wore a black dinner jacket and was soaking up their adoring stares. His eyes roamed the room, smiling at each girl as if she was the love of his life. They practically swooned at the brief attention he paid them. The whole display sickened me.

Adam's blue eyes finally locked with mine, and my breath caught as my stomach fluttered. He smiled and started toward me, sending my pulse racing...in excitement.

Girls moved to intercept him, and he broke his stare with me so he could talk to them. I blinked and wavered slightly on my feet. It was like waking suddenly from a dream to find myself in a nightmare. Because only in a nightmare would I be attracted to this monster.

"All I would take now is a kiss."

Bile burned my throat as I remembered the last thing he'd said to me before his lips had touched mine. He had kissed me to feed me his energy, the same energy he'd said would make me change my mind about him. My skin tightened in revulsion at the knowledge that his power was inside me. I felt soiled and violated, and I wanted to throw up.

I watched the girls flock to Adam, fawning over him like he was a rock star. He greeted each of them with light touches and chaste kisses that made them glow with the love they thought they felt for him.

Ree came up to me and pressed a glass of sparkling water into my hand. I tried to give it back, but she refused to take it.

"You look ill. It will help settle your stomach," she whispered.

"Leaving this hell is the only thing that will help me," I said bitterly.

She hurried away, and I looked for somewhere to set down the glass she'd left with me. I meant what I'd said to the Incubus earlier. Not a morsel of food or drop of water would pass through my lips in this place. God only knew what they would do to me if I was drugged again.

I laid the glass on a table and turned back to the room to come face-to-face with Adam. I stumbled, causing him to grab my arms to steady me. Warmth infused me at his touch, and I had to resist the urge to lean into him.

A battle raged inside of me, between my aversion to another male's touch and my unnatural attraction for him. I knew his power was forcing me to feel this way, but that didn't stop me from feeling like I was betraying Chris.

Disgusted and frightened, I took a step back. He let go of my arms to take one of my hands in his.

He kissed my hand. "You are breathtaking in that dress. I could barely take my eyes off you when I came in."

His eyes lifted to mine, and there was no mistaking the desire in his. Then his gaze fell on my bare throat. Disappointment crossed his face, and his voice was harder when he spoke again.

"You aren't wearing the necklace I gave you. Did you not like it?"

"It was beautiful, but I don't wear jewelry."

I thought of the silver chain I'd started wearing two days ago, and the pleasure I'd felt to see the dove pendant resting against my chest. I hadn't been wearing it when I woke up here, so it must have broken when they'd taken me. Would I ever see it or the man who had given it to me again?

"I'll have to find out what other gifts will please you," Adam said, undeterred. "I have more money than you could dream of, and I'll give you anything your heart desires."

"Even my freedom?"

His sigh was barely perceptible. "Anything but that."

I yanked my hand from his and turned my head to look at the other girls, all of whom were watching Adam with open adoration. Oddly, none of them looked jealous that he'd singled me out. They seemed content to share as long as they had their time with him.

"I've been told you haven't eaten or drunk today. Why?"

My disbelieving gaze swung back to Adam. "Do you really need to ask that after you tricked me and drugged me last night?"

He held up a hand to signal to someone, then looked at me. "I apologize for that. It won't happen again."

I let out a humorless laugh. "Pardon me if I don't believe you."

A mox demon approached us, carrying a tray of hors d'oeuvres, and Adam motioned for me to try one of the little pastries.

My stomach rumbled at the sight and smell of food, but I couldn't bring myself to take it. "No, thank you."

"You have to eat, Beth," he pressed unhappily. "You have to keep up your strength."

"I'm not one of your chosen to be fed and pampered like a prized brood mare," I bit out in a low voice so only he could hear me."

He stared at me, appalled. "Brood mare? I would never disrespect the mothers of my children like that."

"You kidnapped them and forced this on them by taking away their free will. Half of them are not yet eighteen. They're children, and you're going to destroy their lives. How can you live with that?"

"Look at them," he said. "They're happy and living in luxury."

My hands clenched into fists. "They're going to die. Doesn't that bother you at all?"

For the first time, his composure slipped, and he snapped at me. "Of

237

course, it bothers me. I'm not a monster. I would save them all if I could, but even my power is not enough to do that."

"Then why do you do it?"

"It's survival of the species, and the way it's always been done." His voice softened. "I love and honor my females, and they want to bear my children. They will die happy in the knowledge that they have given me sons."

I wanted to scream at him, but I kept my voice low. "They don't want this. You made them think they want it. You stole their lives and their futures, and destroyed their families, and they don't even know it."

He spoke to me like he was talking to a child. "I know you don't understand this yet, but you will soon."

"What I don't understand is why you need to take human girls if you can breed with other demons. These girls don't have to die."

"I can breed with demons, but I have to feed them more of my power to ensure the child is one of my kind. I could only have one or two children that way. With humans, I can have many sons."

I exhaled in defeat. There was no getting through to him when he really believed there was nothing wrong with what he was doing.

I studied the large room. Except for the lack of windows, it resembled a typical drawing room with oriental rugs, fine artwork, and a crystal chandelier. In addition to the door I'd entered through, there was another door that led to a dining room with a long table set for a large party. Incubi stood guard at the door to the hallway, so there was no getting out that way. Maybe there was another door in the dining room that led to a kitchen. The food had to come from somewhere.

Adam leaned close, startling me.

"I can see what you're doing, and it's no use. This lair was built specifically for me. It's underground and heavily fortified with warlock magic. You can't escape, and no one will find it."

"Chris will find me," I declared. "He'll never stop looking for me."

He sighed heavily and placed a hand on the small of my back. "Come. I want to show you something."

I eyed him warily. "What?"

"Our security room. It's just down the hall."

I went with him because the more I knew about this place, the more information I'd have to formulate an escape plan.

At the end of the hall, we stopped at a door with an electronic card reader. Adam swiped a key card, and the lock flashed green. He grabbed the door handle and held the door open for me.

Inside the dimly lit room, two Incubi sat at computer stations similar to the ones we had at the command center. On the wall in front of them were monitors showing the live video feeds from at least twenty security cameras. Some of the cameras were internal, and others showed a backyard, a driveway, and other outside locations.

"Bring up camera four from twenty minutes ago," Adam said.

"Yes, Father," one of the Incubi said.

He typed into his computer, and one of the monitors began playing a recording. The video showed an exterior view of the open front door of a house. At first, nothing happened. Then someone exited the house.

Nikolas.

A cry slipped from me when I saw the person behind him. Even from here, I could see the strain and exhaustion on Chris's face. I put a hand over my mouth as I watched him walk down a wide set of steps. I drank in the sight of him like it had been weeks instead of a day since I last saw him.

The monitor changed to a new camera feed, and I could see Chris and Nikolas walking to their bikes. They weren't alone. I saw Jordan, Mason, Sara, Raoul, Seamus, Niall, and...Rachel. Two more people came into view. Chris's parents.

"No," I whispered when Chris straddled his bike. He couldn't leave.

"The entrance to this place is at the back of the property, and unless you know it's there, it's virtually undetectable," Adam said as I watched Chris ride away.

Tears streamed down my face. He'd been so close, and I hadn't even known it. It was too cruel to bear.

"I didn't feel him," I said, dazed from shock. "Why didn't I feel him?"

"What do you mean?" Adam asked, puzzled.

I stared through blurry eyes at the screen where Chris had been a moment ago. "Our bond. I couldn't feel our bond." My voice broke on the last word, and it felt like my world started to crumble along with it. What did this mean? Had Adam's power weakened my bond with Chris?

"You have a bond with the male even though you aren't mated with him?" Adam asked curiously, oblivious to the pain ripping me apart inside.

I turned on him. "He is my mate," I shouted. "I love him, and nothing you do will ever change that."

"Time changes all things," he said, unaffected by my outburst.

In that moment, I got my first real look at the unfeeling, ruthless monster that hid beneath the good looks and charm. All he cared about was a pretty face at his table and a vessel for his future children. And he'd hurt anyone to get what he wanted.

I lowered my gaze, unable to stomach looking at him for a moment longer.

"I don't feel well. Please, take me back to my room."

"You need to eat," he admonished softly as if we'd been talking about nothing more serious than the weather. "You'll feel better after we dine."

The last thing I wanted was to go back to that room with all those happy, innocent girls fawning over the male who had already sentenced them to die.

"I'd rather be alone."

Adam released an impatient breath. "You are going to be my mate, so you'll dine with me tonight and every night after."

I didn't respond. Nor did I pull away when he took my arm to lead me back to the drawing room. I was too numb to feel anything.

I sat beside Adam through dinner as he smiled and charmed everyone else at the table. I didn't speak unless spoken to, not caring if anyone thought my behavior strange. A small army of mox demons served us, placing course after course in front of us. Adam had spared no expense, and the food looked delicious.

My mouth watered, and my stomach ached with hunger. But I didn't eat a single bite.

Chris

"What do you mean it's a dead end?" I hit the top of the conference table as the rage that had been boiling beneath the surface for days threatened to erupt.

Five days. That was how long it had been since I'd last seen Beth. Five days since I'd held her and kissed her, not knowing it might be the last time I'd ever touch her. I never should have let her go out that day, and now she and I were both paying the price. The Lilin had Beth, and I was a hairsbreadth away from losing my sanity, imagining what he could be doing to her.

"Most of these leads are dead ends," David said calmly from the phone's speaker. "Demon archives are all over the place, and they only started creating their digital library two decades ago. Kelvan has a network of demons helping him track down data, but some of it is still only in written form and not always reliable. But if anyone can make sense of it, it's him. I promise you, this is our only priority right now."

I dragged my hands through my already messy hair and let out a ragged breath. "I know. I'm sorry I yelled at you."

"Don't worry about it. I'd probably do the same in your place."

Nikolas leaned forward on the opposite side of the table. "David, have you had any luck with the property search?"

"Nothing in California. I found a building Jonathan Wells owned in New York, but that was sold ten years ago. Based on what we've found so far, he creates a new identity every thirty years, so he could have property under a different name."

My eyes met Nikolas's, and I knew we were thinking the same thing. The Lilin created a new identity whenever he came out of hiding to breed. That meant it would be even harder to find him, unless David and Kelvan somehow managed to discover a link to his new name.

I picked up my tablet and opened the photos he'd sent days ago. "What about these pictures Kelvan found from New York?" I asked, desperate for something, anything, to keep me from coming apart. "Do we have a positive ID on Jonathan Wells?"

"No. I'm sorry, Chris. I wish I had more for you."

I had to stop myself from throwing the tablet across the room. I'd always considered myself easygoing and even-tempered, until Beth disappeared. Now it was a constant struggle to keep it together. I didn't know how much more of this I could take.

"You're not going to throw that at me, are you?"

I looked up to see Jordan approaching us cautiously. She'd been here constantly since Beth was taken – when she wasn't out running down leads with Raoul. Like everyone else, she was working around the clock to find Beth.

I laid the tablet on the table. "You're safe."

She pulled out the chair beside me and picked up the tablet to scroll through the photos. "What's this? Hey, I know this guy."

My body jerked like I'd been shot. "You know one of these men?"

"I don't know him well. I've seen him around a few times. He's actually a friend of Beth's."

My body froze for several seconds like it was encased in ice. Reaching over, I tapped the face of the dark-haired male in the photo. "Beth knows *him*?"

The last word came out as a growl, causing Jordan's eyes to widen.

"No. I mean...not that one," she stammered.

She pointed to the blond male who was in all the pictures with the male we thought might be the Lilin.

"Him."

I fought to control my breathing. "How do you and Beth know this man?"

"Beth met him at Luna the night we went to the rave. We saw him a few days later while we were out shopping, and she introduced us. He was at Suave the night we all went there, too."

I remembered the blond man kissing Beth's hand that night at the club, and how she and Jordan had seemed to know him. Red tinged my vision. He'd been there. The bastard had been in the same goddamn club, and we'd had no idea. And he'd touched Beth.

"Chris," Nikolas barked.

I looked at him, and he shook his head in warning.

He turned to Jordan, who was watching me warily. "Can you remember the man's name?"

"Adam," she replied instantly. Her brow creased. "Adam...Woods, I think. No. It was Woodward. He said he was a student at UCLA."

"Jesus." I pushed back from the table and began pacing as a new realization hit me like a punch in the gut. "He was stalking her this whole time."

"Who?" Jordan asked. Her eyes went from me to the photo, and an expression of horrified disbelief crossed her face. "This is the Lilin? Adam is the Lilin?"

David's voice came from the phone before anyone could answer her. "You guys want to tell me what's going on?"

"Jordan recognized the blond man in the photos you sent us," Nikolas told him. "He's going by the name Adam Woodward, and he's passing himself off as a UCLA student."

"Shit," David said. "Okay, let me run that name. I doubt he'd give her his real name, but you never know."

I stopped pacing. "How long?"

"Two hours at the most if there's anything to find," David replied. "I'll call you as soon as I know something."

I gripped the back of a chair and stared at the phone for a few seconds after he hung up, trying not to get my hopes up. If this turned out to be another dead end, I wasn't going to handle it well.

"You okay?" Nikolas asked.

I shook my head. "He was under our noses this whole time. Christ, he spent time with Beth. He got to know her before he took her. Why?"

"I don't think he'll hurt her."

Nikolas and I looked at Jordan.

"How do you know that?" Nikolas asked.

She cleared her throat. "The few times I saw him, he seemed really taken with Beth. I think... I think he took her because he likes her."

The metal in the chair buckled under my hands.

Nikolas looked at Jordan. "Contact everyone, and tell them to be ready to move on my word."

"On it," she said, almost running away.

He turned back to me. "You going to be able to hold it together?"

"I will for Beth."

"No one is better at this than David. Give him the time he asked for, and he'll find them."

I inhaled deeply and let it out. "Just promise me one thing. The demon is mine."

Nikolas nodded. "He's yours."

22

Beth

I rubbed at my ankle under the shackle. Even with padding, the thing started to chafe after a day, and I'd been wearing it for three now. The only time it came off was when Ree brought me my meals or to bathe, or when I was required to join Adam for dinner. The rest of the time, I was chained in my room. And they say romance is dead.

It was my own fault they'd put me back in the shackle, but I'd never regret the reason for it. During my second dinner with Adam, I'd managed to slip away through the door in the dining room that led to the kitchen. I'd had no idea where I was going, but I'd led my captors on a chase before they'd cornered me in a supply room.

Weston had caught me, but I'd managed to give him a kick to the groin he wouldn't soon forget. It didn't matter how big and strong a male was. He'd whimper like a little girl when you got him where it hurts. Needless to say, he stayed away from me after that.

Someone knocked softly on the door. I didn't bother to call out because they were coming in whether I wanted them to or not. Judging by how long it had been since Ree had delivered lunch, I figured it was time for dinner.

The door opened, and Ree entered, shutting it behind her. As she did every night, she carried a garment bag that contained whatever Adam had picked out for me to wear to dinner. He liked to dress me up in alluring outfits and pretend we were in some relationship that existed only in his fantasies.

"Hey, Ree."

I'd given up being cool to her by day three. Mox demons were so mild-natured and apologetic about everything that it was impossible to be mean to her. Besides, it wasn't as if my imprisonment was her fault.

She smiled and laid the garment bag on the foot of the bed. "Good evening, Beth. I hope you are well."

"As well as can be expected."

She came around the bed to unlock my shackle, and nodded in approval when she saw my empty lunch plate. Ree was a bit of a worrier, and she'd pleaded with me for two days about my refusal to eat. I'd been drinking water from the bathroom tap so I wouldn't die of thirst. But by day three, my body had started to suffer from my self-imposed starvation. I had a fast metabolism, which meant I needed a lot of nutrients.

It was Ree who'd convinced me I had to eat to keep up my strength. Not eating was the same as slowly killing myself, and I was no quitter. Someday, I'd get an opportunity to escape this place, and I needed to stay strong for that.

My food wasn't drugged, but I'd already learned Adam didn't need to drug me to get what he wanted.

Once I was free of my shackle, I went to shower. I returned to the bedroom to see what I was to wear tonight, and I came up short at the sight of an elegant pink cocktail dress laid out on the bed. It had short sleeves and a modest neckline, and the skirt came all the way to my knees when I put it on. It was nothing like the other dresses he'd sent me and looked more like what the other girls wore.

I studied my reflection. "This is different."

"You look lovely as always," Ree said as she handed me a pair of white shoes.

Slipping on the shoes, I sat in the room's only chair to await our escort to dinner. I watched Ree move around the room, tidying it efficiently, and I couldn't help but be curious about how she'd come to work in Adam's household.

I'd never thought much about the lives of demons like her until I met Sara, probably because I'd been trained to focus on the dangerous ones. Sara had a different way of looking at the world, which was one of the reasons I liked being around her so much.

"Where are you from, Ree? Where is your family?"

She straightened from making the bed and gave me a look of surprise. "You wish to know about me?"

"If you want to tell me."

"There is not much to say." She sat on the edge of the bed with her hands folded in her lap. "I was taken from my family by gulak slavers when I was fourteen. Master bought me, and I've been with him ever since."

She spoke so matter-of-factly, but I could see the trace of sadness in her eyes. How cruel to be taken from her family so young and sold into slavery.

"How long have you been with him?"

"Twenty years."

I pressed my lips together, angry on her behalf.

"Please, don't think I've had a bad life here. I miss my family, but Master has never mistreated me. I could have gone to an owner who was abusive and cruel."

"But you're a slave. You don't have the freedom to leave if you want to."

She shrugged. "I have decided to be content with my lot."

Her voice held a note of resignation, of one who had given up hoping for more out of life. In that moment, I resolved to never let Adam destroy my hope or my fighting spirit. It might take weeks or months or even years, but one day I'd be free again.

Pain lanced me when I thought about being away from Chris for that long. They said a bond could survive a long separation as long as both people wanted it. But did it weaken over time? If it took me years to make my way back to him, would he still want me, knowing who I'd been with that whole time?

"Don't be sad, Beth," Ree said softly. "Master will be a good mate to you."

A loud rap came on the door before I could tell her he would never be my mate, and she hurried to open it. Weston and another Incubus stood there, and there was no mistaking the satisfied expression on Weston's face when he looked at me. Something about it made my stomach knot with dread, and I suddenly didn't want to leave this room.

Weston motioned for me to come, and I complied despite my misgivings. Denying Adam my presence at dinner wasn't an option. I'd tried that on my second night here, and my Incubus guard had threatened to dress me himself and carry me to the dining room if I refused.

We walked down the hallway in our usual formation, with one guard in front of Ree and me and one taking up the rear. As we neared the drawing room, I expected to hear the now familiar murmur of feminine voices, but silence greeted me.

Weston walked past the empty drawing room and opened a door to an office decorated with old mahogany furniture and several Degas paintings. I was meeting Adam here?

I expected Weston to tell me to have a seat, but he went over to the paneled wall and pressed something I couldn't see. A door-sized panel separated from the wall, revealing a narrow stairwell.

A shiver of foreboding went through me as we descended the stairs and entered a short hallway with stone walls and lit by wall sconces. At the end of the hallway was a pair of heavy wooden doors. One of them was slightly ajar, and Weston opened it further, waving me inside.

It was like stepping back in time. I found myself in a sitting room with a stone fireplace on one end. Two chairs and a small sofa sat before the fire, and a large Persian rug covered the stone floor. Colorful tapestries adorned the walls in lieu of windows, and the only light came from the fireplace, a wall sconce, and the tapers on a table set for two.

The cold knot in my stomach grew bigger when I took in the table and the romantic lighting in the room. I knew without asking that we were in Adam's private quarters, and he'd planned an intimate evening for the two of us.

My heart sped up, and I wanted to flee this room. This whole setup told me Adam had decided to take things to the next level. Just the thought of what he might do terrified me.

"Beth, you look absolutely ravishing."

I looked away from the table to see Adam standing in the doorway that led to his bedroom. He was dressed in his usual dinner attire, minus the jacket, and I tried to brace myself for what would happen next.

Warmth flooded me, and my breath quickened as a familiar fluttering started up in my stomach. Adam smiled at me, and the pull to go to him was stronger than ever. My body trembled from fighting his intoxicating power, but I knew once I gave in, it was all over.

Every time I saw him, his influence was stronger than the day before. He was feeding me his power, and the only way to do that was through a kiss. Since I wouldn't willingly kiss him, he had to be coming to my room while I was asleep and doing it without waking me.

The idea that he was kissing me, possibly touching me, while I slept, made my stomach churn, but I was helpless to stop him. I couldn't stay awake twenty-four hours a day, and if I were able to do that, he'd probably go back to drugging me.

Adam took a step into the room and wavered like he was dizzy. He grabbed the doorjamb for support, and Weston immediately moved toward him.

"I'm fine," Adam told his son as he straightened.

Weston didn't look convinced. "Perhaps you should rest. You will need your strength for tomorrow."

Adam patted Weston's back fondly. "I'll be okay once I feed."

Icy tendrils slithered down my spine at his choice of words. He'd said "feed" instead of "eat," and that made me suddenly afraid I wasn't just his dinner companion. Was he planning to feed from me tonight? Because that would mean...

I nearly gagged on the panic and nausea rising up in my throat. Automatically, I took a step back and came up against the hard, unmoving chest of my other guard.

Adam spoke to Ree as if I hadn't just attempted to run.

"Ree, please, tell the kitchen we are ready for our meal."

"Yes, Master."

She bowed and hurried out, leaving me with Adam and my two guards—and a growing pit in my stomach.

"Beth, come sit with me," Adam said as he walked over to the sofa near the fire. He moved slower than normal, and he almost stumbled once.

The guard behind me gave me a not-so-subtle nudge when I didn't move. I forced my legs to cross the room and take a seat as far as I could from Adam on the sofa.

Being this near to him had my emotions in a tug of war. The part of me under his influence wanted to slide across the cushion to him. The rest of me was scanning the room for anything to use as a weapon if he tried to touch me.

Weston went to a side table and poured two glasses of red wine, which he carried over to us. I took mine to appear like I was going along with whatever this was, but I had no intention of drinking it. Something told me if I ever needed a clear head, it would be tonight. And I didn't put it past them to drug me.

Adam accepted his glass. "Thank you. You and Giles may leave now."

Weston frowned, and his gaze flitted to me.

"Are you sure, Father?"

"Yes. I want to spend time alone with Beth." Adam smiled at me. "I think she'll be more comfortable if it's just the two of us."

Weston hesitated, and Adam chuckled.

"I love your devotion, my son, but I think I'll be safe with her. It's not as if she can escape from down here."

"As you wish."

The two Incubi left, and the room was quiet except for the crackle of the fire. I swirled the wine in my glass as I waited for Adam to speak.

"Am I really so repugnant that you can't even look at me?"

I took a breath and lifted my eyes to meet his.

"Are you going to feed from me?"

His eyebrows shot up. "You don't beat around the bush, do you?"

"You didn't answer my question."

"And if I say yes?"

My body tensed, and I had to loosen my grip on the wine glass before I snapped the fragile stem. I tried without success to keep the quiver out of my voice. "You said you would never force me."

He sighed. "I didn't lie. I won't force you."

I let out a trembling breath.

The door opened, and two mox demons entered, carrying covered dishes. They laid the dishes on the table, bowed to us, and left, shutting the door behind them. I heard a scraping sound followed by an ominous click when the locks on the heavy door engaged.

Adam sniffed the air. "Prime rib, my favorite. Shall we eat?"

We went to the table and Adam pulled out my chair for me. I watched him closely as he removed the dish covers and took his seat. He was definitely moving slower, and some of his movements were a little jerky. He'd looked tired a few times in the last five days but nothing like this.

"Are you sick?"

He glanced up from cutting his meat. "No. I'm just a little drained at the moment."

"Drained?"

"You rely on your demon's strength, correct? Have you ever used up too much of it at once?"

I thought about the night I'd dived off the Golden Gate Bridge. "Yes."

"It's the same for me. I used up too much of my energy today, and now I need time to recover. I'll be good in a few hours."

I took a bite of prime rib while I thought about whether or not to ask my next question.

"How did you use up all your energy?"

Adam regarded me for a few seconds before he laid his fork on his plate and gave me his full attention. He looked like he was trying to decide if I was playing an angle or interested in knowing more about him.

"I told you I have to feed my girls daily before and during their pregnancies."

I nodded.

"The closer I get to breeding, I have to give them more of my energy to help them conceive."

I pretended to take a sip of wine to cover my revulsion. I wasn't sure if I managed to hide it, but his expression didn't change.

"Do you have more questions?" he asked. "I'm happy to answer them all."

"What happens tomorrow?"

His eyes grew darker. "I think you already know the answer to that question."

I said nothing as I set my glass down with a trembling hand. Now I knew why there had been no one in the drawing room tonight, and why he'd depleted so much of his energy. He had prepared them to breed with him tomorrow.

I also knew just by looking at him that he didn't have the strength to do that, not without replenishing his energy. I'd seen the hunger in his eyes when he'd entered the room, and it hadn't been for food. He needed to feed from a female, and it was either me or one of his slaves. I had a sick feeling I'd lost the draw, no matter what he'd said a few minutes ago.

"Your face is like an open book," Adam said softly, pulling my gaze back to him.

"Then I don't need to tell you what I'm thinking," I replied in a tight voice as I fought to keep my emotions in check.

"No."

He smiled and stood, coming around the table to me. Even in his weakened state, he was able to reach me before I could push back my chair. He took my hand in a firm but gentle grip, and I had no choice but to stand.

I found myself facing him, our bodies inches apart. Once again, the desire for him flared, stronger this time, and I swayed from the need to move closer to him. But more disturbing than the physical attraction was the emotional one. I knew it wasn't love, but his influence over me made it feel like it was.

My chest ached with a mix of yearning for Adam and devastation over my betrayal of Chris. How could I love Chris and have feelings for this monster? Nothing, no drug or magic or demon power, should be able to come between our love.

"Don't be afraid, love," Adam murmured.

He put his free hand on the back of my head and pulled me closer until our mouths met. Mine opened for him against my will, and he kissed me long and slow. Tears ran unchecked down my cheeks, and I tasted them on our joined lips. My Mori cried out and then shrank away as Adam breathed his energy into me. I was powerless to stop him. After a minute, I wasn't sure I wanted it to stop.

Adam broke the kiss and led me over to the sofa. I went, unresisting, and sat beside him.

He smiled at me, his eyes dark with lust. It should have frightened me, but I felt dazed. The world had taken on a surreal quality, as if this were only a dream I would wake from any second.

"You truly are breathtaking," he said huskily, running his fingers through my hair.

"No...force," I protested weakly.

"No force," he echoed before he kissed me again.

I felt his power flow into me, and a part of my brain registered that he wouldn't need to use force if he continued to feed me like this. The realization made me suck in a sharp breath, and I felt a burst of his power flow into me. Dully, I mused that he wasn't going to have the strength to do anything if he kept giving it to me.

I'm not sure if it was a conscious thought or pure survival instinct driving me. I put my hands on either side of his face and kissed him back until he was breathing heavier. Then I pushed him down until he was lying on the sofa with me half on top of him. He let out a low groan, and I knew I had him where I wanted him.

I inhaled deeply.

The first stream of power was stronger than I'd expected, and it left me lightheaded. I had to take a moment to adjust before I took more from him.

Adam's hand moved to my back, and I felt it at the top of my dress zipper. Panic warred with the sick desire for him his power created, and I drew more power into me.

Two inhales later, Adam's hand stilled.

I pretended not to notice and continued to kiss him as if nothing was wrong. I could feel his energy flowing through my body, strengthening me, as it was meant to. It was a heady sensation, and I felt disgust and exhilaration at the same time. I also felt an almost overwhelming need to give him anything he asked of me.

I sucked in another breath.

Adam broke the kiss, panting. "That's enough, love."

"More," I whispered, going in for another kiss.

"I said enough."

He gripped my shoulders to hold me away, and his arms shook from the effort. My eyes met his, and I saw disbelief then anger cross his face. He pushed me off him, and I tumbled to the floor.

The foreign power filling me made my body feel like it belonged to someone else, and it took me a few seconds to adjust to it. I crawled out of his reach and got to my feet in the center of the room. For a moment, the room spun, and then it felt like I was having the biggest adrenaline rush ever.

Adam sat up slowly and fixed me with a hard stare. "Come here."

I took two steps toward him before I was able to plant my feet. The urge to obey him was almost too much, and I made myself think of Chris to block it out.

"No."

His expression darkened. "Don't make me come to you."

It occurred to me then that he was just sitting there, something the Adam I'd gotten to know would not do. He was paler than normal, too, and the corners of his mouth were pinched.

"Beth, I have been very patient with you, but I think I've let my affection for you cloud my judgement."

I scoffed. "Affection? You don't care about anyone but yourself."

He pushed forward to sit on the edge of the sofa. "I love my children, and I would have come to love you."

I took a step back as he stood. He was steadier than I'd expected him to be, but his movements were slower, more deliberate. He was trying to hide how much I'd weakened him.

He started to walk toward me, and I automatically dropped into a fighting stance. That made him stop and stare at me.

"You would fight *me*?" His laugh was condescending. "I am over two hundred years old and the most powerful of my kind. You're young and weak and –"

"A warrior," I finished proudly. "And I would rather die fighting than let you touch me again."

His mouth curled into a sneer, and he gave up all pretense of being anything but the monster he was.

"I have no intension of killing you, but I will feed from you. I'll need my strength for the coming days, and your energy will sustain me. Don't worry. I promise you'll find it quite enjoyable."

I let my revulsion show. "I'll pass."

He resumed his advance on me. "You don't have a choice."

"We'll see," I shot back as we began to circle each other.

"You're in my lair, which is deep underground, highly secured, and has only one way out. Even if you somehow got away from me and out of my quarters, you wouldn't get within a hundred feet of the exit before one of my sons stopped you and brought you back to me. One way or another, I'll get what I want. I always do."

He was right about one thing. The odds of me escaping this place were almost nonexistent, and I'd given up on the hope of someone coming for me. But I refused to give in to the despair that had pressed down on me since I'd watched Chris ride away from here. And I'd promised myself I would not stop fighting until I had no strength left in me.

A log popped in the fireplace. Startled, Adam swung his head in that direction.

I moved in and sent my fist into his jaw. His head snapped back, and he staggered under the force of the blow.

I stared at my hands, more stunned than he was by the speed and strength of my strike. My eyes met his, which were narrowed in surprise and fury.

He recovered quickly and came at me. I wasn't fast enough to block the attack, and he wrapped his strong hands around my throat in a crushing choke hold.

I panicked for a few seconds as my air was cut off. Then years of training kicked in, and I rammed my hand into his throat just above his sternum. He gasped and loosened his hold on me, and I sent a side kick into his stomach. He stumbled back, and I sucked in precious air.

My throat burned from his bruising grip, but I forgot all about that when I saw Adam's face. His irises had gone completely black and his lips were pulled back in a snarl.

He lunged and hit me hard in the side, sending me into the nearest wall. The air was knocked from me, and I crashed into a small table, sending me and a vase of flowers to the floor.

I cried out as shards of glass cut into my hands and knees. Before I could stand, Adam's hands were in my hair, roughly dragging me backward.

I twisted my body, ignoring the searing pain in my scalp, and tackled him around the waist. He let go of my hair as we went down, and I managed to roll out of his reach. I came to my feet a little unsteadily but faster than he did.

"You're only making this harder on yourself," he said when we faced off again. "I would have made the experience good for you. The more you fight me, the less you are going to enjoy it."

I would have laughed if my ribs weren't hurting so much. I feared he'd cracked one of them with his last hit. He wasn't a skilled fighter, but he had enough strength left in him to slowly beat me down. A few more strikes like that, and it would be all over for me.

His tone softened. "I can see you're hurting, Beth. Stop this, and I'll have someone see to your injuries."

I gritted my teeth. "No."

253

"So be it."

He moved quickly, taking me to the floor. The impact sent pain radiating through my chest, and I gasped for air as he straddled me. Tears of pain and desperation burned my eyes as I tried in vain to buck him off.

He smiled victoriously and grabbed the neckline of my dress. My heart pounded in my ears as terror consumed me. Unable to throw him off, I pulled his head down and butted it hard with mine. It should have hurt, but I was past feeling pain.

I rolled, and he fell facedown on the floor. As soon as I was free, I was on his back with my arm wrapped around his throat, and I held on with every ounce of strength in me.

Someone was screaming, and it took me several seconds to realize it was me. I couldn't stop. I had five days of fear and degradation and helplessness built up inside me, and I screamed it all out. My throat felt raw and my lungs burned, and still, I screamed.

I don't know how long we stayed locked in that position, or when it registered that Adam was no longer moving. Panting, I let him go and rolled to my knees beside him. His head was turned at an awkward angle, telling me I'd broken his neck. His eyes were closed, but I could see the slight rise and fall of his chest as he breathed. A broken neck wouldn't kill him. The only ways to kill an Incubus were silver through the heart, fire, or beheading.

I raised my head and desperately looked around the room. I would find no silver in a demon's lair, and there was no sword to behead him. My eyes fell on the fireplace, and I frantically tried to think of the best way to burn him without burning the place down around me.

That was when I saw it.

I forced myself up and went to pick up the cast iron ash shovel hanging beside the fireplace. Hefting the heavy shovel, I staggered back to Adam to finish what I had started.

As soon as my gruesome job was done, I dropped the bloody shovel and fell to my knees. My stomach revolted, and I threw up until I was dry heaving. Cold enveloped me, and I somehow knew I was going into shock.

I had no strength left to stand, but I had to get as far away as I could from the corpse. I crawled to the corner near the fireplace and huddled with my knees up to my chest. It was a little warmer there, and the couch hid the gory scene from me.

The Lilin was dead by my hand, and he could never again hurt another girl. I rejoiced in that, even though I knew I hadn't saved myself or the girls he'd taken. His sons would come to check on him, and when they did, they'd kill me. They idolized their father. My death would not be a slow or painless one.

Minutes passed, or maybe it was hours, before I heard the first pounding on the door. It was locked, but it wouldn't take long for them to break through.

I pressed my forehead to my knees. Closing my eyes, I barred all thoughts except those of Chris from my mind. And I waited.

23

Chris

"Where is she?" I roared at the Incubus I held by the throat against the wall.

Around us, the bodies of his brethren littered the hallway, but the Incubus showed no fear. He smirked through bloody teeth and let out a rattling laugh.

"Too...late," he rasped.

I rammed my knife into his chest so hard it pinned him to the wall.

"Chris."

Sara's voice cut through the bloodlust consuming me. I ran toward her, barely seeing the faces of the warriors I passed. All I could think about was Beth. I could sense her nearby, but I couldn't locate her. Her presence felt muted, and I was terrified of what that meant. She could be dying, and I couldn't find her to help her.

I found Sara and Nikolas in an office, standing before an open section of wall that led to a set of stairs leading down. I moved past them and raced down the stairs with them close on my heels.

I emerged in a dimly-lit hallway with a set of doors on the other end, and I knew without asking that this was the Lilin's private quarters. We hadn't found him since we'd stormed his lair, and my gut told me he was holed up down here. And he had Beth.

The thought of what he could be doing to her made me almost blind with rage. I hit the doors with the force of a truck, but I didn't even put a crack in them.

"Beth," I bellowed, shoving at the doors with all of my might.

Sara ran up to me. "Stop. You'll hurt yourself."

"She's in there," I snarled, my voice barely recognizable as my Mori came closer to the surface.

"It's warded." Sara waved me away and placed her hand on one of the doors. Blue sparks crackled over the surface of the wood, and there was a blinding white flash as her power obliterated the warlock magic protecting the door.

Solmi, my Mori growled when I felt Beth's presence strong and clear. She was alive and behind this door.

I rammed the door hard with my shoulder, and it cracked under the assault. A second hit and it crashed inward.

The first thing I saw was the body in the center of the room. The head had been hacked off with what looked like a fireplace shovel, and the rug beneath the body was soaked with black demon blood.

"Beth," I shouted, seeing no sign of her.

My eyes fell on the bed visible through the open door of the bedroom, and I nearly choked on the fear of what I would find in that room.

I was halfway across the sitting room when a tiny whimper stopped me cold. I looked toward the sound, and crimson bled into my vision when I saw Beth's bloody and bruised body huddled in a corner. She was barefoot, and the pink dress she wore was ripped and bloody.

Blood roared in my ears as the last of the control I'd been holding onto for days finally slipped. My vision tunneled until all I could see was my mate, looking small and broken on the floor.

Beth's head lifted slowly. Through the curtain of her blonde hair, her tortured gray eyes met mine. A wave of pain came across our bond, pushing through the red haze in my mind. My mate needed me.

I knelt in front of her. My focus never left her, but I was aware of every sound behind me. My body thrummed with feral rage, and I'd kill anyone who came near us.

Neither of us moved or spoke for a long moment. Then she reached out with one hand and touched my face as if she wasn't sure I was real. I placed my shaking hand over hers, holding it against my cheek and letting her touch soothe the beast clawing to break free. For the first time in five days, the unbearable tightness in my chest began to lessen, and I could breathe again.

"Beth," I whispered hoarsely.

Her eyes brimmed with tears that spilled over and left trails through the black blood on her face. She stared at me, silently pleading for what she was unable to put into words.

Letting go of her hand, I sat on the floor and lifted her into my arms. She curled into a tight ball with her face buried against my chest. A single ragged sob escaped her as I wrapped my body protectively around her, and the anguished sound sliced my heart to ribbons.

"I'm here, Dove," I said, my voice hoarse with emotion. "I've got you."

I could hear low voices and movement in the room, but all of my attention was focused on Beth. Nothing else mattered to me. I had no idea what she'd gone through down here, or what lasting effects it would have on her. My sole purpose in life now was to do or be whatever she needed to help her recover. I'd start by taking her away from this hellish place.

Standing with Beth in my arms, I walked to the door where Nikolas stood talking to Sara and Rachel. Rachel put a hand to her mouth to cover her gasp when she saw Beth, and Sara looked like she was trying hard not to cry.

"I'm taking her home," I whispered, not wanting to startle Beth.

Nikolas nodded. He and Sara would stay here and oversee the care of the human girls and the demon slaves we'd recovered. Margot was most likely with them now, and then they'd need to be returned to their families. There were more than enough warriors here to handle that. My only concern was Beth.

"I'm coming with you," Rachel said softly.

We made our way upstairs. Warriors moved out of our way and cast worried looks at Beth as I carried her through the large underground structure. She kept her face pressed to my chest, and I was glad she didn't have to see the blood or the dead Incubi littering the hallway from our short and violent attack on the lair. She'd been through enough tonight.

I climbed the final set of stairs to the exit, a carefully concealed trapdoor in the floor of a utility shed at the back of the Bel Air property. My jaw clenched as I walked through the trees and the house came into view. It gutted me to know I'd been here four days ago, and the whole time, Beth had been a few hundred feet away.

Once Jordan had identified the Lilin, it hadn't taken David long to find out that Henry Durham, who owned this property, supposedly had a grandson named Adam Woodward. That had been all we needed to convince us to come back for a second look at the place.

It was Sara who had suggested that the reason we didn't find anything the first time was because the Lilin might be using warlock glamours. She'd stayed in the house on our first visit, but this time, she'd walked the entire property. She was the one who had discovered the trapdoor in the shed and had neutralized the powerful glamour hiding it.

I'd never be able to repay my cousin for what she'd done here tonight. She would say we're family and she was glad she could help, but she'd given me back my mate. There was no gift more precious than that.

My mother was waiting for us in the driveway with a set of keys in her hand. She gave Beth a tender look and led us to an SUV at the bottom of the driveway. Rachel opened the back door for me, and I climbed in, settling Beth on my lap. The two women took the front, neither saying much as my mother drove us back to the command center.

Beth still hadn't uttered a word by the time we arrived at the house, and her silence scared me. Killing a demon wouldn't upset her. Something far worse had traumatized her, and I couldn't bring myself to think about what had put her in this fragile state.

The women took over as soon as I carried Beth to her bedroom.

"Rachel and I will bathe her and check her for injuries," my mother said when I sat on the bed with Beth in my arms.

"I won't leave her."

I gazed down at the girl I'd feared I would never hold again, and I didn't think I'd ever be able to let her go.

My mother laid a gentle hand on my shoulder, and I looked up into her warm eyes.

"Christian, I know you two need each other, but it's important that we understand the extent of her injuries. You have to let us tend to her."

The meaning in her words sent a knife straight through my chest, and I could only nod helplessly. My protective instincts were riding me hard, and it took a Herculean effort to stand and place Beth in my mother's capable arms.

Rachel ushered me out of the room and shut the door. A few minutes later, I heard water running in the bathroom and the soft murmur of voices.

I didn't move from my spot by the door. The longer I waited, the more my mind replayed images of the scene in the Lilin's quarters and tortured me with thoughts of what might have happened down there.

My hands clenched and unclenched, wanting to rip apart the demon that had hurt my mate. But Beth had dealt out her own justice on the Lilin. I couldn't conceive of how a new warrior had been able to kill such a powerful demon with nothing but a tiny shovel. People were capable of seemingly impossible feats when they were pushed to their limit, and I was afraid what had happened to push Beth to hers.

I was seconds away from knocking on the bedroom door when it finally opened. My mother stepped out and shut it gently behind her. I tried to read her expression to be prepared for what she was going to tell me, but I was too wound up to think clearly.

"She has some cuts and bruises, but otherwise she's unharmed," she said, placing emphasis on the last word.

I sagged against the wall as relief coursed through me. It was a minute before I could speak. "She's talking?"

My mother smiled. "A little. She's going to be okay."

"When can I go in?" I asked roughly.

"In a few minutes. You should use that time to clean up. At least, change out of those clothes."

I looked down at my black-stained shirt and jeans. I didn't want to spend a minute away from Beth, but I couldn't go to her like this.

"My duffle bag is in her room. Can you get it for me?"

My mother went inside and returned with my bag. I used Mason's bathroom to shower, and I was back at Beth's door just as it opened again and Rachel came out, followed by my mother.

"She's asking for you," Rachel said quietly.

I entered the room, and my eyes immediately found Beth lying in the middle of her bed. Her eyes tracked me as I crossed the room and sat on the edge of the bed. Anger boiled in me when I saw the bruises forming on her jaw, but I pushed it down. The last thing she needed now was to see me getting upset.

I wasn't sure what she needed from me, so I took one of her hands in mine. "Are you in pain?"

"No," she whispered. "Will you hold me?"

I lifted the comforter and slid in beside her. I lay on my side facing her, and she came into my arms with her head tucked under my chin. Closing my eyes, I struggled with the sudden onset of emotion at having her safe and in my arms.

Over and over, I found myself thinking about what she must have endured the last five days. Captivity, even for a short time, took a mental toll on a person, even a warrior. Beth's physical injuries would be gone long before she recovered emotionally from her ordeal.

"Chris."

I kissed the top of her head. "Yes."

"I love you."

"I love you, too, Dove."

I rubbed soothing circles on her back, and she let out a little sigh.

"At night...I imagined you holding me like this," she whispered.

A lump lodged in my throat. "You'll never have to imagine it again."

She fell asleep a short while later, but I lay awake for a long time, not willing to give up a second of feeling her beside me. The sky outside was turning pink when I finally gave in to my exhaustion and joined her in sleep.

Beth

"How can you say no to a boot sale, Beth?" Jordan demanded incredulously. "You love boots more than I do, if that's even possible."

I tucked my feet beneath me on the couch and lifted a shoulder. "I'm just not in the mood to shop."

Her gasp was a tad melodramatic. "Okay, who are you, and what have you done with my BFF?"

Mason chuckled from the other end of the couch where he was eating his way through his second bowl of popcorn. We were having a movie day, and I'd let him choose the movies. We'd just finished *Blue Crush*, and we were starting *Point Break*. Surfer movies weren't really my thing, but I had to admit, it didn't get much better than Keanu Reeves and Patrick Swayze.

Chris was supposed to be here with us, but he'd left two hours ago to meet with Nikolas about something. Not that I minded. He'd been pretty much glued to my side since I came home a week ago, and he could probably use some guy time.

Things had been quiet here since the Lilin was killed. Most of the warriors who had come to Los Angeles to join in the hunt had left, including Chris's parents and Rachel. Slowly, life for everyone at the command center had gone back to the way it was before the Lilin had arrived in town. Well, for almost everyone.

I was finding it a little harder to get back into a normal routine. My injuries had healed after a day, but I was off active duty for a month. Council's orders. Chris was on leave, too, and we spent our days training and hanging out together. At night, he slept in my bed, but all he did was hold me. I wished he'd kiss me again, but I didn't know how to tell him that.

I'd told him some of what had happened in the Lilin's lair, but I hadn't been able to bring myself to talk about Adam's plans for me or my last night there. I didn't know how to tell him about Adam feeding me his power, or the attraction for him that had grown stronger every day. How did I tell the man I loved that I hadn't been strong enough to stop myself from having feelings for another male? That I'd kissed another male? Just thinking about it made me want to throw up.

Chris never pressured me to talk about my ordeal. He told me we had all the time in the world, and he was here when I was ready. The Council wanted to know the details of the Lilin's death, but Chris had asked Lord Tristan to get them to back off. The demon was dead, the girls were all safely back with their families, and the threat was over. He told them they'd have to be content with that for now.

"Are you even listening to me?"

I gave Jordan a sheepish smile for having zoned out on her. I'd been doing that a lot lately. "Sorry. What were you saying?"

She huffed. "I said if you don't go, I'll have to drag Sara with me, and you know how much fun she is to shop with."

Mason snorted, and Jordan smacked him on the back of the head.

"Keep that up and I'll make you go with me."

The door opened, cutting off Mason's retort, and Chris entered the guest-house. He came over to me and surprised me by taking my hands and pulling me to my feet.

"What's up?" I asked, puzzled by his actions.

He smiled. "How would you like to go on a little trip?"

My stomach fluttered with excitement. "Where?"

"It's a little place by the ocean. My parents have a house there." He brushed my hair back over my shoulder. "Unless you'd rather stay here."

"No," I said quickly, already imagining Chris and me alone in a house by the ocean.

His smile widened. "Good. Go pack. We're leaving in an hour."

I hurried to my bedroom and stopped in the doorway to turn back to him. "Do I need to dress for warm or cold weather?"

He thought for a moment. "Colder than here."

I waited for him to say more. When he didn't, I frowned. "Are you going to tell me where we're going?"

"Nope," he said with a mischievous little grin.

Jordan helped me pack, and an hour later, Chris drove us to a private hangar at LAX where one of the Mohiri jets was waiting for us. We took off, and I still had no idea where we were headed, even after we'd stopped in Chicago to refuel. All I knew for sure was that we were heading east.

It was early morning when the plane began to descend. We landed at a small airport, and the first thing I noticed as the plane taxied to a hangar was the Canadian flag. It took me a few seconds to recognize the second flag from my world studies.

I turned to Chris and found him watching me with the same pleased smile in place.

"Your parents have a house in Newfoundland?"

I'd always wanted to visit Canada, but I'd thought I would start out west, maybe go hiking in the Rockies. I didn't know that much about the East Coast, but now that I was here, I was eager to explore it.

"They bought it years ago, and they used to visit around once a year. But they haven't been back since they moved to Germany. It's a great place, and a local couple takes care of it for them."

His brow creased with uncertainty. "I thought you might like a change of pace, but if you'd rather go somewhere else, we can."

I smiled and grabbed his hand. "No. I can't wait to see it."

Instead of the usual SUV, there was a black truck waiting for us. Chris stowed our bags in the back of the large double cab, and we set out.

It was barely dawn when we drove through the city. Chris had been here before so he pointed out places of interest we could visit while we were here. When he said there were over two hundred miles of coastal trails for hiking and walking, I could barely sit still. He laughed and told me he thought I'd like that.

We left the city and drove through several small towns before Chris turned onto a gravel driveway. He stopped in front of a white two-story house overlooking the ocean. The house was hidden from the road by trees, and the view was breathtaking.

I got out of the truck and inhaled deeply of the cold ocean air. The breeze was chilly, but the morning sun felt good on my face.

"What do you think?"

"It's beautiful," I breathed, intrigued by some peculiar little black and white birds skimming across the water. I couldn't tell if they were swimming or flying.

He put an arm around me and pulled me close for a quick hug. "Come on. I want to show you the house."

Grabbing our bags from the truck, he went ahead of me to unlock the front door. I expected to enter a cold house, and I was pleasantly surprised to find it toasty warm inside.

"I called the caretakers yesterday and asked them to get the place ready for us," Chris explained as we walked through a big eat-in kitchen. "They stocked the fridge and pantry for us, too."

The living room was nice, and its best feature was the large window over-looking the ocean. There was a fireplace we could use, though the house was heated by a furnace in the basement.

Upstairs, there were three bedrooms and a single bathroom. I wondered aloud how a whole family could get by with one bathroom.

Chris laughed. "Times were different back when this house was built."

He entered the largest bedroom and laid our bags on the queen-size bed. It was covered with a colorful patchwork quilt that had to be handmade.

My stomach did a little flip at the thought of sleeping in this bed with Chris. I didn't know why I was nervous, considering I'd been sharing a bed with him for a week. But something about our trip and this room felt different, more intimate.

To hide my sudden shyness, I walked over to the window, which also looked out over the water. The original owners had really capitalized on the location when they built the house.

"How did your parents find this place?" I asked Chris without looking away from the window.

"They took a trip to the island, and they loved it so much they hired someone to find them a house. My mother would have been happy to stay, but there's not much work for a warrior here."

"I guess not."

I'd learned about the island in my studies. It was one of the few places on Earth that was considered Fae territory. No one knew why the faeries had claimed it as their own, but it had been that way for as long as anyone could remember. They seemed to tolerate our people in small numbers, but no vampire would dare set foot on the island.

Chris joined me at the window. "Do you like the house?"

"I love it." I faced him. "Can we take a look around?"

"We can do anything you want. But first, I'm going to make us some breakfast."

He took my hand in his, and we went downstairs. Chris cooked while I tried the delicious homemade bread and jam provided by the caretakers. I made a note to thank them and let them know how much I'd enjoyed it.

After our meal, we set out on foot to explore the town. The sky was partially overcast, but the sun managed to break through enough to make it a beautiful day. It could have been raining, and I wouldn't have cared as long as I was with Chris.

Living in Los Angeles, I'd gotten used to how strangers avoided interacting with each other in public. It shocked me when most people we passed here called out a greeting. I mentioned it to Chris, and he laughed at my amazement that people could be so friendly.

At noon, we stopped into a quaint little coffee shop for lunch, and Chris teased me about all the baked treats I consumed.

"All this fresh air makes me hungry," I said after I'd eaten two of the little chocolate-covered peanut butter balls. "These are so yummy. You should try one."

His eyes sparkled with laughter. "I will if there are any left when you're done."

When we finished our walking tour of the town, we headed back to the house. We made dinner together, and then we went down to the beach where someone had created a fire pit out of rocks. Chris got a fire going and sat with his back to a small boulder, tugging me down to sit between his legs.

I leaned back against him and sighed happily. This place was far removed from California and all that had happened, and I could feel it working its healing magic on me. "It's so peaceful here."

"We can stay here as long as you want."

I tilted my head to look up at him. "On the beach or the island?"

"Whatever you want."

He lowered his head, and my breath hitched in anticipation of his kiss. Disappointment washed over me when he playfully kissed the tip of my nose. It was sweet and affectionate, like everything else he did for me, but it wasn't enough. I wanted him to kiss me like he used to, like he couldn't get enough of me.

I stared at the fire again without seeing it. What if Chris didn't want me that way anymore? I knew he loved me and he was even more protective of me now, but I was afraid he no longer desired me. I'd been with the Lilin for almost a week. What if that had changed how Chris saw me?

The fire died down, and Chris stood, helping me up. Hand in hand, we walked back to the house and up to the bedroom we were sharing. I brushed my teeth and then changed into my sleep clothes while he was in the bathroom. It was our nightly routine now.

When he came back to the bedroom, I was already in bed, waiting for him. He turned off the light and got in beside me. Wordlessly, he opened his arms, and I went into them.

"Love you," he said.

"Love you back."

I closed my eyes and let the steady sound of his breathing lull me to sleep.

Chris and I spent the next few days exploring the surrounding towns, getting to know the locals, and not taking life too seriously for once. When you are constantly protecting humans from the bad guys, it's easy to forget there is a lot more good than evil in the world. Sometimes, you just need to get away from it all to understand that.

When the caretaker heard how much I loved her bread, a new loaf arrived every morning, along with another bottle of what she called bakeapple jam. She laughingly informed me that a bakeapple was a berry, not an apple, and she offered to give me some to take back with me. She looked insulted when I wanted to pay for it, so I didn't bring it up again.

Every night after dinner, we went down to the beach to sit by the fire. We talked, but only about things we'd done that day or our plans for the next one. Neither of us mentioned what had happened to me, but I could tell Chris was waiting for me to talk about it. On our third night there, I finally found the courage to open up to him.

"He wanted to keep me...as a mate," I said, never taking my eyes off the fire.

I felt Chris stiffen behind me, but he stayed silent, waiting for me to continue.

"I told him I had a mate, but he knew we'd never..." I cleared my throat. "He didn't care that I loved you. He said I'd forget you eventually."

Chris's chest rumbled angrily against my back.

"I could never forget you," I whispered.

His arms tightened around me, and he leaned down to press his cheek to mine. "I know."

I took a deep breath. I had already told him I'd been locked in my room most of the time and that I'd mostly seen Adam at dinner with the other girls. Now that the time had come to tell him the rest, I couldn't seem to find the right words.

Chris rubbed my arms. "You don't have to talk about it if you're not ready."

I took hold of his hands and drew his arms around me again.

"Adam – the Lilin," I amended, because Chris hated to hear me call him by name. "He thought he could use his power to make me love him like the human girls did. He...came to my room when I was asleep and fed his energy to me."

Chris swore, and I could feel his fury simmering beneath the surface. I tensed, waiting for him to stand and move away from me, but he stayed where he was.

"He couldn't make me love him, but I started to..." I couldn't say it. I couldn't hurt him like that.

"You felt a physical attraction," Chris said tenderly.

I nodded stiffly, and he kissed my temple.

"You have nothing to be ashamed of. You were under the influence of a powerful demon."

My eyes filled with angry tears. "It shouldn't have mattered how strong he was. He never should have been able to make me feel those things for him. How can you even touch me, knowing I let him do that to me?"

Chris lifted me and sat me sideways on his lap. I couldn't look at him, so he turned my face toward his. The light from the fire showed me the fierce love shining in his eyes.

"You did not let him do that. He forced it on you."

"But –"

"No buts. A Lilin's power is designed to manipulate emotions, the same way a Master could make you believe whatever they want. They're predators, Dove. I'd be just as susceptible to a Master as you were to the Lilin. Maybe more. Would you think less of me if that happened?"

I sniffled. "No."

His thumb swiped at the wetness on my cheek. "Is this why you didn't want to talk about what happened? You thought it would change how I felt about you?"

I averted my eyes, not wanting to see his disappointment. "Yes."

He pulled me against his chest, and I laid my head on his shoulder.

"I love you, Beth, and nothing will ever change that. Tell me you believe me."

I sighed, feeling lighter and happier than I'd been in almost two weeks. "I believe you."

Chris

Beth relaxed against me. She hadn't been herself since the night I brought her home, and everyone I'd talked to had said she just needed time and love. I'd give her whatever she needed for however long she needed it.

It killed me to know what she'd been going through because of that bastard. He'd messed with her mind and made her believe she'd done something wrong, that she was unworthy of my love. I wanted to bring him back to life so I could be the one to kill him.

She hadn't told me about the night she'd killed the Lilin, but she would when she was ready. It was enough that she'd been able to open up to me about what she was feeling.

I held her close and looked out over the water that sparkled under the full moon. When my mother had suggested this house for a getaway, she'd confided she had always thought there was something magical about the island. Seeing the light come back into Beth's eyes over the last few days, I was starting to believe my mother was right.

Beth lifted her head and looked at me before she leaned in and brushed my lips with hers. It was the first time she'd initiated a kiss since she'd come home, and my breath stalled as I waited to see what she would do next.

She placed her hands on my shoulders and slanted her mouth against mine. I opened to her, letting her take the lead, and nearly lost my mind at the first swipe of her tongue against mine. Fire ignited in my blood, and I stifled a groan when she raked her fingers through my hair and held my head in place as she kissed me slowly and thoroughly.

I protested when her mouth left mine, and she let out a sexy little laugh as she trailed kisses along my jaw. When her tongue traced the shell of my ear, it was all I could do to sit still. I wanted nothing else but to lay her down on this beach and worship every inch of her body.

Hot breath washed over my ear, and the world stopped when she said, "I need…"

"What do you need?" I asked huskily.

"You," she whispered.

I cradled her face in my hands and looked into her beautiful gray eyes. "You have me."

Her teeth tugged at her bottom lip, and her eyes filled with uncertainty. I grazed her lip with my thumb and felt her tremble.

"What is it, Dove?"

"I want to…" She glanced away self-consciously. "I don't know how to make it good for you."

Make it good for me? I stared at her profile for a moment before her words sank in. She was trying to seduce me.

My chest expanded, and I could barely keep the grin off my face. God, I loved this woman.

"It's good because it's you," I said, wishing she'd look at me and see the truth in my eyes.

"I know we have the bond, but you're used to experienced women, and I've never –"

"Stop." I captured her chin with my hand and gently forced her to face me again. "I'm glad you have no experience because it means I am the only man you'll ever have. You may not have noticed it, but I'm a little possessive when it comes to you."

She gave me a small smile. "I might have noticed that."

"Good."

I stood with her in my arms and set her on her feet so I could douse the fire. She laughed when I swung her into my arms again and started walking to the house.

"I can walk, you know," she protested half-heartedly.

"Where's the fun in that?"

I entered the house and carried her straight to our bedroom. When I looked at the bed, I was surprised to suddenly feel nervous. I'd imagined this moment so many times, and I wanted to make it perfect for her.

Setting her on the edge of the bed, I knelt on the floor between her legs, putting my face level with hers. I reached behind her and freed her hair from its ponytail, letting it fall in soft waves around her shoulders. Moonlight poured in through the open curtain, bathing her in a soft glow and making her blonde hair gleam like white gold.

"What?" she asked hesitantly, making me realize I'd been staring at her.

"You are so beautiful."

I put a hand on the back of her head and pulled her toward me as I leaned in to taste her sweet mouth again. She met me eagerly, and what started as tender soon became hungry and urgent. Without breaking the kiss, I removed her coat and then my own. I had her shirt unbuttoned before I pulled back, panting.

"Am I going too fast?"

Her answer was to grab the bottom of my thin sweater. I raised my arms, and she pulled it over my head, throwing it somewhere behind me. I smiled and returned the favor, freeing her from her shirt. Nudging her chin up with my nose, I gained access to her throat and leisurely tasted every inch of her skin down to the swell of her breasts. The sight of them rising and falling with each quick breath nearly undid me, but I forced myself to stop and make sure she was still with me.

"Beth?"

"Don't stop," she said in a low throaty voice that sent a bolt of raw lust through me.

I pressed light kisses above the cups of her delicate satin bra as my fingers found the tiny clasp at the front. My heart raced like it was my first time when I moved the cups aside and bared her to me.

"Perfection," I whispered roughly as I dipped my head again.

Her fingers dug into my shoulders, and I almost growled with satisfaction to be the first – and the only – male to know her body and to give her pleasure.

Lifting my head, I met her heavy-lidded eyes. I gently pushed her down on the bed, and she looked up at me with so much love and trust that I suddenly found it hard to breathe.

I kept my gaze locked with hers as I removed her short boots then unbuttoned her jeans and eased them over her hips and down her long legs. Reverently, I ran my hands from her ankles to her thighs and hooked my thumbs in the top of her panties.

She let out a small gasp. "Wait."

My hands stilled.

"I want to see you."

I smiled and stood, my hands going to the button of my jeans as I kicked off my boots. She rubbed her lips together nervously, and I expected her to look away. But her eyes followed the journey of my hands as I unfastened my jeans and pushed them down. I stepped out of them and watched her for any sign she wanted me to stop. Seeing none, I lost my last piece of clothing and stood there as her gaze moved over me like a caress.

"Can a male be beautiful, too?" she asked when her eyes settled on my face again. "Because that's what you are."

I leaned over her, bracing my arms on either side of her head.

"I'll be whatever you want," I murmured as she pulled me down for another searing kiss.

Mine, Solmi, mine, my Mori chanted impatiently as my mouth left hers, and I began a slow, thorough exploration of her body. I took my time, learning every curve and hollow, and reveling in each breathy moan I drew from her. I could have spent hours just adoring her and bringing her pleasure.

"Chris," she said thickly.

I looked up to see tears shimmering in her eyes. "What's wrong?"

"I'm so happy."

I gave her a wicked little smile. "And I plan to make you happy every night for the rest of our lives."

She laughed and wiped her eyes. "As long as I can make you happy, too."

"I don't think that will be a problem." I shifted my body, and desire flared in her eyes again.

"Chris," she whispered.

"Yes, Dove?"

"My Mori is going crazy. Is that normal?"

"Mine, too. They'll calm down soon."

I settled my body over hers and lowered my head to trail kisses over her face. When my mouth covered hers again, she responded with a hunger that rivaled my own. Her eyes locked with mine as I made love to her, and I knew that no matter how long I lived, I'd never see anything as beautiful as she was in the moment our Mori joined forever.

It was sometime in the wee hours of the morning when we finally curled up together under the covers, sated and content. Beth lay with her back to my chest and her head on my arm. Her fingers toyed with my hand that lay against her stomach.

"Can't sleep?" I asked her.

"I can't stop thinking. I keep expecting to wake up and find out this was all a dream."

I nipped her bare shoulder with my teeth, and she sucked in a sharp breath. "Does that feel like a dream?" I asked, pressing my lips to her soft skin.

She rolled over to face me, her hair falling over her shoulder in wild disarray and her face still glowing from hours of lovemaking. My body stirred again, and I knew I'd never get enough of her.

She gave me a sexy little smile as her hand traveled down my chest and stomach, eliciting a growl from me.

"No, this feels very real," she murmured.

"You're insatiable."

Her lips grazed my jaw. "And you're mine."

I lowered my head enough for our lips to meet. "Say it again."

"You. Are. Mine." She punctuated each word with a kiss. Then she pushed me onto my back and rose up on one elbow.

I think I'm a little possessive about you, too.

I grinned and pulled her mouth down to mine.

I'm all yours.

EPILOGUE

Beth

O*ne year later*
    "How much you want to bet she runs him down before this is over?"

I laughed and elbowed Chris in the side. "That's not nice. And she's doing much better than yesterday."

"Ow! I'm just calling it as I see it."

"You're terrible. And you're going to lose because he's too fast to get run over."

I turned my gaze back to Sara, who was slowly navigating the long driveway on her new Ducati Monster. Nikolas had bought her the smaller, lightweight model months ago, but he hadn't wanted to risk teaching her to ride in the city. He'd had it shipped home to Westhorne for when they finished up in New York. Sara was eager to learn to ride, but I didn't think Nikolas was enjoying it as much. He was beside her the second the bike wobbled even a tiny bit. I had to admit, it was fun to watch the two of them.

Chris moved behind me and tugged me back against him. Trapping me in the circle of his arms, he nuzzled my neck beneath my ear, making it hard to pay attention to anything but him.

"What do I get when I win?" he asked against my ear.

"Um..."

For a moment, I completely forgot what I wanted to say. It amazed me that he could still render me speechless after a year together.

"No fair. You know I can't think when you do that."

His husky laugh made my knees weak.

"Okay. If I win, you have to polish all my weapons tonight."

I shrugged. Polishing blades was easy enough.

"And if I win, you can wash the Harley."

"Deal." He nipped at my ear lobe. *Did I mention, there are no clothes allowed?*

I rolled my eyes. *You have a one-track mind.*

A shout and a string of Russian pulled us from our little bubble. I looked for our friends and found Nikolas rubbing his shin and wearing a pained expression. Sara was beside him on her bike, and her words carried to us.

"Sorry! Did that hurt?"

Laughter rumbled from Chris's chest, and I couldn't help but join in. Our mirth earned us a dark look from Nikolas, which only made us laugh harder.

When I'd first met Nikolas, that scowl would have made me want to run and hide. After a year working and living with him and Sara, he was more like a big brother than the legendary warrior who used to intimidate the crap out of me.

Chris and I had gone back to California after two amazing weeks in Newfoundland, but only to pack our things. Los Angeles didn't hold the same appeal for me anymore, so we'd talked about it and decided to join Sara and Nikolas in New York. Nikolas had been glad for our help with the new command center, and the four of us had quickly become a tight-knit group.

I still saw Mason, although not as much as I would like. After Raoul took over the Los Angeles command center, Mason had decided to stay there. He loved the beach, and he got lots of fighting action once things went back to normal after the Lilin died. His and Brock's bromance was still going strong, and the two of them were planning a trip to Hawaii to catch some "real waves."

"Whenever you're ready to polish my weapons, let me know," Chris said suggestively.

"Is that what we're calling it now?"

I grinned at Jordan as she strolled toward us. I missed having her around all the time. She had spent Christmas with us in New York, but she'd told me she was a California girl at heart. She thrived on the nightlife and the fighting, and every week we heard a new story about her latest escapade. She was quickly building a reputation as a bit of a hellion, to our amusement and to the dismay of the Council. People were calling her a female Nikolas, and it was a title she wore with pride.

"Beth just lost a little wager we had," Chris informed her smugly.

"Technically, I didn't lose. You said Sara would run him down. He's still standing."

Jordan snorted. "Does Nikolas know you guys are taking bets on his life now?"

Chris let me go and held up his hands.

"Hey, he knew what he was getting into when he said he wanted to teach Sara to drive a motorcycle."

"I heard that," Sara called as she and Nikolas headed in our direction.

They didn't get very far before two huge black, furry beasts came bounding across the grounds toward them. Sara handed her helmet to Nikolas and went to hug her hounds. Her hellhounds. She talked about Hugo and Woolf all the time, but even after being at Westhorne for three days, I was still getting used to seeing them in the flesh.

Sara used her sleeve to wipe slobber from her face.

"All right. Go find Niall, and see if he needs help on patrol."

The hellhounds panted excitedly and took off into the woods. I could only imagine the look on Niall's face when those two brutes came after him.

Sara saw us watching her, and she shrugged. "He shouldn't have made fun of my driving yesterday if he didn't want retribution."

Chris chuckled. "I remember when you were such a sweet girl."

"When was that?" Nikolas deadpanned.

Sara punched him in the arm, and everyone laughed.

"Now that the driving lesson is over for today, let's talk about going to Boise tonight," Jordan said.

Sara groaned. "You don't get enough clubbing in Los Angeles?"

Jordan put her hands on her hips. "This isn't about clubbing. It's about having fun with my BFFs before they desert me again."

"We're going to Miami, not China," I said. "And you could always come with us. I hear they have a great nightlife there."

We were spending two weeks at Westhorne before we started our next assignment, which was to establish the new command center in Miami. The Council was so pleased with the success of the first two centers they had plans to create them in major cities around the world. It looked like Sara and I were going to get in some of that traveling we wanted to do.

Chris took my arm and smiled at the others.

"Whatever you guys decide is okay with us. Now if you'll excuse us, Beth and I have plans for the rest of the afternoon."

Fated

"We do?" I asked as we walked away from our friends.

"Not really," he said when we were out of earshot. "I just wanted to spend some time alone with you. Let's go for a walk."

We crossed the grounds and entered the woods. Geographically, West-horne was a lot like Longstone, surrounded by woods and miles from the nearest town. I already loved it here.

It didn't take long for me to realize where we were headed. Sara had taken me to see the lake on my first day here. Sure enough, we arrived there five minutes later.

"It's beautiful here," I said as we strolled near the edge of the water. "So peaceful."

He pointed across the small lake. "See that spot over there between the two big oak trees? That's where Nikolas plans to build their house when we finish with the Miami job."

"I can't believe Sara didn't mention it. She loves this lake."

"She doesn't know yet. He's going to tell her today."

I wished I could see Sara's face when Nikolas dropped his surprise on her. "She's going to flip. Not that I can blame her. It's gorgeous here."

He stopped walking and faced me, wearing a smile that told me he was up to something.

"How would you feel about us being their neighbors?"

I gaped at him for a full ten seconds before I saw he was serious.

"You want to build a house here?"

He smiled. "If that's what you want. Nikolas and I thought it would be nice for the four of us to have a private place to come home to between jobs. And since this whole valley is protected by Fae wards and hellhounds, it's safe to –"

"Yes!"

I threw my arms around his neck and kissed him soundly. When neither of us was steady on our feet, we sank to the grass and made out like teenagers until the not-too-distant bark of a hellhound reminded us this place wasn't *that* private.

Sitting on the grass with my back to Chris's chest, I pictured a pretty little house nestled in the trees with a deck overlooking the water. I saw Chris and me sitting on our deck waving to Sara and Nikolas in their own house across the lake. The daydream changed, and I saw little blonde and brunette children playing together while we looked on. Warmth filled me, and I heaved a sigh of pure bliss.

Chris rested his chin on my shoulder. "By the way, do you know what today is?"

I frowned. Our one-year anniversary was last month, and I couldn't think of anything else.

"No. What is it?"

"Exactly fifteen years ago today, you and I met."

I gasped. "Oh, my God, you're right. You remembered the date?"

He hugged me tighter. "I told you, Dove. I remember everything about you. Meeting you is something I could never forget."

I thought back to that day, but I couldn't remember much beyond the heat of the fire and the smoke burning my nose and throat. And Chris. Most of my memories of that day were a blur except for him. The moment I'd looked up into his eyes, I'd felt safe, and when he'd held me, I'd known that was where I belonged.

"Do you know, I think I fell in love with you a little that day?" I said.

Chris nodded slowly. "That explains why you're so crazy about me."

"Whatever." I rolled my eyes even though he couldn't see them. "Don't you believe in love at first sight?"

"I don't know, but I do believe I was supposed to go to that building. Whether it was fate or some higher power at work, I was meant to find you."

I smiled dreamily. I loved it when he said things like that. "And now, I'm your mate."

He pressed a kiss to the corner of my mouth.

"Now, you're my everything."

~ The End ~

BONUS SCENE

If you have jumped ahead to read this scene before Fated, I encourage you to read the book first. The events in the bonus scene take place after Fated, so the scene will be much more enjoyable after you've read the book.

I filled the wood bin on the porch with the last armload of firewood, then stood back to survey my work. Sara loved a good fire, and ours was going almost constantly since the temperature had dropped below zero. I'd spent the better part of the morning cutting and splitting enough wood to fill our shed, and to keep my mate warm through the holidays. And if it wasn't enough, there was always body heat.

Smiling, I knocked snow from my boots before I opened the door and entered the cabin. My nose was immediately greeted by the smell of ginger-bread, and I looked at the two racks of cookies cooling on the counter. My lips twitched. At least this batch wasn't burnt. She was getting better with her baking.

Sara was going all out in her determination to make our first Christmas at the lake a special one. I kept telling her it was already perfect, but that hadn't slowed her down. She'd been in a whirlwind of decorating, gift-wrapping, and meal planning for at least two weeks, and she was wearing herself out. I'd caught her yawning at breakfast today, but she'd refused to go back to bed as I'd suggested. I'd be glad when she could slow down and just enjoy the holiday.

Her voice drew me to the living room, and I came up short at the sight before me. She was sitting on the floor, talking to an imp that stood on the coffee table, wearing...clothes?

The imp gestured at his body and let out a series of indignant squeaks. I had no idea what he was saying, but Sara seemed to understand his rant.

"Eliot and Orwell are just teasing you. I think you look very handsome," she said earnestly.

The imp stopped making noises and looked down at his outfit. He smoothed his hands over the fabric of his tiny blue shirt and adjusted the collar. If I didn't know better, I'd say he was preening himself for her.

He pointed at his feet and let out another squeak.

Sara smiled. "You don't have to wear the shoes, although I think you'd look quite dashing in them."

He stared at her for a moment, and then he looked at a pair of tiny black shoes sitting on the coffee table. Bending, he picked up the shoes and jumped off the table.

He hit the floor running, which was a good thing because Oscar had apparently been lying in wait behind the couch. The grey tabby darted out, but the imp was too fast for him. The little fiend made it safely to the minia- ture house in the corner of the room that Sara had made for them. A few seconds after he slammed the door, he appeared in one of the plastic windows, making rude gestures at the cat.

A laugh slipped from me. Only in our house would you see an imp wearing actual clothes and flipping the bird at a cat.

Sara turned her warm smile on me. "All done?"

"We have enough wood to last us through the blizzard of the century," I said as I walked toward her. I hooked a thumb towards the imp house. "What's the deal with the clothes?"

"I told them they could come to dinner tonight, but they had to dress for it. None of that lifting their loincloths to flash the guests. Nate still hasn't gotten over that from Thanksgiving."

I grinned down at her. "Yes, I imagine getting the full Monty from a six-inch demon while you're carving a turkey is enough to traumatize anyone."

I scooped her up from the floor, and sat on the couch with her on my lap. I couldn't enter a room she was in without touching her. Not that I'd ever try to deny myself the pleasure of holding her.

Laughter bubbled from her. "Caveman."

I nuzzled her throat and she made a happy sound. She leaned in and sniffed at my sweater.

"Hmmm. I love the smell of snow and fresh-cut wood on my man."

Her warm lips brushed the skin above my collar, and a fire ignited low in my belly. One kiss was all it took to awaken my hunger for her, and the holiday season had made my beautiful mate even more amorous than usual. Not that I was complaining.

I stifled an impatient groan as her lips travelled with maddening slowness, up my throat to my jaw. I loved it when she touched me, but all I wanted now was to taste her sweet mouth.

When her lips finally met mine, I took over. Cradling her face in my hands, I kissed her slowly until her hand slipped under my sweater to caress my bare stomach. I let out a soft growl and deepened the kiss as her exploring hand made my abs tighten.

I pulled back to gaze into her heavy-lidded eyes.

"Tell me I have time to take you upstairs."

She gave me a rueful smile. "They could arrive any minute."

I groaned and pressed my lips to the sensitive spot beneath her ear, as I lamented the fact that these were the last few minutes we'd have our home to ourselves for the next week.

"You're okay with them coming for Christmas, right?"

I lifted my head and kissed the tip of her nose. "Of course. I just like having you all to myself."

She rested her head against my shoulder with a happy sigh. For a few minutes, we sat like that, with the only sounds coming from the occasional crack of the logs in the fireplace.

My gaze swept the room, which Sara had lovingly decorated with mistletoe and real spruce garland she and Beth had made. To one side of the fireplace stood the ten-foot Douglas fir I'd put up yesterday. Nate had sent Sara all their family Christmas ornaments, and she'd delighted in hanging each one on the tree. I'd had the honor of stringing the lights and placing the star at the top. Then we'd stood back and admired the first Christmas tree in our new home.

Sara moved to get up. "Oh, I forgot to put the presents under the tree."

"Plenty of time for that," I said, enjoying our quiet time too much to let her go yet. She gave up without a fight, which told me she was happy to stay where she was.

Her fingers began to toy with my sweater. "The snow's been coming down thick for over an hour. Do you think they'll make it before the roads get bad?"

"Stop worrying. Chris has driven in snow plenty of times."

As if on cue, a chorus of deep barks broke the peaceful quiet. I enhanced my hearing and picked up the sound of an approaching vehicle.

"They're here!"

Sara scrambled off my lap and ran to the window that made up one whole side of the room. It overlooked the lake and gave us a clear view of the narrow gravel road that now connected the lake with the stronghold. I would have preferred no road, but we'd needed a way to get the truckloads of logs and building supplies here. And I didn't want Sara to have to walk all the way to the stronghold whenever she needed to, especially in the winter.

Outside, the ground and trees were coated in a thick layer of snow, while fat snowflakes drifted down. Sara had hoped for a white Christmas, and she was getting her wish, plus some.

Two large black shapes bounded past the house, sending up a spray of powdered snow as they raced around like excited puppies. Hugo and Woolf stopped and stared at the road for a few seconds before they began braying loud enough for the people in Butler Falls to hear them.

Turning from the window, Sara ran to the closet by the front door and grabbed her coat and boots. I chuckled when she nearly tipped over in her haste to tug on the boots. She flashed me a wide smile, and was out the door before she'd even pulled her coat on.

I followed her along the well-beaten path by the water to the clearing near the mouth of the road. Across the lake, the door to Chris and Beth's cabin opened and Beth stepped out, waving, before she started toward us.

As soon as Hugo and Woolf saw us, they ran circles around us. Laughing, Sara told them to go patrol and they took off around the lake. Hellhounds were bred to guard and protect, and they needed work to keep them occupied. Sara had taught them to guard the lake, and they loved going on patrol. They'd stay out there until she called them in.

When we heard the crunch of tires on gravel, Sara almost began jumping up and down in her excitement. As much as I loved having her to myself, I would never deny her this happiness. She was still coming to terms with the knowledge that she would outlive Nate and her friends, and she wanted to make every moment with them count. I wanted that for her, too.

A black SUV came into view and stopped at the clearing. Chris got out, along with Roland and Emma.

"You made it!" Sara squealed as she ran to them and practically jumped into Roland's arms. Laughing, he hugged her back before setting her on her feet again so she could tackle Emma.

I'd seen Emma a few times since she and Roland mated, but it still amazed me how far she had come from the pale, terrified girl we'd brought home to Westhorne two years ago. In the beginning, I'd had my doubts she would recover fully from the horrors she'd suffered. But no one seeing her now would ever suspect she had such a dark past. Her face glowed with happiness as she and Sara embraced like they hadn't seen each other in years.

Roland turned to me with a smile. "Thanks for sending the plane. You're going to spoil us for normal travel."

"We figured if you were coming all this way to spend Christmas with us, it was the least we could do."

"It's a good thing we left when we did," Emma said. "We heard Portland is snowed in."

"I was worried the weather would be bad in Boise, too." Sara linked her arm through Emma's. "I'm so glad you guys are here. I wish Peter and Shannon could have come."

"They really wanted to." Roland grinned at her. "You should see Pete. He's already a basket case and they still have a month to go."

Sara shook her head in wonder. "I still can't believe Peter is going to be a dad. It feels like just yesterday the three of us were having sleepovers. Now look at us."

"Now we're just a bunch of boring old mated couples," Chris joked.

Beth poked him in the side. "You better not be calling me boring, mister."

He smirked at her. "Never, Dove. Especially not after this morning when you –"

She gasped and slapped a hand over his mouth. He responded by pulling her into his arms and kissing her as if they were alone.

"*And* that's our cue to leave," Sara announced. "Don't mind those two. They'll come up for air eventually."

Roland laughed and went to the back of the SUV to grab their bags. I took one from him and we called goodbye to Chris and Beth as we set off toward our place.

"Damn, Nikolas."

Roland let out a whistle as he stared at our two-story log cabin, with its massive stone chimney and tiered deck that led down to a dock on the lake. Another smaller deck on the second floor was connected to the master suite so we could enjoy the lake without leaving our bedroom.

"Wait'll you see inside," Sara called over her shoulder as she and Emma walked ahead of us. "I don't know how I'm going to leave here when it's time to go to the next job."

"We can stay here as long as you want," I reminded her.

After successfully establishing command centers in Los Angeles, New York, and Miami, we were due for a vacation. I liked the work and I didn't mind the travel, but Sara missed home and her pets when we were away for long stretches. I had to admit, I liked having a place to ourselves for a while.

The four of us entered the cabin, and Emma made an appreciative sound as she looked up at the high ceiling and exposed beams. Her gaze swept the wide-open space to the large kitchen that was a blend of rustic charm and modern appliances.

"This place is beautiful!"

Sara smiled widely at her. "Thanks. Come on, I'll show you around."

She took Emma on a tour of the place, and I showed Roland to the guest room on the first floor. We left their bags in the room and returned to the kitchen, where he went straight for the cookies.

"No burnt bottoms. She's getting better," he said before he popped one in his mouth.

"I heard that," Sara called from the stairs.

Roland snickered and stole another cookie.

The girls returned and the four of us settled in the living room to catch up. Sara talked to them at least once a week, but they never ran out of things to talk about. She liked hearing about the pack and life back in New Hastings, and she told them stories about New York and Miami. I noticed she avoided any mention of vampires out of concern for Emma's feelings. No matter what my mate did, she was always thinking of others.

Emma smiled at us. "I can't believe we're here. I just love everything about this place."

Sara leaned her head on my shoulder. "I'm glad you like it. And I hope that means I won't have to twist your arm to get you to visit again."

"Are you kidding? You'll be lucky to get me to leave."

"Stay as long as you want," Sara said around a yawn. She let out a small laugh. "Sorry. I was up a bit too late last night wrapping presents."

I laid an arm across her shoulders. "She's been running around all week. And now she's going to do nothing but relax and have fun."

"Sounds like a plan to me," Roland agreed.

The distant braying of the hellhounds heralded the arrival of a new visitor. A minute later, I heard the thump of boots on the porch, and I went to get the door. I smiled when I saw the blonde warrior, her hair covered in snow and her arms full of presents.

Jordan grinned and shoved the presents at me. "Merry Christmas!"

Twin squeals came from behind me, and I moved aside as Sara and Emma rushed past me.

"When did you get home?" Sara asked. "I wasn't sure if you were going to come."

"Got in about an hour ago. I have to tell you it's weird being back in my old room."

I carried the presents to the living room and laid them under the tree. Everyone said their hellos and I decided to leave the girls to their reunion.

"Drink?" I asked Roland.

"Yeah."

The two of us headed to the kitchen, where I handed him a beer and poured a glass of Macallan for me. Before I'd taken a sip of my drink, the door opened again and Beth burst in, followed by Chris. She hurried to the living room to join Sara and the others.

Chris poured himself a drink and raised his glass to me. "To surviving our first Christmas at the lake."

"Surviving?"

He swung his free hand toward the living room. "You forget the last time Beth, Sara, and Jordan partied together?"

Roland laughed. "We're in the woods, in a snowstorm, miles from the nearest town. What trouble could they get into here?"

"You had to ask that." I picked up the bottle of Scotch and topped off my and Chris's glasses. "To our survival."

"I don't think she's ever looked this content," Nate said to me a few hours later as he carved the prime rib that had been done to perfection by the West-horne cooks.

I followed his gaze to Sara, who was placing serving bowls on the dining room table. She radiated happiness, and she was humming softly as she moved the centerpiece to make way for the food. Every now and then, her eyes would lift to take in the friends and family gathered in the living room, and a new smile would curve her mouth.

My eyes found Tristan, standing by the window talking quietly to Madeline, who looked unsure of herself for the first time. I don't know who was more surprised when Sara had invited her mother to Christmas Eve dinner, and I hadn't expected Madeline to accept. They'd talked a few times since they were reunited, and Sara had forgiven Madeline for the things in their past, but they weren't close. Sara's invitation told me she was ready to take the first step in building a new relationship with her mother. Madeline being here said she wanted that, too.

"I think you're right," I said, helping Nate arrange slices of meat on the serving platter he'd given us as a housewarming gift. The dish had been passed down from Sara's great-grandmother, and Sara had cried when Nate said her father would have given it to her when she married.

I carried the platter of meat to the table and placed it where Sara told me to. I couldn't resist giving her a quick kiss on the lips before I called to our guests.

"Dinner is served."

Roland jumped up from the couch. "Thank God, I'm –"

A loud crash came from behind me, and the cabin shook. I spun to see something come through the kitchen window, sending glass everywhere.

My body tensed for a fight, and it took me several seconds to realize we weren't under attack. I stared at the top of the pine tree now poking through the window above the sink.

"Don't worry. We'll have that patched up in no time," I said, turning to Sara, only to find she was no longer beside me.

I scanned the room, but she was nowhere in sight. Where could she have gone that fast?

"Sara," I called.

Nothing.

I walked to the bottom of the stairs. "Sara?"

Still nothing.

That was when it hit me.

I couldn't feel her.

I sped to the door and opened it. On the porch lay Hugo and Woolf, and they lifted their heads when I ran outside. Seeing them there only intensified my alarm. They would never let Sara leave without following her. I looked at the clean snow beyond the porch. No one had walked there in at least an hour.

"Nikolas, what's wrong?" Tristan said from behind me.

I stared at him as an icy knot of dread formed in my gut. "Sara's gone."

"What do you mean? She was just here." He spun and looked at the room. "She has to be here."

"I can't feel her."

Jumping off the porch, I circled the cabin, calling Sara's name. Farther away, I could hear the others spreading out, calling for her, too.

Hugo and Woolf followed me and the more worried I got, the louder they whined. They knew something was wrong.

I looked at the two hellhounds. "Find Sara."

Instantly, they transformed from tame pets to deadly beasts out to protect their master. Growls issued from their snarling mouths as they plunged into the trees. I followed them, hoping they'd pick up her scent, but after ten minutes, I split off to search on my own. I could cover ground a lot faster without them.

As I circled the lake, I had the most awful feeling of déjà vu, and I couldn't help but remember the last time I'd searched the woods for Sara in a snowstorm.

No. This is not the same.

This whole valley was protected by Fae wards, and there was no way a vampire could get past them. It just wasn't possible. And no one had entered the house and taken her. She'd left on her own. But why? And where was she?

Solmi, growled my agitated Mori as I reached the front of the lake with no sign of Sara.

Tristan and Chris intercepted me by the vehicles.

"Nothing?" Tristan asked, his brow creased with worry.

"No."

"Beth and Jordan ran to the stronghold, and Roland and Madeline are searching the woods," Chris said. "She can't have gone far."

My mouth suddenly went dry. "Not unless she...transported."

As soon as the words left my mouth, I knew I was right. There was no other explanation for her disappearance. My stomach twisted. She could be anywhere in the world.

Chris and Tristan stared at me.

"You think she transported?" Chris asked. "But why?"

I dragged a hand through my wet hair. "I don't know. Eldeorin had said her jumps are most likely triggered by emotions. I just don't know what could have made her jump this time."

"Maybe the crash frightened her," Tristan suggested, and I could tell by his expression he didn't even believe that. It took a lot more than loud noise to scare Sara.

I heard running feet and turned to see Nate coming toward us, his face a mask of worry.

"You haven't found her?"

Before I could answer, every window in our cabin lit with a brilliant white flash. My Mori began to flutter wildly.

Sara.

I ran to the cabin and burst through the door, skidding to a stop at the sight of Sara standing in the kitchen, shivering and wet from head to toe. She looked at me with eyes that mirrored my own relief.

"Nikolas," she said between chattering teeth.

I went to her and pulled her into my arms, feeling the cold seeping from her body. "God, Sara. You scared the hell out of me."

"M-me too," she stammered.

Picking her up, I looked at Chris and Tristan, who had followed me. "I'm taking her upstairs. Let everyone know she's back."

Without waiting for a reply, I carried Sara to our bathroom where I started the shower and quickly stripped off her wet clothes. She didn't say much as I placed her under the hot spray and then toweled her off a few minutes later. There would be time to ask her what happened once she was warm and dry.

In our room, I helped her into dry clothes, but she insisted on drying her hair herself. When she was done, we lay together in the middle of our big bed, propped up on pillows. I pulled a warm throw over her, and she settled against me with a weary sigh.

"I'm sorry I scared you," she said quietly.

I rubbed her arm. "What happened? Where did you go?"

"I don't know. I mean, I know I jumped, but I didn't mean to. I have no idea where I went. There was just woods and snow." She shivered. "I couldn't feel you and that scared me more than anything else."

I hugged her tighter, not wanting her to see how much her words worried me. Was something happening to her power again to make her lose control of it this way?

"I knew walking around in the dark wouldn't help, so I kept trying to jump back here. And then suddenly I was home."

"Do you know what made you do it?" I asked as I ran my hand through her soft hair. "Was it the crash?"

"I don't think so, but it happened so fast."

I stared at the snow swirling outside the window, trying not to think of what could have happened if she hadn't been able to bring herself back here. Even more frightening was the possibility of it happening again. It was enough for me to say the words I never thought I'd utter.

"I think you should call for Eldeorin."

Sara leaned away to look up at me with wide eyes. "You're serious?"

"You jumped to the middle of nowhere in a snowstorm, for no good reason. He's the best one to explain it, and to know how to stop it from happening again."

"I know, but you can't stand Eldeorin."

I stroked her cheek with my thumb. "I love you a lot more than I dislike him."

She smiled and raised her face for a kiss. I happily obliged her.

"I love you, too," she murmured against my lips.

Pulling away from me, she closed her eyes. I watched her eyelids flicker as she concentrated on reaching out to Eldeorin in the way he'd taught her. I didn't like her having any connection to the faerie, but in this moment, I was grateful. If anyone could help her, he could.

She opened her eyes and rested her head against my shoulder again. "He'll be here soon."

We lay there quietly, listening to the muted sounds from the rest of the house. Tristan and Chris would have already removed the tree by now and covered the window. Knowing Nate, he'd have all the food wrapped and waiting for us to come downstairs. Sara had wanted tonight to be perfect, and I'd do my best to ensure she got her Christmas dinner after we talked to Eldeorin.

As if thinking about the faerie had summoned him, he suddenly appeared in the middle of our bedroom. He looked at the two of us on the bed and smirked.

"Well now. This is different. I'm down for a threesome, but you are the last pair I'd expected to –"

"Eldeorin!"

Sara sat up, scowling at the faerie. His grin faded and he took a step toward the bed.

"You are unwell."

She tucked her hair behind her ears. "Do I look that bad?"

"No, I can feel it." He held out a hand. "I'm sensing small fluctuations in your magic. It reminds me of when you went through liannan, only not as drastic."

The mention of Sara's liannan sent a chill through me. Her power had grown exponentially in a matter of days, and she night have died if Eldeorin hadn't shown up. Only an induced coma could help her body adjust to the changes in her power.

Sara sucked in a breath and moved away from me. Her fearful expression told me she was afraid of losing control of her power like she had during her liannan.

"You think her power is growing again?" I asked Eldeorin, keeping my voice level to reassure her.

He rubbed his chin. "It's hard to say. Sara's unlike full-blooded Fae, and we can only guess how her magic will progress. Tell me what happened tonight."

Sara told him how she'd jumped without meaning to, and he nodded thoughtfully.

"You consciously jumped back to the house?"

"Yes."

Her answer pleased him. "Very good. You'll be jumping with ease in no time."

"What about the fluctuations you felt? Am I losing control of my power again?"

Her voice trembled and I wanted to go to her, but I knew she wouldn't let me near her if there was the slightest chance of her hurting me.

Eldeorin smiled. "I'm sure it's nothing we can't fix, Cousin."

Her shoulders sagged in relief.

He looked at me. "I'll need to link with Sara to determine what the problem is. It might cause her to have some minor outbursts of magic, so it would be best if you leave us."

The last thing I wanted to do was leave Sara when she looked so distraught, but she needed his help more than she needed me right now.

"I'll be downstairs," I told her.

She gave me a brave smile. "Okay."

I walked out, shutting the bedroom door behind me, and went downstairs where I was met with worried faces and a flurry of questions.

"She's okay," I said in a low voice. "Eldeorin is with her now, and he's going to figure out what caused her to jump like that."

I looked at the kitchen window, which was now covered by a tarp. As I'd thought, someone had cleaned up the glass and debris, and wrapped up all the food. There wasn't anything for me to do but wait, not that I would have gone far from Sara.

Unable to sit still, I paced the area at the bottom of the stairs, while the others talked quietly among themselves. I didn't want to think about the possibility of Sara enduring what she had during her liannan. It had been so difficult for her, emotionally and physically, and she'd had to train hard just to regain control of her power. I sent up a silent prayer that she didn't have to go through that again.

Almost an hour passed before I heard our bedroom door open, and Eldeorin appeared at the top of the stairs. His face gave nothing away when his eyes found mine.

"You can come up now."

I took the stairs two at a time, and ran into our bedroom. Sara stood near the French doors, looking out at the snow, so I couldn't see her face.

"Sara?"

Seconds passed before she turned to look at me, wearing a slightly dazed expression. Dread churned in my stomach, and I took a step toward her.

"What is it?

"It's..." The dazed look left her eyes and she smiled. For a moment, her body seemed to be surrounded by a soft white glow.

I shot Eldeorin a questioning look and found him smiling, too.

"It seems congratulations are in order."

"What?" I asked dumbly.

I swung my gaze back to Sara, and she wordlessly laid a hand over her stomach. It took me a few seconds to register what she was telling me. My knees weakened and I had to grip the post at the foot of the bed to stay on my feet.

My eyes lifted to meet hers again, and she nodded at my unspoken question.

I went to her and cupped her face in my hands. Her green eyes brimmed with happy tears, and I brushed them away as they fell.

"A baby?" I said hoarsely. "We're having a baby?"

"Yes," she whispered.

My chest expanded as an indescribable joy filled me, and I reached down to splay my hand across her flat stomach that would soon grow round with our child.

Slipping my other hand behind her head, I pulled her to me and kissed her with a fierce tenderness that left us both breathless. I was about to pick her up and carry her to the bed when a throat cleared behind me, reminding me we weren't alone.

"I'll be leaving now," Eldeorin said, sounding amused. "Sara, I'll be by in a few days to check on you. But from what I can see, she's healthy and strong."

"She?" I turned to him, stunned. "You can already tell it's a girl?"

"Only a female child would inherit Sara's magic, and this one's already a strong little thing. She's the one who sent them off on their little adventure tonight."

I stared at him, reeling from the news, and he shot me a devilish grin.

"Rest up, Daddy. You're going to need it."

ABOUT THE AUTHOR

When she is not writing, Karen Lynch can be found reading or baking. A native of Newfoundland, Canada, she currently lives in Charlotte, North Carolina with her cats and two crazy lovable German Shepherds: Rudy and Sophie.

Made in the USA
Las Vegas, NV
12 May 2022

48805149R00173